M000283190

Romantic, meticulously observed, historically fascinating and musically, highly literate. Fiona Mountain understands everything about the fine folk art of storytelling. *The Keeper of Songs* is a wonderful tale, exquisitely told, showing a deep empathy with the landscape of the Peak District and the traditional music that has emanated from it. Fiona creates a world of romance, detail and heartfelt emotion.

   - BBC Radio Presenter and writer, Mark Radcliffe

The depth of Fiona's research for this book, is evident in her thoughtful and magical portrayal of the stories deep within our old songs. She is a natural diviner of the worlds that dwell within them, both real and fictional and she has created a novel that reveals more secrets than one knew a song could ever keep.

   - Sam Lee, Author of *The Nightingale, Notes on a Songbird*

With such a lightness of touch and meticulous attention to detail, surely Fiona Mountain must have cleaned the chandeliers of Chatsworth in a former life? *The Keeper of Songs* is a well crafted and heart-rending tale of love and loss woven skillfully across multiple generational divides, and throughout, her love for Chatsworth and the beautiful Peak District shines through. A gripping read; I loved it!

   - Christine Robinson, Author of *Chatsworth, the Housekeeper's Tips, Tales & Tipples'*

It's been a great pleasure to read *The Keeper of Songs*, and I know it's a book that will stay with me for a long time. Fiona Mountain's own fascination with the power and resonance of music and folklore is evident as the threads of the story slowly weave together, and the lost lives and lost loves, the secrets and lies, the misunderstandings and the regrets, resolve themselves - though not without grief - into a satisfying conclusion. Her meticulous research takes us from the depths of the caves of Castleton to the majesty of Chatsworth House, but it's folk music that drives the narrative - the ancient songs, telling tales of tragedy and true love, that generations of singers have kept alive to this day.

- Jane Sanderson, Author of *Mix Tape*

THE KEEPER OF SONGS

FIONA MOUNTAIN

SNOWGLOBE
BOOKS

First published in Great Britain in 2021 by SnowGlobe Books
Copyright © Fiona Mountain 2021

The moral right of Fiona Mountain to be identified as the author of this work has been asserted in accordance with the Copyright, Design and Patents Act of 1988.
All rights reserved. No part of this publication may be reproduced, stored in a retrieval system, or transmitted in any form or by any means, electronic, mechanical, photocopying, recording or otherwise without the prior permission of the copyright owner.
This is a work of fiction. Names, characters, business, places, events and incidents are either the products of the author's imagination or used in a fictitious manner.

Print ISBN: 978-1-8384246-8-8
Ebook ISBN: 978-1-8384246-9-5

A CIP catalogue of this book is available from the British Library.

ABOUT THE AUTHOR

Fiona Mountain grew up in Sheffield and moved to London aged eighteen, where she worked for the BBC in the press office for Radio 1.

She has written five previous novels, which have been published around the world, including America, Canada, Australia, Italy, Germany, Holland, Japan and Thailand. Fiona's first novel, *Isabella,* was shortlisted for the Romantic Novel of the Year Award and *Bloodline* is the winner of the prestigious Mary Higgins Clark Award from the Mystery Writers of America.

You can find out more information about Fiona Mountain and her books at fionamountain.com
Or follow Fiona on Facebook, Twitter and Instagram.

facebook.com/NovelistFionaMountain

twitter.com/FionaMountain

instagram.com/fionamountainwriter

ALSO BY FIONA MOUNTAIN

ISABELLA

PALE AS THE DEAD

BLOODLINE

LADY OF THE BUTTERFLIES

CAVALIER QUEEN

For Daniel, James, Gabriel, Kezia and Scarlett,
May you always find the gold

Over moors and valleys deep, through the Dark Peak and the White
There two tragic lovers sleep in gritstone, blood, and lime.

Henry & Clara, Bella Hardy

'There's no point looking back,' my Mum, Silva, used to say. 'You're not going that way.'

Which is a bit ironic, because she grew up, and then went on to work, at Chatsworth House, the most beautiful and famous stately home in England, a place that's steeped in centuries of the richest history. It's a place that inspires respect and love for the past.

I understand now though, that my mother had good reasons for wanting to leave her own past behind her. But she came to understand that people live freer and happier lives if only they understand the sort of history that's never taught in schools. The private history of our own parents and grandparents and great-grandparents. The history of the ordinary, extraordinary people who made us who we are.

There are so many things that can be passed down through the generations. So many legacies that you can hand on to your children and your children's children, so many gifts which might be bequeathed to you, sometimes inadvertently. The colour of your eyes and hair and the shape of your mouth. A wild imagination maybe, or skilful hands, a voice to sing with. A kind nature or a fear of the dark. There are heirlooms too, jewellery and antiques, rare and valuable objects, and other treasures that are valuable purely for sentimental reasons. There are also the old stories and songs.

And something else. Another legacy, dark and hidden. Bad things that have happened, events that were too distressing and overwhelming to be resolved in one person's lifetime.Some of us are burdened by age-old debts that sooner or later, must be repaid.

PART I

CHAPTER ONE
MOLLY, 1967

Molly Marrison sits on the wooden stool barefoot, strumming a Gibson guitar. She can be no more than seventeen years old, willow-thin, with a silky cascade of long, straight, black hair. High cheek bones, big, dark eyes. Anyone can tell she's nervous but there's a stillness about her, a quiet power. In her flowing, diaphanous skirts, her bangles and beads, she's like a pagan, half vagabond gypsy, half Medieval princess. She's beautiful beyond words, like a girl from his dreams, a girl Leonard Cohen might write songs about.

'I think I'm in love,' Pete sighs.

'Lust you mean.' Mike chuckles. 'She's cool,' he agrees.

John wants both his friends to shut up, so he can just listen to her.

Molly is singing a haunting ballad of love and death, based on a local legend that's well known here in Castelton and all over the Peak District. John Brightmore remembers singing it at a school concert, when he was about twelve years old. Only he didn't sing it like this. Nothing like. It tells of two runaway lovers, called Henry and Clara, who were murdered one moonlit night as they rode through Winnats Pass on their way to the wedding chapel. It happened over two hundred years ago but Molly Marrison makes the tragedy of doomed young love completely her own, makes it seem as if the terrible crime was committed only yesterday and to people she knew well. She might have been one of the victims even, a ghost now, singing from beyond the grave. She gives the age-old song the soothing quality of a lullaby and the dark power of an incantation.

John is spellbound. No exaggeration. The hairs on the back of his neck are standing on end. He loves music, passionately believes in its transformative power, the way it can make you feel things you've not felt before, see the world from completely different angles, but in his eighteen years on this earth, he's never experienced anything like this. It's overwhelming. Her voice. Her face. Her spirit. She sounds like nobody else, looks like nobody else. So different to all the savvy chicks with their geometric haircuts and Mary Quant micro-mini skirts.

Molly introduces another song. 'It's about a poor lady who got led astray by a handsome rogue and found she was in a lot of trouble. But I'm sure she survived. We all do, you know.'

John smiles at her words and she locks her eyes with his across the crowd, sings directly to him, pouring out her heart to a total stranger. She's just a teenager but she sings as if her soul is old, full of longing and loss. It's like a fist squeezing John's heart and he's swamped with a need to take her in his arms and protect her. He's never felt like this before, not with any girl but the irony is that this girl looks like she wouldn't welcome any offer of protection. There's a vulnerability about her, for sure, but at the same time, she has such courage and charisma. John's so proud just to have given her a stage.

This whole night had been his crazy idea, dreamt up after a few pints with his pals up at the Castle Inn.

'We should start our own Cavern Club,' he'd said, imagining a rival to the famous basement music venue in Liverpool, where the Beatles first played. After all, Castleton is famous the world over, for its impressive caves and caverns, so it's a wonder nobody had thought of it before. Pete and Mike, the other members of John's band, are both Castleton lads.

John lives over at Chatsworth and everyone there has some interest in history. Impossible not to really, when you're surrounded by such a wealth of it every day. George Ashwell, a wily old tenant farmer on the estate, Derbyshire born and bred, once told John how Peak Cavern, as well as being a popular tourist attraction celebrated for having the most imposing entrance of any cave in Britain, also has fantastic acoustics.

'Apparently, a choir of tinker children sang there long ago and one Christmas, a brass band played traditional carols,' John had enthused to his friends, already picturing lights and amps and the cave mouth towering above them like a dark cathedral of rock.

So, the Peak Cavern Club was formed and a date set for the first 'happening'. Entry was to be free, everyone welcome, local performers given the opportunity to contribute a song or two. They'd no budget for a sound system but John was undeterred, decided the music should be unplugged anyway. Pete designed fly posters, which were printed and handed round town, stuck on lamp posts and on the wooden bus shelter in the High Street. It created a real buzz. Nothing much happens in Castleton, so this first gathering of the Peak Cavern Club was eagerly anticipated.

The makeshift stage is a square of carpet thrown over a couple of wooden pallets. A bar has been built from beer kegs, donated by the Castle Inn and someone's painted a canvas backdrop of spiders, rainbows and stars. A small, beaten-up generator powers lights that illuminate the cave mouth with dim pools of purple, blue and green. Everyone is smoking, so there are dots of orange light flitting like fireflies and it's so cold in this underworld that breath turns to mist, combining with the smoke to create a sort of shifting, illuminated fog. The mysterious, mystical atmosphere, suits Molly Marrison perfectly.

John tears his eyes from her to take in the whole scene and he sees that everyone is entranced. It sends shivers down his spine, it really does, because he knows he's witnessing something remarkable, that if this girl doesn't go on to sing in front of thousands, it will be a crime. She comes to the end of her last song and there's a second or two of stunned silence before people start applauding, whistling, whooping.

It's then that John notices one of the girls in the audience. Standing at the back of the cave, she's the only one not clapping. John knows her. Or rather he knows of her. Sukey Miller. She dated Mike for a few weeks last summer. She dresses like the mini-skirted dolly-birds who spend their time at wild parties which end up with lots of drugs and people disappearing off to bedrooms. But Mike said all Sukey ever talked about was getting married. She flashes John a sexy smile, like someone trying too hard, but he thinks how she looks like a bit like Nancy Sinatra, in her boots that are made for walkin'. Sukey's boots are the white, mid-calf go-go boots that are all the rage. She has great legs, he can't help but notice.

Molly Marrison steps down from the stage, disappearing once more into the small crowd, as if, away from the spotlight, she becomes invisible. She's totally out of his league.

He's made this 'happening' happen tonight and it feels so great, the best feeling ever. To have created something out of nothing, an event for people to enjoy. John's dad is a shepherd and it's always been assumed that John will follow in his footsteps, but he's very sociable and he's in his element in places like this. Live music - there's no bigger thrill. He's never felt so alive, so glad to be alive. All he needs is a girl to share it all with, someone special. That would be the icing on the cake, but John's been told, by his friends and family, that he has a tendency to romanticise girls, put them on pedestals and then he gets disillusioned and heartbroken when things don't work out. Being with the right person is the best thing in the world and being with the wrong person is the worst, his mother warned. His parents have been married for twenty-two years and according to them both, they've had their ups and downs, have had to learn to take the rough with the smooth. His dad says it's been mostly up and smooth and totally worth the ride anyway. John wants the same. One day.

As he makes his way to the bar, he sees Molly Marrison and, wonder of wonders, she's looking right at him again, with those huge dark eyes of hers. Can he find a way to tell her, without it sounding corny as hell, that she has the voice of an angel?

'Can I buy you a drink?' he manages to ask her.

Molly cups her hand around her Camel cigarette as she lights it, flicking her eyes up at him. 'Drinking's boring,' she says teasingly, blowing a lazy smoke ring. 'It's what old people do.'

'Right,' he chuckles, running his fingers through his shaggy, black hair. So this girl is funny, as well as talented and beautiful. He notices she has a book of Baudelaire's poetry, poking out of her canvas shoulder bag.

'D'you have any dope?' she asks.

He shakes his head. 'Nope'

Pete Jackson appears out of nowhere, offers Molly a drag on his joint and they start talking. Bad boy Pete in his beaten up leather jacket. He always gets the girls, damn him.

Someone lays their hand on John's arm. Sukey. She says something to him but everyone is talking now and he can't hear her. He tilts his head so she can speak into his ear and her pale pink lips brush his skin.

'I can sing too, you know.' Her voice is breathy and she flutters impossibly long, false eyelashes at him. 'I'm actually really good.'

Sukey has hazel eyes, gold hair cut in a stylishly heavy fringe over dark brows. A bottle blonde then, not that John cares about things like that. She's trying to look like the Bond girl in *Thunderball*, all bikinis and power play.

So many girls say they can sing but hardly any actually can, when it comes down to it. 'Next time then, hey?'

With his stubbly beard and faded blue jeans, John knows he couldn't look less like a musical impresario but Sukey gazes up at him, as if he's the bee's knees.

'That a promise?' She lisps.

''S up to you,' he smiles. 'Anyone can ask for a floor spot, like Molly just did. That's kinda the whole idea.'

'It's genius to use the Cavern for live music,' Molly says suddenly.

'Thanks.' He looks down at his boots, scuffs them on the packed earth floor. 'Tonight has given me lots more ideas,' he adds, modestly.

'Such as?' Molly sounds genuinely intrigued.

He looks up from his feet. 'There's a really special place at Chatsworth, where I live. A little private theatre, up in the tower in the north wing. The most amazing venue.'

'Wow. I'd love to see it.'

'Honestly?'

'Honestly.'

CHAPTER TWO

SILVA - 2002

For all of us, I think, there are certain events in our lives, certain days, that become watersheds, splitting the years absolutely, changing everything, changing us, so profoundly, that from then on there's a distinct before and after. The 8th of January 2002, turned out to be one of those days for me. My memory of those hours is like a photograph album filled with a series of disjointed snapshots.

I remember that I was standing at the top of the scaffolding tower, beneath the magnificent chandelier that hangs in the great dining room at Chatsworth House. Thousands of freshly washed lead crystal droplets tinkled and shimmered, like galaxies of stars just above my head.

'Care for something well and you make it sparkle,' I commented.

'Anyone ever told you you're kooky,' laughed Lizzie Ludlam, my colleague and friend, calling up from the ground below.

'And a dab hand at cleaning chandeliers.' We both were by now. We'd been doing it for long enough.

'You off to the forge when we finish here?' Lizzie asked.

'I am.' No change there. I'd started blacksmithing in my late teens, inspired in no small part, by all the historic ironwork I spent so many hours cleaning. By that score though, I might have become passionate about ceramics or sculpting, portrait painting, carpentry. I might have taken up gilding or stonemasonry. But from the moment our Head Housekeeper, Bea Waterfield, told me the story of Vulcan, Roman God of flames and the forge, I guess my course was set. Me and Vulcan. We've a lot in common. I spent most afternoons at the smithy, playing with fire, hammering hot metal. It was very therapeutic.

'Any exciting plans for this evening?' Lizzie asked.

'Cooking toad in the hole for me and my dad.' It was his favourite meal and I made it about once a week. Left to my own devices, I'd have been happy with a bowl of soup, or a fish finger sandwich, if I was really pushing the boat out, but home-cooked meals made my dad happy and I'd been making toad in the hole for him since I was eleven. I'd been trying to make him happy since then too. I'd even learnt to make fluffy Yorkshire puddings from scratch and I made a mental note to remember to pick up flour for the batter, along with the sausages, from the Farm Shop on my way home.

'Friday night is fish night,' Lizzie said. 'We're off to the chippy. You make me feel like such a sloth.'

'Sloths are cute,' I assured her.

With her glossy, curly, short blonde hair, shapely figure and huge personality, Lizzie had a dash of Hollywood silver-screen glamour about her. Even with no make-up and wearing a white polo shirt, jeans and scuffed trainers, she managed to look like Veronica Lake.

'I don't have the energy to cook when I've been working all day,' she said.

'If you can call this work, hey.' I reached up to fasten a tiny screw into the bottom tier of the chandelier. I loved my job. What was there not to love? I was part of the twenty-strong housekeeping team at the most beautiful and famous stately home in England and I spent every day surrounded by so much beauty and history. It was no exaggeration to say that the master craftsmen and women who'd made this house one of the most spectacular in the world, were my heroes. I'd studied them: the carpenters and stone masons, the painters and blacksmiths, especially the blacksmiths, who'd left their mark over the years. I felt privileged to be entrusted with caring for the thousands of treasures they'd left behind for us.

Cleaning the magnificent chandeliers was an intricate operation that took two people at least two days to complete, so it was only done once a year, when every one of the rooms at Chatsworth underwent a thorough deep clean. This must have been about the tenth time Lizzie and I had undertaken the task together, so we had our routine well worked out. One by one, I'd unhooked each chain of droplets, packed them in cloth and handed them down to Lizzie, who'd washed them in a bucket of warm water, frothed with pure soap flakes. She had then rinsed them in another bucket of clean water and laid them out to dry on a trestle table, covered in soft towels, all labelled, so we didn't lose track of tiers and sections. We replaced any of the little brass pins that had become brittle or black and while they were drying, the chandelier was dusted with a brush and vacuum. Then we reassembled the droplets in reverse order to how they came off, due to the outer pieces overhanging the inner.

'You look like a circus trapeze artist up there,' Lizzie told me. 'Or Catwoman maybe, what with your rope of black hair and lissome bod. It's a good look.'

It wasn't a look as such. I tied my hair back in a French plait just to keep it out of the way and I was wearing Converse high-tops, black leggings and a black jumper, just because they were warm, practical and inconspicuous. I had two sets of outfits in my wardrobe: one for when I was feeling confident and another for when I wanted to hide in the shadows. For no identifiable reason, today was a shadow day.

'Anyway, I thought you were going to come to the gym with me last night,' I teased. 'What happened to your New Year's resolutions?'

All Chatsworth staff had use of a well-equipped gym at the back of the estate office and club, located in the red brick Georgian building in the park, which had once been a coaching inn. Every January Lizzie stated that she was going to come with me three times a week but her good intentions always went by the wayside by about the middle of the month.

'I was knackered once Carys and Maria were in bed. When it came down to it, cuddling up on the sofa with Joe, with a bottle of wine and a big bowl of cheese and onion crisps, somehow seemed far more appealing than sweating on a treadmill.'

'I can see why.'

'You need to find someone to cuddle.'

'I have Tijou. The cuddliest spaniel a girl could ever wish for.'

'Did you ring Joe's friend from uni?'

'Not yet. Not had time.'

'I give up.'

It was a wonder she'd not done that long ago, bless her. Lizzie was always trying to find me a man, complaining that I was way too picky. There was probably some truth in that.

'Drinks tomorrow anyway?' Lizzie said. 'Freya's free.'

'Freya's always free for socialising.' I looked forward to our girly get-togethers too. I stood back to admire our work. 'Nearly done.'

Even unlit, the chandelier was stunning. It gave the dining room an old-world elegance and grandeur, like a chamber from a fairytale castle. The textile team had recently replaced the scarlet damask that lined the walls and hung drapes in scarlet Indian silk at the windows.

More snapshots.

I remember that Annie Ollerenshaw, one of the older housemaids, was up a ladder cleaning the huge panes of glass which framed the most beautiful views of the frosty lawns and mighty Emperor Fountain.

I remember the silver steward, Hector, setting out gleaming cutlery on the thirty-foot-long dining table. He'd explained to me that the forks were all turned with their prongs face down on the snowy linen tablecloth because in bygone days, a lady's or gentleman's lacy cuffs, might otherwise catch on them. I loved knowing things like that.

I remember this timeless scene being disturbed by Ted Waterfield, Bea's husband, striding through the huge double doors and across the oriental carpet, in his anachronistic baseball cap and blue boiler-suit. In his late fifties, balding and sturdy with a cheery, round face, Ted was the most unflappable person, but he didn't appear so unflappable now.

He flicked a glance up at me.

16

'Morning Ted.'

He didn't even smile back, which was so unlike him. Even from above, I noticed a sheen of sweat on his brow, despite it being freezing cold in the dining room as usual. Had he been running? Surely not? Ted never ran. Lizzie frowned as he made a beeline for Bea. She was at the far end of the room, carefully dusting the Chatsworth Tazza, a huge dish made of Blue John gemstone.

Ted took off his cap and Bea set down her cleaning cloth, to give him her full attention. He said something and her hand flew to her mouth. They spoke for a moment, then she squeezed his arm, as if to console him and started walking towards me and Lizzie.

Bea Waterfield, my boss, had been Head Housekeeper at Chatsworth for twenty-five years, but dressed in a turquoise turtleneck and dark slacks, she looked trim and youthful. The benefits of an active job, she claimed. I often thought how she'd come to resemble the lovely objects she'd taken care of for so long. She had silvery hair, a pretty porcelain complexion, china-blue eyes and a heart of gold; plus a stony displeasure if people didn't do their job to her exacting standards. She was energetic and efficient, even in the way she walked.

She stopped now, at the foot of the scaffold tower, feet neatly placed together in her court shoes, hands lightly clasped, her face turned upwards.

'Could you come down for a moment please, Silva.' Her expression was so kind and concerned that it doused my whole body with cold dread.

'Sure,' I said, glancing at Lizzie, who looked equally anxious. I climbed down the ladder inside the scaffold tower and jumped off the final rungs to stand in front of Bea. 'What's wrong?'

'Let's go to my office, shall we?'

The Housekeeper's Office was in the North Wing and was more like a comfy drawing room than a place of work, full of tasteful, antique mahogany furnishings, with a high corniced ceiling, walls covered in pretty floral-patterned wallpaper and the floor covered in a faded, wool rug. Bea invited me to sit beside the fireplace and busied herself making a pot of tea. She put a spoonful of sugar into my cup, even though she knew I didn't take sugar. The tinkling of the spoon against the bone china rang like an alarm. Bea took the upholstered armchair opposite me but she perched forward in it, as though it was the most uncomfortable seat imaginable.

'Is it my dad?' I asked, my heart kicking with panic. That would explain why Ted had come running. I knew from the look on Bea's face that I'd guessed right. 'What's happened to him? Where is he?'

'John didn't turn up for work this morning,' Bea began carefully. 'In all the thirty years Ted has worked with him, he's never been so much as five minutes late. Even when your Mum…when things were tough for him, so naturally Ted was concerned. He tried to phone him but got no answer. When John still hadn't shown up by ten o' clock, Ted went round to his cottage.'

I wrapped my fingers around my cup but its warmth was no comfort. My heart was pumping hard, yet I felt dizzy and cold, as if no blood was reaching my head or my fingers. I was going to faint or be sick. I felt as if I was ten years old again. I knew how this ended. I'd been here before. No. My dad would never just leave without telling me where he was going. He'd never put me through something like that again, even if I was no longer a child. It was fine. Nothing bad had happened to him.

'John wasn't in the house but the back door was unlocked, so Ted went out to the shed. He could hear music playing.' Bea took a breath. 'Your dad had collapsed on the floor. Ted called 999 but he'd stopped breathing. Ted's a trained first aider, was able to give mouth-to-mouth, do all the right things.' She broke off. 'The paramedics were there within ten minutes. Tried to restart his heart.'

My own heart had stopped, while my head filled with images from television hospital dramas; flashing blue lights, defibrillators and the horrible jerking of lifeless limbs.

'It worked,' Bea said. 'Your dad came round.'

'But?' My voice was a cracked whisper.

'They were lifting him into the ambulance and...' Bea shook her head, looked as if there was a pain behind her eyes. 'Dear Silva, there's no easy way to break this to you.' She reached out and gripped my hand, as if to stop me sliding over the edge of a cliff. Too late. A falling sensation, as if the ground had opened up. My legs were trembling uncontrollably. 'I'm so, so sorry, love. They weren't able to save him.'

'What d'you mean?'

Bea seemed reluctant to say the words and of course, I knew what they were. I knew. But I had to hear nonetheless, or it couldn't be true.

'John is de...your dad died,' she said quietly.

'No.' I shook my head, my mouth dry as ash. 'No.' I pulled back, as if distancing myself from the person who'd delivered the news might push it away, make it not be real. 'Where is he?'

'The ambulance took him.'

'Took him where?'

'The hospital, I assume.'

A flare of hope. 'Then they've not given up.' But of

course, the hospital had a mortuary. My dad could not be lying in a mortuary. It was so absurd.

'It's just so awful. Such a terrible shock.' Bea dashed a tear from her cheek.

I jumped to my feet, went to fetch her a tissue from the box on the sideboard and she accepted it with a small, apologetic smile because of course, it should have been the other way round. It should have been her, comforting me. It should have been me who was crying. Only I didn't feel like crying. I felt nothing now. Nothing at all. It was as if I was dressed in a suit of armour and the arrowhead that Bea had just fired at me, had bounced right off. I felt like an actress rehearsing a scene; trying to work out how I should be feeling, rather than just feeling.

My dad couldn't be dead. I'd seen him just yesterday and he'd been right as rain. Half an hour ago, I'd been thinking about buying sausages, to make his toad in the hole, for heaven's sake. Half an hour ago I was looking forward to listening to him natter about his day.

Bea looked weighed down, as if she'd more bad news to impart.

'There's something you've not told me?'

She let out a deep breath. 'When your dad came to, just for that brief moment, he was asking for someone.'

My heart shot up into my throat. I couldn't bear this. 'Sukey? He wanted to see my mother?' He'd died wanting to see her, one more time.

But Bea shook her head.

'Me? He was asking for me?'

'No love.' Bea sounded as if she was apologising on his behalf.

I frowned. 'Who then?' Who else was there?

'Someone called Molly.'

'Molly? I don't know anyone called Molly.' Who the hell was Molly?

She looked as confused as I felt. 'Ted said that those were your dad's last words. He said it seemed very important to him, that you get the message, so Ted insisted I pass it on to you right away. Your dad's last wish: Tell Silva. Find Molly.'

CHAPTER THREE

Tell Silva. Find Molly.
What are you on about, Dad? Who is she? Who the hell is Molly? How do I find her? Why on earth? I felt so cross with him. I desperately wanted to talk to him.

I turned my old blue Jeep in the direction of Pilsley village, only a couple of miles away from Chatsworth House, on the edge of the estate. It had snowed just after Christmas and with temperatures not rising much above freezing since then, patches of snow had lingered and turned to ice, making the winding country lanes slippy. I wasn't generally a fast driver but now I drove faster than was wise, faster than was necessary and I felt the wheels slip and slide. I chucked the Jeep into four-wheel drive. My dad had chosen it for me because it was built like a tank, he said, would keep me safe on the country roads. I put my foot down. But what was the hurry? I just needed to get to dad's cottage. I couldn't, wouldn't believe he wasn't there as usual. That he wasn't…anywhere on this earth. How could that be? The lanes, lit by the headlights, were like the corridors of a haunted house. Nothing felt real. Nothing made any sense. My dad had been there my whole life and for so long, it had been just the two of us.

When I'd seen him yesterday, he'd been up a stepladder in the State Bedchamber, helping Lara, from the textile department, to take down the salmon pink drapes from the ornate four poster bed.

His greeting was typical: 'Look out, here comes trouble.' We'd chatted about this and that and then he'd said, 'Don't work too hard, love.'

Those were the last words I'd ever hear him say. But not the last words he'd ever said. *Tell Silva. Find Molly.*

I started making mental lists because lists were comforting. What do you need to do when someone dies? Organise a funeral. Register the death. What else?

The houses in Pilsley were all tied houses, meaning they were occupied by people who worked or had once worked, on the estate. I parked outside Dad's cottage, in the middle of a small terrace at the edge of the village green. I unlocked the front door with my own key, the one Dad had insisted I keep, even after I moved out because his home was always my home, he said. It wasn't particularly odd to find the cottage empty because my dad spent most of the time in his shed. I crossed the tiny back garden, past the potted plants and mossy wooden bench and bits of wood stacked against the wall. As I pushed open the shed door, the certainty grew stronger, that I'd find him standing there at his workbench with a mug of tea on the go and half a packet of chocolate digestives, ready to give me a big, warm hug. Radio 4 would be playing in the background; disembodied voices having intelligent conversations.

But Ted had heard music, which made no sense. My dad never listened to music, claimed he had no ear for it.

As one of Chatsworth's odd-job-men, or oddmen as they were affectionately called, he spent all day fixing things and he was so good at it that he was in constant demand from neighbours and friends during his time off. He was never without a screwdriver in his hand: mending broken legs on chairs, repairing radios, kettles, toasters. People were always bringing him stuff to patch up and he was hopeless at saying no.

If only he'd been able to mend himself. But he'd stopped taking care of his health after my mother, Sukey, left us. What had really happened all those years ago? Maybe I'd never know. His memories were out of reach now, erased. I suddenly regretted not sitting him down, just once and asking him the questions I could now never ask. We should have talked, really talked, while we still had the chance. It was too late now. Too late.

Without the welcoming orange glow from the little three-bar electric radiator, the shed was bitterly cold. I turned my eyes from my dad's saggy old armchair and went straight to the workbench where there was half-drunk tea, in his favourite mug. I'd given it to him for Father's Day when I was about twelve years old. The words 'Best Dad in the World' were printed on it in cartoon letters, faded over time. The tea had grown cold, its surface mottled and the mug looked unbearably poignant and forlorn. I touched it, thinking how my dad's fingers had touched it too. Just a few hours ago. A lifetime ago.

He'd been fixing a vintage record player for Bea and Ted's teenage daughter, Jasmine. There was a liquorice-black disk beneath the needle, an album cover laid face down on the bench beside it.

I picked up the album sleeve. Molly Marrison, it said, in swirly, hippy graphics. *Died for Love*. It had meant nothing to me when Bea said the name but now, seeing it written down, the shape of the letters, I felt a weird stir of recognition.

Molly.

I turned the sleeve over. And stopped breathing.

The girl in the photograph was in soft focus, dressed in green velvet and lace with a sunset behind her, the sky a blaze of yellow, orange and red. She had long, straight black hair and a strong, serene face. Her skin was dusky, with high cheekbones that made her look like a Cherokee. She seemed to be in a trance. Her dark sage's eyes looked right through me. I'd seen another photograph of her in this shed, years ago.

I found the knob on the record player and turned it on, watched the black disc begin to spin. I lifted the needle arm, gliding the stylus on the end of my finger, lowering it gently into the outermost groove.

An expectant crackle of static, then an astonishingly beautiful voice filled the cold air. It was pure and warm, like chocolate and gold, though the song was weighted with such awful sorrow and despair. An elegy. I hadn't read the titles of the tracks but I didn't need to. I knew this song.

Over moors and valleys deep, through the Dark Peak and the White
There two tragic lovers sleep in gritstone, blood, and lime.

It was *The Runaway Lovers.*

All this time I'd been running from the past, only to find, like a child in a twisted fairytale, that I'd been going in a circle, had ended up right back where I began. I hadn't thought about Robbie Nightingale for so long. I'd not allowed myself to think of him. I'd decided that it could never have worked out for us. His arms had once felt like the safest place I knew, my harbour and shelter from the storm. Until I realised that maybe I was the storm.

I had vowed never to regret. Never to worry that I'd made the most terrible mistake of my life. I tried not to wonder: what if? Side by side, they're the most powerful two words in the world, aren't they? What if?

Now, all my resolve fell away. I wanted to hear his voice. I needed to hear his voice: talking to me, teasing me, singing to me, it didn't matter which. I missed him, with a hollowed-out ache, as if my vital organs had been replaced by holes. Robbie had been my best friend. Who was I kidding? He'd been so much more than a friend. For a time, when I was a kid and then a troubled teen, he'd meant everything to me. My whole world had revolved around him.

I could just pick up the phone and call him.

No. I couldn't.

As I watched the black disc spinning, spinning, spinning, the years fell away and time spun backwards. I was ten years old again and my world was about to shatter, to change forever, in the most terrible way that a child's world could change.

CHAPTER FOUR

SILVA - 1978

I instantly blamed myself for the way things turned out, and I went on blaming myself. If only I hadn't gone to the Christmas party, I might have been able to stop my mum from doing what she did. I might at least have understood.

But I did go to the party. Of course I did.

It was one of the most magical traditions at Chatsworth. The children from the village primary school were all invited up to the House for a special celebration, presided over by the Duke and Duchess of Devonshire and by Father Christmas himself. Our parents all came too and it was the highlight of the season for my mum, the chance to dress up and hobnob with nobility.

There were twenty of us kids, aged between five and eleven, and we travelled the three short miles from school in a trailer with slatted wooden benches down each side, drawn by Naomi and Sally, the faithful old Chatsworth shire horses. Weathermen had been predicting a harsh winter but the gabled Victorian schoolhouse looked as pretty as a

Christmas card as the horse-drawn carriage, of sorts, drew away. There was the deep stillness that heavy snow always brought, amplifying our excited chatter. Pilsley wasn't as chocolate-box perfect as the other two villages on the Chatsworth estate but all the buildings were distinguished by the elegant dark turquoise paintwork, known as Chatsworth Blue. Along with the village shop, there was a post office, a bright red telephone box and a quaint old coaching inn, the Devonshire Arms.

We passed the cottage where I lived with my parents, in the middle of a terraced row that faced out onto the village green, opposite the old Smithy House. The cottages were hundreds of years old and their original thatched roofs had long been replaced by slates but were now blanketed with snow as thick as thatch. Windows glowed with golden lamp-light and the green itself was no longer green. It was popu-lated by snowmen, in a range of shapes and sizes and jaunty scarves and hats. My dad and I had spent all Saturday morning shaping ours and I'd made him a little snow dog, a terrier, to keep him company.

There was a light on in the upstairs widow and I imag-ined my mum, sitting in front of the mirror at her kidney-shaped dressing table, getting dressed for the party. She never left the house without her hair flicked with a curling wand, her eyes shadowed with blue powder, lips glossy red.

As we trundled round Pilsley Green, I saw a lady, who was definitely not my mum, coming out of our front door. She had black hair and was wearing a bottle-green coat with an orange scarf thrown over her shoulder. Head down, she was hurrying as if she couldn't get away fast enough. I knew nearly everyone who lived and worked at Chatsworth and I didn't recognise this person. Who was she? Might her visit be connected to the horrible row my parents had had last night? The nasty things my mother had shouted? It made my eyes sting with tears, just trying not to think about it. I quickly brushed the tears away.

'Are you OK, Silva?' my teacher asked softly, leaning forward, a concerned look on her face.

I nodded.

'Are you warm enough?'

'Yes thank you, Miss.'

We were all wrapped in woolly hats and scarves and Mrs Nightingale was clutching the plastic envelope, full of paper snowflakes. Every year, children from the school made decorations, to adorn the enormous tree in the Painted Hall and this year, Mrs Nightingale had taught us how to cut out snowflakes from paper.

She'd sat us all down, cross-legged, in a semi-circle on the square of blue carpet, in the corner of the classroom where she'd taken her seat in her wooden armchair. She was so pretty, like a silhouette of a girl on a cameo, with an oval-shaped face and thick auburn hair, piled messily on her head. It was easy to imagine her wearing a ball gown with a velvet choker around her throat, but in reality, she tended to wear long jersey dresses the colour of rust and moss, that hugged her slender body and flowed down to her ankles. She looked as if she should play a harp and she had the most soothing voice, especially when she told stories, which she did often. Like now, when even an art lesson had begun with a pretty tale. She'd waited until we were all sitting quietly around her, then she told a story. She said it was a true story, about a man called Snowflake Bentley and that it had been told to her by her eldest son, Robbie.

'Snowflake Bentley lived at the beginning of the century, in a place called Vermont in New England,' Mrs Nightingale began, in her sing-song voice. 'It's called New England but it's a long way away from this old England where we live. It's in America, at the other side of the Atlantic Ocean. In New England, every year, there are drifts of snow that last for months. And Snowflake Bentley went out in the deep snow every day and found a way of taking pictures of snowflakes, hundreds of them, using an old camera and a microscope. He was fascinated by snowflakes,' Mrs Nightingale said 'because he saw that each and every one, is beautiful and unique. Just like children and the people they grow up to become.'

She held up the open book, showing amazingly intricate, glittering white shapes on black backgrounds. I couldn't believe they were real snowflakes. They made me think of lace and leaf skeletons, frost flowers on the window. When the other children went back to their desks, I waited patiently and asked if I could look at the book up close.

'Wonderful, aren't they?' Mrs Nightingale said softly, as I leafed through the thick, glossy pages, stopping to take in each image. At the front of the book, her son had signed his name in bold blue letters. Robbie. The shape of his signature was as pleasing to me as the shapes of the snowflakes. What sort of boy would own such a book? How wonderful it would be to have a big brother like that. I'd always longed for a brother or a sister, big or little. I hated being an only child.

'Since we don't have a camera or a magnifying glass, we'll have to improvise,' Mrs Nightingale had said, when we were all seated back at our desks. She handed out paper, pencils and scissors and showed us how to make the cutouts. It was exciting to use the paper to make something in 3D rather than just drawing on it.

Step one, start with a square; step two, fold diagonally.

Fold the triangle in half, then a third. Cut the top off and draw a pattern. Cut it out and unfold. Ta-dah! A snowflake.

I screwed mine up.

'Why did you do that?' Mrs Nightingale asked gently, coming over to my table.

'It wasn't any good.'

'Oh, that's not true, Silva. It was lovely.'

'It was much better than mine,' said Mrs Nightingale's daughter, Freya.

Freya was a year younger than me but we were in the same class because there were only two classes in the whole school. A cheery little lass, who talked about ponies incessantly and had won lots of rosettes, she had a freckled nose and bouncy red curls, several shades brighter than her mum's.

I smiled my thanks at her but the trouble was, that my snowflake looked nothing like the photographs in Mrs Nightingale's book and I knew I could do better.

'Here. Have another go,' my teacher suggested, handing over a fresh piece of paper.

I glanced up as I worked and saw out of the classroom window, that it was snowing again, as if we'd made it snow by making snowflakes, like mad scientists conjuring up lightning with a chemical reaction. I drew a pattern that was more curly and complex and the result was better, still not great but it would have to do because I didn't want to disappoint Mrs Nightingale by having nothing to take with me to the party. I was always disappointing people. My mum was bitterly disappointed if I didn't get ten out of ten for my times tables and spelling tests or win the obstacle race on sports day. Dad said she just liked to show off to the other mums. I did my best and I often got eight out of ten in the tests and came second or third in sports races, but still, nothing I ever did was good enough. Nothing I ever did made my mum want to hug me and play with me, like other mums did. A paper snowflake was certainly not going to do the trick, since she said art was a complete waste of time. I wasn't allowed to make things at home because Mum said that, mostly, I just made a mess.

The teacher took a reel of white cotton from a box and proceeded to cut off lengths for us to tie in loops through one of the points of the snowflakes.

I looked at the cotton and then at my snowflake and I bit my lip, wondering if it was quite right.

'Penny for your thoughts,' Mrs Nightingale said.

She always encouraged us to speak up, so I did. 'Shouldn't we use green cotton instead of white?'

'That's such a dumb idea,' sniggered one of the boys. 'It won't match.'

Mrs Nightingale ignored him. 'Why do you think green would be best, Silva?'

'It needs to blend in with the Christmas tree that the snowflakes are going to be hung on, rather than with the snowflakes themselves. So it looks like they're falling.'

'Excellent idea.' Mrs Nightingale reached for the green cotton reel, slotting the white one back in the box. 'Thank you, Silva.'

She told us to write our names on the back of our snowflake and then she collected them all up and carefully ironed them, one by one. She'd put the snowflakes in the plastic envelope to keep them dry; to be handed back to their creators when we arrived at the House.

The shire horses were drawing the trailer through the golden gates, Chatsworth's grand entrance, that lead to the long, wide drive, that wound up through the deer park, now blanketed with white. I liked gates: the way they're like a barrier and an invitation, a welcome and a warning.

These gates stood over twelve feet tall, were six feet wide, made of wrought iron and partially gilded. Perfectly symmetrical, they were adorned with leaves, shields and gold scrolls. The shire horses were plodding but even so, they were moving too fast for me. I wished I'd brought my sketch pad. My brain was always bubbling over with ideas which sometimes kept me awake at night and I realised that if I could copy some of the intricacies of the ironwork, if I drew half-moons and petals and lozenges, it would turn into the prettiest paper snowflake ever.

But we'd already left the gates behind and now came the magic moment, when Chatsworth House first came into sight, the view captured on a million picture-postcards, that were sent all over the world. There it stood, so magnificent between the woods and the water, with the three arches of Paine's Bridge crossing the river before it. Chatsworth had once been called the Palace of the Peak and it was easy to see why, with its huge, gilded windows and the fountains and statues in the manicured garden, while behind, rose a dramatically contrasting backdrop of densely wooded hills and bleak outcrops of gritstone crags, surrounded by wild and desolate heather moorland. My dad always told me never to take it for granted, that we were fortunate enough to actually live here, in this wonderful place.

The trailer trundled up to the courtyard, which was bordered by the impressive stone stables with another fountain in the centre. Icicles dripped crystal spears and daggers. The horses came to a halt, blowing smoke from their noses, snorting and tossing their heads, making their bridles jangle. The sides of the trailer were let down for us all to clamber out. Mrs Nightingale made us line up in twos, crocodile formation, to enter the House through the North Entrance Hall, which was lit by the welcoming blaze of a huge log fire. The reflection of the flames danced on Roman statues and on the gigantic oil painting of a ruined abbey that hung above the massive hearth. We walked along the North Corridor, nearly two dozen little footsteps ringing out on the elaborate geometric floor. It was composed of coloured marbles, like a rainbow version of the Yellow Brick Road, taking us to the Painted Hall.

The largest and grandest room of all the large and grand rooms at Chatsworth, the Painted Hall was filled with illusion. A triumphal archway graced the top of a wide staircase and the black and white marble floor spread out like the giant chessboard from Wonderland. It was very dramatic and theatrical, especially today, when the hall was decked for Christmas. Dozens of bay trees had been arranged around the room with tangerines fixed by invisible wires, to make them look like orange trees. It was a Chatsworth tradition and the tangerines gave off the most wonderful zesty, Christmassy scent.

All the parents were gathered in groups by long trestle tables that were laden with a feast: sausages-on-sticks, gingerbread men, cupcakes and jellies. Other adults waited by the towering pine tree, decorated with twinkling lights and glittering baubles. My friends were squealing and running across the checkerboard floor to join their mums and dads. I stood quiet and still in the middle of it all, fighting down a surge of panic, because I'd searched all the faces, all the groups of grown-ups. My mum wasn't here.

I blinked away hot, stinging tears. I was not going to cry in front of everybody. I was not.

'In this house, always remember to look up,' my dad kept telling me. So I turned my face to the ceiling now, to stop the tears from spilling and the sumptuous painted murals and frescoes swirled above me. The scenes of Roman emperors gleamed as fresh and bright as if they'd been painted only yesterday.

'Where's your mum, Silva?' Mrs Nightingale inquired.

I wiped at my eyes with my fingers. 'I don't know, Miss.'

'How about your dad? He works here, doesn't he?'

I nodded. 'He's one of the oddmen.'

I could see that Mrs Nightingale was trying not to giggle because I'd used the funny name for odd-job-men but said it so seriously. She opened the envelope of snowflakes, searched through them and handed over my snowflake. 'How about you hang yours on first. It's the best one,' she added, confidingly.

I felt really proud as I walked over to the huge tree, clutching my snowflake in my hand. I took my time, selecting a good branch, while the other children all lined up behind me. I reached up on tiptoe and carefully, with a sense of ceremony, I threaded the green cotton loop onto a branch.

There.

'How pretty it looks, Silva,' Duchess Deborah told me.

'Thank you, Your Grace.'

The duchess looked pretty too, in her dark-grey tailored wool jacket and pleated skirt, which matched her perfectly styled grey hair. Standing beside his wife, the Duke was smart, in a brass-buttoned blazer and festive tie. For over four hundred years, Chatsworth had been owned by the Cavendish family, a line currently led by the 11th Duke and Duchess Deborah. The Great and The Good, my dad called them. I always wondered which was which. I especially loved the duchess, who seemed to be both a very good and a very great lady. She had a string of pearls round her neck and matching pearls in her ears and she always looked like the Queen. Mum loved to tell people that our duchess was one of the legendary Mitford sisters, known as Debo. Her boundless energy and enthusiasm had saved Chatsworth from having to be sold after the war but she wasn't too grand to work behind the counter selling tickets. She did have a grand voice though and a way of putting people in their place, just with a look. 'Now John,' I'd heard her scold. But my dad didn't mind; he'd do anything for her. We all would.

The House Comptroller, Mr Bradwell, was a tall and imposing man with a short beard and salt-and-pepper grey hair and he made us all hush. Everyone listened to Mr Bradwell. We'd not dare do otherwise. He was very important, in charge of the entire household, the buildings, gardens and lakes and everything to do with opening the House to the public too - the ticket sellers and car park attendants. It was also his job to arrange parties.

'I've been in touch with Father Christmas on my radio,' he said. 'The sleigh is about an hour away, so you've plenty of time.'

I sat down next to Freya, who tucked into the party food with gusto. I took a bite of sausage roll but I wasn't hungry. I was still hoping that my mum would show up in time to see Father Christmas arrive.

She didn't though. She missed it all. When Santa had finished giving out presents from his sack, I wondered what I was supposed to do, since there was nobody to take me home. I worried then, that something terrible had happened.

CHAPTER FIVE

'You'd better come with us,' Mrs Nightingale said to me, seeing me sitting forlornly on the bottom step of the wide, red-carpeted staircase.

I was tracing the metal scrolls in the balustrade with my finger and clutching the packet of modelling clay Father Christmas had given to me, somehow knowing that modelling clay was what I wanted, more than anything in the world. I wanted to show it to my dad, only he couldn't be found either. But as well as being doubly anxious now, I was excited to ride in Mrs Nightingale's bright yellow Triumph and go back to her house.

The Nightingales lived in Beeley village, which lay at the foot of a moor of the same name, looking out over Lindop Wood. With old houses built of mellow stone, narrow lanes, ancient trees and a little boutique hotel on the snowy banks of the stream, it was idyllically picturesque.

Brook House was a farmhouse that had lost its farm, but was still surrounded by an acre of land with a ramshackle stone barn and fruit trees, their branches curtseying low under the snow. The house itself was three centuries old and inside its sturdy walls was a warren of comfortable rooms and higgledy-piggledy nooks and crannies, the ceilings low and ribbed with heavy oak-beams, like the hull of a sailing ship. At the heart of the house was a big kitchen with a scrubbed pine table and cream-coloured cooking range throwing out warmth. I felt much calmer, just being here. I told myself that everything would be alright.

At Chatsworth House, antiques coexisted with modern art, whereas Brook Farm seemed to be in a time warp, with nothing modern at all; every piece of furniture looked as if it had its own long history. There was also an array of obscure musical instruments in the corner of the living room.

'The gong's from the Hebrides and the Uilleann pipes are Irish,' Freya said, seeing me eyeing them. 'They're Robbie's.'

On the deep window ledge there was a photo of a lad in school uniform. He had grey-blue eyes and a mop of curly brown hair and he was leaning against a tree, his tie half-undone and his school blazer slung over his shoulder, hooked on his finger.

'That was taken near our house on Lewis,' Freya said.

'Where's Lewis.'

'It's an island off Scotland. We used to live there.'

'Where d'you like best, there or here?'

With no hesitation, Freya said: 'Here.'

A pile of books was stacked by the sofa: heavy tomes about mythology and folklore, music and history.

'Mum works as a teacher and she enjoys studying, herself,' Freya said. 'She even likes taking exams. Dad says he wishes me and Robbie were more like her.' She giggled.

'Robbie took a maths test last week and he got detention because he wrote song lyrics all over the paper.'

My eyes were drawn back to the photo. 'What was the song?'

Freya shrugged, frowned, as if I'd just asked the daftest question.

Where was Robbie now, I wondered? The wind had got up, rattling the windowpanes. We scoffed a plateful of flapjacks and Freya played a tinkly tune on the grand piano. Mrs Nightingale came and told me that she'd spoken to my dad, who'd be round later to pick me up. Meantime, I was to stay for dinner. So everything was going to be fine.

'Let's paint our nails,' Freya suggested. 'Something Christmassy? Red or gold? You should have gold, since you're called Silva.'

'OK,' I said. My name wasn't spelt like the colour but everyone always assumed it was.

We knelt on the carpet and Freya started work on my right hand. She'd done four fingers when she got a blob of varnish on my white school shirt. I tried to rub it off with my thumb but that only made it worse. 'I'd better wash it,' I said. My mum would kill me if it was stained.

'The bathroom's on the first floor landing.'

As I walked through the hall, I heard someone singing, a lone male voice, drifting down from high up in the house, melodious and unaccompanied.

Over moors and valleys deep, through the Dark Peak and the White
There two tragic lovers sleep in gritstone, blood, and lime.

I instantly forgot all about the splodge of glitter on my top and I followed the song, as if summoned by it. I walked up two flights of uncarpeted, worn, wooden stairs and along a narrow corridor, then up another creaky, winding stair-case. I came to an empty attic room - empty, all except for a young boy and a tape deck. I recognised him from the photograph downstairs. He was wearing faded blue jeans and a dark blue jumper and his feet were bare; bony toes which were not pale white like mine, but softly tanned, as if he often went barefoot. He was sitting cross-legged beneath the skylight on a worn rug, a pair of headphones clamped over brown curls. He was scribbling away with a biro in a spiral bound notebook, which was opened on the floor in front of him.

I stood back in the shadows beside the doorway so I could listen to him and watch without interrupting. He looked to be in a world of his own. He stopped the tape, pressed rewind or fast forward, then hit the play button. He jotted something down and pressed pause again, sang another refrain. I realised that he was learning the song he was listening to.

Clara, such a tender girl, virtuous and fair to see
Daughter of a wealthy Lord, but cruel as death was he
Suitors rich and mighty came, all for Clara's favour strove
But only one, with fortunes none, young Henry stole her love

Experience had taught me, only last night in fact, that no good at all came from snooping and besides, it felt all wrong. But I couldn't bring myself to go. I felt inexplicably drawn to him, almost like an ill person craves food containing the right vitamins to make them feel better.

The song was about a girl and boy, who'd been murdered on their way to be married. Unaccompanied, it sounded like nothing I'd ever heard before and it had a grip-ping narrative that made me want to go on listening, just to hear how the story ended. The way he sang, set up vibrations inside my body. Made me feel as if I was inside his thoughts. He seemed to inhabit the song and the story and he'd transported me with him, into that dramatic, other world. More than that, the melody of the song and the words, stirred something in me, as if I'd known them all my life.

Come my Clara, let's be gone, slipping silent out of sight
From your fathers house we'll steal into this moonless night
Fast they rode to lands unknown, through the Dark Peak and the White
Seeking for a place renown for pitying young loves plight

Far, far away, Freya was calling my name.

Robbie looked up. I gasped, sprang back, but it was too late. He'd seen me standing there, staring at him and it was as if I'd intruded on an intensely private moment; as if I'd walked in on him when he'd just stepped out of the shower and had caught sight of him stark naked. But he smiled at me and I smiled back. Then I turned and bolted downstairs.

Mrs Nightingale placed a huge bowl of steaming soup on the table. 'Cock-a-leekie.'

'That's Scottish for chicken and leek,' Freya translated, helpfully.

'It smells delicious,' I said honestly.

'They used to serve the chicken whole, sitting in the soup,' Mrs Nightingale told me.

'How would you eat it?' asked Freya, wrinkling her nose.

'By ripping it apart with your fingers I imagine,' Mr Nightingale offered. 'Don't go getting ideas, litt'un,' he said with a wink across the table to Ewan, Freya's younger brother. Mr Nightingale was a big, bearded man with a kindly smile. He'd just come home from work in the Chatsworth gardens and kicked off his snowy wellington boots, before washing his reddened hands in the deep butler sink. He dried them on a towel, all the while chatting about the challenges of feeding the deer in the park during the cold spell, and two of the gardeners he worked with, named Bill and Ben.

'The Flower Pot Men,' Ewan chimed.

'They really are,' Mrs Nightingale smiled. 'I had a lovely chat to Bill the other day about his younger sister, Mary, who was a famous singer in the late Forties, apparently. I never knew.'

'That's because because Bill's sole topic of conversation is normally about planting and harvesting plants guided by the position of the moon,' Mr Nightingale said. 'He's an interesting chap. Very deep and mystical.'

'Robbie should talk to him about his sister,' Mrs Nightingale said, as she ladled soup into my bowl. She turned to Freya: 'Where's he got to now anyway? Your brother?'

'Where d'you think?'

'Be a poppet and run up and fetch him, would you, darling?' Mrs Nightingale turned to me: 'It's my fault. There's this ballad that my mother used to sing, called *The Runaway Lovers*, about a young couple in the eighteenth century, who eloped from Scotland and were ambushed as they were riding through Winnats Pass. Clara's saddle is in the little museum in Castleton and was given to the curator by my great-grandfather, Jack Willis. One of his ancestors got hold of it, when he was working here at Chatsworth as a groom, at the time of the murder.'

'I'm going to work with ponies too,' Freya said.

'So you keep telling us, love. The Dukes of Devonshire owned all the land in Castleton back then,' Mrs Nightingale added, 'so the riderless horses were brought to the Chatsworth stables. Anyway, Robbie's become quite obsessed by that song, just as I was.'

'Why are they called the Duke and Duchess of Devonshire, when they live in Derbyshire?' asked Ewan. He was about five years old, with white-blonde hair, and was dressed in stripy dungarees.

'It's just a title, sweetie, given to the first Duke by the king,' Mrs Nightingale told him.

'Are you related to Florence Nightingale?' I asked. We'd learnt in a school history lesson, how Florence lived in Derbyshire before she went to nurse wounded soldiers with her lamp.

'My cousins grew up in the house where Florence was born,' Mr Nightingale explained.

If you were ill, Mr Nightingale was just the sort of person you'd want to have looking after you. I thought how nursing and gardening were similar jobs, all about nurturing living things.

Robbie bounded downstairs and slid into the chair beside me, which was good, because it meant I didn't have to face him.

'This is Silva,' Mrs Nightingale said to him.

'Hi-ho, Silver.' He threw me the sunniest smile. 'Sorry. Bet people say that to you all the time.'

'Actually, you're the first.'

He looked really pleased to hear it.

'It's Silva spelt with an A, not E-R though,' Mrs Nightingale told her eldest son.

'It means from the woods,' I said quietly. 'My dad said I came from the woods.'

Robbie smiled again. 'That's awesome. But do people always spell it wrong?'

'Yeah and they're always telling me that a girl called Silver should have fair hair.'

Mrs Nightingale stroked my head. 'Instead, it's glossy and dark as a raven's wing.'

'That's a description straight from a story book, Mum,' Robbie said. 'You so have to write one.' He reached for the butter, to butter his bread, just as there was an almighty gust of wind. The lights flickered off, then back on, then went out and stayed out.

Power cuts were common in the outlying villages of the Peak District and you had to be prepared. At home, my dad kept torches loaded with batteries but Mrs Nightingale's emergency remedy was more traditional. She fetched matches and lit a candle, then used that to light more candles, so that the whole kitchen was illuminated with flickering gold light. It was as if we'd slipped back into another era and were seeing the farmhouse as it used to be long ago, with golden gleams on old wooden beams, and pools of darkness and unlit corners, where ghosts might loiter and hide.

'Someone tell us a story then,' Mrs Nightingale said, sitting back down at the table with a sense of occasion, as if she relished power cuts and the modern, electric light had stifled her somehow. She was looking at Robbie expectantly, as if he was the one with all the stories.

Robbie leant back in his chair, his profile gilded. With his broad shoulders, curly hair and his strong, straight nose, wide eyes and full mouth, he looked just like one of the Roman statues from the sculpture gallery at Chatsworth. I decided the Nightingales were the most beautiful and fascinating family I'd ever met.

'I've been listening to that tape about the Runaway Lovers,' Robbie said.

His mother pushed her soup bowl aside and sat forward with her elbows on the table, her chin propped on her hands. 'And?'

'I can't stop thinking about it.'

'It has everything, doesn't it? It's a romance and a murder story and a ghost story, all in one. A mystery too. I mean, we don't even know who Henry and Clara were, or where they came from.'

'What actually happened to them?' I had to ask.

Robbie turned to me. 'D'you scare easily?'

I wondered why he even had to ask because it was as if he knew me; knew everything there was to know about me, could read my thoughts. I shook my head. I felt only a delicious sense of anticipation. I wanted to hear this story, even if it were to terrify the living daylights out of me.

'Excuse me,' said Robbie's dad, scraping his chair legs back on the flagstones as he stood. He picked up his mug of tea and a candlestick before retreating to his study, as if he'd heard this family legend plenty of times.

'Clara was an aristocratic lady from Scotland, whose father had forbidden her to marry Henry,' Robbie began, in a softly compelling storyteller's voice, not unlike his mother's. 'They planned to elope to the little chapel at Peak Forest, where young couples could get married without their parents' consent. But Derbyshire was a dangerous and desolate country back then. Big Moor, which you have to cross to get here from Sheffield, was described as a wasteland and a howling wilderness. As Henry and Clara rode side-by-side through Winnats Pass, under the moonlight, they were set upon by a gang of miners, dragged from their horses, robbed and brutally murdered. Their bodies were thrown into a disused mine and their skeletons weren't found until years later but their spirits haunted the lonely glen. Still do. Their screams can still be heard and the galloping of horses' hooves. The murderers were never caught but they didn't escape justice. It's considered bad form to mention their names because there are family members still living in Castleton, who are ashamed of being descended from them. Four died in horrible ways and the fifth man confessed on his deathbed. God's retribution. Or so the story goes.'

'What do you mean?' Mrs Nightingale asked. 'So the story goes?'

'Well it's a famous folk tale, Mum. It's been passed on through so many generations, by long chains of people, so it might not all be true.'

A knock at the door made me jump out of my skin, but it was just my dad, come to take me home.

'Thanks for having me,' I said to Mrs Nightingale, as I quickly pulled on my boots and coat. They were lovely and warm and dry because she'd taken the trouble to put them by the range. She was like the kind mother in the Ladybird 'Learn to Read' books, that I still had on my bookcase from when I was smaller. Stories about how Peter and Jane's mum took them shopping and cooked nice food and tucked them up in bed at night. My own mum never did any of those things. She just said: Never have kids. They'll ruin your life.

'You're welcome any time, Silva,' Mrs Nightingale said. 'I mean that. Just come over whenever you want.' She stroked my hair again. 'Have a lovely Christmas.'

'You too. Merry Christmas.'

'Where's Mum?' I asked my dad, as I crunched after him down the snowy, moonlit garden path.

He said nothing and went on saying nothing as I climbed into the passenger seat of our old green Ford Cortina. He banged the door shut, put the key in the ignition and my eyes flew to his face, searching for the dad I knew and loved, the one who told terrible jokes and was able to calmly rescue people, when their guttering fell down or a pipe sprang a leak. But alarmingly, there was no sign of that person. He looked crumpled, his features fallen in somehow, like the roof of an old house that sagged in the middle.

He sat there beside me in the driver's seat but he didn't start the engine, even though it was freezing cold. He didn't seem to notice the temperature. He seemed to have forgotten that I was even there and forgotten what to do with the key. Our breath was misting the car windows and I shivered. Dad's shoulders slumped and he turned to face me at last. The crinkles round his dark eyes, which deepened when he smiled, now looked deep in a different way, as if he'd aged ten years in ten hours.

'Silva, there's something I need to tell you.'

I swallowed. 'About Mum?'

He rubbed at his forehead as if to dislodge something. 'Yes, love.' His voice was as heavy as a stone sinking to the bottom of a well.

'What about her?'

'She's gone.'

'What do you mean, gone? Gone where?'

'I don't know, Sweetheart.'

I twisted round in my seat to face him. 'Well, when will she be back?'

'I don't know that either.'

'Tonight? Tomorrow? Next week?' Surely she'd not be gone as long as a week? 'You must have some idea.'

He shook his head.

'But she will be back for Christmas?'

'I don't know.'

I was shaking uncontrollably now, my knees knocking together like a cartoon character. I felt all wobbly and there was a nasty taste in my mouth. This couldn't be happening. What my dad was saying wasn't true. But he'd not lie about something like this?

I swallowed hard. 'She is…coming back? Eventually, I mean?'

'I don't know.'

Why did he keep saying he didn't know? He had to know. Adults were supposed to know things, have answers, and if he didn't, then we needed to find out. He needed to start the car. Right now. We had to get back home. Maybe Mum had just popped out somewhere, not thought to mention it and was back already.

'She's taken her clothes,' Dad said, his voice ragged. 'Make-up. Shoes. Hairdryer. The lot.'

'Dad. We have to call the police.'

Now he turned the key and the engine spluttered to life. The headlights lit up the snow, making it sparkle as if scattered with diamond dust. 'She's a grown woman, Silva. If she wants to leave, she can leave.'

My granny Ivy came round. Dad's mum. She rustled us up some lamb chops but I sat pushing the meat and bones around on my plate, tears streaming down my face, trying not to snivel. Dad ate fast, businesslike, then rinsed his plate under the kitchen tap and left it to dry on the draining board. He hurried out of the kitchen as if he had much to do, but in reality, I think he didn't know what to do at all.

My granny offered me her handkerchief, ironed and scented with lavender. 'Don't cry, Silva,' she said, 'there's a good girl. You don't want to upset your dad.'

I didn't want to upset him at all, so I wiped my eyes, my nose, tried to control myself.

'Come and help me wash up,' Granny cajoled.

I stuffed the handkerchief up the sleeve of my jumper, as she handed me a tea towel and I dried our plates, knives, forks and the pans. I put them all away neatly.

After Granny had gone home and my dad had gone to his shed, I had to find something else to do, so I set about tidying and cleaning our cottage from top to bottom. I found Marigold gloves under the sink and attacked the kitchen and bathroom with bleach. I found a duster and polished the furniture with lemon-scented polish, until it shone and I mopped the floors with lavender-scented cleaning fluid. My dad was a big believer in elbow grease, so I used plenty and I vacuumed, as if my life depended on it. I wasn't sure I was doing anything right, which detergents to use for what but I scrubbed the inside of the fridge and rearranged the knives and forks in the cutlery drawer. While I was at it, I dusted the skirting boards. I dragged out my wardrobe and the sideboard and brushed away the cobwebs that had gathered behind them. I did all the ironing piled in the basket. By the time I was done, the whole house shone and the air smelt of springtime.

I wanted everything nice for my mum to come home to.

She never did come home but I carried on cleaning. Dad wasn't chauvinistic at all but he did belong to a generation that automatically left housework to womenfolk. He'd occasionally whizzed round with the Hoover on a Saturday, to keep Mum sweet but after she'd gone, he'd lost heart in pretty much everything. He stopped caring for himself, let alone the cleaning. So, despite being just a kid, I took responsibility for keeping us both fed and ensuring everywhere was spotless. I got good at seeing what needed to be done.

I always remembered what my granny had said. It became my motto. *You don't want to upset your dad.*

So from that day on, if I felt sad or scared, I just plastered a smile on my face, told myself to take it on the chin and get on with things. I made it my responsibility to make things better for my dad, not worse. There was a hooligan inside me, wanting to shout and scream about what had happened to us but I kept her quiet. Granny Ivy had always disapproved of my mum for her shouting; said that ladies never raised their voices. So when I felt anger boiling up inside me, I learnt to push it back down, bottle things up.

When my dad was working in his shed and couldn't see me, I stood at our front window for ages, willing my mum to walk up the lane and across the green. If I imagined it hard enough, maybe it could actually happen. I was always listening out for the sound of the garden gate, the front door opening, the sound of her voice calling out hello.

Each day that passed without that happening, the fury and grief built and built inside me, but I never let it show. Instead, I turned it inwards, where I felt it grow bigger and hotter, filling my whole body, like the lava in a volcano, the fire at the centre of the earth - ready to erupt one day.

CHAPTER SIX

SILVA - 2002

'I know you cooked for your dad, rather than for yourself,' Bea said, standing outside the door of my cottage, holding an earthenware casserole dish. 'So my worry is, that you won't bother now and you'll waste away.'

Tijou's nose was all a twitch and the little spaniel jumped up my leg as I took the heavy pot. It was still warm and gave off mouthwatering smells that made my stomach gurgle. I realised I'd not eaten anything out of an oven since my dad died, had been existing on toast and bananas and pots of tea. 'It's really kind of you, Bea.'

Everyone had been incredibly kind. The news of my dad's sudden death had spread lightening-fast around Chatsworth. Robbie's mother, Flora Nightingale, arrived with pink camellias cut specially by her husband, Hugh, from the glasshouse and my colleague Lizzie and her eldest daughter, Carys, had come round with cookies they'd baked together especially. When I went to buy milk at the local shop, half a dozen people stopped to give me hugs. This was the very best part of living in such a tight-knit community.

'Kettle on?' Bea asked, stroking Tijou's big floppy ears but tutting at him, as if he was spoilt and disobedient, which he was. I hated telling him off because he always looked so dejected.

I set the dish on the pine table, next to the Blue John vase which was filled with the camellias.

'How's Ted?' I asked, taking a bottle of milk from the fridge, along with the box of Lizzie's cookies.

Bea didn't answer and when I turned to find out why, I saw that she'd picked up the record that I'd found in my dad's shed and had propped up on the dresser. I'd brought it back with me because if I was going to do as he had asked and find this person called Molly, this seemed like a vital clue, the only clue I had, in fact.

Bea was staring at the photograph.

'What is it?' I asked.

'I've seen her before,' she said. 'Here. At Chatsworth. I'm sure of it.' She looked up at me. 'It was years ago but she was definitely here. With your dad. And your mother.'

CHAPTER SEVEN

MOLLY - 1967

Living only a few miles from Chatsworth, Molly has been here on family outings and once on a school trip, but with John Brightmore showing her around, it's as if she's seeing it all for the first time.

The sweeping drive is finished with crushed gravel chippings that give it a soft pinky-brown appearance, very different to the hard navy blue of the main road beyond the golden gates, out in the real world. The old turf that covers the park is grazed short by cattle and fallow deer, so it's like an endless lawn with clusters of trees, beneath which the animals shelter from the sun. Chatsworth House itself is a gilded fairytale palace. John is not at all like other boys and it's no wonder, growing up in such an extraordinary place.

When she came to Chatsworth before, Molly had shared the House with car loads of families and coach loads of pensioners and foreign tourists but now, the magnificent rooms are enveloped in a rarefied silence, a waiting stillness that makes Molly almost hold her breath. Everything looks grander with no clicking cameras and chattering voices. It's as if they've stepped into another world, slipped back in time to a more genteel era. This place. It's like a little slice of paradise.

'There's an hour to go before the doors open,' John says, glancing at his watch.

'How come you're allowed in?' asks Sukey, sulkily.

Really, Molly doesn't know why the other girl was so keen to come today.

Molly had practically invited herself here, mostly because she wanted an excuse to spend more time with John. He looked like Jesus, with his shaggy hair and stubbly beard, his kind, wise eyes and gentle manner. He wants to change the world and is certain music holds the key. He cares about the planet, hates the Vietnam War, admires Martin Luther King and, after talking to him for five minutes in Peak Cavern, Molly had decided he was quite wonderful, someone she wanted to get to know much better.

He'd told her how she could catch the bus to Chatsworth and somehow, Sukey Miller ended up coming too.

Both girls attend Hope Valley Secondary School and they'd say they're friends but Molly doesn't entirely trust Sukey, who she knows can be two-faced and spiteful, behind people's backs. She's never quite sure if she's a friend or enemy. A frenemy. On the bus, the girls talked about music. Like most girls, Sukey is heavily into the Beatles but Molly's favourite group is The Doors. She has a poster of Jim Morrison on her bedroom wall, smouldering eyes and no shirt, his arms outstretched with staple holes in his ribs, from when the poster had been stuck into the centre of *Honey* magazine. The talk had moved onto boys.

'The pill is the best invention, don't you think?' Molly

said. 'So unfair it's only available to married women or we could sleep with a different boy every night if we wanted to.'

'But you just want to sleep with John Brightmore?' Sukey asked.

Molly had blushed. 'I didn't say that.'

'You didn't need to,' Sukey smirked. 'It's clear as day. I don't blame you,' she added, saccharine-sweet now. 'He's to die for.'

He met the girls at the bus stop near Edensor.

'I'm allowed in the House because my mum is one of the housemaids here,' John explains now, with obvious pride.

'Housemaid. That sounds quaint,' Molly flirts. 'But I wonder, should people be allowed to have servants these days?'

'You're a socialist, are you?' John asks her, as if he doesn't really mind what ideology she follows.

She giggles and he looks surprised, as if he's forgotten she has a sense of humour, half expects her to be as melancholy in everyday life as she was onstage, singing those old, sad songs. 'I guess I'm just an idealist,' she says.

'You're a folk singer, so obviously you're an idealist.'

'I've never been called a folk singer before.'

'Ha, well, I'm sure you're going to get called it a lot. And my mum may be called a housemaid but never a servant. You'll be pleased to know, there are no servants here any longer. Only staff.' John introduces them to one of the young maids who's busy brushing the ironwork on the staircase. 'This is Bea,' he says.

Bea says hello.

'The Duke calls them all his colleagues,' John says. 'It's a great place to work.'

'D'you want to work here too?'

'My dad's a shepherd on the estate, so the expectation is that I'll do the same.'

There's an outdoorsy, ruggedness about John, befitting someone who might work on the land. 'I can see you as a shepherd.'

'Can you? I can't.' He laughs, a warm, genuine laugh. 'It's far too lonely. Living here has given me an appreciation for beautiful buildings and I'd love to study architecture,' he tells her shyly, as if he's not used to sharing his dreams with anyone but has an urge to share them with her. 'I'd like to see the Colosseum and the Alhambra and the Taj Mahal.' She senses she's the first person to whom he's said any of this and it gives her a nice feeling and a wish to share her dreams in return.

'I want to live in London,' she tells him. She's read, in the *Melody Maker*, all about the folk-dens in Soho and Richmond and in her head, London - Swinging London - is the epicentre of music, so that's where she wants to be. 'I want to dance till dawn and hang out in Carnaby Street.' She can imagine doing that with John. It's crazy. They've literally only just met but she feels so easy in his company, as if she's known him for ages.

'This way,' John says.

Sukey flicks her hair and struts ahead. She's wearing her white boots and a teeny-tiny red miniskirt and Molly notices how John's eyes are drawn to her long legs and shapely backside. Sukey's tactics for attracting male attention may be a bit obvious but they seem to work a treat. Men can be so gullible.

Molly is wearing floral-patterned velvet flared trousers she made herself, copied from a pair she saw in Sheffield's hippest boutique, Sheffield's only boutique in fact. The

North's answer to Chelsea's Granny Takes a Trip. It's called: Lift up Your Skirts and Fly, inspired by the lyrics of a Marc Bolan song. Tucked behind the Town Hall on Norfolk Street, it has a music hall air about it with three dark red walls and one white one, painted with a gigantic, psychedelic flower decoration. Every week, the owner, a local entrepreneur, takes a trip up to Carnaby Street to buy stock and every Saturday morning, a line of eager youngsters wait outside, to see what he's brought back. Molly loves going there. She tries on all these clothes that she can never in a million years afford - romantic bohemian blouses that look like they come from the vintage shops in Haight-Ashbury in San Francisco. She studies the designs, then hunts around in thrift shops for fabrics, so she can run up copies on the treadle Singer sewing machine her grandma keeps in the corner of her bedroom.

John must see that both girls are in competition for his attention but who will he choose? It's hard to tell because he's inscrutable but so cute with his messy hair and broad shoulders and kind, brown eyes. They're the colour of milk chocolate and just as sweet.

Molly had been aware of John's gaze focused on her when she was singing in Peak Cavern. She'd looked back at him through the crowd and it was like a scene from a film. Something thrilling and new stirred inside her. Up there on stage, singing songs and playing her guitar, she felt bewitching. She'd first noticed John earlier, when the cave was being prepared for the concert and she'd liked the way he'd seemed quietly in command, calmly directing the bartenders and the lighting guys. When she found out that he was the one who'd organised the whole event, she'd wanted to thank him. It had been her first proper gig and it had felt like a revelation. She'd found her place in the world, her purpose in life and it was all down to him.

After they'd got talking, Molly had learnt that he was a musician too. Not a very good one, he'd claimed. 'I prefer to be backstage, encouraging other people to use their talent,' he'd said.

She thought it was the most generous, unselfish thing she'd ever heard. He'd told her he was a rock climber too and she liked the intrepidness of that.

'I'm scared of heights,' Molly had admitted.

'The trick is never to look down.'

Now he tells her: 'At Chatsworth, you must always remember to look up.' He takes her gently by the shoulders to make her stand still.

Molly tilts her face, as if to catch the warmth of the sun but above her is the extraordinarily vivid painted ceiling, a swirl of heroic Roman centurions and emperors in chariots, naked women, cloaks, shields and billowing white clouds. She can still feel the warmth of John's hands on her shoulders and the warmth of his gaze now resting on her face, as if he'd far rather study her profile. Of course, he's seen these magnificent paintings hundreds of times but she has the sense that he's enjoying seeing the House he clearly loves so much, through her eyes.

'My Gran cleans our school,' Molly says. 'She'd think that she'd died and gone to heaven, if she could dust and vacuum somewhere like this, instead of classrooms and smelly sports halls.'

John laughs as he leads the girls past the marble chapel and the magnificent library, then along a service corridor, that's used as a kind of storeroom with ladders and lamp shades and empty picture frames, stacked against a bare stone wall that's lined with long, metal heating ducts.

'The public aren't allowed in this part of the House,' John says, as they reach a narrow stone staircase. Above is the Belvedere Tower but before they get that far up the tower, tucked away on the second floor, is a door which John unlocks with a brass key, ushering the girls into a tiny, scarlet theatre.

'Private theatres like this are usually only found in European palaces,' John says proudly. 'It used to be the ballroom,' he adds. 'Sorry. I sound like a tour guide.'

Molly guesses he's trying to impress her and she is impressed. She looks down at the stage, framed with red velvet curtains and a proscenium arch decorated with trompe l'oeil, that gives the impression of ornately decorated plasterwork and tasselled drapery. Above the doorway is a gilded balcony.

'How old is it?'

'It's Edwardian,' John says.

'It's beautiful,' Molly breathes.

'I've already asked the duchess if we could have a concert here one day.'

She turns to him, daring to hope that she might be allowed to sing here. It would be amazing, like a dream. 'What did she say?'

'Sadly, it's not been used as a theatre for ages,' John says. 'Just for storing textiles and as a workshop for making curtains and cushions and suchlike.'

'What a pity.' Now he's mentioned it, Molly notices long rolls of fabric lying across the rows of seats in the stalls. A Singer sewing machine, just like the one she uses to makes clothes at home, is set up on a table at the back of the auditorium, surrounded by cardboard boxes of cotton reels and binding tape. The exquisite little theatre is like a sleeping beauty, awaiting its reawakening.

John looks sad to have disappointed her. 'We're already planning next month's Peak Cavern Club though,' he says tentatively. 'Will you come back? Sing again?'

She turns to face him, leans with her hands against the back row of red seats. 'I wasn't intending to sing last week,' she admits. 'I only came to watch.'

'But you brought your guitar along, just in case?'

'I never go anywhere without it,' she smiles. 'After the first singers did their floor spots, I thought, hey, why not? I'm as good as them.' She hoped that didn't sound cocky. 'You never know what you can do until you give it a try, right? So I plucked up the courage.'

'I'm so glad you did. You were…magnificent.'

'My mouth went dry and I've never been so terrified in all my life,' she confesses 'But then when I started singing, it felt so natural, so amazing, actually. It was like coming home. I realised that something had been missing from my life and now I'd found it. When everyone applauded, I knew that although it was scary, I'd always want to do it.'

Sukey huffs, as if to say she thinks Molly is being terribly pretentious but Molly feels sure that John won't think badly of her and right now, that's all that matters to her. His opinion is all that counts.

'I felt as if I was tapping into something ancestral. You know what I mean?'

'I'm not sure I do, to be honest, but I'd like to learn.'

He looks at her, as if she's the most intriguing person and he wishes that they could go on talking for hours, forever. She wishes they were alone. If only the other girl was not there with them, John might have invited Molly to sit with him in the back row of the empty theatre. He might have kissed her. She might have kissed him. Of course, she's kissed other boys at school. Gone further than kissing, truth be told, but none of them were particularly memorable experiences. She knows somehow, that kissing John Bright-more here, in this lovely little theatre, would have been totally different, something she would vividly remember, even as an old lady. She wants to make lots of magical memories like that, for her whole life to be full of magic.

On the way back down the stone stairs, Molly pauses by a huge window which, at first glance, appears like spectac-ular stained glass. Not an image of saints and angels and Christ on the cross, as you'd expect to find in a church but a giant geometric pattern, multiple leaded squares set within a larger square frame. However, it's not stained and it's not glass.

'It's made of Blue John,' John tells her. 'From your hometown.'

The caves under Treak Cliff Hill, at the edge of Castle-ton, are the only place in the world where the beautiful Blue John gemstone can be found.

'Your name's John and my second name's Miller,' Sukey simpers. 'There's a vein of Blue John actually named after my family.'

Miller happens to be one of the most common surnames in Castleton, so that's no proof of any family link to the history of Blue John and John, is also the most common name in England, so hardly worthy of note either. But Molly is too kind to point any of that out, even though Sukey is starting to really get on her nerves. She's so obvi-ous, desperately trying to establish any link with John, to get him to like her better. *Please don't let him.*

The squares in the window have been cut and hewn very thin, so that the spring sunlight shines through, illumi-nating the distinctive zigzag pattern in the famous gemstone, a glorious array of shades, from deepest purple to palest lilac, rich amber to snowy white. Molly's mind drifts and she's soon miles away, wondering how the window was made, who made it and how, so it takes her a moment to tune in to what Sukey is telling John now.

'One of my great-great-grandparents made amazing Blue John vases,' Sukey is saying. 'We still have one of them.'

Molly can't believe her ears, she really can't.

'That's pretty cool,' John replies.

Sukey glances at Molly with a truly icy coldness, then turns to John with her sweetest smile, as if she's flipped a switch. 'You'll have to come see it. It's in my bedroom.'

Thankfully, John doesn't respond to that and Molly's heart sings.

He leads them down the stone stairs and back out into the warm sun, where the first cars are parking up in the visitors' car park and the ticket attendants are at their stations. Molly doesn't want to leave Chatsworth, doesn't want to leave him. He's said he's organising another concert but that's weeks away and she can't wait weeks until she sees him again, she just can't.

'Thank you so much for showing us round,' Sukey says to him as they walk back to the bus stop, where their bus is already waiting under a big tree, engine rumbling, passengers climbing aboard.

'My pleasure.'

Sukey jumps onto the bus, swings herself into a seat by the window and props her chin on her hand, in a way that's designed to look sultry, like a model on a fashion shoot.

'The gardens here are lovely,' John says quickly, quietly, as Molly boards. 'You could come again, maybe next week, for a picnic? Just you.'

'I'd like that,' she says, trying to play it cool, though her heart is fluttering like mad. She suddenly feels so much lighter, in both senses of the word: less heavy and lit up inside.

John looks as if he's just won a million pounds on the Premium Bonds. 'See you next week then.'

CHAPTER EIGHT

SILVA - 2002

'G rand resting place for an odd-job-man,' my dad once joked, knowing where he was to be buried when the time came. With its stone pillars, arches and marble monuments, St Peter's Church was certainly grand, its Victorian Gothic spire dominating Edensor village. And Dad was to have the most illustrious company. At the top of the sloping, tree-lined churchyard were the Devonshire tombs. Kathleen Kennedy, sister of American President, J.F Kennedy, was buried there amongst several dukes, one of whom she'd married. Former head gardener, Joseph Paxton, was there too. His memorial was the grandest of all and it made a good shelter for the piebald Jacob's sheep which were penned there, doing their job keeping the grass cropped and tidy. It had tickled my dad to know that he, who hung picture hooks and curtain poles, as he put it, would be spending all eternity, beside the man responsible for building the celebrated Crystal Palace in London.

St Peter's was very spacious for a village church but still it was packed, people squeezed onto pews and crowded in at the back. Staff from Chatsworth past and present: gardeners and tenant farmers, housemen and housemaids, chefs and accountants. Near the front, were Bea and Ted and their two teenage children, Aidan and Jasmine, owner of the record player my dad had been fixing. Lizzie was there with her husband, Joe Ludlam, Manager of the Farm Shop and also her parents, Abe and Megan Morton, who were employed as Farm Manager and Head Room Guide respectively. A few rows behind them, were Lara Frost, from textiles, and the young park keeper, Chris Hibbert, who'd often shared a pint with my dad. Retired gardener, Bill Hawksworth, was there with his younger counterpart, Ben Grindy. They were joined by joiner Phil, who nodded his head at me by way of a greeting. Matthew Redfearn, who'd recently been promoted to the post of Keeper of Collections, was seated beside the Duke and Duchess, who were dressed immaculately in smart black tailored suits.

The welcoming address was delivered by Reverend Bramwell, the fresh-faced vicar, who delivered sermons in a softly spoken voice that held everyone's attention far better than if he'd been booming at them from the pulpit. As he spoke now of John Brightmore and the afterlife, there was the sound of sniffling, noses being blown, the occasional muffled sob. I'd known my father was well loved but still, seeing this outpouring of emotion was so touching. I just wished he could have been here to enjoy it, to see everyone. How he'd have loved it. He loved people. Liked nothing better than a good gathering and a knees up. It would be so much better to have a funeral just before a person died, while they could still attend, to hear all the nice things people said about them. Maybe everyone should organise a thanksgiving for their own life when they reached a certain age, but what age? My dad had not made his sixtieth birthday.

When the vicar had asked me if I'd like to give a tribute, of course I'd said yes. I was an only child and my dad had no other close relations. Well, that was not strictly true. He had a wife. Somewhere. But what were the chances of her turning up to bid him a fond farewell with a eulogy? To be fair, how would Sukey even know her husband had died? I did feel guilty, for having made no effort to contact her, but then I felt a surge of white-hot rage. It burst over me like a tsunami, until I managed to suppress it. Sukey clearly had no wish to be contacted by me. And in any case, it wasn't Sukey who my dad had asked me to find at the end, was it?

As the first hymn was sung, I wondered how I was going to stand in front of all these people and talk about my dad. The voices around me fell silent, everyone sat down with a rustle of coats and shuffling shoes. I remained standing, made myself put one foot in front of the other to walk down the aisle. I climbed the steps to the carved white and black alabaster pulpit and unfolded the notes I'd made, on a page torn from my sketchbook. I gripped the thick, creamy paper, which quivered in my trembling hand, the writing swimming before my eyes, just jumbled letters. I refolded the notes, looked out into the waiting faces, tucked my hair behind my ear. A deep breath.

'My dad listened to the farming programme on Radio 4, every morning,' I began. 'His own father had been a tenant farmer here at Chatsworth and my dad had worked for a while as a farmhand, but he always said he was a people person, liked company too much to spend all day on his own in a tractor or tending a flock of sheep. Aside from telling very bad jokes, what gave him the most pleasure and satisfaction, was helping people and mending things. People just used to leave broken stuff on our doorstep and he'd take them out to his shed and find a way to fix them. "Leave it with me, it'll be as good as new."' I could hear my dad saying those immortal lines, as if he was standing right beside me.

'When I was little, I thought he was a hero because he fixed my Sony Walkman and Mrs Ollerenshaw's guttering, all before breakfast one Sunday morning. And I was right. He was a hero. He could mend just about anything. But he couldn't mend himself.' I bit my lip to stop it from trembling. 'A heart is just a pump after all. An extraordinary pump, that went on pumping every minute of every day, for fifty-four years. It should have gone on for another quarter-century at least.'

My voice wobbled and I had to pause.

'My dad loved Chatsworth and historic buildings,' I continued after a moment. 'He was born here and I know he had every intention of dying here.' I fought back tears now, took a moment to compose myself before I went on. 'You're all here because you loved him,' I struggled on. 'I think it would be so amazing, an amazing legacy, if we all tried to be more like him. Just do something in his memory, every day.' I managed a smile. 'I'm not saying fix a kettle or anything complicated like that, but do something to help someone and make their life a little better. My dad would really like that. In fact, to use one of his favourite phrases, he'd be chuffed to bits.'

Someone, very softy, started applauding. It was such a surprising sound in the subdued church. Were you supposed to applaud at a funeral? I looked up and around at the packed pews. People were smiling, so clearly nobody thought it inappropriate. Then I saw that it was none other than Robbie Nightingale. He was sitting with his family over on the left, partially hidden by one of the stone pillars. I couldn't believe it. I couldn't believe Robbie had come back. He was right here. Robbie.

Blinded by the sight of his lovely face, I stumbled on my way back to the front pew, fell back against the hard wood, thoughts racing, my cheeks inexplicably burning. I stared down at the decorative floor tiles, adorned with fleur-de-lys, roses, birds, lions.

More hymns were sung: *Nearer, My God, to Thee* and *The Old Rugged Cross*. And all I could hear was Robbie's beautiful, warm baritone. He was a great believer in the power of singing to connect people, to celebrate or to offer comfort and hope, in times of sorrow or distress, so it might have been that he was actually singing a little louder and with more conviction than everyone else. Or was it just that I was as attuned to him as ever? I responded to the sound of his voice as I always had. It was a salve to my soul, like a heavy snowfall in the night, lying peacefully over everything and making the world beautiful and pure once again. A touch of magic. Robbie Nightingale. I read somewhere that D H Lawrence described the nightingale's song as brightest sound in all the world, like stars darting. Yes.

When I stood at the church door beside Reverend Bramwell, to thank the mourners as they filed slowly past, people had such heart-warming things to say.

'Your dad was a true gent, even when he was just a lad,' said retired housemaid, Maggie Ashwell.

'He rescued me from many a blown fuse,' said Trish Dodridge, who worked on the cheese counter in the Farm Shop.

'Salt of the earth,' said Robbie's dad. Praise indeed, from Chatsworth's head gardener.

Many of the women had red-rimmed eyes from weeping, including Lizzie and Bea. Poor Ted looked crushed.

Then Robbie was standing there in front of me and his dark lashes were spiked with tears. The same smokey-grey-blue eyes, curly hair, the same easy manner and open smile. Yet he looked different to the image of him I'd carried in my head. Taller. He was easily six foot now and his shoulders had broadened. It was four years since I'd last seen him and whilst he'd obviously not grown since then, for me, he'd been frozen in time. I still expected him to look as he had, that last summer we were together, when we were still teenagers. He was wearing a black waistcoat and white shirt and he looked as if he came from a different century.

He leant in towards me, as if he wanted to pull me close and instinctively, as if he was the moon and I was the tide, some invisible force drew me towards him. I caught a faint waft of his cologne, a sweetly familiar mix of herbs and citrus. Too much. I made myself draw back, only a fraction but enough to send a clear message. Rather than hold me, he just took hold of my hand, achingly polite and formal, only he held me as if he didn't ever want to let me go. Or was it just wishful thinking? There was no question that the warmth of his hand holding mine gave me more comfort than the tightest hug from anyone else.

'It's good of you to come, Robbie.'

'Of course I came,' he said. 'Is there anything I can do?'

Where to start? *Just stay and talk to me. Keep holding my hand.*

'That was a beautiful tribute you gave.'

'Thanks. I just wish I'd said all those things to my dad, while I had the chance.'

'You didn't need to say it, Silly. He knew how much you loved him.'

Only Robbie had ever shortened my name to Silly. Only

he had ever been allowed to call me that. To be fair, nobody else had ever dared try. It has been his invention, all his, and he made Silly sound like the sweetest, most complimentary word.

Knowing our history, everyone was pretending not to watch us, while watching us closely all the same. Bea was standing directly behind Robbie, waiting for her turn to give me her condolences, so he let go of my hand, moved on. 'Catch ya later,' he said.

Later alligator, I said to myself. The way we'd parted when we were kids.

I flinched as the first clod of peaty earth hit the wooden coffin lid, breaking into brown-black crumbs. I still felt like I was in a movie. Did people really throw clods of earth on to coffin lids? Seemingly, they really did. The weather was suitably dramatic and funereal with low, grey, scudding clouds. The wind was icy but it wasn't just my cheeks and fingers that were numbed, it was my whole soul. I couldn't escape the belief that this was all a charade and the wooden box was empty.

The vicar had said that burial ceremonies were generally reserved for close family members but Freya had offered to come too. She'd always felt like my family, even though of course she was Robbie's sister, not mine. Everyone used to take it for granted, that Robbie and I would belong to the same family one day. My dad had even sent a Christmas card to Robbie one year, addressed, 'to my future son-in-law.'

Following in her mother's footsteps, Freya had gone to teacher training college, then taught for a while in a tough inner city primary school in Manchester but after marrying Sam, a sound engineer from BBC radio, the lure of Chatsworth had been too strong and she'd come home, seven years ago. She was now mother to a little four-year-old boy called Dylan and held the grand title of Education Co-ordinator at the Chatsworth farmyard, which basically meant organising activities for the parties of children, who came on school trips to learn about where their food came from. Meanwhile, Sam was working with the Chatsworth events team, in charge of audiovisuals.

Freya, Lizzie and I met up at least once a week, for wine, chips and gossip at the Devonshire Arms, when Freya invariably entertained us with tales of the real perils of working with animals and children. For instance, how the Duchess said watching the incredulous tots watching the cows being milked was better than any theatre. She'd once asked a little boy from Sheffield what he thought and he said it was the most disgusting thing he'd ever seen and vowed never to drink milk again.

'Thanks for being here,' I said to Freya, as we turned and walked back through the graveyard.

'I would say it's a pleasure but that sounds all wrong. You know what I mean though?'

'I do.'

Freya linked her arm through mine. She'd not said one word about her brother turning up, but what was there to say? Robbie was a kind person. He'd known my dad since he was a lad. He'd come to pay his respects. That was all. He'd be gone again soon, back to Scotland and the new life he'd built for himself there with a woman called Catrina, a rich divorcee he'd met on a plane to America, who played the fiddle. Everyone was expecting them to announce their engagement soon.

The old tombstones in the graveyard staggered like drunkards, the names that had once been etched on them, now lost to the winds and frost, replaced by green and white blooms of lichen and moss that looked like tiny fireworks exploding against a dusky sky. The engravings that were still visible all said much the same. Beloved mother. Adored son. Precious sister. Dearest brother. In the end, that's how we're all remembered. Not by status and wealth, not by fame or achievements, but by our relationships to the people we have loved and been loved by. Everyone is defined by family. In the end, that's all that matters.

It felt as if I had no family left but that was not true. I did still have a mother out there, somewhere. She should have been here with me. I swallowed down another burst of rage, felt it burn my insides like toxins. Of course it was Sukey I really needed to find. Not Molly. But if I found Sukey, I'd have to face it all, confront all the unresolved anger and painful questions. I'd have to talk to her about that night, all those years ago. I'd have to talk about what I'd overheard her say. I'd have to find out what it was that she'd done and why she had gone away and never come back. Had it been my fault?

CHAPTER NINE

I'd been given two weeks' compassionate leave from work but I found it impossible to sleep beyond six-thirty and I was up and dressed by seven as usual. I took Tijou for a walk to Queen Mary's Bower, then went to the gym for an hour. Then, since I wasn't cleaning Chatsworth, I came home and started deep cleaning my kitchen. It didn't need cleaning but I needed to clean it. I needed to keep busy, so I didn't have time to think about my dad, who had gone forever or about Robbie, who had come back, but only for a while.

I know some people hate cleaning and find it repetitive, dull and dissatisfying, but I am not one of those people. Since I'd started cleaning after Sukey left, there had always been comfort for me in the simple, repetitive tasks of wiping down, putting things in order, when all else felt completely disordered.

I could have gone to the forge instead, but it was not that kind of release I was looking for right now. I'd never told anyone this, but my obsession with blacksmithing had started with a story that Bea had told me when I was a youngster, waiting around by the magnificent wrought iron staircase in the Painted Hall, for my dad to finish work.

'The Roman God and patron saint of blacksmiths is Vulcan,' Bea had said, coming to stand quietly at my side. 'When his mother, Juno, first saw him, she found him so ugly she threw him from the top of Mount Etna.'

Bea told me how the fall left Vulcan with a lame leg, how he was raised by nymphs in a cavern beneath the volcano. He learnt to harvest burning embers from its molten core and use them to heat metallic ores he mined from his subterranean den, which he fashioned into arms and jewellery. Word soon spread, and his extraordinary skills attracted the attention of the gods. Vulcan created Jupiter's fabled lightning bolts and Mercury's winged helmet.

'Vulcan's mother hurt him,' Bea finished gently. 'But he took that hurt and used it, found a way to use his wounds and scars to make something beautiful.'

From then on, I'd gravitated to the little smithy in the corner of the old stables at Chatsworth. The unmistakable smell of scorched coke, metallic dust, sweat and damp earth. Things that should have repelled me, but the noise and grime, the fire and sparks, only drew me in. I'd stand for ages, watching Eli Strutt at the anvil. When the metal turned cherry-red it was soft as clay, only you couldn't touch it to mould it. I was fascinated by how Eli respected the material he worked, as if it was a living, breathing thing, he had to coax and cajole with the exertion of a little controlled strength when needed, like a gentleman from a historical romance might ride a high-spirited stallion.

'Want to have a go?' Eli had asked me one day.

'Now?' I'd replied, wide eyed.

He handed me the hammer with a cheeky grin. 'Strike while the iron's hot.'

He'd taught me how to stand at the anvil with my legs slightly apart, how to let the weight of the hammer create its own force and I'd loved every second. Years later, when Robbie had gone and I'd started working at Chatsworth, I'd gone back to Eli and asked him if I could be his apprentice. Working with fire, hammers and an anvil, was the best way I knew of dealing with the volcano of rage and pain I felt at the core of me, the overwhelming feelings of resentment and loss that otherwise threatened to erupt and cause all kinds of damage and destruction in my life.

Cleaning, on the other hand, made me feel rooted, safer and more secure.

My job as a housemaid at Chatsworth came with a little cottage in Edensor, tucked in the shelter of St Peter's Church. Half-way between Pilsley and Beeley, Edensor was even more idyllic than the other two estate villages. Well named. Eden. It had sixty-three dwellings of varying architectural style, a result, so it was said, of Joseph Paxton presenting the sixth Dwith a range of choices. Unable to make up his mind, the Duke requested some of each. Consequently, the cottages featured Norman arches, Tudor chimneys, castellated turrets, Swiss-style roofs and Italianate windows, all with lovely little English country gardens. It was like living on the most beautiful film set.

I'd fallen in love with Guide Cottage, so called because it was once the meeting hall for the local girl guides, before I'd even opened the front door. It was like a romantic, miniature version of Brook House with hollyhocks in the garden, a range in the kitchen, low beamed ceilings and deep, cosy window seats, that were perfect for curling up with a sketchbook.

Dad had taught me lots of DIY skills over the years and I'd redecorated all the rooms myself. I knew what to do with Polyfilla, sandpaper and masking tape and I spent my weekends with a brush and roller, painting the thick walls buttery white. I'd borrowed Dad's power tools and his crowbar and letting rip in the living room, I had discovered a historic bread-oven hidden behind the plasterboard. I sanded and waxed the old elm floorboards in my bedroom and Don Turner, the Chatsworth plumber, helped me install a claw-footed bath I'd unearthed in a local reclamation yard. I bought old, framed pictures, a mismatched dinner service and a squishy old sofa, clad in faded tartan.

'You could make a shack look chic,' Flora Nightingale told me, when she brought round azaleas for the Blue John vase, which stood in pride of place on the mantelpiece.

I'd felt like a child playing house, only without my favourite playmate.

I'd met Robbie's girlfriend, Catrina, once, four years ago.

Catching up over glasses of mulled wine in the Devonshire Arms, Freya had let slip that her brother would be home that Christmas. 'You should just tell him,' she'd said.

'Tell him what.'

'That you still love him.'

I nearly choked on my warm, spiced wine. 'Is it so obvious?'

'Yep,' she nodded. 'Plain as the nose on my face. And you know Robbie won't ever do anything about it.'

'Won't he?'

'I love my brother dearly but his go with the flow attitude to life is infuriating,' Freya grumbled. 'It's all very well and an attractive quality in its own way, up to a point, I guess, if you like that kinda thing.' She looked sceptical. 'But doesn't it drive you nuts?'

'Not really.' I laughed. 'Actually yes, it totally does.'

'Well then.'

I might have taken Freya's advice, taken matters into my own hands but a couple of days later, I'd been dusting in the Music Room when in he walked with a strawberry blonde. She looked as if she'd gone to a huge effort to make it look as if she'd gone to no effort at all, was casually dressed in a boxy blazer, high-waisted jeans and white pumps and she stood so close to Robbie that when she tilted her head coquettishly, examining the famous violin from a different angle, her permed, red-gold hair fell over his shoulder. It was irrational and unfair of me and not at all helpful or grown-up, but I hated her on sight, I really did.

'Who played it?' Catrina asked, in a mild Scottish accent.

'It's not real,' Robbie said. 'Just an illusion.'

'You're kidding me.'

'He's not,' I pinned on a smile, made myself walk over to them. 'It's trompe l'oeil.' The painted violin appeared to hang from a real metal peg on the door. 'It's convincing though, isn't it? Visitors are always asking us who originally owned it.'

Catrina frowned at the illusory violin, glanced warily at Robbie, as if she feared the pair of us might be playing a practical joke at her expense.

'This is Silva,' Robbie smiled. 'Silva, this is Catrina.'

'I guessed who you were,' Catrina said, voice clipped. 'Robbie's told me all about you.'

'Has he?' I cocked an eyebrow, glanced at Robbie, who looked unusually awkward.

'At least a painted violin is one less thing for you to dust,' Catrina commented, managing in those few words, to make being a housemaid at Chatsworth sound no better than scrubbing public lavatories all day.

I could have told her that we were conservation assistants but I couldn't be bothered. I didn't need to impress her. 'There's still plenty to keep me busy.' I smiled sweetly, twirling my little hogs-hair brush. 'So I'd best get on. It was nice meeting you.'

A few days after that encounter, just before New Year, I'd been over at Brook House and couldn't help but notice that a new musical instrument had joined Robbie's expansive collection in the corner of the living room. Taking pride of place near the Christmas tree was a kind of violin, but with more strings, flame-shaped holes and a scroll in the shape of a blindfolded angel. It was undeniably beautiful but to me it became an ugly, hostile thing, as soon as I knew where it had come from.

'What's that?' I asked him.

'A viola.'

'Not a normal one?'

'It's called a viola d'amore.'

I laughed. 'Violin of love? Let me guess. Your girlfriend gave it to you? Christmas present?'

'Yeah.' He'd looked sheepish.

'Where's she gone then?'

'Back home to Scotland, for Hogmanay.'

'May I?'

'Sure.'

I picked up the viola, which protested at my touch with a discordant twang. 'It looks old and very expensive. It must have cost her a fortune. Freya did say Catrina's loaded.'

'You're jealous?' Robbie sounded delighted. 'You are. Admit it. You're jealous of her.'

I was going to admit no such thing, not even to myself. I'd been in love with Robbie, once, a long time ago. I'd probably always love him but I'd had my chance and I'd well and truly blown it. Nobody but myself to blame.

'Why's it called a viola d'amore?' He seemed unwilling to say and I sensed we were teetering on the brink of a pointless argument, which would only make us both miserable. But I had to push it. 'Tell me.'

'The blindfolded angel is…'

'Cupid? It's Cupid, isn't…?'

Robbie shut me up, by suddenly taking my face between his warm hands and kissing me. It was the most passionate, fierce kiss, almost angry, his mouth so hard against mine I could feel his teeth. I hooked my fingers in the belt loops of his jeans and pulled him closer.

'Are you trying to break my ribs?' he asked.

I let him go. 'Don't say another word.'

'We…'

'There is no we. Or us. It's too late.'

'It's never too late,' he said.

'But it is.'

'Don't look back, you're not going that way?' These were not his words but mine; ones I'd used often enough. He repeated them with resignation.

I didn't know what to say to that, so neither of us said anything more and he turned and walked away. Next morning, he was gone, back to Scotland for Hogmanay too. Back to his girlfriend.

I'd done some research, torturing myself really and I found out from Matthew Redfearn, Chatsworth's chief curator and a font of knowledge on antiques, that a viola d'amore had two sets of strings: seven playing strings and seven vibrating strings, which supposedly trembled in unison. I'd been tormented by that idea, especially when I heard that when he wasn't away travelling Robbie lived with Catrina in the house she'd purchased with the proceeds of her divorce settlement, in a smart district of Edinburgh. Freya told me, scornfully, how Catrina liked telling her posh, professional friends she was shacked up with a sexy, hippy singer.

There was a knock at the door now, just as I was putting the mop and bucket away and Tijou scampered into the hall, his nails skittering on the floorboards, tail wagging excitedly. Perhaps he was expecting to see my dad. How long did it take a dog to forget a person, to accept they were never coming home? Were dogs better at it than children?

'Hi,' Robbie said, to me or to Tijou, or to both of us.

Tijou licked his hand. He didn't know Robbie from Adam but treated every stranger as a long-lost friend and potential playmate.

'Hi,' I said. I'd not changed out of my gym clothes. My hair was tied back in a messy ponytail and I was wearing faded, grey joggers and a skimpy vest top. I needed a shower. Why should that matter? It mattered. 'Come in.'

He'd brought a box of Danish pastries from the Farm Shop, so I filled the kettle for coffee, took down plates from the cupboard over the sink. My heart had gone haywire. After all this time, how could Robbie Nightingale do that to me? How could he have miraculously appeared in my kitchen, normal as normal can be, bearing treats?

Waiting for the kettle to boil gave me the chance to take

a proper look at him. I'd been too distracted at the funeral, when the sheer shock of seeing him there, along with everything else, had prevented me from taking much in.

He was dressed in clompy, black boots, faded blue jeans and a shirt with faint blue stripes and a granddad collar. It was crumpled, untucked and open at the neck and with his messy curls, his overall appearance was a bit dishevelled, as ever. It made me think of a review I'd read, of a concert he'd given in Scotland. The journalist had written how Robbie understood how to sing traditional songs and translate them into a rock context. How he could sing unaccompanied or front an electric band if he wanted to. How he looked like a rock star. To me, he looked older. A man, not the boy I'd loved and he carried with him the exoticism of a seasoned traveller, as if the sights he'd seen, the many adventures and experiences he'd inevitably had over the years, had altered him inexorably, which of course they must have done. I'd known that's what would happen. That's why I'd done what I did. I felt vindicated. It had been the right decision after all.

'You look different,' he said.

Whereas I'd not been anywhere much and my adventures had been few and far between. He was just being nice. 'Well, I'm not a schoolgirl any longer.'

'I hear you're an artist.'

I laughed at how grand that sounded. 'I'm a housemaid, Robbie.' Which was actually pretty grand, given that I was a housemaid at Chatsworth, but all the same…

'Part time artist, then.'

'Spare time, more like.'

He shrugged, as if to say that made no difference. He bit into one of the pastries, cupping his hand underneath it to catch the crumbs. I handed him a plate. 'Thanks.' He grinned. 'So what are you?' He asked. Painter? Potter? Sculptor? Mum and Freya wouldn't say. They told me I had to ask you myself.'

'Blacksmith.'

I'd expected him to chuckle, look incredulous, assume I was having him on, as did almost everyone. When I used to hang out with Robbie, I was all set to be a ceramicist or a sculptor maybe. I'd expected to have to try and explain to him why I'd changed direction, as I'd done to countless people on countless occasions.

I always left out the part about Vulcan, just focussed on how the hammer Eli Strutt held in his hand fascinated me, the way he bent the glowing metal into shape, sparks flashing. How the fire, the red-hot metal, the opportunity to bash away on an anvil and make a work of art, the dramatic combination of beauty and brutality had been instantly irresistible to me. Eli had been delighted to share his forge, tools and skills with me, seemed genuinely thrilled a young person was taking such an interest in his ancient craft. 'Never mind that you're a girl, eh,' he liked to say, with a wink. Eli actually had a female ancestor, Martha, who'd been a blacksmith. I loved hearing about her.

But I didn't have to explain any of this to Robbie. He seemed to understand and to be genuinely delighted by my answer.

'A blacksmith,' he said. 'Course you are.'

'What's that supposed to mean?'

He set down the plate, swung himself up to sit on the kitchen counter. Making himself at home. 'I mean it's perfect. It suits you perfectly.'

'How come?'

His looked as if he feared he'd dug himself into a massive, great hole.

I faced him, hands on hips. 'How?' I challenged, not about to let him off the hook. 'Go on. Tell me what you mean, Nightingale.'

'When you were younger, you were like a sort of... erm...Trojan horse.'

I spluttered a laugh. 'A...what?' I knew he'd not intended to be mean to me but that sounded pretty mean, to be honest. 'If my history serves me right, a Trojan horse is something which disguises its true intent, right? An innocent appearing container used to bypass defences but hiding something destructive?' How did we get so personal so fast? It was wonderful in a way. We'd not had a proper conversation for years but he could say things to me, nobody else would ever dream of saying and get away scot-free. 'That sounds very rude.'

'What I mean is...on the surface, you're this sweet, smiling, super neat and organised, efficient person with huge dimples and a notebook of lists. You like tidying and ticking things off and being in total control. But you keep so much hidden away inside you. Underneath that calm, very competent and controlled exterior, there's someone wilder and darker and far more dangerous.'

'Is that right?' But I could see what he was getting at. I was well brought up, a well-behaved little girl, who'd never really turned into an angry, angsty teen. Should have done.

Don't cry, Silva. You don't want to upset your dad.

It turned out time was not always such a great healer, in the way people are so keen to say it is. My mother's abandonment, the renewed rejection, year upon year, when she failed to send so much as a birthday card. None of it got any easier to cope with as the years passed. In many ways, it was far harder to deal with at sixteen than it had been at ten but I didn't want to worry my dad or cause him any trouble, when he had enough to contend with. So I'd made it my mission to cheer him up as best I could, convince him that I was perfectly fine, not affected at all by what had happened. I'd cultivated an outward personality that was very capable and carefree. I was described in school reports as a quiet and considerate member of the class, very conscientious, bright and polite. That was outside though. Inside, I felt mutinous, burning with a sort of fizzy, hot energy, I was storing up for some later use. Then I'd got hooked on blacksmithing and had started going to the forge. Just in time. Spend too much time angry and it eats away at your soul. I'd become fascinated with robotics, in particular the idea of transformers, the new cartoon and toys that every kid wanted for Christmas at that time. On the outside they were one thing and inside, something completely different. I understood what that felt like.

But I'd never fooled Robbie. He had shown me what it meant to be properly loved for who I was, not who I thought I ought to be. He was the only one who'd seen right through me to what was hidden inside. I still just couldn't believe that he'd had the nerve to come right out and say it.

'You're angry with me now,' he said. 'I've offended you. I'm sorry. I didn't mean to.'

I didn't have to ask him how he liked his coffee. Sweet and black. I handed a steaming mug to him. 'I'm not offended, Robbie.'

'No?'

'Honestly, no.'

He gently pushed a Danish pastry at me and I took it, bit into it. An explosion of sweetness on my tongue. Custard and almonds.

'You've never heard from your mum then?' he asked. 'Not in all this time?'

The camellias were dying in the Blue John vase, shedding petals. I whipped them out, dumped them in the pedal bin, scooped up all the fallen petals and dumped them too. 'Never, in all this time.'

He blew across his hot drink, sipped it, clearly weighing up what to say next, whether to say it. 'I did wonder if you might have tracked her down…you know…if she might have wanted to come to the funeral.'

My hackles rose. What right had he to tell me what I should have done? OK, he wasn't telling me anything as such, just tentatively suggesting, but still, he'd touched a raw nerve. He'd always challenged me, been straight with me and I'd liked him for that, loved him for it. So very much.

'To be honest, I did think about it,' I admitted. 'But in my defence, it wasn't her that dad wanted, at the end.'

'What d'you mean?'

I'd not planned to talk to Robbie about any of this but I wanted to talk to someone. Wanted to talk to him. It made so much sense to ask him too, given his line of work: 'Does the name Molly Marrison mean anything to you?'

'Should it?'

'Wait here a sec.' I reached for the album that I'd tucked into the plate rack. I handed it to Robbie. 'So when he died, Dad was fixing a record player and this was playing.'

My brain had been gnawing away at the possible sequence of events. Had my dad needed to test the record player was working properly, before he gave it back to Jasmine and chosen to listen to that particular album? Or had temporarily having a record player to hand, given him an excuse to listen to a record he'd not heard for years? Either way, had Molly Marrison's voice caused some kind of emotional and physical rupture? I'd never know.

I'd brought the record player back home with me too,

intending to return it, in good working order now, to Jasmine. Until then, it was standing on the kitchen counter, so I was able to play Robbie the opening track.

Over moors and valleys deep, through the Dark Peak and the White
There two tragic lovers sleep in gritstone, blood, and lime.

We listened together as Molly's haunting voice filled the space between us, summoning up the ghosts of the Runaway Lovers. Henry and Clara had lived and loved and died, over two centuries ago, but Molly sang as if she grieved for them, as if she felt their plight on an intensely personal level. There was outrage in her voice for the waste of it all, for their stolen future.

In Winnats Pass so dark and deep, five murderess miners lingered there
And lost in love, this hapless two were caught so unaware
Long, young Henry struggled brave, fought with every breath of
power
'Till at last his strength is gone, all in that midnight hour

They'd been planning a life together and the thieves had not just robbed them of their money but their lives, days of joy, love, children, of the chance to grow old together. The melody and the lyrics as Molly sang them, evoked all the glamorous romance and courage of two idealistic young people, head over heels in love, who were willing to risk it all, would rather sacrifice comfort and wealth and respectability and leave their homes and their families hundreds of miles behind, venture into the dangerous unknown, just to be together. It was incredibly affecting. I could see them, riding in the moonlight, side by side, dressed in rich swirling cloaks.

I knew Robbie saw them too. 'It's the song you used to sing.'

'I still sing it,' he said. 'But not like this.'

I stopped talking, let him concentrate on the final verse. On the vital silence before the final verse.

Shamed and damned, blood on their hands,
An eye for an eye, a life for a life,
A widow, where once was a wife,
Then from the darkness of Waterhull,
Something so rare and beautiful
With this ring, I give you a song to sing.

Suddenly, there was a new light in his eyes, as if he'd struck gold.

'What?' I asked, warily.

'I've never heard that part,' he said in wonderment, as the track ended and the needle arm lifted. 'There are lots of versions of *The Runaway Lovers* out there, but I've never heard anything remotely like this. I'd love to know where Molly learnt it.'

'Might she have just, you know, made it up? Don't you always say that old songs should change and evolve, because that's the way they live on?'

'I do.' He looked amazed that I'd listened and remembered that. Pleased too. 'Lots of old ballads exist in many forms. There are over a hundred different versions of *The Bold Grenadier*, which is sometimes also called *One Morning in May*, and that's just in this country, for instance.' I could tell he was thinking out loud, processing. 'The American versions sometimes include an extra verse, a warning to women to be wary among men. Stories and songs are gradually altered as they are passed from person to person, down the generations. Musicians record new versions of them, want to retell stories in their own voices. But…'

'But?'

'It would be odd to stay totally faithful to the tradition of an existing song, the way Molly has done, and then just tack a completely new verse on the end, one with such cryptic lyrics.'

'Well, my dad asked me to find her. So when I do, if I do, I'll be sure to ask her about it for you.'

'Your dad asked you to find her?'

'He did.'

'Why would he do that?'

I shrugged. 'Your guess is as good as mine.' What would I even say to this girl, a middle-aged woman now? It was a ludicrous situation, really it was.

'You're going to track her down?'

'I have to try, don't I? I mean, it's the last thing my dad asked me to do. The last thing I can ever do for him.'

'Dying wishes,' Robbie said. 'The most powerful wishes of all.'

'To be honest, I'm intrigued to meet her.' Increasingly, talking about it to Robbie now, I sensed an important family mystery here, one I definitely needed to solve for myself, as well as for my dad. Somehow.

I picked up the dishcloth and Robbie's cup, started wiping away the ringed coffee stain it had left on the work surface, waiting for him to tease me for being a neat freak, wanting him to tease me. He didn't. He just put his hand over mine to make me stop and his touch made my whole body soften, relax, as if my heart had opened up and warm honey had been poured into it. I stared at our two hands. Our skin tone was the same, slightly tanned.

'D'you think your dad loved her and lost her somehow?' Robbie asked softly.

His words were weighted with meaning but I did my best to shrug them off. 'Unlikely.'

'I've thought about us a lot,' he said.

And there it was. Our own stolen future was suddenly hanging between us, like another achingly sad love song.

'Have you?' I asked him.

'Have you?' he asked me.

I turned away from him and very neatly folded the dish-cloth. I rinsed our two cups under the tap, one by one, set them upside down on the draining board, side by side. 'Are you and Catrina still vibrating in unison?'

'Ha. I'm not sure we ever did that.'

I turned back to him. 'I assumed, since you met in midair, that you two had lots in common, shared a wander-lust at least?'

'She prefers to call it wanderlove,' he said wryly.

I pulled a face, managed to resist the urge to mime sticking my fingers down my throat. 'Honestly?'

Robbie chuckled. 'What about you? You with anyone?'

'Nope. I'm free and single and still just about young enough to enjoy it.'

'You were always so determined not to need anybody,' he said. 'And you know, that's perfectly fine. Admirable. Except.'

'Here we go.'

I knew he blamed me for the end of our relationship. Technically it was fair enough, since I was to blame. We'd both been so young and he'd needed things from me that I'd not been able to give then. Namely my heart. I'd opened up to him more than to anyone, before or since, but still I couldn't let him in. I understood the psychology of it a little better now. My expectation was that people who were supposed to love me, would end up hurting me. That everyone left, in the end. And Robbie. Well, I'd realised that summer, he was someone who could never be relied upon to stay anywhere for long. And I was OK with that.

I loved him and he loved me and we had lots in common but in the end, it turned out we actually wanted totally different things. I wanted to stay in Chatsworth and Robbie wanted to leave. I wanted to feel secure and he wanted adventure. I wanted a home and he wanted to wander. I think I was half in love with his family and I wanted to be cosseted in the lovely, cosy safety of it, while all he wanted was to break free. He wanted to escape the very thing I wanted to be held by.

It was way cooler to be an adventurous wanderer, than a stay-at-home type and even if home happened to be somewhere as special and lovely as Chatsworth, I worried it meant I was lacking in courage or ambition or some sparkly, appealing quality like that. I'd tried to be a different person but that's always a bad idea, doomed to failure.

I'd not wanted to hold Robbie back. No doubt he'd decided that I'd pushed him away.

I folded my arms. 'Are you seriously expecting me to believe you'd have been happy to stay here with me, in Derbyshire, rather than go chasing after your dreams? No need to answer that.' On the spur of the moment, I decided to tell him at least one of the secrets I'd kept to myself all these years. Now my dad was gone, there was no need to hide it any longer. 'I did try to find her ages ago. My mother, I mean.'

'You did?' He looked incredulous. 'How? When?

'Right after she went away.'

'What are you talking about?'

'Me and my dad. We always want to fix things for people. He fixed kettles and I wanted to fix him, even when I was just a kid. After Sukey left, he was so miserable, just moping about and I couldn't bear it. I thought maybe she didn't realise how much he really loved her. Maybe he didn't even realise how much he loved her himself. I'd always wanted to be one of Charlie's Angels.' I smiled. 'I never missed an episode, remember? I fancied being the dark-haired, sassy one, can't remember her name.'

'Sabrina?'

I laughed. 'That's impressive. Anyway, I decided to be a detective, like Sabrina, and track Sukey down. I figured if I could just find her, I could tell her how much my dad missed her and she'd come home. Simple.'

'So despite everything, Silva Brightmore, you're an incurable romantic.'

'Yeah, well. I went to see her friend, Helen, who worked with her in the Orangery shop. She told me Sukey had a brother called Simon, who lived in Buxton, who she'd not spoken to for years. I found his number in the telephone directory and I rang him.'

Robbie's eyebrows lifted. 'You were what, ten? And you rang a total stranger? Out of the blue?

'I did and d'you know what he said? "Let sleeping dogs lie, lass. For your father's sake, let it go."

'How come you never told me this?'

'I never told anyone.'

'I'm not anyone,' he said softly.

'No.'

'Let sleeping dogs lie.' He scooped Tijou into his arms, looked into his big doleful eyes 'What did that mean?'

'I have no idea. But he scared me.'

'Simon says.' A game we used to play, like all kids.

91

'Simon says let it go, so I let it go.'

Tijou wriggled and stuck out his long, pink tongue, tried to lick Robbie's nose.

I laughed. 'He likes you.'

'I suspect he likes everyone. How old is he?' Robbie asked, depositing Tijou back on the floor.

'He was four on the 1st of July.'

'He has a birthday?'

'Well of course.'

'I thought he was a puppy still.'

'He acts like one.' It struck me that they were similar characters, Robbie and Tijou. Sweet natured, playful, energetic and friendly. 'You could come for a walk with us sometime, if you like.'

'I would like.'

'How do I even go about finding Molly?' I asked him, picking up the threads of our previous conversation. 'Where do I start? I've no idea. The record company who put out that album doesn't even exist anymore, I don't think. Ted has known Dad forever and obviously the name Molly meant nothing to him. Bea does think she saw her here at Chatsworth once though.'

Now Robbie had picked up the album sleeve, appeared to study the credits on the back, then he flipped it over and spent far longer studying the photo on the front, just as Bea had done. 'The local history library would be worth checking out. If she was from around here and released an album, there's bound to be something about her in the local press, reviews of concerts, of the record itself, that sort of thing.'

'Good idea. Thanks.'

Robbie handed the record to me, face up. 'Don't look at the photo.'

Which left only the swirly graphics, Molly's name and the title of the album. That jolt of familiarity again. 'What am I looking at then?'

'Molly and Johnny?' Robbie said it with a soft sort of awe in his voice, respect.

I stared back at him now, my spine tingling. 'Molly and Johnny,' I echoed, my eyes wide. 'No.' I half shook my head. 'No way.'

My Dad had always been John to me, never Johnny. That's all I'd ever heard anyone call him. Sukey had called him John. My Grandma Ivy had called him John. Ted had called him John. His friends had all called him John. Everyone at Chatsworth called him John. Nobody ever called him Johnny. Nobody I'd ever known, at least.

'You remember then?' Robbie asked me.

Molly. That's why the name had rung a weird and distant bell when I'd first seen it written down. But it had been so out of context. 'Of course I remember.'

CHAPTER TEN

SILVA - 1984

'More kindling,' I said, handing sheets of newspaper to Robbie to scrunch for the barbecue.

I slid my eyes sideways to watch him as we worked, standing side-by-side at the fire pit at the bottom of the old orchard at Brook House. Robbie had grown tall but so had I. I was leggy, like a tap dancer, according to Robbie's mum. She said she could easily see me on stage with a cane, in a top hat and fishnet tights. Robbie had looked at me oddly when she said that, as if he'd turned shy all of a sudden. His face had changed shape recently too. He was all angles and curls now. In a few months, he'd be eighteen. He was about to take his driving test and his A'levels. If he got the right grades in his exams, he'd be going to Edinburgh University in the Autumn, to study music and anthropology. I was going to miss him dreadfully, not that I was ever going to let him know that, of course. I wasn't going to think about it now. We had the whole summer ahead of us.

Having coaxed the flames to life, we watched them leap and lick. There were flames dancing in my body too, a hot, quivering sensation, low in my belly. It was not unpleasant, just confusing. We'd done this countless times. I'd lit countless fires with Robbie. Nothing had really changed, only lately, somehow, everything had changed. I used to be so easy around him and now I wasn't. The air between us felt deliciously charged.

'You've got soot on your nose,' he told me.

'Have I?'

'Have now,' he said, dabbing my nose end with his finger.

I stuck my hand in the bag of charcoal and he ducked out of the way but not quite fast enough and I smudged his cheekbone. 'There. You look like a chimney sweep. Or a Masai warrior.'

'Honestly.' Robbie's dad tutted affectionately. 'How old are you two?'

'Seventeen,' Robbie said.

'Sixteen,' I said.

'Would never have guessed. You still act like a pair of little kids.'

Only not. Because as a little kid, I used to wish so hard that I had a big brother like Robbie and over time, my wish had been granted because he'd become just like a brother to me. For the most part, he'd treated me as if I was part of the furniture, except for when he wanted someone to tease and torment. I used to love it when he teased me in the way he teased his sister because it made me feel accepted and included. But now it had the opposite effect and I felt a bit rejected, dejected. On the one hand I wanted nothing to change between us, ever, but at the same time there was a new undercurrent of turbulence and longing inside me. I was sixteen and everything felt new and too raw.

'I'll go and see if Freya and your mum need any help,' I said, needing to escape.

'Too late.'

Freya was on her way across the daisy-strewn lawn, in her jodhpurs and blue flip-flops, carrying a glass dish of marinated chicken drumsticks. 'Is it time to put the food on yet?'

'Only if you want your sausages incinerated,' Robbie told her. 'You muppet.'

The three of us loved the silliness of The Muppet Show and Robbie did a brilliant impression of Kermit the Frog. I knew that it was crucial to wait for the smoking coals to turn white but Freya had never got the hang of that.

'It'll be a good hour before it's all cooked,' said Robbie's dad, or Hugh as he insisted I call him now. 'You young folk could take the dogs for a walk.'

'You mean, please could we walk them?' Robbie smiled.

'OK, clever clogs. It would be helpful,' Hugh replied.

'No problem.' Robbie went to rouse the pair of golden retrievers from where they were dozing in a sunspot by the back door. 'Skye,' he called. 'Lewis. Here boys.' Robbie's mother's love for all things Scottish had inspired her choice of names, not just for her children but also their dogs. She'd told me her own mother had been the same, which was why she was called Flora, although there was also Flora's Temple in Chatsworth's garden, so her name connected her to here as well as to the Highlands.

'You coming then, scamp?' Robbie asked his brother, slinging his guitar strap over his shoulder.

'Need to practise my bowling.' Ewan was cricket-mad.

'Please yourself,' Robbie said, good-naturedly.

He didn't ask if I was coming or not, took it as a given. Did he think I always tagged along with him? Did I always tag along? Very probably. But his company was not the only attraction.

I'd fallen into a routine of going over to Brook House most weekends and often as not, while lunch was being prepared, I went off exploring with Robbie, his brother and sister and the Nightingales' dogs. We were the Famous Four.

Chatsworth's gardens were a magical playground, a hundred and five acres of fountains and waterfalls, lakes and secret glens. We'd built dens in the trees and dams in the streams, played hide and seek in the rock garden, lost each other in the maze. We'd dodged the spray from the plume of the mighty Emperor fountain and cycled down the wide Broad Walk, the sunlight flickering through the trees, like light from a cine projector. On hot summer days, we skinny dipped in the lakes up in Stand Wood and I tried not to stare at Robbie's long brown back and white buttocks. It felt safer to keep our clothes on and cool off in the Willow Tree fountain. An artificial tree of copper, it was made as a practical joke, when it was first 'planted' before the Civil War. There it stood in the rock garden, unnoticed until, all of a sudden, rain sprang from its hollow tubed branches, the shower giving the exact appearance of a weeping willow. We'd lived at Chatsworth too long to be caught unawares but that didn't lessen the fun.

Today though, Robbie was heading in the opposite direction. 'Wait 'till you see what they've just found.'

The south end of the garden, neglected and overgrown since the Second World War, was soon to be restored by the gardening team, under the direction of the Duchess and Robbie led the way to a place which he said had been known as azalea dell. It was like a woodland glen with dense trees and ferns and a meandering stream, its banks covered in a mass of bright-faced azaleas and sky-blue rhododen-drons, that gave off an intoxicating scent.

Robbie plucked two of the purple azaleas.

'Dad would kill you if he saw you doing that,' Freya scolded.

'One or two won't hurt.' He stuck a flower in his sister's hair, then tucked the other behind my ear. When his fingers brushed my cheek, it was like sherbet exploding all over my skin.

'Look at you two,' Robbie said, looking only at me.

'Sisters,' his sister said, slipping her arm around my waist and tilting her head towards my bony brown shoulder.

I knew very well that nobody could ever mistake the two of us for sisters. Freya was my best friend but we were different in every way. Freya was tiny and curvy whereas I was tall and lean. Freya was a rosette-winning show-jumper now, while I spent all my free time sketching and making things out of clay or glue.

'If Silva really was my sister, she'd be your sister too,' Freya said to Robbie with a mischievous gleam in her eyes. 'How would you like that, huh?'

Robbie threw a stick for the dogs to chase. 'I'd not mind,' he said but as if he would actually mind very much. He flashed a glance at me that was like a coded message, as if he wanted me to understand what he meant. I wasn't at all sure I did but I didn't want him to think of me as a sister any longer either. I wanted…it made me hot just to think about it.

Robbie kicked off his trainers.

'What are you doing now, you loon?' Freya asked.

'Going barefoot,' he said.

'You're such a hippie,' Freya scoffed.

'Give it a go,' Robbie gently urged me, as if he wanted

to share the experience with me, as if it was very important to him that I shared it. 'The soles of our feet are the most sensitive part of our body. It will blow your mind.'

When I stepped out of my sandals, Freya rolled her eyes.

I had to watch where I was putting my feet, not only to avoid nettles but to see what I was treading in, whereas Robbie walked in his bare feet, as if he was walking on carpet. He knew how to avoid the boggy spots, stepped round protruding tree roots and rocks as if by instinct. Eyes to the ground, I saw all kinds of things. The wild garlic flowers were still wrapped up, waiting to split open but wood anemones and celandines had sprung out of the woodland floor. The texture of the floor was damply soft with leaf mould and moss, and it was like walking on a sandy beach, covered in seaweed after the tide had just gone out. It was like a dream of perfect childhood, freedom and innocence; the kind of childhood I'd want for my own children, if I ever had any. Ages ago, when I was at nursery playing with dolls, I'd pictured myself with a whole brood of babies but now, that was like a dream that had faded on waking, in the harsh light of morning. I could no longer see myself as a mother, or a wife. Heaven forbid. I'd be a hopeless mother, hopeless wife. Just look at my role model. Were we alike?

Sometimes I pretended I could remember my mum, but I was kidding myself. I could no longer remember the sound of her voice and her face had faded, grown blurry. All I had left were fragments. Sukey drinking wine out of a mug. Sukey painting her nails pink. Sukey yelling at me for getting glue on the table, when I'd been making a model of Chatsworth House out of lollipop sticks and matchsticks. I'd learnt to watch her face, to be on permanent high alert for the smallest changes in her expression, in order to avoid trouble. I knew how to gauge the mood of a room before I walked into it, so I could tell if she was displeased with me, before she had time to start yelling. I learnt to do my bit to keep the peace. But that particular time, I'd been so absorbed in making the model of Chatsworth that I'd completely missed the warning signs.

It was as if she'd died now, only worse because if a person died, they had no choice about leaving people behind. She'd given birth to me, spooned porridge into my mouth, held my hand when I first learnt to walk. How could she just go? Why didn't she take me with her? I couldn't make sense of it, but I refused to dwell on it any longer. Waste of energy. I'd decided a while ago, the best way to manage the hurt was just to stop waiting, stop caring.

The meandering path we were now following seemed to have no purpose at all, except to be followed.

'Where *are* we going?' Freya demanded as we crossed a little rustic wooden bridge.

'Wait and see,' Robbie told her cheerily.

We looped round into an arboretum of conifers and pine trees with sunlit glades of long, pale-green grass between the trees. There were towering giant redwoods, Norfolk Island pines, a cedar of Lebanon, as well as beautiful Brewer's spruce trees. They had a drooping, melancholic appearance, as if the boughs were draped in veils of green lace and I took a mental snapshot to sketch later. This was one thing that had not changed at all since I was a little girl. I still noticed shapes and patterns, drawing endless inspiration from the wealth of manmade and natural beauty in the House and gardens of Chatsworth. In English class I'd written an essay about how nature created shape and form and colour as much as any of the great artists and master craftsmen at Chatsworth House. My teacher gave me an A for it.

Ahead was an exquisite little lake sheltered by trees, mirrored in its tranquil surface. The whole place reverberated with a cacophony of birdsong, liquid trills of thrushes and blackbirds, invisible, high up in the canopy. Nestled within a cluster of ancient oak trees, set back a little from the edge of the water was a granite folly that looked like a hobbit house.

'Wow, what is that?'

'A grotto,' Robbie told me. 'Built two hundred years ago, for Duchess Georgiana.'

There were more rhododendrons among the rocks above the grotto, these with blood-red flowers on a dark-red stem, like polished mahogany.

Freya threw a stick into the lake for the dogs to chase and Lewis belly-flopped with an almighty splash. We three humans ran to the edge of the pond as the dog scrambled out and shook himself, drenching us with droplets of water from his golden fur.

'Thanks buddy.' Robbie smiled. He swung himself up onto the bough of a huge Douglas Fir, which hung over the water and sat with his legs dangling like a rodeo rider. 'Those old oaks over there are the outliers of Sherwood Forest.'

'Robbie Hood.' I rested my hand on the tree trunk, looked up into his adorable face, framed by fresh gold-green leaves, the sunlight catching in his brown curls and picking out chestnut highlights. 'Where's your bow and arrow?'

'Sadly, I never had one.'

'You poor, deprived child.'

'Totally.' He swung himself down, landed with a soft thud on the ground beside me. 'Come see inside.'

Freya and I followed him as he ducked through the entrance of the grotto, into a rectangular stone den. The walls were lined with stalactites and stalagmites like a real cave but he was already leading the way, up to a tiny wooden bandstand that had been built atop it. A slate roof sheltered a circular bench made from a tree trunk, adorned with graffiti. Ed & Lucy, Zak 4 Beth, O heart T. It felt as though we were in a gathering place. People had met here before and left their mark and seemingly, their reason for coming had been love, as well as music.

'So cool,' I said.

'I knew you'd like it,' Robbie smiled, sitting down on the bench with his guitar beside him.

'It's basically graffiti,' Freya commented.

'Only no rude symbols,' I noted.

'Maybe people can't bring themselves to carve anything rude into a tree,' Robbie said.

'Robbie, you're such a hopeless romantic,' his sister sighed.

One of the inscriptions stood out from all the rest, particularly noticeable because it looked like considerable time, effort and skill, had been taken to carve it. The heart was drawn in perfect proportion, the pair of curves at the top were sensually female and the pointed end dramatically flicked, like a teardrop. The two names inside it were pierced by an arrow.

I traced the carving with my fingertip. 'Molly & Johnny. Who were they, I wonder? What happened to them? I wonder if they're still together.'

'Living happily ever after, with a couple of kids and a dog?' Robbie asked.

'Is that your definition of happiness?'

'Is it yours?'

It probably was, to be honest. 'Absolutely not,' I dismissed quickly. 'Far too boring and conventional.'

'You could never be boring and conventional.'

The way he was looking at me, made my insides fizz. I said: 'I'm not sure I even believe there's any such thing as being happily married.'

'Blimey. When did you become such a cynic?'

I plonked myself down bedside Robbie and picked up his guitar. Cradling it in my lap, I tried to strum a tune. 'I always wanted to learn to play guitar.'

'Why didn't you?'

'My dad's not interested in music. Never listens to it.'

Robbie looked incredulous. 'What? Never?'

'No, never.'

'Well it's never too late.' He put his left hand over mine, manoeuvred my fingers, one by one, showing me where to place them on the frets. He had beautiful long, slender fingers, lightly tanned and I loved looking at them touching mine. 'Strum,' he instructed.

I strummed.

He moved my fingers for me again.

I recognised the tune, just about. Led Zeppelin's *Thank You.*

I impressed myself by how easily I remembered the positioning of the different chords. Tentatively, I sang to Robbie about how I'd still be loving him if the sun stopped shining, how if the mountains crashed into the sea, there would still be the two of us.

'You've a very sweet singing voice,' he told me softly.

'Thanks.'

'Sweet as a nightingale.'

'Stop messing with my head,' I ordered him. 'Because frankly, it's messy enough already.'

'You really don't want to be a Nightingale, one day?' He sounded deadly serious now and it made my heart gallop.

'You two should carve your names here.' Freya teased. 'Robbie loves Silva. Silva loves Robbie.'

Robbie chucked one of his trainers at his sister and it bounced off her shoulder. 'Shut up, you.'

Freya released a peal of wicked laughter, picked up the trainer and lobbed it right back at him.

Silva loves Robbie.

Was this love that I was feeling? It was disconcerting, whatever it was. Not at all how I'd imagined love would be. It made me feel unsafe.

Had Molly felt unsafe here?

CHAPTER ELEVEN

MOLLY - 1967

'But it's not my birthday,' Molly says, holding the gift, wrapped in sapphire blue tissue paper and gold ribbon, which John has just given to her.

'Who said presents should be reserved for birthdays?'

John is always giving her things, love letters, poems, flowers and trinkets. Molly unties the ribbon, unfolds the paper. Inside is a glossy white box and inside the box, is a beautiful perfume bottle, fluted golden glass, curved like a seashell with a transparent blue glass stopper shaped like a fan. Shalimar, it says, on a gold badge.

'Created in memory of the greatest love story,' John tells her gently. 'Named after the Gardens of Shalimar, the favourite place of the girl who inspired the Taj Mahal, the most romantic building in the world.'

Molly draws out the stopper, holds the bottle to her nose. It's a very grown-up fragrance, sensual and oriental with notes of iris, jasmine and rose.

'Put some on,' John urges.

She dabs scent on her wrist, behind her ears. She's read

in a magazine, that perfume needs to be applied to pulse points and she feels very sophisticated. It's the loveliest gift that anyone has ever given to her. John helps his father at weekends, lambing and moving the sheep but he doesn't earn much and this must have cost him a fortune. She's literally lost for words, so she doesn't try to find any. Instead, she leans forward, pivoting at her hips and snakes her long, thin, brown arms round John's neck as she kisses him on his mouth.

His arms slip around her waist, pulling her closer, so her small breasts are pressed up against his chest. He inhales and murmurs: 'You smell wonderful.'

They're getting good at kissing, having spent hours practising. They've been meeting here all summer, in this hidden spot they discovered at the edge of the Chatsworth gardens, so overgrown nobody else knows it even exists. There's a small lake ringed with old trees and hidden in the trees is a grotto, made of granite boulders. John found out it had been built for Duchess Georgiana, to resemble the Castleton caves, filled with the gemstones she liked to collect.

'Home from home for you,' he'd told Molly. It even has a little space designed especially for musicians, for on top of the Grotto is a tiny bandstand.

Sometimes, Molly bakes cakes and they bring a picnic but today, she has just brought her guitar. It's sitting beside her now, on the bank of the lake. All the colours seem exaggerated, like technicolour. The sky dark-blue, the light a rich golden, and the trees are a lush almost unearthly green, reflecting perfectly in the still, mirrored water. Molly is wearing a strappy sundress and she can feel the sun prickling her thin shoulders. Thankfully, her olive skin hardly ever burns.

'I feel bad that I don't have a present for you too,' she says.

'You don't need to give me anything.' He softly kisses her mouth, her eyelids, her neck. 'Except your heart.'

She's given that to him already but she wants to give him her body too. She's aching to give herself to him and she knows he wants her, as much as she wants him. She doesn't know for sure what a willy actually does but she desperately wants to find out. Deep down, she's scared though, despite all her bravado. She's scared of getting pregnant. Scared of her gran finding out. Molly's mother, Esme, died giving birth to her and it's her Granny Lavinia who's raised her. Her father is a softie. It's Lavinia who rules the roost. She's always scolding Molly and Molly's dad too, telling him he's setting his daughter a bad example with his easy-going, free-spirited ways.

Molly loves her granny very much but she's old-school; so strict, it drives Molly mad. Lavinia's abiding values are moderation in all things, good manners, hard work and education, so it's bad enough that Molly is playing in seedy folk clubs, dressed in rags, as her granny calls her gypsy clothes. For a girl to be a folk singer is tantamount to being a prostitute, in Lavinia's eyes. Molly travels on the bus to the Wayfarers in Manchester, the Barley Mow in Sheffield. In the two months since the first Peak Cavern gig, she's has built up quite a following. When her granny tried to stop her singing, she'd threatened to leave home. She meant it too. She really did.

Molly has repeatedly been warned by Granny Lavinia, in the strongest possible terms, against the new sexual immorality, she claims she's seeing everywhere, a slippery slope that will lead to an abyss. She'd be more than furious if she knew Molly has been sneaking off to meet John. If she knew what the pair of them get up to, when nobody's watching. Her grandmother's only instruction about the opposite sex: 'Until you're married, don't let a man touch you.'

Molly wants to be touched by John. She's read the naughty bits in *Lady Chatterley's Lover* and *Forever Amber.* She smuggled copies of both books into school, covered in brown paper, read them avidly with her friends. She wants to experience the ecstasy and wild physical pleasure described in the pages of those banned novels. She wants to be free, to lose herself in passion, and find herself. She wants to go all the way with John.

'The Duke told me something really exciting today,' he says.

'What's that?'

'His friend, the Duke of Bedford, is organising a big concert on his estate at Woburn Abbey, at the end of August. Our Duke thought I'd be interested because of the Peak Cavern Club and everything but there's been nothing like it in this country before. It's going to be held outside and it's going to go on for three days. Three whole days, just imagine? It'll be like Monterey, right here in England.'

They'd read the news reports from the Monterey Pop Festival, in *Melody Maker* a few weeks ago. The Who, the Grateful Dead and Jimi Hendrix blasting out *Wild Thing* and then pouring lighter fluid all over his black Fender Stratocaster and setting it ablaze.

John fishes a small poster from the back pocket of his jeans, unfolds it and hands it to her. 'Take a look.'

She reads aloud: 'The Festival of the Flower Children.'

The photographs from Monterey showed thousands of orchids from Hawaii, American cops wearing orchids in their motorcycle helmets.

'Apparently the Duchess of Bedford thinks it's an actual flower show they're hosting,' John chuckles. 'She's going to have the shock of her life.'

'She is.' Molly read the strap-lines: 'The World's Largest Love-In. Free incense and sparklers.'

'Look who's playing,' John says. 'The Faces, The Kinks. Marmalade.'

Molly lowers the poster into her lap, fixes him with her huge black eyes. 'Johnny, we have to go.'

He laughs.

'This is no laughing matter. Don't you want to go?'

'Yes. But. How ever will we afford it?'

'Good question.' She chews her lip. 'I have hardly any money and I assume you don't either now, since you blew it all on my lovely present?'

'Tickets are three pounds. And it's not just the ticket price. We have to find a way to get there.'

'Where is Woburn anyway?'

'Bedfordshire? Buckinghamshire? Somewhere down south at any rate.'

Molly has never been further than Sheffield. 'We can hitch a ride. It'll be an adventure.'

He laughs at her determination and resourcefulness. 'But even if we get there Moll, how do we get in?'

'We have to find a way. Think, Johnny, think.'

'Johnny? I like being Johnny. Ah but it's too hot to think,' he groans, flopping back on the grass.

'Let's swim then,' she says, jumping to her feet. Her head is too busy to be in a body that's still. She has to go to Woburn. To be surrounded by music, by musicians, by people who love music, for three whole wonderful days. To go there with Johnny, away from his parents and her grand-mother, away from restrictions. Oh, what heaven. She's already walking towards the lake, kicking off her shoes, peeling her dress off over her head.

'What are you doing?'

'What's it look like?'

She reaches both arms round her back and unhooks her bra, lets it drop on the grass and then dives headfirst into the water, squealing at the shock of the cold.

Underwater, she strikes out for the deep centre of the pond, where she breaks the sunlit surface, then pushes into a sleek front crawl. When she reaches the far bank, she flips over, graceful as a mermaid and glides on her back, her face turned to the darkening sky. There are black clouds sailing overhead and her long hair swirls around her head, like a black cloud in the water. John catches her as she floats past him. She turns herself vertical, her feet on the bottom of the pond, and he gazes at the small, white triangles of her breasts beneath the water. He takes hold of her waist, pulling her closer, so she can feel the warmth of him in the cool water. She wraps her arms around his neck and pulls herself up his body, hooking her legs around his hips. She kisses him as the first drops of rain fall on their faces. They ignore it for a while, then swim back to the bank, haul themselves out onto dry land just as the heavens open, a sudden deluge of huge, fat raindrops.

'The bandstand,' John shouts.

They grab their clothes, Molly's guitar and the bottle of perfume, dash up the damp grassy slope, laughing and breathless as they reach shelter, beneath the conical slate roof. They sit side-by-side on the bench and watch the rain falling like a silvery curtain, hammering a tattoo on the roof.

'It's like being inside a waterfall,' Molly says. Her clothes are damp, her skin dimpled with goosebumps, her long, wet hair clinging to her bony brown shoulders, but she loves it.

'We're going to be here for ages.'

Good, she thinks because there's nowhere on earth she'd rather be. 'Give me your penknife,' she tells Johnny.

She tosses her long, wet hair over her shoulder, as she kneels by the bench and starts carving.

'What are you doing?'

'Wait and see.'

She carves the letter J first, the rest of his name and then an M. She links their names with an ampersand and then encircles the whole with a heart, pierced by an arrow.

'It's going to be here for years and years,' she says. 'Like a work of art.'

'It is a work of art,' he tells her, when finally it's done. 'It's by far the most artistic graffiti I've ever seen.'

The newly exposed wood is honey gold against the aged and weathered surface. 'You're the first person who's ever called me Johnny.'

'First and last. Promise. You can be John to everyone else and Johnny just for me.'

Her hair is dripping down her back, soaking her t-shirt. She shivers and he takes off his shirt, drapes it around her shoulders. 'When I'm with you, I feel like a totally different person,' he says. 'A better person.' He takes hold of her hands. The nails on her left hand are cut short for pressing frets while on her right hand they are long, for strumming. He strokes them. 'I love how your hands are so different.'

The rain has eased off to a soft patter. Molly picks up her guitar. She tunes the strings, then plays with open tunings. She likes to imagine the musicians who might have played here in the little bandstand, over the centuries. Violinists and flautists maybe. A little brass band. Or maybe it was just a folly and she is the first person ever to bring a real musical instrument here.

Johnny watches her fingers move on the fretboard.

At the folk clubs her repertoire includes: *The Runaway Lovers*; *She Moves through The Fair* and a new song by Sandy Denny, that she taped off the radio, *Who Knows Where the Time Goes?* She's obsessed with that song, loves the Celtic overtones in the lyrics. Next, she sings a song she's written herself, called *Lady of the Lake*. She's been practising it in her bedroom, is planning to sing it at the next Cavern Club but she wants to give Johnny a sneak preview.

'What d'you think?' She asks, when she comes to the end of the song.

'I think I love you.'

'I meant, what do you think of the song?'

'I think it will be hard to share you.' Suddenly he looks so sad and serious.

'What are you talking about?'

'I fell in love with you when I heard you sing. Everyone falls in love with you when they hear you sing. And you need to be heard by thousands.'

'Jealousy is old-fashioned,' she tells him. 'This is the age of Aquarius, remember? Peace and love. The times they are a-changing.'

'What does that even mean?'

'It means,' she smacks a kiss on his mouth, 'girls like me, can go out and drink in pubs, travel, stay out all night. We can do anything we want.'

'Whatever would your granny say?'

'My granny was born on Queen Victoria's birthday. Nuff said.'

'Really?'

'Really. Falling madly in love, being a couple, then being unfaithful and having your heart broken by some guy and feeling betrayed, those days are gone, thank God,' Molly tells him. 'It's 1967. We're tearing up the old world and making a new one. Jealousy and possessiveness and all of that, they're abolished. Nobody belongs to anybody anymore.'

'Do you honestly believe all that?'

She knows it's what she's supposed to believe but does she believe it? 'Let's not talk about it.' She touches his cheek with her fingertips. 'I'm the only person who gets to call you Johnny and you…you're the only person who gets to hear songs I write myself.'

'Everyone needs to hear your songs.'

'Actually, they don't. If you want credibility, it's way cooler to find a song from a traditional source, than to actually write anything.' This she does know for certain.

'You're the coolest person,' Johnny says. 'And you're going to be so successful.'

'You really think so?' She wants success so badly, sometimes it makes her breathless.

'I really think so.'

That's what gives her the idea. The most amazing idea. She sets the guitar aside and focusses on his face. 'You have a two-track tape recorder, right?'

'I do.'

'Then we shall go to the Festival.'

'Are you my fairy godmother?'

'Will you help me make a demo tape?'

'Of course I'll help you. Any way I can.'

She feels powerful again, so free and excited, in love with her own future and the infinite possibilities that lie ahead. People talk about losing your virginity but she wants to give hers away, like the most precious gift that's hers to give. She's too old to be a virgin anyway. She clambers onto his lap, wrapping her arms and legs around him, as the damp curtain of her hair trails over his skin like seaweed.

'On second thoughts, you're more like a mermaid than a fairy godmother,' he says with a groan. 'Or a siren, sent to lure me to my doom with the sweetness of your song. I think you should get off me, before it's too late.'

But instead she wantonly hitches herself closer, gazes deep into his eyes. His pupils are dilated with desire that matches her own. 'Wouldn't this be a good way to go?' She softly teases, bending her head towards him to nibble his ear lobe. 'Don't you want to do this?'

'D'you mean with you?'

'No with some other girl. Yes, with me.'

'You know I want to,' he says, his voice thick with desire.

'Well then. Kiss me.'

They kiss gently, then more intently, his stubble rubbing her cheek. She takes his hand and places it on her breast, still kissing.

'We can't do it here,' he moans. 'I want it to be right.'

'This feels completely right to me,' she whispers.

PART II

CHAPTER TWELVE

SILVA - 1984

Sitting cross-legged with my sketchbook, in the saggy old armchair in my dad's shed, I doodled an arrow, rubbed out some lines, made alterations. I'd always enjoyed designing things, then trying to find a practical way to turn the images I'd created on paper into real 3D objects. I was going to surprise Robbie with a bow and arrow, since he said he'd never had one. How hard could it be to make one? Only I got distracted, drew a heart around the arrow, artfully curved and flicked like Molly & Johnny's heart. I doodled Robbie's name inside it, then my own. Robbie & Silva. They looked good together.

Stop daydreaming. Never gonna happen. Which was a good thing, right? Some of my school-friends had had boyfriends and the relationships seemed to involve more pain than gain. They lasted a few months at best, before they just fizzled out or else turned petty or bitter. I couldn't bear for that to happen to me and Robbie. In any case, he was leaving soon. Do not fall in love with him, I instructed myself. Whatever you do, do not fall in love. Because if I did, how could I deal with being left behind?

I bit into my honey sandwich, then twisted my hair into a bun, stabbed it with the pencil to hold it in place. I assembled the basic kit I'd need to get going. Saw, knife, the tree branch I'd picked up on the walk back from the grotto. I sawed the branch to a length of about fifty inches, began trimming the bark. It was like a kind of meditation. The world shrank to the action of my fingers. How did people cope with life, if they couldn't lose themselves in creating something?

Sandpaper, I needed sandpaper. Where would my dad keep sandpaper? It was anyone's guess. The shed was a mess. I itched to fetch the broom and a cloth, give it a good scrub and sweep, arrange the tools tidily. Make it a nicer place for him just to be. But he always claimed he liked it just as it was and knew where to find everything. He'd be furious with me, if I started meddling in here.

I hunted around, crouching to look under the workbench, in the tool-box. There was a big wooden cupboard screwed to the wall and I dragged over a little three-legged stool, so I could reach. On top of the cupboard was a battered old leather travelling case. I tugged it out, dislodging a decade of dust, cobwebs and desiccated flies, which rained down around my head. I dusted myself down, deposited the trunk on the bench, flipped the rusty catches and opened it, releasing a waft of musty smell. All that was inside was a large, mummified object, wrapped in an old woollen blanket. I lifted it out and unwound it.

Nearly a foot tall, it looked like a vase, only with a kind of lid. Maybe not a vase then. It was made of a material that looked uncannily like Blue John, a rare gemstone we'd learnt about in geography lessons. But most of the knowledge I had of it came from Chatsworth, because we had a huge collection of Blue John here. In the eighteenth century, Duchess Georgiana had a passion for it. The thing about Blue John is that it's only found only in one place in the whole world: in the caves under a hill in Castleton, a few miles away. It was distinguished by the extraordinary zig-zag banding of purple, lilac and white and that unmistakeable pattern ran around the perimeter of this vase, the colour varying, from violet to cream and hazy gold. I'd only ever seen tiny pieces of Blue John for sale in the local gift shops. Earrings and pendants and pretty little bowls which sold for hundreds of pounds each. But this was something else. It was just like the precious antique ornaments in the collection at Chatsworth. In the light from the naked bulb that dangled above the workbench, the colours gleamed with jewel-like intensity.

I let out a breath. 'Holy shit.'

What on earth was it doing here? Why keep something as gorgeous as this hidden away? It was wrong, on every level. Wrong not to have it out on display and wrong to store it in a shed. It wasn't exactly the most secure of places although, in a way, it was hidden in plain sight. Nobody would look for something so valuable in a garden shed.

I could no longer see my mother's face properly or hear her voice but her parting words were scorched onto my psyche like scar tissue. I'd grown around them, so they were a part of who I was. Sometimes I felt as if they'd actually altered my DNA. I'd put the actual memory in a box and padlocked it, then buried it deep inside me, like toxic waste. But it had a long half-life and the poison kept escaping, burning me all over again.

I heard her so clearly.

You're thick as thieves, the pair of you. Though of course it's me who's the thief isn't it? That's how you see me now. A thief. Who stole what wasn't mine.

I slammed the lid down on the memory, blotting out the sound of the even more venomous words that had followed. Might this extraordinary object be what my parents had been rowing about that night? Might my mother have stolen it? I didn't know what to think. I didn't want to think at all. I wanted to forget I'd ever seen it.

Too late.

'What the devil are you doing?' My dad was standing in the doorway in his checkered pyjamas and slippers, back-lit by the moonlight, so his face was shadowed and dark. His voice sounded shadowed and dark too. I felt like a thief myself, caught redhanded with stolen goods and in my shock I nearly dropped it. 'No need to look so terrified, love,' he corrected softly. 'By rights, that's yours.'

'Mine?'

Dad walked over, looked at the ornament, then at me. 'It was your mother's,' he said, with touching reverence. 'She wanted you to have it. When you turned eighteen. I've been keeping it for you, 'till then.'

I frowned, sceptical. Did my mum really love me enough, to leave me something so rare and precious? Did she really care enough, to want me to have such an amazing and unique gift for my milestone birthday? Despite all that I'd heard her say on that terrible night? It didn't stack up. How did Sukey even come to own something like this in the first place?'

'It's a family heirloom,' Dad said. 'Your mother was born and raised in Castleton and her family came from there.'

'How come I never knew that?'

'Apparently that was made by one of her ancestors. One

of your ancestors, in other words. Some great-great-grand-parent or other.'

'Really?' Could that be true? 'Wow.'

'I know. Pretty impressive, huh? You may as well have it now. What difference is a few months going to make, eh?'

'A few years, more like,' I smiled. 'I'm only sixteen Dad, in case you forgot.'

'You've always acted way older than your years, Petal. I expect you've had to. Sorry about that.'

We never ever talked about things like this. It was as if the appearance of the Blue John was making him all mushy and maudlin. 'You're all right, Dad.'

I studied the vase more closely, carefully removed the finial, saw that it was hollowed out, a receptacle.

'I understand it's called a candle-vase,' he explained. 'For holding flowers in summer and candles in winter.'

'Neat.' I immediately saw how the finial had been inge-niously designed, so it could be inverted to hold a candle.

'We need to find a good spot for it.'

'Can we put it in the living room?'

'Put it wherever you like, Sweetie-Pie.'

I didn't trust myself to carry it inside, so I went to rewrap it in the blanket and as I did so, a small photograph with crimped edges fluttered out, like a butterfly released from a chrysalis. A black and white image of two girls, sitting together on the grass. There was an outdoor stage in the background and young people were lounging around smoking, dancing, with feathers and flowers in their hair. Some had painted faces like children at a village fete. You could tell it was a bright, sunny day somehow, even in monochrome. A music festival. It looked like a music festival.

One of the girls was definitely Sukey and her friend was

very striking, with long straight, dark hair and big, dark, heavy-lidded eyes. Her skin was dusky, making her look like an American Indian and her lacy clothes made her look even more exotic. Who was she? I turned the photo over, hoping for something written on the back of it but it was blank.

Dad was busy inspecting the branch that I'd been whittling. It might make him sad to see the photo. He was always sad though, hard to see how this could make matters worse. And I need to know more. 'It's Mum, isn't it?'

He stared at the image for the longest time but he didn't take it from me, as if he didn't dare touch it. 'Yes,' he said eventually. 'It's your mum.' His voice cracked, as if he might cry but he curled his hand into a fist, put it against his mouth and pretended to cough.

'Who's the other girl? Was she Mum's friend?'

He nodded, as if that was all he could manage.

'What's her name?'

He cleared his throat. 'Can't remember.'

He really was a dreadfully bad liar. Why would he lie about a thing like that though? 'D'you think they stayed in touch? Might she know where mum is? Might we ask her?'

'No.'

'OK.' It was not OK. Far from it, but I was so good at pretending that all was fine.

I wanted to keep the photo; I had so few of her but my dad took it off me, pushed it into his pyjama pocket. He sniffed, wiped his eyes with the back of his hand. 'What are you doing out here in the middle of the night anyway, lovey?'

'Making a bow and arrow.'

'Ask a silly question, expect a silly answer.' He smiled. 'Well, I'll leave you to it. I'm off back to bed.' He never stayed up late any longer. Too tired, he said. Too old. He acted like he was pushing seventy, not forty.

'Sleep tight, Dad.'

He dived under the bench, rummaged in a plastic bag, produced a sheet of sandpaper. 'I expect you'll be needing this.'

I laughed. 'Well anticipated. Thanks.'

'You're welcome.' He kissed the top of my head, spoke quietly into my hair: 'The real tragedy, is that your mother has the most amazing daughter and she doesn't know you.'

I didn't know her either but I had at least learnt something new about her. She came from Castleton and her ancestors had been fine craftsmen. That was something. More than something. I hugged it close as I shaped and sanded the bow.

CHAPTER THIRTEEN

Next weekend, walking over to Beeley to give Robbie his present, I met him in the lane by the brook, walking the dogs.

'You look like Diana,' he said. 'Striding across the fields with a bow slung over your shoulder.'

'She's a goddess right?' Chatsworth's most famous painting showed Duchess Georgiana as Diana, wildly emerging from stormy clouds, her hair a cloud around her face and a floating organza gown billowing behind her. It was a wonderful painting. My favourite. 'I'll go with that.' I slipped the bow off my arm, handed it to him. 'It's for you. I mean. I made it for you.'

He looked astonished. 'No way. It's awesome. That's so sweet of you.'

I shrugged. 'You said you never had one so…well…now you do.' I felt acutely embarrassed, as if the gesture was too much. Had I just exposed myself, revealed how much I idolised him?

Maybe I had, because he dipped his head and kissed me.

Just a fleeting kiss on my cheek but the feeling of his lips on my skin left me breathless and stunned. It was the same way I felt when I was about eleven years old and tried to climb the apple tree after him, lost my footing and fell two feet. That brief hiatus when there was no air in my lungs. Part of me just wanted to run away, as far and as fast as I could.

But clearly Robbie wasn't going to let me do any such thing. 'Hey, there's a vacancy come up for a waitress at the Devonshire Arms. You should go for it, Silly. You'd be great.'

I cleared my throat, tried to clear my head. 'You think?'

'Definitely.'

The Devonshire Arms was an atmospheric eighteenth-century coaching inn in Beeley, with low beams, flagstone floors and exposed stone walls, known for serving hearty local food and cask ales. It was run by Ed Fletcher, a trendy Mancunian, who would no doubt be good fun to work with. It would also be great to earn money of my own.

'I guess I might as well apply.' My decision obviously had nothing at all to do with the fact that Robbie also worked there.

The interview was the following Friday, straight after school, but I wished I'd gone home to change first. Sitting on a barstool opposite me, Ed looked like a member of Joy Division, wearing skinny black trousers and a peacoat and I felt so gauche, in my pleated school skirt and tie, but he didn't treat me like a kid.

'I came to Chatsworth when I was your age, to work as a kitchen porter,' he said chattily. 'My folks dropped me off with my battered suitcase and drove away, left me in tears. It was my first time away from home and I only intended to stay a few months, get some experience, work out what I wanted to do with my life. That was five years ago. Anyway, the job's yours.'

'Oh, OK,' I laughed. 'That's great. Thanks.'

He stuck out his hand for me to shake on it. 'Robbie's given you the most glowing reference ever. First shift Saturday? He can show you the ropes.'

Robbie showed me how to use the dishwasher and the cash register, how to pull a pint with a good head on it. Then later, when we were both standing at tables, taking orders for steak pie or beer-battered haddock, he kept catching my eye and smiling over at me and it made the evening feel enchanted, even if I was mostly wiping down tables and stacking dirty plates.

Ed said I was the tidiest waitress he'd ever had on his team and I started looking forward to going to work, as other people might look forward to a party.

The staff wore a uniform of sorts: black Levis, tan leather belt and white t-shirt. I had to tie my hair back in a ponytail, plait or ballerina's bun, so there wasn't much scope for individuality but I did my best, experimented with make-up in front of the bathroom mirror, outlining my eyes with kohl and shadowing them in smokey grey, aiming for a sultry, edgy look. I bought some small hooped silver earrings from Top Shop and sometimes I wore a silver snowflake on a leather choker, that Robbie's mum had given to me as a Christmas present. Robbie told me I looked pretty but I'd heard him say the same to Lizzie Morton, one of the other waitresses. Lizzie and I were at school together and Lizzie had always been pretty, in a sporty, cheerleader-y sort of way with long, straight gold hair, caramel skin and an athletic figure. She'd already declared that she was madly in love with Robbie.

She rested her chin on the broom handle and gazed at him across the restaurant, as if he was a pop star on a poster. 'He's a singer, isn't he?' She sighed dreamily.

'Kind of.'

Some weekends, Robbie caught a train to London, to visit the archives at a place called Cecil Sharp House, where he learnt more about traditional songs. He'd sung a few of them for us, late one night in the Cavendish Hall, the red brick Georgian building near Edensor, where Chatsworth staff went to socialise and swim and play pool, beneath an ornately barrelled ceiling. He'd talked passionately about how folk songs are the oldest music we have, how they connect us to our past and Lizzie said she loved listening to him talk. She loved talking to him too and she was not the only one.

Working alongside him at the pub, I got to see how girls literally flocked round him and poured out their hearts. He didn't do anything to encourage them and he seemed oblivious to how much attention he attracted, but they all liked talking to him. Talking and talking. The customers, young and old, male and female, all loved him too, even though he spent far too long chatting to them to be very efficient with their orders.

He had a knack for getting people to tell him their stories. One Sunday afternoon, two elderly ladies in silk scarves told him all about how Duchess Evelyn, wife of the ninth Duke, used to carry a hammer to scare woodworm away from the antiques. Blacksmith, Eli Strutt, regaled him with a tale from the day President John F Kennedy arrived in a helicopter, to visit his sister Kick's grave in Edensor churchyard.

'What did you think about that?' Robbie asked, as he served Eli his egg and cress sandwiches.

'Not much, lad. The wind from that machine blew my chickens away and I've not seen 'em since.'

Laying out cutlery at the next table, I burst out laughing.

'It's Midsummer's Day tomorrow,' Robbie said, unhooking my denim jacket from the peg and handing it to me at the end of our shift. 'Want to come for a drive with me?'

I shrugged on my jacket. 'A drive?'

'I passed my test, remember?'

'Yeah but there's just one slight problem. You don't have a car.'

'I can take my mum's.'

'Will she let you?'

'If I ask nicely.'

Robbie always asked nicely, made it pretty impossible for anyone to refuse him anything. It was annoying! 'Will Freya come? Ewan?'

Robbie looked confused. 'D'you want them to come?'

Why had I even suggested that? What an idiot. 'I don't mind,' I said. 'Where will we go?'

'You choose.'

The first place that came into my head: 'Castleton.'

I'd been wanting to go, ever since I'd found the Blue John but I could hardly ask my dad to take me. Bad enough that he had to see the candle-vase every day. I'd put it on the window ledge in the living room, kept it filled with flowers from the cutting garden: roses, peonies, azaleas. It had become a strange little ritual, like an act of remembrance for a person who'd not died. Which was surely the precise reason it made Dad so sad. He did his best to hide it, made a point of commenting on how lovely the flowers looked but

I could read him too well after years of watching and worrying over every shadow that crossed his face. I'd taken the vase up to my room, to save him from having to see it but he'd missed it immediately, insisted I bring it straight back downstairs again. No way could I ask him to go with me to Castleton. He was far too busy anyway, helping to organise the first ever country fair at Chatsworth, due to take place later in the summer. He and the rest of the staff had to sort out logistics for spillover carparks, food stalls, signage, fencing for the main ring.

Robbie could take me to Castleton though and much as I loved his sister and brother, I so hoped they wouldn't come.

CHAPTER FOURTEEN

Robbie picked me up outside my house, in Mrs Nightingale's red Renault and it was just him. Just him and me. For the whole day. Bliss.

When I was a little girl, leaving the gilded oasis of Chatsworth and venturing out through the golden gates into the wilds of Derbyshire, had felt like leaving behind an enchanted land and stepping out into the dangerous real world. But not today. Today, as I gazed out at the expanse of moorland and the rocky escarpments, known locally as 'edges', that defined the landscape of the Peak District, I felt a joyous sense of freedom. The moors were ablaze with heather, a lush sea of purple as far as the eye could see and a sweet heathery scent wafted through the open window of the car.

Just me and Robbie, all day. I still couldn't believe it.

Though he'd admitted, after we'd set off and there was no way out, that it was only the second time he'd been behind the wheel without an experienced driver alongside him in the passenger seat, I felt quite safe with him, even if he did put his foot down, took corners like a rally driver and stalled at the crossroads, twice. But only good things could happen today. There was literally nowhere else I would rather be.

We drove through the villages of Baslow, Claver and Grindleford, passing the wooded river valley of Padley Gorge and on into Hathersage.

Robbie braked, changed gear and we jolted. 'Sorry.' Then: 'Your dad used to climb, didn't he?'

'Yeah.'

Hathersage was an epicentre for climbing, overlooked on the east side by the spectacular escarpment of Stanage Edge, while the dramatic line of gritstone outcrops, Curbar, Froggatt and Gardoms, stretched for twelve miles north and south, an almost continuous wall of rock.

'Didn't you go with him?' Robbie remembered.

'Once.'

'Did you like it?'

'I loved it.' I must have been about thirteen and Dad said I was a natural, instinctively knowing how to breathe and use my bodyweight to balance. 'Dad got scared though, told me how many people died climbing each year. He always wants to wrap me in cottonwool.'

'That's understandable. You're all he has.'

I glanced at Robbie's profile, loving him for being so sympathetic and wise. I was about to tell him about the other side of my family, the mysterious grandparent who'd made the Blue John candle-vase, but we'd already dropped down into the Hope Valley and Castleton.

As Chatsworth had been known as the Palace of the Peaks, so Castleton was once the Gem of the Peaks but they were starkly different places. Once the heart of the Royal Forest, Castleton lay at the edge of the Dark Peak, an area of gritstone and crags and the town was ringed by brooding hills. The crumbling ruins of Peveril Castle had stood guarding the town, since the days of William the Conqueror and beneath it, was the vast gaping mouth of Peak Cavern, otherwise known as the Devil's Arse, considered at one time to be a gateway to the underworld.

We parked by the tourist information office, walked up past the gift shops and cafes that lined the narrow winding High Street. It had rained in the night but during the course of the morning, the rainclouds had been blown away by a brisk breeze and the sun was trying to make an appearance, turning the pavements bright and shiny. It was typical weather for the Peak District in summer and the day-trippers were undeterred. A little girl in pigtails and red wellington boots, was jumping in puddles as she held on tight to her mother's hand. It gave me a familiar pang of loneliness which always confused me. I was never sure whether I wanted to be the little girl with her mother or to be a mother with a little girl of my own. Was it my mother I was still longing for, despite my best efforts to forget all about her or the chance to be a mother, despite consistently declaring to everyone, myself included, that motherhood was not for me?

The fleeting touch of Robbie's hand in the small of my back, gently steering me in the right direction, felt like coming home to a warm fire. Sometimes, I felt like a cartoon character who'd run headlong over a cliff. I was frantically pedalling my legs in thin air, knowing that soon I'd come crashing down. But might there be someone there to catch me, if I was prepared to trust him? So maybe it wasn't the little girl in wellies who confused me, it was

Robbie because he made me want things I'd decided were far too dangerous to want.

Sometimes I got so tired of living in my own head. It would be great to take a break, not escape to a different physical place but a different headspace. That would be the best holiday of all, wouldn't it? But it's true what they say: wherever you go, you take yourself with you.

We entered Winnats Pass, rugged precipices rearing up on either side of the narrow, winding chasm. There was some beauty to soften the bleakness, since the steep sides of the pass were cloaked in green, spangled here and there with the purple-blue petals of flowers which grew scattered among the mossy crags. But still, it was a place full of foreboding, like a scene from a fantasy story. I was used to walking in the Peaks. It had given me good lungs and muscles but the steepness of the incline here, pulled at my calf muscles.

'No wonder it used to be called the Wind Gates,' Robbie smiled, as I wrapped my denim jacket tighter around me, shivering from the gusts that funnelled between the towering pinnacles. 'Derbyshire place names are wonderful, aren't they?' he added. 'I mean, we're on the road to Chapel-en-le-Frith, so we could be in France, except we've just passed the Devil's Arse, which is about as northern as you get. Your dad told me that the area in front of the Devil's Arse is called Duel Yard or Jewel Yard, nobody knows which but either way, there must be a great story attached to it.'

'Your mind works in such a peculiar way,' I told him. I loved it though. The way he noticed little things and somehow saw a bigger picture.

'Mam Tor,' he said, pointing to the mound that towered above us. 'Mother Mountain.'

'We learnt all about that at school. It was also called the

Shivering Mountain.' On account of the fact that it was said to keep up a constant trembling and this caused the rocks it was made of to crumble to pieces, especially in winter after a hard frost, when great tons of stones came tumbling down the mountain sides with an ominous rattling that sounded like torrential rain. The vast southern face fell away, leaving a great scar and the trees and cottages at its base were entirely buried beneath the slips. I shivered again myself. 'I'm not gonna lie. This place spooks the hell out of me.'

Robbie laughed. 'And we're not even in the caves yet. It's not too late to back out.'

Right in front of us was the sign for Treak Cliff Cavern, steep steps up the side of the hill. Robbie chuckled as I strode on ahead with purpose, following a party of school-children in raincoats and rucksacks, talking in French.

At the top, a young guide sold us tickets and led the way to the entrance of the cave. He introduced himself as Nate and he looked like a landlocked surfer. His complexion was darkly tanned and he had bleached blond hair, drawn back in a ponytail, a pierced eyebrow and a tattoo of an eagle on the inside of his right wrist. He saw that we were all fitted with yellow hard hats, as if we were builders on a construction site and then he took us through a low, narrow doorway, which he said was the way the orig-inal mine had been entered, back in the eighteenth century.

A little over thirty metres from the entrance, we entered the first chamber, where a vein of Blue John was immedi-ately visible in the roof when Nate shone his torch there. The distinctive purple rock was the same colour as the flowers out on the hillside, threaded with bands of white and amber.

'There are fourteen different veins of Blue John and this

one here is part of the Treak Cliff Blue Vein,' Nate said. 'One of the most beautiful and most valuable.'

I craned my neck for a better look, wondering which vein my candle-vase was made of? 'Is Blue John still mined here?'

'Some,' Nate said. 'We take out no more than half a ton a year, now. Enough to make small pieces of jewellery.'

'When would a piece this big have been made?' I used the space between my hands to show him a rough measurement of the candle-vase.

'Mid to late 1700s, I'd say. That was when Blue John became massively popular and huge amounts were mined then.'

The schoolchildren were getting restless, noise levels rising, so Nate led us deeper.

'I didn't know you were so interested in Blue John,' Robbie said.

'I found something made of it in my dad's shed. A candle-vase. Sukey wanted me to have it when I turned eighteen but Dad's let me have it early.'

'Your mum gave you a birthday present?'

'I know. Crazy hey. Who'd have believed it? Dad said it was made by one of my great-great-grandparents.'

'So that's why you wanted to come here?'

'Partly. And Dad said Sukey grew up in Castleton. I never knew that before.'

'She must have come down here herself then, lots of times.'

'I suppose she must.' I waited to see if that made me feel closer to her but disappointingly, it didn't. Not in the slightest.

We were in an intricate maze of underground passages now, alternatively narrowing and widening. The walls were lined with glistening minerals, milky-white and yellow and slippery green, like the inside of an alien. There was the constant drip of moisture and rush of water through hidden channels.

'Amazing, that something as pretty as Blue John, came out of somewhere so creepy,' I said.

'Beauty often comes from darkness. Don't you think?'

'I've never really thought about it like that.'

'I mean, lots of artists and poets and composers are tortured souls aren't they or at least they've suffered some degree of trauma or heartbreak?'

'Do you think you need to have suffered, to be creative then? Does it help?'

'Good question.'

The passage opened out into a great soaring chamber, higher than a house.

'Welcome to the Witch's Cave,' Nate announced, flicking a switch to take out the main electric light. Sure enough, the distinct shadow of a witch riding a broomstick was revealed on the far wall, greeted by gasps from the children.

'That's brilliant,' I breathed. I'd always liked looking for shapes in clouds and the whorls of tree-trunks.

From here, we entered a pure fantasy world. Glittering grottos of translucent rock formations. Sweeps of stalactite draperies that gleamed like frozen crystal waterfalls. Nate explained to the schoolchildren, how stalactites and stalagmites grow towards each other with infinite slowness. 'Those two over there are three centimetres apart now but they've been reaching out to each other for over a million years and they won't touch for another hundred thousand.'

'That's the saddest love story I ever heard,' Robbie whispered to me and under the cover of the cavern's darkness, he moved closer to me, until our shoulders were touching. He reached out and took hold of my hand, then slipped his fingers through mine, enmeshing them together. It felt heart-healing, the most wonderful thing that had ever happened to me.

CHAPTER FIFTEEN

Back out on the hillside, black clouds were gathering and Robbie kept hold of my hand.

'I've never forgotten that story you told me,' I said. 'The Runaway Lovers who were murdered here, on their way to be married.'

'On moonlit nights, people say they can see Clara's ghost. A girl in a long cape all stitched with gold, is sometimes seen flitting between the rocks. When it's windy, you can still hear her screams.'

'Stop it,' I scolded. Even without a mystery and a murder story attached to it, Winnats Pass would be an eerie, menacing place.

'People have heard her weeping and begging the vicious miners to spare her life and the life of the boy she was going to marry,' Robbie went on in a theatrical voice. 'Horses' hooves are heard galloping up the pass but no horses have ever been seen.'

I shuddered. 'Aren't you afraid of ghosts?'

'I like to think they exist: a reminder of the layers of

history beneath our feet, old stories that refuse to be forgotten.'

'I love that idea. Such a great way to look at it.'

I wasn't usually a person to let my imagination get the better of me; I made sure I kept my feet on the ground at all times, but I sensed something sinister here. As if Winnats Pass was not just haunted by the souls of dead lovers but by the ghosts of the miners who had lain in wait and so brutally killed them. It was like watching a movie unfold or being locked in a lucid dream. I felt their presence, could almost see the malevolent faces of five desperate men, wielding pickaxes, eyes filled with murderous greed.

'Hey, are you all right?' Robbie squeezed my hand. 'I didn't mean to scare you.'

'Oh, yes you did,' I smiled. 'I'm fine.' But I walked a little faster, practically dragging him after me.

At the bottom of the Pass, Robbie led me through a door, into a small, dimly lit museum, with glass display cabinets ranged around the walls. 'Since we're here. You have to see this.'

The glass cabinets were filled with mining artefacts, tools used to extract lead ore from the hillside: winches, ropes, picks and crushing stones.

'They must be the same tools used to mine Blue John,' Robbie said. 'Some of them might have belonged to your great-grandparents.' He sounded awed by that idea. 'Look,' he said. 'Over there.'

In a glass display cabinet, tucked away in the far corner, was a very ornate and old leather saddle. It was fitted for a lady to ride, with silver spurs and saddle bags. A little note pinned beside it said it was made of hand-stitched, red Moroccan leather. The red had faded now to a dusty, dusky pink but it was easy to imagine how opulent it would once have looked. There was something intensely poignant about it. The story was no longer just a murder ballad. The physical evidence of Clara's saddle made it powerfully real all of a sudden. Two young lovers had died here, in the most horrific way.

There was a printed plaque affixed to the wall beside the cabinet.

In the year 1768, a young lady and gentleman, each mounted on a fine horse, were journeying to the chapel of Peak Forest to be married, but in Winnats Pass they were seized by five miners, dragged into a barn and robbed of a great sum of money. In vain, the lady begged them to spare her lover; vainly he strove to defend her but to no avail. While one villain cut the gentleman's throat another drove a pickaxe into the lady's head. The horses were found, some days after with their saddles and bridles still on them, in that great waste of Peak Forest. They were taken to Chatsworth as 'waifs', the Duke of Devonshire being Lord of the Manor. For many years the saddles were preserved at Chatsworth. The murder remained a secret until the death of the last of the murderers; but they did not go unpunished. One fell down Winnats and was killed on the spot. Another was crushed to death by a stone which fell upon him, near the place where the poor victims were buried. A third became a suicide; a fourth, after many attempts to destroy himself, died raging mad; and the fifth, after suffering torments of remorse and despair could not expire till he had confessed his sins and disclosed the particulars of the horrid deed.

I remembered Robbie saying how nobody ever spoke the names of these five murderers out loud because even two hundred years later, the crime still brought shame upon their families. All the same, the names were listed beneath.

In contrast, the two runaways were simply referred to as Henry and Clara. Henry who? Clara who?

One other name leapt out at me.

The saddle was obtained for this museum, from a Mr Jack Willis of Grindleford Bridge, whose ancestor obtained it at Chatsworth House, where he had been working as a groom at the time of the murder.

Mr Willis. Robbie's great-grandfather. Strange that we both had family history connected not just to Chatsworth but to Castleton too. To Winnats Pass, to be precise.

'Hey look, Robbie. Your Great-Grandpa Jack gets a mention too.'

But he'd wandered over to the counter, was reading a small poster tacked to the cork noticeboard. I went to stand with him, saw that it was an advertisement for a concert at the Rambler Inn in Edale. A local folk-singer named Percy of the Peaks.

'D'you have to hurry home?' Robbie asked me.

'No,' I said, perhaps a little too quickly. The date for the concert was tonight and my heart was already skipping ahead, hoping that Robbie might want to go, might invite me to go with him. We could have a drink at the pub, listen to the music, stay out late. It would be like a proper date.

'How about it?'

'Sounds great,' I said, cool as a cucumber.

As we walked back into town, I paused at the bow window of a little Blue John gift shop. In the way that little girls are typically drawn to anything pink and fluffy and many women are supposedly unable to resist the sparkle of diamonds, I seemed innately attracted to Blue John. I loved the idea that this fascination might, in part, be due to basic genetics, some kind of ancestral memory.

The shop had shut for the day but the window was still half lit, enough to see the display of pendants and rings through the security grille. Even in the dim light, the variety in the colouring of the stone was stunning. As well as jewellery, there were little bowls and goblets and obelisks, so delicately wrought, as to be almost translucent. They were priced at several hundred pounds each and they were minute, compared to my lovely candle-vase.

Robbie stooped to peer through the window with me, his head close to mine, curls tickling my face. If I turned my head a fraction, our mouths would be close enough for a kiss. I swallowed, wanting him to kiss me, more than I'd ever wanted anything in my whole life.

He asked: 'Which one d'you like best?'

Without hesitation, I pointed to one of the rings. The zig zag striation that ran right across the middle of it was so precise it could've been drawn with a geometric instrument. The colours were a blend of regal purple and cloudy white with a streak of old gold so, it almost outshone the gilding in which it was set. 'That one,' I said.

The price on the tag was astronomical - more than I earned in a whole year.

The shop next door was still open and Robbie dragged me inside. There was a carousel of pendants and he checked which one caught my eye, unhooked it and before I could say anything, he'd taken it to the counter and paid for it.

'There you go,' he said, handing it to me. 'Sorry it's not wrapped up.'

'Oh, Robbie. I love it. Thank you so much.'

I freed it from it's packaging, went to hang it round my

neck and Robbie helped me, moving behind me and fastening the clasp, while I scooped my heavy hair out of the way. His fingers tingled and tickled, made me giggle and the lady behind the till smiled at us, as if touched by a little scene of young love. Love had never been mentioned though and technically we were only friends.

I fingered the pendant, felt it resting coolly against my throat. Twee to say I was never going to take it off. But. I was never going to take it off.

We still had two hours to kill before the concert, so we found a cafe tucked off the High Street and ordered mugs of hot chocolate, which the plump, grey-haired waitress brought to our table, complete with marshmallows and a swirly dollop of cream.

I spooned melting marshmallows into my mouth. 'D'you think she thinks we're school kids?'

'Some of us still are school kids,' Robbie reminded me.

Under the table, I tapped his shin with my boot. 'Oi.' I popped another marshmallow into my mouth. 'Two more years,' I groaned.

'All those A grades to collect.'

'No guarantee I'll get any. Depends how hard I work.'

'You work harder than anyone I know.'

'You calling me a swot? Just because you sail through your exams, barely doing any work at all.'

'That's not fair. I do lots.'

'Yeah right.'

'So are you going to go to art college?' he asked me. 'My mum says you definitely should.'

'I'm not sure,' I said. 'I'm not really good enough.'

'Course you are, Silly. You've got bags of talent.'

'Thanks. But what if I don't?'

'You love it all, don't you? I mean, how long do you

spend at Chatsworth, staring at all the statues and paintings?' He looked at me with a sort of bemused affection. 'Until you pointed it out to me, I'd not noticed how it's the way the light falls on it, that makes that painted violin in the music room look so real and until you made me look at her properly the other day, I hadn't really appreciated how amazing the Vestal Virgin is: the way the marble is carved so you can see her face through the veil and everything. I didn't know that Raffaelle Monti made her or that he was inspired by something that was found in Pompeii.'

'I've always loved the Vestal Virgin. Mrs Waterfield introduced her to me when I was about seven.'

'That's just it, Silly. You're always chatting to the house-keeper and the maids.'

'When I was little, Mrs Waterfield used to look after me while I was waiting for my dad to finish work. I like watching the maids with all their different brushes and cloths. It's kinda peaceful, you know? A couple of summers ago, Maggie Ashwell let me help her wax the bronze statue of Endymion. I swear she had as many brushes as a portrait painter, all with different bristles but she used an actual toothbrush to get between his toes! First, we had to give him a good clean to get all the bird poo and moss off. Then we dried him with a special cloth and rubbed him all over with wax. I had the best time.'

'I bet you did.' Robbie grinned. 'You rubbed him all over?'

'I did. And yes, he's stark naked. And no, I didn't blush then and you'll notice that I'm not blushing now. Not in the slightest.'

'You're shameless.'

'Evidently.'

'And your heroes are stonemasons and sculptors and

blacksmiths? For a sixteen-year-old girl, you have to agree that's…unusual.'

'Is that a polite way of telling me I'm weird?'

'Weird and wonderful.'

'Well saved.'

'Wouldn't you love to make beautiful things, that people come to see in galleries and exhibitions?'

'Long way to go. Most of what I make is rubbish.'

'Nothing you do is rubbish.'

'Thanks.' He'd become my greatest champion. How did that happen? 'But you're biased.'

'My bow and arrow. See? That's a beautiful thing.'

'Pleased you like it.'

'I love it. It works really well too.'

'I like making things that are beautiful as well as useful.'

'Like the candle-vase?'

'Yes. I guess.' I didn't want to admit that my mother's gift might influence my preferences to that extent.

'So what do you want from life?' Robbie asked. It felt like a loaded question.

I rested my chin in my hand and cocked an eyebrow at him. 'You assume that being a girl, what I most want, ultimately, is children, a family?'

'You honestly don't want that?'

'I honestly don't.'

'Never?'

'Never.'

'We'd have cute kids, you and me.'

'Would we now?'

'What would we call them? Come on, play along.'

'Kizzy,' I said. 'After that little gypsy girl, in that TV programme.'

'Raffi,' Robbie said. 'After Raffaelle Monti and because we'd have the most angelic little boy.'

I did secretly love it, when he painted pictures of our imaginary future like this, but I couldn't bring myself to let on. 'Artists are supposed to crave freedom and shun domesticity,' I argued archly. 'Musicians too.'

He looked thoughtful. 'If your mum was born and brought up here, there might be people who still remember her,' he said, giving the impression he'd totally changed the subject, only it didn't feel that way somehow.

'I still remember her.' Albeit vaguely, it had to be said.

Robbie lowered his eyes, focused on his cup. He took a breath, seemed to hold it for a moment as if about to dive into something. 'Have you ever thought about asking around, you know, trying to find her?'

I put down my spoon, said levelly: 'She doesn't want me to find her. She knows exactly where I am. She could get in touch with me so easily, if she wanted to.'

'It's about what you want too though,' he said very gently.

'I want to look forward, not back,' I said firmly. 'What's the point in looking back? We're not going that way.'

He gave a small approving nod. 'Good on you. I like that attitude. In fact. It's a great attitude.'

'But?'

He folded his arms on the table, leant forward on them. 'Don't you think that sometimes you need to look back? Understand and make peace with the past, before you can move on? What's that quote we learnt in English lessons? The past is never dead, it's not even past.'

'Ohh, hark at you. Very profound.'

He smiled. 'Can't you feel it though? Time fading in and out? The past as part of the present?

'Like tectonic plates, rubbing up against each other.'

'Yes, exactly.'

We had the most random conversations. We could start off talking about our favourite flavour of ice cream and then move on to something deep and philosophical. He made me feel like the most amusing and clever person. As well as larking about with him, climbing trees and splashing in the lakes and the willow tree fountain, I loved spending time alone with him and just talking to him like this. I loved the way that words and thoughts flowed between us so easily. Usually, I loved the feeling that gave me, that I was connected to him on some unfathomable level but right now, it scared me too, how close he was to a truth I didn't want to even consider. That constant, nagging sense, that something vital was missing from my life, someone who'd left a void inside me, that nothing had ever come close to filling and maybe never would. Sometimes I felt my mother's presence and her absence so acutely. Because Sukey was not there, she was always there, casting the longest shadow.

It's about what you want too.

I couldn't tell Robbie the real reason why I didn't ever want to find Sukey. I could never tell him or tell anyone, the awful things I'd overheard her say about me, that last night before she left. I was too ashamed to talk about it. If I even let it back into my head, it made me feel insignificant and worthless, that there must be something very wrong with me, something broken and unlovable. I'd buried it, shoved it deep down inside me, as deep as the Blue John buried under Treak Cliff Hill, only not beautiful, but very ugly. 'Can we talk about something else?'

'OK. Can I tell you something?'

'Go ahead.' I wanted to know everything there was to know about him but he looked up at me with those grey-blue eyes that were like the smoke and sea mist and I had a pang of dread. What if he confided in me, that he had feelings for another girl?

'My dad's not my dad,' he said.

I sat up straight. 'What?'

'I have a missing parent too, like you do.'

'But…where is he? Who is he?'

'He's a poet from the Isle of Lewis. His name's Jim Munro and my Mum met him when she was at uni. She fell in love with him and married him, before her twenty-first birthday.'

'Wait.' He was going too fast. 'Your mum was married before?'

'They went to live on Lewis and I was born there. And I think they were happy, for a time. But then, just after Freya was born, my dad, Jim, he started screwing around with the music teacher from the primary school and after a couple of years, he just upped sticks and left one morning, when Mum had gone to pick up Freya from nursery. He never even said goodbye. Just packed up and went. A bit like your mum did.'

'I'm so sorry.' I touched the back of his hand where it lay on the table. I wanted to hug him. He looked like he needed a hug. 'How old were you?'

'Seven. Nearly eight. A bad age.'

'Is there a good one?'

'Freya was three, so she doesn't remember much. I do though. My grandparents came up to Scotland and brought all three of us back here. Mum was in a bad way. Not sleeping, not eating, crying all the time or just sitting and staring off into space, which was worse than the crying. Then after about a year or so, she got together with my stepdad.'

I had to reorganise my brain, to accommodate this news that Robbie and Freya were not Hugh Nightingale's children. That Robbie's family was just as mixed up as my own, in its own way. That he was half Scottish? 'So. Your name's really Robbie Munro?'

Robbie shook his head. 'Hugh adopted me and Freya. He's a good man, wanted us to be a proper family. Which means I could choose to be either Robbie Nightingale or Robbie Munro. But Robbie Munro feels like someone else. And my stepdad has been more of a dad to me, than my real dad.'

But he still described Jim Munro as his real dad. 'I used to think your family was so normal.'

'Sorry to disappoint you.'

'Oh, I'm not disappointed at all.'

Robbie cracked a laugh.

'Sorry.' I grimaced. 'That came out all wrong. Normal is the wrong word, anyhow. Your family is so lovely. I've always thought you and your brother and sister had a perfect upbringing.'

'Perfect how?'

How to explain that Brook House for me was like a deep green dream, old apple trees and dark folk songs. Your parents are so kind and welcoming. And brilliantly eccentric. Your mum offering endless cups of tea and cake, just the sweetest person but interesting too with her books and stories. And your dad knows all about plants and trees and the seasons. They give you so much respect and freedom.'

'You've evidently studied us very closely.'

'I have. It's true. But I totally missed this.'

What he'd just told me made me feel more bonded to him than ever. 'I tend to mistrust people who've always had things go well for them,' I said. 'They make me feel isolated and weird.'

'I understand.'

'I know you do. I have always felt that you did. Now I understand why.'

We were the only customers left in the cafe. The waitress had stacked all the other chairs onto tables, was sweeping crumbs up off the floor and dropping hints.

'I think she's telling us it's time to go,' I whispered.

Robbie asked for our bill and put his hand in his pocket. I did the same.

'I'll get it,' he said.

'Let's split it. I have a job now you know, my own money.'

'Yeah but it's still all right to let people do things for you.'

'I do.'

'You do not. It's like you see it as a sign of weakness or something.'

I placed some coins on the table.

He tutted at me. 'You're impossible.'

'I'm independent. So, do you ever see your dad?' I asked, as we started to walk back towards the car park.

'Occasionally, yeah. I always knew I was in serious trouble when he showed up. Crisis fatherhood. It was worse than useless.'

'It's good that you can talk to him though.' I envied him that.

'Sure, I can talk to him and he can talk to me. When I was fourteen, he told me what a disappointment I am to him. I said to him: "You know what Dad, you're a big disappointment to me too." I told him how selfish he was. I told him how what he did was going to affect the rest of my life. I think it probably doesn't matter so much if your parents split up, so long as they both stick around in their kids' lives and are basically civil to each other. But if they aren't kind or aren't there, then it's not just your childhood and adolescence that's different. Adulthood is different too. Relationships; the decision to marry or not; to have children or not; the kind of parent you'll be, it's all different. The whole trajectory of a person's life is altered.' He made it sound as if he was speaking for me, as well as for himself, trying to articulate what I might be feeling or at least to open up the conversation properly, so that I could tell him. But I didn't want to talk about myself or any of that stuff. I never did. I was far more interested in him.

'You actually said all that to your dad?'

'I actually did.'

'How did he take it?'

'Not well.'

'Did it make you feel better though, getting it off your chest?'

'Sort of.'

'It makes it hard to believe in happily ever after,' I said, as we got into the car.

'But do you want to believe in it?' Robbie twisted round in the driver's seat and locked his eyes with mine and I felt something electrifying dart through me, like a laser beam of light and heat shooting from my heart, all the way down to my toes. 'Because I want to believe in it. Not in spite of it all but because of it.'

It was in his nature to analyse and it was so typical of him, to take the messy past, accept it and work with it, turn negatives into positives. To look forward even as he looked back. I wished I could be more like him. I didn't know how to answer and I didn't have to answer because it happened then, the thing I'd been longing for and dreaming about for so long but had thought might only ever be a dream.

He brushed a lock of hair away from my face with his

fingertips and made me feel as if an electric current was running up my spine. He leant towards me and pressed his mouth firmly and tenderly against mine. I was sixteen years old and it was the first time I'd ever been kissed. I'd lain awake in bed in the dark and fantasised about what it would be like to be kissed by Robbie Nightingale, to have his hands on my skin, but nothing could have prepared me for the reality. His touch made me quiver to the depths of my being.

I didn't know what to do but my body took over. Instinctively I put my hands on either side of his rib cage, pressed myself against him and some part of me floated above, watching the two of us. We were making out in his car, like kids did in the movies but the movies were so tame by comparison. They gave no hint that it felt like this.

There were a million butterflies fluttering in my belly, fireworks going off inside my chest and my stomach and my head. His hair smelt of fresh air and his kisses tasted very mildly and sweetly of the chocolate we'd just drunk. I couldn't breathe. I felt as if I was drowning in wonderfulness. It was as if a door had been opened for me and I could see through, into a new and exciting adult world. I couldn't enter just yet but it was all there, waiting for me.

He slipped his hand inside my t-shirt, hooked his thumb under my bra and his tongue slid into my mouth. My whole body exploded, every atom animated. When he drew away, I wanted to clutch him, cry out: don't stop.

CHAPTER SIXTEEN

E dale was separated from Castleton by the Great Ridge and it took us half an hour to drive round it to The Rambler Inn.

A traditional pub with a summer beer garden, roaring log fires in winter, real ales on tap and a menu that featured pie and chips, The Rambler was hugely popular amongst walkers on the Pennine Way. But it wasn't just ramblers who came to The Rambler. It'd also become a famous venue for live music, hosting acts every week, folk musicians and fiddlers mostly. By the bar, the wall was full of framed black and white photographs, musicians and bands who'd played here over the years. Many of the photos were signed and while Robbie ordered drinks, I studied the faces.

Towards the far end of the wall, one face grabbed my attention. There was no mistaking her. It was the girl from the photograph, the girl who'd been sitting beside Sukey on the grass, in the sunshine at the music festival years ago. In this photo, she was cradling a guitar, enigmatic and serene in a long, white, lacy dress with a flamenco-style skirt.

There was an autograph of sorts, in the bottom right-hand corner but it was more like a symbol. It had been done with a black marker pen and might have been four petals of a flower or a four-leafed clover maybe. The four petals or leaves, were all slanted upwards, so they looked like two hearts placed side by side, their tips almost but not quite adjoined.

'Excuse me,' I said to one of the barmen.

He was young, with a ponytail and long-sleeved t-shirt under a short-sleeved one, a faded drawing of Johnny Cash on the front. 'What can I get you?'

I pointed to the photo. 'D'you know who she is?'

He took a look. 'Sorry. Bit before my time. She's gorgeous, whoever she is.'

'She is,' I agreed, then felt the sudden need to add: 'My mum was friends with her.'

'Cool,' the barman said. 'You're gorgeous too,' he murmured. 'Just sayin'.'

'Thanks.'

'I hope your boyfriend appreciates you.'

'I don't have a...oh!' I grinned. 'I hope so too.'

Percy of the Peaks looked to be at least seventy years old, lean as a whippet and silver-haired, his face peat-brown and leathery, like a fisherman. Wearing a woollen blue waistcoat with brass buttons, he walked on stage alone and a hush descended as he sat himself down on a wooden stool, closed his eyes and with no preamble and no instrument to accompany him, he started to sing.

Be not frightened of our fashion,
Though we seem a tattered nation,
Give us ribbons, bells and saffron linen,
And all the world is ours to win in.

There was something wonderful about listening to such an old voice. It was tremulous but not with age. It seemed to vibrate with pure, raw emotion. It felt as intimate as if he had turned the little stage into his living room.

'That's an old, old song, from a long, long time ago,' Percy began. 'From the days when the Duke of Devonshire allowed gypsies and tinkers to live in the Devil's Arse. You'll have heard how there was a whole village inside the cave, where the rain never falls and the sun never shines. No law-abiding person who was born and brought up in Castleton would ever venture near the Devil's Arse. All lived in fear and dread that it served as a gateway to the underworld, to hell itself. Not just because of its name and the rude noises that it produced from its bowels, after it rained but because it became a notorious gathering place for gypsies, rogues and vagabonds. It's said that the secret language of thieves cant was created there, at a meeting between Cock Lorel, the most infamous knave that ever lived, and the King of the Gypsies. Those tinkers and vagabonds are my people,' Percy announced with pride. 'Will you listen to another song?'

'We'll listen all night,' one woman called out appreciatively from the other side of the bar.

Percy started to sing once more and then abruptly stopped again, mid song. 'I learnt that one from my grandfather, who always spoke it as a poem.'

So that's what he did with the remaining verses. Verses that were weighted with everything there was to know about rejection and forgiveness. His was a voice to get lost in. When he sang again, the words seemed to come straight from his heart, as if he knew exactly how it felt to be deceived in love, overwhelmed by the darkest grief. But much more than that, it was as if he was channelling all these universal human aches, as if he was singing, not just for himself but for everyone and perhaps for that reason, the songs, though full of longing and sorrow, were extraordinarily uplifting.

If I was a scholar, could handle my pen,
Just one private letter to him I would send.
I'd write and I'd tell him of my grief and woe
And far o'er the oceans with my true love I would go.

I'd never known either of my grandfathers, but I'd have loved to have had one just like Percy. 'He's wonderful,' I said to Robbie at the end, when the old man had left the stage.

But everything that night was beyond wonderful to me. The whole world appeared in soft focus and at the same time, every sensation was sharpened, heightened, all the colours luminous. Robbie had stood close beside me during the whole concert and I'd been acutely aware his arm looped easily around my waist, the warm pressure of his fingers, resting just above my hip bone. I could still taste his kiss, still feel his mouth on mine. I kept touching the little pendant hanging round my neck. I was certain that Percy's songs had affected me so much because now I understood them. Now I knew what singers and poets meant, when they spoke of longing and passion and heartache.

The songs had clearly touched Robbie too but it wasn't enough for him just to listen. 'I'd love to talk to him,' he said.

'Let's go and find him.'

'What? Now?'

'Yes now. Why not?'

The barman in the Johnny Cash T-shirt said he thought Percy had gone up onto Kinder Scout.

'Kinder?' I was astonished. The path that led up to the plateau began just opposite the Rambler Inn but it was an infamously arduous hike. 'Can he walk that far?'

'He might be old but he's amazingly fit and hardy.'

'But it'll be dark soon.'

'Not that soon,' the barman shrugged. 'And I don't expect a bit of dark would bother him.'

'Come on then,' I said to Robbie.

'Up Kinder? You don't mind?'

'This is important to you, right?'

'Yes.'

'Then it's important to me too. Let's get a move on.'

The evening air was velvety soft, scented with sun-dried grass and flowers and we walked for a while in silence, just breathing it all in. 'It's weird when it's light so late,' I said eventually.

'Did you know, that Midsummer Eve is one of the spirit nights?' Robbie told me. 'When boundaries between worlds are weakened and men are subject to fairy tricks.'

'Where d'you learn all this stuff?'

'From old songs. Where else?'

'What else d'you know?'

'The Aboriginals believe their ancestors wandered their continent singing out the name of everything: birds, animals, plants, rocks and so they sang the world into existence.'

'That's beautiful.'

'When I climb a tree or sing a folk song, it's the same

feeling,' Robbie said. 'I feel rooted to the earth and to the past.'

I thought how he was impossible to define: combined the spirit of a poet and a scholar and an explorer, all in one.

We'd reached the wide, bleak moorland plateau. It was dotted with freakishly shaped stones, carved and polished by wind and rain. Huge, weathered boulders and pillars that appeared to have fallen from the sky. Shaped like props from sci-fi movies, they resembled giant fossilised snails, upturned teeth, asteroids. The ground around them was tufted with fluffy cotton-grass and patches of sphagnum moss, while overhead in the orange sky, soared the black shadow of a peregrine falcon.

In this strange moonscape, Percy sat alone, using a granite rock as a seat, leisurely smoking a pipe, beneath the saffron and coral sunset. He'd lit a small fire out of a pile of twigs and he exuded inner peace. He didn't seem at all surprised to see us.

'Evening,' he said.

'Good evening,' Robbie replied. 'We've come from The Rambler.'

'I know where you're from, lad. Sit yourself down.'

There being no seats, Robbie went to sit cross-legged on the ground in front of the old man, while I knelt to the side.

'Your concert was wonderful,' Robbie said.

'Pleased you enjoyed it.'

'Will you teach me your songs?' Robbie asked, straight up.

Percy leisurely sucked his pipe. 'Well now, I know hundreds of songs.'

'I want to learn them all.'

His eyes twinkled. 'How about you sing something for me first, eh?'

The song Robbie sang was achingly lovely but Percy told him, bluntly, that he was singing it all wrong.

'Will you show me the right way?'

Much as he'd done at the Rambler, Percy closed his eyes and began to sing and I hardly dared move, hardly dared breathe. I flicked my eyes from Percy to Robbie. Watching Robbie was as interesting as watching the old man. He was entranced, his gaze intent upon Percy's craggy face, as if he was using not just his ears to listen but all his senses. I knew he was noting every intonation, every rhythmic lilt, half mouthing the words, as if to absorb them.

'Who taught that to you?' Robbie asked, when Percy broke off.

'My grandpa.'

'What else did he teach you?'

I could hear the old man's mind working, cogs of memory turning, as he dragged up jumbled fragments from the past, not just from his personal memory but from an inherited memory; from his subconscious. He sang a strange lament about a world weary traveller called Spencer the Rover.

The night being approaching to the woods he resorted,
With woodbine and ivy his bed for to make,
He dreamt about sighing, lamenting and crying,
Go home to your children and rambling forsake.

I watched him twisting the large pewter ring he wore on his left hand. It looked old and ornate, was embossed with an elaborate crest. The backs of his hands were mottled and his veins stood out like blue pipes.

At the end of the song, Robbie said: 'I've heard that one before.'

'Who else sings it?' asked Percy, sounding most put out that someone had got there before him.

'A docker in the East End, name of Davey Cook. Peter Kennedy made a recording of him, for the BBC. But the way the melody changed, from the first to the second verse. That's different.'

'Ah, well now, that's my invention,' Percy grinned, enjoying himself. 'Did Davey Cook sing one about the headless horsemen?'

'He didn't.'

'Goes back thousands of years it does.'

As he sang, Robbie listened, barely blinking, as though he'd been allowed a glimpse of a precious treasure that might disappear if he didn't show due respect. It was hard to tell who was happiest to be with whom.

The fire had gone out of the sky. How long had we been there? It was like the mirror-opposite of a fantasy story, where time stands still in the real world, while the hero disappears through a wardrobe or down a rabbit hole. Here, it felt as if we'd slipped away from reality just for a moment, when in fact, an hour or more had passed.

'D'you know the song about the Runaway Lovers?' I asked Percy.

'I don't ever sing that one.' Percy's eyes were deep, denim-blue and now they looked into my own eyes with a piercing directness. 'There's a Romany legend,' he said, 'about a gypsy blacksmith, who was tasked by a Roman legionnaire to forge twelve large nails. Have you heard it?'

I shook my head.

Percy leant towards me. 'The smith did as he was bid, only to learn when it was done, that the nails were to be used to fix Christ and the robbers to their crosses. But three of the nails were stolen and hidden by the gypsy's relations, so the three victims were fastened with only three nails apiece, saving them all much pain. However, an angry mob, discovering that the nails that executed Jesus were gypsy work, drove the smith and his kin from their land and they've been doomed to wandering and persecution ever since. But the young thief passed the foot of the cross as he fled and Jesus blessed him. For their service to the Son of God, the gypsies were made immune to damnation for the sin of theft.'

The hairs on my arms were standing on end. My mother was suddenly there with us on the plateau.

You're thick as thieves, the pair of you. Though of course it's me who's the thief isn't it? That's how you see me now. A thief. Who stole what wasn't mine.

It was as if Percy was psychic and knew things about me, about my family; things I didn't know myself, shameful things, maybe criminal. As if somehow, he had heard my parents rowing that fateful night before Sukey went away. I swallowed, my mouth dry as ash. 'That's a powerful story.'

'Aye, it is that.' Percy looked at me for a long moment, as if to get the measure of me. 'It's a story about learning to see through the eyes of a skull. About debts from the past that are carried forward, in order to be repaid. Just remember that. In a few years time, it might make more sense to ye.' He gazed into the fire for a moment, prodded it with a stick. 'You should jump over it. Both of ye. It brings good fortune, a good marriage and children.'

'Oh, Silva doesn't believe in marriage,' Robbie said.

CHAPTER SEVENTEEN

The concert was my idea. Before Robbie left home, I wanted him to share some of the songs he'd spent the summer learning from Percy, recording, studying and preserving them on a little Uher cassette machine he'd bought secondhand. He'd spent hours and hours in Percy's company, long days and evenings.

'They're our songs,' I reasoned, pressing my palms against his chest while he held me. 'Derbyshire songs. Our heritage. It's not fair, if some random crowd in a folk club up in Scotland, get to hear you sing them before we do.'

'Silly, you really care that much?'

'Damn right I do. Where can we have a concert though? How about The Club?'

There'd been a few gigs there over the years, most recently a rhythm and blues band from Stoney Middleton. But Robbie didn't want to play in The Club. Instead, he asked the Duchess for permission to hold a small gathering in the Chatsworth gardens and she readily agreed. So it was to take place round a campfire, at the Grotto Pond, on the night before the Country Fair.

'It'll bring people together, in the simple way that they've come together for thousands of years,' Robbie said. 'Around the fire with food, drink, music and good company.'

'It's perfect,' I agreed.

The Grotto Pond had always felt like an enchanted secret garden but now, trees around the clearing had been strung with fairy-lights and glowing lanterns and swags of multi-coloured cloth bunting. There was an iron fire-pit, scattered all around with hay bales and sawn off logs to sit on, some upturned to make stools and others lying lengthways as rustic benches. They were arranged in an intimate, informal circle around a collection of instruments: tribal-looking drums and a double bass. There was a sense of ritual and ceremony, the atmosphere mystical and ancient, like being lost in a dream.

A little bar had been set up under an awning beneath the trees, facing the pond and there were about two dozen people already gathered in the clearing. Bea and Arthur Waterfield had brought their baby daughter, Jasmine. Ed from the Devonshire Arms, was chatting to Trish from the Farm Shop and Bill Hawksworth, the gardener. There were a few faces I didn't recognise: people who must have come from further afield. Freya was there with her mother, Flora. Her red curls were pulled back off her face, restrained in a loose chignon and she looked very alluring, in a silky amber dress and gold, jewelled flip-flops, her buttery freckles grown more pronounced in the summer sun. I wished I'd dressed up more; I was just wearing jeans and Docs and a strappy, navy blue camisole, my hair fastened back in a loose plait.

My former colleague from the pub, Lizzie, was there with her mother, Megan, too. They looked so similar, both in sundresses and dark glasses. They were drinking bottles of cider and laughing together, like they were each other's best friend. Perhaps they were. Megan was one of the room guides and Lizzie had just started work as a housemaid at Chatsworth, so they were colleagues now as well. I imagined them chatting about their jobs and about life, over a pot of tea. I wished my dad had come. He said he was going to and then he said he'd be so busy at the Country Fair tomorrow, he needed an early night. So he'd ducked out, not before letting slip that he'd once organised a concert himself. Which I found almost impossible to imagine.

Robbie was talking to Kirk, the barman from the Rambler Inn who, it transpired, played percussion. A Danish girl called Sofie, who Robbie had got chatting to at a gig in Manchester, was tuning her double bass.

'Drink,' Freya said.

'Is that an instruction or a question?' I laughed. 'I'll get them.'

Nobody bothered to check people's ages, so I joined the small queue at the bar, paid for three bottles of Mexican beer with wedges of lime in the neck. I wandered over to rejoin Freya and Flora at the fire pit.

We clinked bottles. 'Cheers.'

'So, how's it going with you and my big brother?' Freya asked.

We'd made no secret of the fact that we were seeing each other and Lizzie had told me I was the luckiest girl in the world. I felt very lucky. And strange. Time had taken on new dimensions. Hours seemed to hurtle by when Robbie and I were together but when I was apart from him, they crawled and my self-restraint was constantly challenged. I couldn't let myself hog the telephone and let my fingers dial his number every evening. I couldn't let my feet take me where they most wanted to go; couldn't just happen to be randomly passing by Brook House, at all hours. I didn't like the feeling that my heart was shaped like a begging bowl. Mostly though, I was walking on air.

'It's going great,' I said.

'Finally,' Freya grinned. 'You're perfect for each other.'

I sipped my drink, watching the flames. There was something so exultant about fires, the leaping and dancing, faces glowing golden in the red and orange gleams, the primeval smell of woodsmoke.

Kirk had drawn a sawn-off log up to the drums to use as a stool and as he sat himself down, everyone else took it as their cue to take their seats.

Robbie walked into the circle, as if he'd been performing in front of an audience his whole life. He started to sing with no microphone and no musical accompaniment, just as Percy did. My skin broke out in goosebumps as it had done the first time I'd heard him, that Christmas when I was ten years old. I recognised the song immediately. This was not a song that Percy had taught Robbie, but the song that had started it all. *The Runaway Lovers.*

Over moors and valleys deep, through the Dark Peak and the White
There two tragic lovers sleep in gritstone, blood, and lime.

His unadorned singing gave the foreground to the drama and I'd forgotten how starkly beautiful it was. As Robbie had matured, his voice had grown both deeper and sweeter, an intimate, confiding baritone with a tough edge, which did perfect justice to the violent poignancy of the romantic ballad.

After the first verse, Robbie was joined by the drums and double bass and I saw him anew. He was my Robbie, the

Robbie I'd known since childhood, who'd been like a brother to me. The Robbie who'd kissed me in the front seat of his mum's Renault. The Robbie who lay close beside me on his single bed, while we listened to records in the dark, till we fell asleep like two spoons. He was the same person I'd sat for hours chatting to, here by the Grotto Pond, the same smile, the same enthusiasm and animated way of speaking. But he was also this other Robbie. There was an aura about him. No ego. But something bigger. Not only was he blessed with a rare talent as a singer and storyteller but there was something otherworldly about him, as if he was tapping into something spiritual and primitive. Here, in the wooded glade, he seemed totally at home, at one with nature. He belonged to a fabled land of Celtic twilights, wildflower meadows and mossy graveyards. A world of mystery and tragedy.

'That's a local song,' Robbie said, when he reached the end, his speaking voice as hypnotic as his singing. 'It's about something that happened very close to here.'

He explained how traditional songs had always been sung a-cappella and then he sang another song of lost love and I saw that his talent was to take people on a journey with him. There was a quality in him, in the way he sang, of creating an experience, where the listener and the song, seemed to be totally interconnected and it was spine-tingling. I felt as if I was falling and at the same time, soaring. There seemed to be within him such a need to heal, to pierce the heart of all who listened.

There is a flower I have heard people say
They grow by night and fade by day
Now if that flower I could find
It would cure my heart and ease my mind

This song was like nothing I'd ever heard before. It was fresh and immediate and at the same time ancient. The instrumentation, when it was there, was stirring, yet eerily restrained.

Robbie's voice was like candlelight, soft and warm, calming and mystical. You were supposed to stare into the heart of a candle flame, to meditate and soothe a troubled soul and his voice had the same effect on me.

My friends and other lovelorn teenagers all over Britain, were making compilation tapes for each other, to express feelings they couldn't put into words, as well as Bruce Springsteen and Jennifer Rush and Foreigner. They were pretending that *Dancing in the Dark*, *The Power of Love* and *I Want to Know what Love Is*, were all about them. They were listening to the charts and choosing a song that would be their song. But I didn't need the Chart Show. I didn't need Foreigner and Jennifer Rush. I had these ancient songs and Robbie himself singing them to me.

I could barely listen, barely breathe. The songs seemed to me like prayers and the emotion in Robbie's voice and in the unbearable, eerie desolation of the melody and lyrics, bypassed my normal defences, called to emotions buried deep inside me, liberating the uncomfortable feelings which normally I kept safely locked away. It touched every nerve. My chest tightened and my throat hurt. Tears welled in my eyes. I couldn't remember the last time I'd cried but now I let the tears fall down my cheeks unchecked, too spellbound even to brush them away. It felt cleansing and healing. The most amazing release. I saw Bill Hawksworth wipe tears away from his eyes too, as if the songs had affected him deeply, and I remembered Robbie's mum saying that his sister had been a famous singer.

The song ended and Robbie spoke for a while about

Percy, his eyes fixed on something or someone directly behind me. I looked over my shoulder and there was Percy himself, sitting on a fallen log beneath an old oak tree.

'Percy believes that when he's singing a song from centuries ago, all the people who sang it before him are there, standing behind him,' Robbie said. 'The travellers and tinkers and farm labourers and their wives, who kept the songs alive for us.'

I shivered, but in a pleasurable way, as if unseen fingers were gently stroking the tender skin on the insides of my arms. Robbie was a time-traveller, channelling voices from the past, people who were long gone, who seemed to share all the same concerns as those alive today. I knew I'd carry images from tonight with me, all of my life. I knew that no matter how long I lived, nothing would ever look cooler or lovelier to me, than Robbie Nightingale singing ancient songs by the campfire in Chatsworth's twilit wood.

Soon, too soon, everyone was applauding. Surely that wasn't the end? It was though and Robbie was standing amidst a cluster of people who were crowding around him, keen to talk to him or perhaps even ask for his autograph. He was like our local hero. It made me smile.

I went to talk to Percy, who hadn't moved, was sitting on the log where he'd been all night, smoking his pipe in quiet contemplation. The fading heat of the day and left behind a heavy dew.

'Our boy did well,' Percy said to me.

'He did.' I liked that Percy had called Robbie our boy.

Robbie had quickly and politely excused himself from his admirers and came to join us. He pulled up a log and we both sat opposite Percy.

'I'm so glad you came,' Robbie said, grasping his friend's free hand in both of his. 'But I wished you'd sung too.'

'Not my place,' Percy pronounced. Then he did the most extraordinary thing. He dragged the ornate pewter ring off his finger. 'Hold out yer hand,' he said, and as if he was conducting a ceremony, he solemnly placed the ring in Robbie's palm. He waited a moment then said: 'It's been passed down through my family, along with the songs. It's yours now.'

'I can't take this.'

'You can, son. I insist. There's nobody else, you see.'

'What about your children, grandchildren?'

'I've five grandsons and two granddaughters and half a dozen great-grandchildren and I'm right proud of them all but they never think to ask me about the old songs, the old ways. They're not interested.' Percy's eyes misted. 'There was a time when I was hopeful, when it looked like there was one…but no. The old songs are our history. These songs say we matter enough to have a story to pass on. Without them, we're nothing. Songs can live on, even if singers don't. But we need someone to carry them for us. I've been waiting for you,' he said. 'These songs are my family jewels. You won't let them be forgotten, will you?'

'I won't,' Robbie solemnly promised. He slid the ring onto his index finger, where it seemed to fit perfectly and instantly gave him a new gravitas.

'So,' Percy smiled, a solemn yet boyish smile. 'You're now the Keeper of Songs.'

'The Keeper of Songs,' I repeated. 'That's lovely.'

'I'll be on my way,' Percy said, pushing himself to his feet, as if his job here was done.

'How are you getting home?' Robbie asked.

'Ach, don't you worry yourself about that, lad. I brought my old banger. Parked it in the lane, back there.'

We watched him walk away, disappearing into the dark

trees. Then we wandered over to the bar, where there was hardly any queue. Robbie ordered two cups of mead, handed over a jangle of coins he'd dug from his pocket, gave me one of the plastic cups. I sipped at something that was like rich, liquid gold.

'D'you like it?'

'Mmm. It's like drinking nectar. I loved every second of tonight,' I said. 'It was so beautiful, Robbie, just amazing.'

'So are you,' he said. 'You're beautiful and amazing.'

I'd never been very comfortable accepting compliments but I was trying to get better at it. I dug at the ground with the toe of my boot, flicked my eyes up at him. 'Thanks,' I said. Why couldn't I just enjoy the flirtation? Why did I immediately wonder if he felt free to flirt, to say these lovely things to me now because his escape route was already planned? The summer was nearly over. He'd passed his exams and was definitely leaving soon.

'You do belong here of course,' he said.

'At Chatsworth?' While he was born to go off on adventures?

'I meant right here, in the trees. Silva. Meaning from the forest. The wildwood and the Greenwood. Where stories also come from. Robin Hood and King Arthur. Myths and legends.'

'Haha. That's me, a legend in my own lunchtime.'

'I remember when my mum first mentioned a little girl called Silva,' Robbie smiled. 'I expected to be meeting a woodland sprite or a pixie and instead, I met a little Amazon, a girl with a warrior soul.'

I laughed. That was not how I saw myself at all. Increasingly, Robbie talked about wanting to travel, meet all sorts of different and interesting people. He was a wanderer, an adventurer, far braver than me. Whereas I liked being here, at home, surrounded by familiar places, familiar faces. I was a true child of Chatsworth, where the Cavendish family motto was 'safe through caution'.

'I always liked your name too,' I said. 'Nightingale. It's a very appropriate name, given that you're a singer and all.'

'One who sings in the woods at night.'

'True.'

There's Robbie Burns too. The bard of Scotland. I did actually start singing out of duty to my name.'

'Really?'

'No but it makes a good story, hey?'

I laughed.

'I read how there are nearly six hundred folk songs with nightingales in them. In stories and legends and poems, they're symbols of melancholy and bittersweet love.' His eyes twinkled at me. 'Also dubious morality and disorder in the dark.'

'Is that right? And what do nightingales look like? I don't think I've ever seen one.'

'They're like big, handsome brown robins.'

'Hmmm. And their behaviour?'

'They're very polite,' he said. 'Also wistful, worldly and wild. They're summer visitors. Fly all the way from sub-Saharan Africa.'

'Travellers then.'

'A nightingale's beautiful song has only one purpose, you know,' he added with his sexy, mischievous grin. 'They sing to seduce females.'

'Do they indeed?' I enjoyed flirting with him, wanted to carry on. The mead was strong, going straight to my head but I wanted more of that too. More love, more life, more everything. I jiggled my empty glass at him. 'I need a refill.'

Everyone else had gone and the summer darkness had settled around the log that we were sitting on by the little fire. We were wrapped in a single woollen blanket, sitting close together beneath it, shoulders touching. The musicians had packed up their instruments but the bunting and the lanterns had been left hanging in the trees and Robbie kept topping up our cups of mead, from a cask he'd nicked from behind the bar. I threw a fresh log onto the flames.

'Percy said we should jump over it,' Robbie said.

'For a good marriage and children,' I remembered. I shrugged off the blanket and stood up. 'All right then.'

'I was joking,' Robbie said.

The fear of losing him, coupled with some devilment in me that night, made me say: 'Well too bad, I'm not.'

'You're not seriously…'

I made a quick judgement, took a running leap. I was light and long-legged, agile and strong and I cleared the fire effortlessly. I spun round, the rope of my hair swishing like a lasso. Robbie was poised to jump too and he landed beside me, caught me, as if he needed to steady himself against me. 'You're a loony,' he said.

'You too, evidently.'

'Are you tired?'

'No,' I decided. 'You?'

'A bit.'

'Shall we head back then?'

'Or shall we just stay here?'

'All night?'

'I like camping out in the woods,' Robbie said. 'It's peaceful, being away from other people. Most other people,' he qualified.

And yet he was always so chatty and gregarious. 'You're such a contradiction.'

'And you're not?'

'I'm very uncomplicated.'

'Yeah, right.' He gazed at me. 'Everything's so much better when it's done outside, don't you think? Food tastes better, music is sweeter, wild swimming is the very best kind...' he left something hanging, as if there was a fourth activity that should also be enjoyed out in the open.

'You sleep better under the stars too?' I asked softly.

'I do,' he said, as if sleeping was the last thing on his mind.

He made a bed for us out of our jackets and the wool blanket, more a nest really and we lay down together on our backs, on the downy grass and moss, gazing up at the canopy of dark leaves and beyond, to the star-spangled sky. He'd slipped his arm under my shoulders and I was worried it would go numb, so after a while I turned on my side, facing him. He didn't move his arm but tightened it around me. I looked into his grey-blue eyes and it was as if wisps of smoke from the campfire were held in them, an ancient, storyteller's magic.

'My dad said I talk to you in my sleep,' I told him. My room was right next to his and the plasterboard wall was thin.

'My sister says I talk to you,' Robbie said. 'We had to share a tent when we went camping.'

The way he looked at me, made me think of a word from a Jane Austen novel. Ardent. His gaze was gentle and ardent.

'I love your face,' he said, stroking my cheek. 'I've never seen so many characters in one face.'

'What d'you mean?'

'When you laugh, your eyes smile and you look so impish and young, like a little girl at the circus. But when you're lost in thought, you look all wistful and sophisticated, like you should be at a cocktail party.'

'Well I definitely prefer circuses to cocktail parties.'

'Me too.' He moved closer, so our noses were almost touching. 'I love you,' he whispered.

Used carelessly, those three famous little words, could sound so commonplace and trite, wholly lacking in meaning but I knew Robbie would use them only with great consideration. Suddenly, the night had become momentous.

'I love you too.'

Though I hoped I'd say that again in my life, this would always be the first time and the words felt powerful, dangerous even, like a dark charm or a spell, that might open hidden doors, invoke angels or demons.

I thought later, how making love was the best way to describe what we did. We used our bodies to create something beautiful. We kissed, gently and then not so gently. He ran his hands under my t-shirt and over me and it was as if he was a sculptor, shaping me. I did the same to him. And then we were no longer two bodies but one complete being and we lay with our limbs tangled, curled up together, like babes in the wood, by the dying embers of the campfire.

I woke just after dawn, before Robbie. My head was resting on his shoulder, my plait of hair snaking over his arm, which was flung across my waist so I couldn't move. I didn't want to move, was careful not to rouse him. The new day felt as perfect as a day could be, full of possibility. That rare sense of being exactly where I was meant to be, with the person I was meant to be with. Everything right with the world. What if life didn't get any better than this? Suddenly the past no longer mattered, lost all its power over me. My mother had wrecked my family but with Robbie, I might make a new family.

There was something so sweet and intimate about just lying close beside him and watching him sleep. His lips moved slightly, as though he was silently singing the verses of a song that had come to him from out of the darkness and soon, all the woodland birds had joined in with a rousing chorus. There were birds singing in the trees all around us, singing their hearts out, as if in celebration. The loveliest serenade.

Robbie had once told me, how storytelling was almost as important to human beings as breathing. That stories had always been told around campfires and how, throughout the ages, there was one motif that continually recurred: the journey into the woods to find the dark but life-giving secret within. I had sat beside a woodland campfire with him and it was as if I'd been shown a life-giving secret. Something mystical and magical but it was so much more than that. It was as if, by loving me, Robbie had taught me a different way of seeing, of hearing, of just being. Or perhaps not a new way at all but a very old way. I'd never seen stars shimmer quite so brightly or heard birds sing so sweetly.

The night had been a reminder or a revelation, that the world could be beyond beautiful. Or else it was an other-worldly encounter, that allowed us to slip, just briefly, into a realm somewhere just beyond real life or back in time, to a simpler world. Or maybe, it was all of those things. It made me think of the beauty of Blue John stone, buried deep inside the dark, dank caves in Castleton. Beauty that came from the darkness. I thought of the young lovers who'd come here in the past, Molly and Johnny, whoever they were.

The sleeve of Robbie's shirt had ridden up, exposing a tattoo on the inside of his right wrist. A date. It was written in swirly, old-fashioned script, like a date on an old letter or document, a relic of the past. Except that it was a futuristic date. 21st November 2025. Years from now. Robbie would be what? In his fifties. Me too. Impossible to imagine. What would he look like? Where would we both be? Scary.

I ran my fingers lightly over the black markings on his skin and he opened his eyes. 'When did you have this done?'

'A few weeks ago.'

'What is it?'

'A date.'

'I can see that.' I flipped over onto my stomach, bent my elbow to rest my head on my hand, looking down at him. 'What's significant about it?'

'I'll tell you, one day.'

'Tell me now,' I demanded but I knew he wasn't going to explain.

'One day,' he said again, climbing to his feet. 'Meantime, let's go to the fair, shall we?' He reached out his hand to help me up.

'Will I still know you in 2025?' I couldn't bear to think he wouldn't still be in my life.

Robbie regarded me almost sadly. 'I have a feeling that might be up to you.'

CHAPTER EIGHTEEN

Paine's Bridge was the perfect place to watch as a red and yellow hot air balloon lifted off from the park into the silvery blue sky, marking the start of the first Chatsworth Country Fair and we arrived at the main ring in time for the colourful opening ceremony. Members of the Household Cavalry, Grenadiers and Scots Guards, marched in their smart, bright uniforms, to the rousing sound of brass bands and military drums.

Robbie held my hand as we wandered round the food stalls, breathing in delicious aromas. We shared a slice of Bakewell tart, a far cry from the original, local Bakewell pudding, and drank cloudy traditional lemonade from the Farm Shop's own stall. There was so much to see and do. Hundreds of animals were taking part in the fair: falconry displays, gun-dog trials and Freya riding a bay dressage horse in the Grand Ring, looking dashing in her blue jacket, white breeches and glossy black riding boots. She won a red rosette, then came with us to watch a hilarious event, that involved sheepdogs herding ducks. Robbie kept up a running commentary and Freya and I fell about laughing. I couldn't remember ever having laughed so much.

Robbie stood behind me and slipped his arms around my waist. He kissed the top of my head and suddenly the bubble burst. It felt as if I was in a scene from a romantic movie and I felt like an imposter, as if I was acting the part of a girlfriend. There was a demon perched on my shoulder, whispering: *You can't do this. You don't know how.* I had no clear memory of what it was like, to live in a happy family home with two parents who loved or cared for each other. Even when Sukey was around, all I really remembered was tension, shouting. I had no script to follow, except for stories in books and films. I leant back against Robbie's body, felt the warmth of his chest through the thin material of his shirt and my t-shirt. He tucked my head under his chin and held me tighter. So what if my parents had ended up fighting all the time? I was having the loveliest day. I could write my own script.

We found Flora watching Highland dancing, then went in search of my dad, who'd been drawn to the parade of vintage steam engines. He was admiring an old-fashioned threshing machine with Maggie and George Ashwell, elderly housekeeper and tenant farmer, who, though nearing seventy, were holding hands like youngsters. George was leaning on a knobbly walking stick, wearing a cloth cap and Maggie was in a smart, tailored blazer, like one the Duchess might wear. They looked mismatched and also perfectly suited to each other, like two trees grafted together. My heart squeezed. Could Robbie and I be like them, in a few decades? Could we?

It was then that I saw her. In the queue by the stall selling candy-floss was Sukey's friend, Helen. She'd moved away to Harrogate years ago but she looked just the same.

Her short hair was totally grey but she wore it in a trendy, spiky style with big black sunglasses on top of her head. She'd always had a liking for chunky, bold necklaces and earrings and in her figure-hugging orange dress and high heels, she looked a bit intimidating. She'd always been a bit intimidating.

It took a moment for recognition to dawn and Helen's smile was wary. She'd reached the front of the queue and handed over some coins, was given a cloud of pink candy-floss, which she turned and gave to a little girl waiting, in pink shorts and a t-shirt with a unicorn on the front. A granddaughter? Helen exchanged a few words with a young woman in white jeans and a red jacket, who was clearly the little girl's mother. Helen's daughter? Three generations, on a family outing. Helen began walking over to where I was standing.

'It's Silva, isn't it? Sukey's daughter.'

'Yes,' I said. Biologically, that was factual.

'This is Robbie,' I said to Helen.

'Pleased to meet you.' She turned back to me, asked stiffly: 'How are you?'

'Good, thanks. How are you?'

'Life's treated me well. How old are you now? Seventeen?'

'Sixteen.'

'Starting sixth form?'

'I'm planning to go to art college.'

Was I? It was news to me. Why on earth had I come out with that? As if I needed to impress my mother's friend, as if the news might get passed on.

'You were always very creative and clever and good at sports too,' Helen said. 'Such a good all-rounder.'

But nothing I'd ever done had made Sukey proud of me. 'That's nice of you to say,' I said.

The pleasantries over, there was a lull in the conversation.

'I had a postcard from her,' Helen said. 'That's all.'

'Sukey sent you a postcard?'

'From Bloomingdales, in New York. Or rather, it was of Bloomingdale's.'

Of? From? What was the difference? Helen and Sukey's friendship seemed to revolve around shops. They'd both worked in the Chatsworth gift shop, had regularly gone on trips together, to the department stores in Sheffield and once or twice, up to London for the January sales.

It was as if someone had pulled a trigger, releasing a jet of emotion which knocked me off balance, tumbling me backwards into a dark hole, where I'd be forced to relive the shock and confusion I'd first experienced when my dad told me that my mother had gone. I was trembling, my legs felt weak as water. Robbie slipped his arm around my shoulders and I was so grateful for the solid strength of him.

'Me and Sukey used to talk of going to Bloomingdales one day,' Helen said.

'So she wanted to let you know she'd been?'

'If she did go. She'd not written much on the back of the card. Just something along the lines of, saw this and thought of you. It was all rather odd. The postcard wasn't posted in New York. I checked, because I was curious to know what had happened to her, where she'd gone. There was a Royal Mail postage stamp on the back and a Chester-field postmark.'

'Chesterfield?'

'Yes.'

'When was this?'

'Two, maybe three years ago. I'm sorry,' Helen said. 'I'm guessing from the look on your face, that you never heard from her?'

'No.' I felt angry, vulnerable and deeply ashamed. To be seen to matter so little to someone, to whom I should matter so much.

'She was my friend,' Helen said with caution, as if she was edging her way forward onto thin ice, 'but I can't pretend to condone what she did, running off like that and never getting in touch with you. It's not natural. It's despicable. It's the very worst thing a mother can do. She might have had her reasons for leaving of course, I accept that. She might well have had her reasons for not taking you with her at the time but there's no reason, no excuse, for not keeping in touch with you. Never even sending you a birthday card. That's unforgivable, in my book. I'm so, so sorry.' She made it sound as if she was apologising on behalf of her one time friend.

'It's not your fault,' I said.

'The postcard was so typical of her,' Helen added.

'What d'you mean?'

'She always was a fantasist, your mum. All show and pretend. To listen to her, you'd think she was blissfully happy, that she and your dad were Romeo and Juliet: that he adored her and she adored him and they had a perfect life, a perfect family, that we should all envy and want to emulate. And then she went and walked out on it all. Why? I never could fathom. So it would be just like her, to want me to think that she was living it up in New York City, while all the while she was living down the road in Chesterfield. Anyway, I'm glad to see you looking so well. You were such a brave little lady. Give my regards to your dad.'

'I will.'

I watched as Helen teetered back across the grass to her daughter and granddaughter, resuming their family day out. The little girl came hurtling towards her, brandishing the stick of candy-floss.

My mother's voice was in my head, echoing down the years: *Games of happy families. I can't do this anymore. I've had enough.*

'Are you OK?' Robbie asked me gently.

I nodded. But I was not OK. Far from it. I felt like a spectre at the feast, as if I alone was standing in shadows, while everyone else was enjoying the sunshine, all the fun of the fair. I was suddenly all alone, in a dark place. Or maybe the darkness was inside me. I felt as if all the years I'd worked so hard to bury the past, put it behind me and move forward, had been a complete waste of time and effort. It had been right there beside me, keeping me company every step of the way. *The past is not dead, it is not even past.* It still had the power to wind and wound me. There was no escaping it.

The brass bands and the voice over the tannoy faded out, as the voices clamouring in my head grew louder.

Helen didn't know why Sukey had gone. But maybe deep down, I had always known.

It had been the worst argument I'd ever heard between my parents, which was saying something, since they rowed viciously all the time, rows that went on for days, weeks.

My bedroom was right next-door to theirs, so I'd caught every word.

'I was young and I made a mistake,' my mother yelled.

'And God knows I've been paying the price ever since. Must you keep punishing me.'

'I'm not punishing you.'

I preferred it when she slammed doors, banged about with the pans in the kitchen, threw plates and smashed them even. It was better than when they shouted at each other, turning words into weapons. I wondered if I should pour Mum a glass of wine. She did like a glass or two of wine in the evening and when she was in the bath, when she was cooking and even first thing in the morning, when was putting her make up on and curling her hair with the electric wand. But last time I suggested that my dad had shaken his head, said: 'Best not encourage her, love.' He often complained that my mother drank, as well as spent, too much.

I crept out of my room, onto the landing. The door to my parents' bedroom wasn't quite shut. Through the gap I could see my mum, sitting up in bed, in her pink silky dressing gown, resting her blonde head against the padded, mink-coloured velour headboard, a crystal wineglass in her hand, lipstick smudged. So she didn't need wine taking to her then, she already had a drink. There was an open bottle on the bedside table.

'Why is she coming here?'

'You know very well.'

She put the glass to her lips, tipped her head back and emptied it. 'I don't see that what I did was so wrong,' she said spitefully, as if the wine was a deadly venom she might spit back out.

I was worried that in a minute, my dad would tell her to calm down and that would only make matters a million times worse. But whatever he said or did was always wrong. I'd often wondered how my parents had got together in the first place. People had shapes, which had nothing to do with the shapes of their bodies but their personalities. And my parents just didn't fit together. There was no symmetry or balance. Sukey was like a cactus, all hard and spiky and unapproachable, whereas my dad was slouchy and inviting, like a pair of old shoes.

'It was wrong on every level.'

'You're a self-righteous arse,' Sukey screamed.

'And you, Sue, are a criminal.'

'Don't call me Sue.'

I thought it was funny, that my mum found the plainer and more common version of her name, more offensive than being called a criminal. She didn't like to think of herself as plain or common. But a criminal? Was she happy with that? What crime had she committed?

'Do you know what's worst of all?' Sukey asked. 'I can see the hate in your eyes now, yes hate. Don't say it's not true because you know that it is.'

I willed him: Say it's not true, Dad. Tell Mum she's wrong and you don't hate her.

'It's Christmas,' he said. There was a crack of doom in his voice.

'I know it's bloody Christmas. Games of happy families. I can't do this anymore. I've had enough.'

Sukey flicked her hair and tilted her chin, sticking her nose up in the air in a defiant challenge. It was a classic look of hers that made her appear terribly snooty. 'You got yourself into this mess in the first place. Let's not forget that.'

There was a deathly silence. I noticed that the whites of my mother's eyes were not white at all but pinky-red, as if she'd been crying. No, crying didn't do that to you, did it? It made the rims of your eyes sore and red, not your actual eyeballs. Was she sick?

'That was below the belt,' my dad said eventually.

'It's what's below your belt that ruined my life.'

'For pity's sake woman, keep your voice down.'

'Why should I?'

'Silva.' My dad said my name very softly. 'She has ears, you know.'

'Oh, it's all about her. You've always been thick as thieves, the pair of you. Though of course it's me who's the thief, isn't it? That's how you see me now. A thief. Who stole what wasn't mine.'

Sukey turned her head towards the door and I tried to step back, out of sight but my legs wouldn't work. I was riveted to the spot. I couldn't have moved, even if the house was on fire, burning down around me. It felt as if it was. Everything going up in flames.

Sukey gave no sign she'd seen anyone. She looked straight through me, as if there was no pale-faced little girl on the landing, as if I didn't exist and I felt as if I really didn't, as if I'd lost all substance, dissolved into thin air, like a snowflake landing on wet ground.

'What do I care about her?' Sukey snarled. 'I wish she'd never been born.'

CHAPTER NINETEEN

Walking through the Park on a blustery Monday afternoon, I was surprised to see George Ashwell wandering around under the trees, a pretty, white, lace-edged pillowcase trailing from his hand. He bent down, used a trowel to scoop up what looked like deer droppings, and dropped them into the pillowcase. I wondered if he was OK.

'Morning Mr Ashwell.'

'I'm determined to beat Abe Morton to a trophy at the horticultural show this year,' he said, as if that explained everything. 'My old man used to swear deer dung is better for growing tomatoes, than sheep droppings.' He touched his finger to his nose. 'Bit more upmarket, you know. By rights they should be in a hessian sack of course, but I've not got one, so I borrowed one of the wife's pillowcases. I'll be in big trouble later but what can you do? I'll just pop it into the water butt and she might never know.'

I laughed. 'Your secret's safe with me.'

'I doubt I'll beat the old bugger. Abe knows his onions

and the rest of his veg. But one year, he'll slip up and I'll be right there, behind him.'

The horticultural show had been an annual fixture of estate life for forty years. Held in the Cavendish Hall, the competition to determine who'd grown the best fruit and veg and produced the best cakes and pickles, was friendly and light-hearted, up to a point. The judges had exacting standards and there was real rivalry for the trophies.

'Good luck,' I said.

'Cheers, m'dear.'

I walked on, kicking up drifts of leaves. Traffic light leaves, Robbie called them. Orange and red and dark green. In a few weeks, the grotto pond would be ablaze with scarlet and gold but he wouldn't be there to see it and it struck me, as it never had before, that autumn was a time of endings. The trees were attempting to demonstrate how lovely it could be to let things go, only they were failing to convince me. I was on my way to say goodbye to Robbie. Again. I'd already said goodbye to him once yesterday, at a farewell Sunday lunch at Brook House but then he'd asked me to come for a picnic with him.

'Didn't you know, summer's over,' I'd said.

'Let's pretend it's not, for just one more day.'

Typical. I felt older and wiser, realising that being in love only seemed to make people happy for a small proportion of time. It could bring just as much doubt and misery or the anticipation of misery.

We'd agreed to meet at the Farm Shop and I was there early, had time to visit the ladies loos to check the mirror, make sure I didn't look too windswept. I was wearing dark red lipstick that was perhaps a little too much for a daytime walk but I'd balanced things out with a casual outfit, tight black jeans and grungy red and black flannel shirt and my black Docs. I'd washed my hair in shampoo that smelt of coconut and left it falling free over my shoulders, beneath a woolly beanie hat. I made myself smile, wanting Robbie to remember me looking cheerful.

He was standing waiting for me, by the fire that was blazing in the former harness room.

Built in the old shire horse stud farm, the Farm Shop was a cross between the Harrods Food Hall and a traditional village baker, butcher and grocer, the staff all dressed in blue aprons and straw boaters. It had been the Duchess's idea to sell beef, lamb and venison from the Chatsworth farms, direct to customers and the shop had steadily expanded year on year with a delicatessen and a patisserie, shelves that stocked a mouthwatering array of gourmet treats. Delicious smells of fresh baked bread made my stomach rumble.

It felt oddly domesticated to be buying groceries with Robbie, sharing a shopping basket, as if we were an old married couple. I picked out sausage rolls and custard tarts because I knew they were his favourites, then we went to the cheese counter and he asked for brie, which he knew I liked to eat with crusty rolls. It was amazing the little details we knew about each other, built up over so many years. But his tastes would inevitably change when he went away, no doubt mine would too. As we both grew up, we'd grow apart.

We were served by Trish, who'd worked on the cheese counter since the shop first opened. In her early sixties, she was small and motherly, had an uncanny knack of remembering the names of everyone's family members, as well as what they were all doing. She wished Robbie good luck at university, sneaking a little box of locally made chocolates into our bag as a farewell treat.

Armed with our goodies, we made our way down the road from Pilsley towards Edensor, me matching Robbie's stride or him matching mine. We'd walked together so often, it was impossible to tell whose stride it had been in the first place. Before we became lovers, he'd been like my brother. That felt like such a special thing. To be best friends. To have grown up together. To know someone inside out. How would I ever feel so close to someone again?

We turned left opposite Edensor, over the brow of The Crobbs, where Chatsworth's herd of Limousin cows were grazing with the fallow deer, beneath russet trees, wrapped in gossamer medieval mist. I thought of all the carefree snowy days, we'd spent sledging on The Crobbs, in what already felt like a different life.

For once, neither of us suggested we go to the grotto pond, as if we'd already left that part of our story behind us. Instead, we went down to the river. Robbie started walking faster, almost as if he wanted to get away.

We crossed the Derwent and came to Queen Mary's Bower, a curious little moated building by the river with a square squat tower, a broad flight of stone steps and picturesque parapets covered in ivy. When Mary Queen of Scots was brought as a prisoner to Chatsworth, she'd supposedly been allowed to take the air in the building, which had been surrounded then by water gardens, preventing rescuers from reaching her. Now, it made a sheltered spot for a picnic. Robbie went to sit on the mossy steps and I sat myself down beside him.

He flipped the top off a bottle of damson wine, which he must have borrowed from his parents' drink cabinet. He handed it to me with a smile that made me feel I'd lost a layer of skin, as if he could see right inside my soul. I wished it was as pure and good as his. Lately, sometimes, I was aware of a seam of darkness running inside me. I felt inexplicably black and angry to the core of me, as if I was harbouring something nasty, had ingested festering poison. Where as he...he was the finest person I knew. Perhaps I should tell him so, only it would probably embarrass him, embarrass me more.

'I've decided I'm not going to university,' he announced.

That I had not been expecting and hope surged. 'Wow. Why?'

He looked over towards the river. 'Percy says, still water grows stagnant and flowing streams run clear.'

I swigged some wine, passed the bottle back to him. 'What did he mean?'

'That even if you're on the right track, you'll still get run over, if you just sit still.'

'That makes so much more sense.'

He chuckled. 'We were talking about the joys of the open road.' He knocked back some wine. 'What a good life Percy's ancestors must have had, the tinkers and pedlars. All those songs about rovers and wanderers.'

'You and your gypsy soul.'

'I keep telling my dad, that all those who wander are not lost.'

'And who are we to argue with Tolkien?'

'Exactly.' He drank more wine. 'I've been reading all about song collectors. There's a whole tradition of it, going back to Victorian times. A guy called Alan Lomax, travelled round America and the Appalachians and James Madison Carpenter drove all over Scotland in an Austin Seven. Took him six years. He collected thousands of songs from hundreds of singers, all recorded on wax cylinders. I'd love to do something like that.'

It felt as if the sky was falling in. I was engulfed by a new kind of loneliness and emptiness. 'You want to go off and travel round Scotland for six years?'

'Maybe not quite that long.' He knocked his shoulder against mine. 'You could come with me.'

I saw how we'd already grown apart without me even noticing. It didn't take him leaving, for it to happen. What he wanted now, since meeting Percy, was the exact opposite of what I wanted. I couldn't imagine the life he'd described, constantly travelling from place to place, living out of a rucksack. Planes and trains and buses and long road trips. It would be fun for a holiday, or a month even, but any longer and I'd be miserable. At the same time, I was going to be so miserable here without him.

If only I could make him love Chatsworth as much as I did. Lately, I'd come to really appreciate this extraordinarily special place we called home. I wanted to take Robbie's hand, right now, have him walk back with me towards the House. To stand with me, at the end of the nine-hundred-foot-long Canal Pond, where we'd be presented with the famous view of the south facade, as captured on thousands of tourist snapshots. The long, rectangular body of water was set a few inches higher than the south lawn, so when Chatsworth House was viewed from the end of the pond, it appeared to rise from the glassy water: a magnificent mansion with windows gilded in gold leaf, floating above its own reflection with the mighty Emperor fountain, playing at the north end of the canal. He said that I made him look and see things. Could I make him see that there was nowhere else like Chatsworth? Like any teenager, I'd sometimes longed to live in a city, where there was a bit more action. But Chatsworth was more than just my home, it was a part of me. From his shepherd father, my dad had learnt about hefting, a traditional method of managing communally grazed flocks of sheep on large areas of unfenced common land. Initially, sheep had to be kept in place by constant shepherding but over time they learnt where to go, passing the behaviour from ewe to lamb, over succeeding generations. My dad said that lots of families were hefted to Chatsworth. Our family was one of them. There had been Brightmores on the estate for centuries. Robbie's family was the same.

'We're so lucky to have grown up here,' I reminded him.

'We are.'

'If I ever do have children, I'd want them to grow up here too.'

He looked at me, wide-eyed.

I held up a finger. 'If. I said if. You used to want that too,' I ventured. 'Kizzy and Raffi? Our imaginary future children? You've changed your mind about all that?'

'No. It's just that spending time with Percy has just shown me what I want to do with my life. I want to find more people like him.' He looked at me intently, as if willing me to be on his side, as if my opinion really mattered to him. 'People say how all the old source singers are nearly all gone, that it's too late to collect any more old songs. But I've listened to recordings made in the 1950s of ten-year-old Romany gypsies and if they were young then, then they will still be alive for a few more years yet, won't they? I want to find them, the gypsies and travellers, descendants of the Scots, who were dispersed by the Highland Clearances. Indigenous people, all over the world. I need more than manuscripts and recordings. I want to knock on doors and caravans, be a song hunter, then play the old songs to new audiences.'

I rolled my eyes. 'Trust you.'

'What d'you mean?'

'You can't just be like everyone else and say you want to go off travelling, to see the world and find yourself and broaden your mind or whatever. You have to have a quest. Which is annoying because it means I can't tease you, for just looking for an excuse to bunk off and take a long holiday. Where will you go anyway, aside from Scotland of course?'

He shrugged, popped a piece of fluffy roll into his mouth. 'Wherever the mood takes me. Africa? Australia? America?'

'But it must be somewhere that begins with the letter A, right?' What was I doing? I hated the tone of my voice, scratchy and sarcastic.

I could tell that Robbie didn't appreciate my flippancy right now. There was nothing to be flippant about. I'd almost got used to the idea of him going to Edinburgh, just a train ride away but at this talk of him going off to another continent, something opened up inside me, a yawning sense of loss. I felt as if I'd been turned inside out, so all my vulnerabilities were suddenly on the outside, exposed. Even though I'd never had a boy I liked go off travelling before, it was a pain that felt uncomfortably familiar, like an unpleasant echo. I felt as if I was being dragged back yet again, kicking and screaming, to somewhere I didn't ever want to revisit. The intensity of emotion took me by surprise. I didn't know how to curb or control it. I was going to lose him and I couldn't bear it but there was nothing I could do about it.

'You're so clever. It would be such a waste to give up studying.' Damn. That had come out all wrong too.

'Jeez,' he sighed. 'You sound like my parents.' He snapped off a stem of grass, twirled it in his fingers. 'I thought you'd understand. I thought you felt the same way.'

'Honestly? Whatever gave you that idea?'

Why was I being so confrontational? This was Robbie,

my Robbie, my best friend, who I loved so very dearly. I felt like I might cry. *Do not cry. You will not cry.*

'I figured you feel as stuck here as I do.'

'You have me all wrong.'

'Evidently.'

I felt so lonely because if he didn't understand me, then who would? 'How can you know so little about me?'

'Maybe because there's a huge sign stuck to your forehead that says "closed".'

'Ouch.' I stared at him, incredulous.

Another young couple were strolling down by the river. Holding hands and wearing walking boots and fleeces. They were evidently on a romantic ramble. They glanced across at us, hearing raised voices. They think we're having a tiff, I thought. We are having a tiff. I was sure the girl grasped her boyfriend's hand a little tighter, seeming smug. Perhaps they'd driven out for the afternoon from Sheffield, planned to stop off at a country pub on their way back home. I was so jealous of them, it made my head feel like it was being crushed in a vice. I pressed the heel of my hands into my eyes, hoping Robbie would think specs of dust had blown into them, making them water.

'Come with me,' Robbie said.

'Yeah right.'

'I mean it.'

'No. You don't.'

'I do.'

'I'd get really homesick.' *Ok, so now you sound about five years old.*

'I feel homesick wherever I am,' Robbie said.

'Then we're not at all alike. Sorry to disappoint you.'

'You could never disappoint me.'

I took his face in my hands, pulled it to mine, felt his

warm cheeks. Then I was kissing him and he was kissing me back. Deep and tender, it was very different to all the kisses that had gone before. The first kiss had felt like the start of something wonderful and the ones that had followed had brought us closer, but this was an ending. It was a sorrowful, farewell kiss. The last time I'd ever kiss him. *Don't think that way.* At the very least, it was probably the last time I was going to see him, for months.

'You look so sad,' he said, stroking my hair away from my face. 'Are you crying?'

I shook my head. 'No.' *Definitely not crying.*

'Are you going to miss me?' He sounded hopeful. 'You are, aren't you?'

'I don't miss people.'

Just shut up, I told myself. *Shut up. Shut up.*

'Bloody hell, Silva. You're so snarky sometimes.'

'Sorry about that.'

'I'll miss you,' he said. 'Lots.'

'No, you won't. Not for long.'

'You could at least come and visit me, in…wherever.'

'You can't go to wherever. It doesn't begin with an A.' Terrible joke but he had the good grace to smile.

'We can write to each other,' he suggested, surely just trying to placate me now.

'Every week?' I asked sarcastically.

'Every day, if you like.'

I allowed myself, just for a moment, to try and imagine it and it was so easy. I could picture myself sitting down each night, at the little desk in my bedroom, where I did my homework. I'd neglect my studies and spend far too long writing long, intense letters, covering ten sides of paper, pouring out my heart, trying to reach out to him, ending with crosses for kisses, not too many, three maybe. Then I'd carefully fold the letter and put it in an envelope, resisting the urge to write SWALK on the back. Sealed with a loving kiss. Carefully, I'd write Robbie's name and an address that was not his home address on the front, sticking on stamps, pushing it into the postbox and half wishing I could travel with it.

Then the interminable waiting. Waiting each morning for the postman to bring replies that never came or came too infrequently; over-analysing every word he wrote back to me and all the words that may or may not be hidden between the lines. Waiting for the phone to ring. Waiting for Robbie to come home. Missing him like crazy. Wanting to spend every minute of every day with him, just as I did now but knowing he was hundreds of miles away from me. Thinking about him all the time and knowing he was not thinking about me. Imagining him passing through random towns, drinking with drifters in a bar somewhere, playing his guitar and singing to a host of admiring foreign girls with fascinating stories to tell him. Nights in hotels and motels. Camping on beaches, under the stars. Places I'd never seen, could barely even imagine. And I'd have so little to tell him by comparison, my life would seem so small and dull to him. I'd feel insecure and he'd start feeling trapped and resentful that I was being too needy. And he'd meet someone else, someone as freewheeling as he was and I would be cut up with jealousy. It could go only one way. We'd end up falling out, not even friends any longer, hating each other even.

'So will you write to me?' he tried again. 'If I write to you?'

'No.'

He half laughed at me, as if unable to believe I was being serious. 'You don't mean that?'

'I do mean it, Robbie.'

'Just…no?'

'Yes.'

'I don't understand.'

I needed to make him understand me, only I had an annoying feeling that I didn't even understand myself. Not really. It was as if this storm of emotions that was battering me was not really connected to this current set of circumstances but was drawing its energy from some other source. I needed to make him not hate me for it, at the very least. We'd go our separate ways and it was no great Shakespearian tragedy. It felt brutal, like the end of the world, but it was just reality, just life. I wanted to be noble: If you love someone, let them go.

'Robbie, this summer has been…amazing. Totally amazing. I'll literally remember it for the rest of my life. If I ever do have children, I'll tell them all about my lovely first boyfriend.'

'Stop it,' he said. 'That's just too sad.'

'It's not sad. We had a great summer. But now, it's over. And that's fine. It's totally fine. Because we have all these special memories, don't we?' I willed him to get it. 'Let's not spoil everything. Let's not try to drag it out. Can't we just accept this for what it was? A teenage fling. We'll always know each other, always be part of each other's lives. We'll always be friends.'

'A teenage fling?' He looked at me, incredulous and wounded, as if, inexplicably with no provocation, I'd punched him in the gut. 'Is that all it was for you?

'No. But,' I sighed, deflated. 'I think, deep down, we've always wanted totally different things.'

'What do you want? Because I'm not sure I even know.'

'I'm not sure I know either, which is half the problem?'

'I thought you loved me.'

'I do love you.'

'Then how can you just end this? Why?'

'Because you're going away,' I almost shouted, utterly exasperated with him now. 'You'll be meeting hundreds of new people. Lots of other girls. You want to have an adventure,' I ran on, becoming more sure of myself and my motivation, feeling wise and self-sacrificing. 'I want you to have the most amazing adventure, Robbie. I do. I don't want to hold you back. I want you to be free to enjoy it, all of it.'

'I'd enjoy it more, knowing that you were still mine.'

'Yours? Do you believe people can own one another?'

'Not own, no. Wrong word. You can't belong to another person. But you can belong together.' He reached for my hands, grasped them in both of his. 'We belong together.'

That was such a lovely thing to say. The sweetest thing ever. I wanted him to hug me, so tight it obliterated the terror of losing him.

But one of us had to be sensible and realistic and it was clearly not going to be him. I knew I was doing the right thing. 'Why are you making this so hard?'

'Why are you?'

'Because.'

'Because what?'

I took one of my hands from him, let him keep the other. 'Because it's…just…impossible.'

'Nothing is impossible.'

I sighed. Sometimes his undaunted optimism was lovely and sometimes it was maddening. 'This idea of yours, that we can say together, when we're miles apart. It makes no sense.'

'It makes perfect sense to me.'

'That's because you're an idealist.'

'What's so wrong with that?'

'One of us needs to be realistic. It won't work. It just won't. We both know we're not going to go on writing letters to each other every week, when we never get to see each other, from one week to the next.'

'Do we know that?'

'Yes,' I said. 'I think that if we are honest, we do know. We might keep it up for a month or two and then the letters will tail off, stop altogether. What's the point?'

'If you put it like that,' he said flatly, letting go of my other hand now, standing up, 'There's no point at all.'

I almost grabbed hold of him again, shouted at him: I hate waiting for letters. Or for people to call. I hate waiting for someone to come back.

I stood too and he took hold of my shoulders, rested his brow against mine, just for a moment. 'I will come back,' he said. 'I'm not like your mother.'

'What?' I sprang back, felt a flash of red-hot rage and shame. As if he'd caught me out. 'This has got nothing to do with her.'

'It has everything to do with her. But I'm not like her. I promise you. I will come back. Don't you believe me?'

'I believe you mean it right now but you'll change. It won't be the same.'

'Nothing ever stays the same.'

He made that sound so exciting, whereas I was inclined to see change as sad and scary and he made me feel the lesser person for feeling that way, which annoyed me. He made me feel inadequate for not being more like him, for wanting to stay when he wanted to go. Did he see me as lacking in courage, a dull person even, because I was not so adventurous and free spirited? In which case we were certainly done.

'You're asking me to wait for you?'

'Yeah,' he said simply. 'I guess I am.'

'I can't. I'm sorry, Robbie. I just can't do that. I don't think it's fair of you to ask it of me. And it's not fair of me to ask it of you either.'

Where had it all gone wrong? He was supposed to end up thinking I was being mature and sensible and selfless.

I had the silliest urge to ask him for a recording of his songs. I wanted a compilation tape after all. I needed a soundtrack for this summer, anthems to conjure the scenes. I wanted to have his voice in my headphones, to listen to on my Sony Walkman, under the covers in bed at night.

'So I guess this is goodbye?' He sounded hurt but entirely accepting of my decision. I didn't want him to accept it. I wanted him to argue with me, fight for me.

I said: 'Yes, I guess it is.'

CHAPTER TWENTY

I was in The Club, playing pool with my dad. I didn't want to be there. It was one of the places I used to hang out with Robbie and even the pock-pock sound of the balls reminded me of him. Trouble was, everywhere reminded me of him: the willow tree fountain, the Devonshire Arms, the grotto pond. He was everywhere and nowhere.

I knocked back shandy, wishing it was something stronger. Spirits preferably. I needed spirits. Spirit.

I'd missed Robbie the minute I left him sitting on the steps of Queen Mary's Bower. As I walked away from him, it felt as if whatever it was that connected my heart to his, was being pulled tighter and tighter, until it snapped.

I'd got ready for bed that night, tidied all my clothes away, brushed my teeth, wiped the mascara off my face with lotion and cotton wool. Standing in front of the bathroom mirror, all I saw was him, goofing around with his friends on their last day of school; their first day of freedom, their school-ties like bandanas around their heads, felt-tip autographs all over their white school-shirts. Some over-confident sixth former had painted Robbie's cheeks with stripes of her lipstick, like warpaint. I'd watched him swigging from a bottle of Bacardi, looking wild and unruly and I think I'd felt it even then: that already he'd left me behind.

I tried to focus on my own reflection, to be objective about the face that stared back at me. I'd never thought of myself as beautiful or even pretty. Striking, was the word Flora had once used to describe me. Dark eyes, full mouth, big dimples, small, upturned nose, lightly tanned skin. But what difference did any of that make? He'd meet hundreds of beautiful and bright young girls on his travels and they were all bound to fall instantly in love with him. It was all inevitable though. The summer had ended, as everything must end. Life had taught me to accept transiency. Nothing was permanent.

I ran my hands lightly over my body, which was as long and lean as an adolescent boy's. A runner's body, that almost won cross-country races at school. But I wished I looked stronger, more athletic. I wished my legs were more muscular, instead of long and skinny.

How would I go through a whole day without seeing him? How would I cope with knowing that I couldn't just walk over to Beeley and be near him, talk to him?

I climbed under the duvet, snapped off the light, squeezed my eyes tight, to stop the tears. I needed to toughen up. I'd join the gym maybe. Grow more muscles, get fitter, stronger. It would be something positive to do.

My dad knocked at the door.

'Come in,' I told him, flicking the light back on, wiping my face on the sheet and dragging myself up on the pillows.

He came to sit on the edge of the bed, making the mattress dip and the springs creak. 'Did you have a nice picnic?'

'It was good.'

'Your Robbie's a good lad.'

'He's not mine, Dad.'

'You could do a lot worse.'

'It's not as if I'm going to marry him or anyone.'

'No?' He patted my hand. 'You might well change your mind about that in a few years time. I'd like nothing more than to see you happy and settled.'

'Ha. Well, I'm not sure Robbie's ever going to be a settling type.'

'But you love him.' It was not a question.

'Dad. He's leaving.'

'So? Just because someone isn't here, that doesn't mean you stop loving them.'

'Shouldn't you be advising me that I'm too young for a serious relationship?'

He stroked my cheek with the back of his fingers, gently took hold of my chin and turned my face to make me look at him straight. 'That night Robbie slept here, in the summer. I know he didn't sleep on the sofa.'

'Dad, we didn't…'

'Hush. I came to say goodnight and there he was, in your bed. It's a narrow bed, too narrow for two people. You were on the outside edge and you rolled over and you'd have fallen off, bang, only in his sleep, Robbie reached out his arm and pulled you in. In his sleep. What a thing. Now what does that tell you?'

'I don't know, Dad.'

'You've got a special bond. Sweetheart, listen to me. The saddest thing in the whole world, is if you meet the right person at the wrong time and then you let them slip away. If you don't know what you've got, until it's gone.'

'Oh, Dad.'

'No matter that he's going away. If you love him, wait for him. That's my advice. But then, what do I know?'

I'd noticed how Dad used that phrase a lot these days. Whenever he gave me any advice or passed on words of wisdom, he always qualified it: *But then, what do I know?*

I bit my lip. 'Is that what you're doing? Are you waiting for Mum?'

He was silent for a long moment and then he said: 'I suppose I am.' It seemed to astonish him to realise it. 'I suppose that I am. I was always so in love with your mother. After all these years, I'm still waiting for her to come back to me.'

His eyes were wet with tears and I thought how Sukey didn't deserve someone like him, to wait for her. He was such a good person. He'd taught me so much, done his very best to make me resilient, to prepare me for life and its knocks. But there was one thing he'd taught me inadvertently: I could never tell him that I didn't want to be like him, that I had a horror of ending up like him. The one thing I would never allow myself to do, was to wait for someone. I'd already done it for long enough and I would never, ever again put myself in the position my dad was still in. I would never allow anyone else to have that kind of hold over me. I would never love someone who was absent. I'd made such an effort to be independent and strong and I wouldn't let anyone undo all my hard work, make me feel abandoned again.

Dad gently prodded me with his cue. 'Your turn.'

'Sorry Dad.'

I needed to stop thinking about Robbie. He was gone.

My game had been off from the start, when I'd potted two of Dad's balls and failed to hit my own. *Concentrate.*

My fingers kept absently reaching for my bare neck, searching for something that was no longer there. I'd taken off the Blue John pendant as soon as I came home from the picnic, pushed it to the bottom of a drawer. I'd taken down all the photos I'd tacked to the noticeboard on my bedroom wall. Robbie up a tree, larking about one Christmas with a reindeer headdress. My favourite one, taken during a dog walk up on Gardom's Edge, showed a stunning cloud inversion in the valley below, so that it looked as if we'd been floating in the sky above the crags.

I'd borrowed lots of his clothes, still had a dark grey sweater, frayed at the cuffs, and a navy blue t-shirt. They smelt of him and when I held them up to my face, I could breathe him in. My head was stuffed with information, now rendered useless. He liked olives on pizza, one sugar in black coffee, strong brewed tea. He'd read *The Lord of the Rings* trilogy, three times. His favourite colour was green and his favourite month was May.

Dad bounced the black ball off the cushion, straight into a hole. He set down his cue, looking unhappy to have won so easily. 'Time for chips?'

'Great, Dad.'

I idly studied the notices on the back wall, while I waited for him to come back from the bar.

Great country houses had always been a source of employment for the local community and Chatsworth was keeping this tradition alive. There were always lots of job advertisements: gardeners, kitchen porters, car park attendants - and a housemaid. I read that one all the way through, then again more slowly.

Lizzie was a housemaid now and she said it sounded like

a job from a different century. I had a sudden, vivid memory of Sukey, stretching out with her stockinged feet up on the sofa, in front of the television, every Saturday evening. She refused to watch *Coronation Street* like everyone else. 'Too common,' she said. She far preferred *Upstairs Downstairs*, which chronicled the lives and fortunes of the Bellamy family and their below-stairs servants, in Edwardian London. I could see her now, with her crystal wineglass in her hand, saying: 'People love this programme so much because they think houses like that, don't exist anymore with butlers and chauffeurs and footmen and housemaids and whatnot, all the gossip and goings on. But they do still exist. The chauffeurs might have been swapped for car park attendants and telephonists and the downstairs people are called staff instead of servants but otherwise, it's just the same. And we live here.'

It was easy to forget how big Chatsworth was. Three hundred rooms, thirty-five thousand acres, over sixty farms and three villages. It took nearly three hundred people to keep it all running smoothly: curators and conservationists; park keepers and foresters; people who worked in the admin, finance and marketing offices and in the cafes and shops. I knew most of them by name. Since I was a kid and my dad took me to work with him, I'd enjoyed chatting to housekeeper, Bea Waterfield, and to the housemaids, asking them what they were doing and why. I found that I really loved the idea of becoming one of them, just like my grandmother Ivy and her own mother, my great-grandmother. It felt such an obvious thing for me to do.

The advertisement detailed the qualities of the ideal applicant. It explained that housemaids were also conservation assistants. So first and foremost, the candidate needed to have an appreciation for beautiful objects and be able to handle them with the utmost care. Other requirements for the role were being fit and energetic with a capacity for hard work, plus a keen interest in the heritage of Chatsworth. Could there be a job better suited to me?

I'd been going backstage at Chatsworth, as my dad called it, for as long as I could remember. I'd had fish and chips in the men's mess room with Dad, on numerous occasions and had lived to tell the tale. Lurking in the bowels of Chatsworth, it had become the maintenance team's HQ, when the House was reorganised after the war. It was a hub, where the men ate and had their break; where everything was discussed off the record, from football to staff rotas. I used to think it was called a mess room because it was such a mess! But I really liked being there all the same, even if I did itch to get my gloves on and give it all a really good scrub, or a jet-wash maybe. The women's staff room couldn't have been a greater contrast with neatly ironed gingham table-cloths, placemats, fancy homemade cakes and chatter about embroidery and making jam. Bea Waterfield or Maggie Ashwell, had taken me there sometimes and I loved that so much. The cosiness and home comforts. I knew, from Maggie, that the visitor route through the House, was half a mile long and had to be vacuumed and dusted every morning. There were a hundred rooms that had to be kept clean and tidy. None of that put me off at all.

Suddenly, I wanted to burn my exercise books. I couldn't go back in September, to blackboards and classrooms and writing essays. I wanted to earn my own money. Not just a few pounds from waitressing on a Saturday, but a proper wage. I wanted to get a job and get on with life.

'I might apply,' I said, when my dad came back with the chips and started reading over my shoulder.

'Quit school?'

'Yes.' I turned to him, braced myself for a lecture.

'I thought you were all set to do A Levels, go to art college.'

'I'm not sure I ever actually wanted any of that.'

'Do whatever makes you happy, Petal.' He offered me the chips. 'Housemaid. It's a great job and you're made for it. You're not just good at cleaning, you actually like cleaning.' He ruffled my hair, as if I was still a toddler. 'Peculiar girl that you are.'

I took a chip, dipped it in ketchup, loving him for being so relaxed but also feeling suddenly rudderless. He was my dad. He was supposed to tell me what to do. 'You really think I should go for it?'

He reread the advert. 'The hours are ideal. Eight till eleven. You'd still have plenty of time to concentrate on your art in the afternoons.'

PART III

CHAPTER TWENTY-ONE
SILVA - 2002

Robbie appeared in the doorway of the smithy, just as I was going through my regular little ritual, firing up the forge and boiling the kettle, two of the tasks with which I began work each afternoon, after I'd finished working up at the House.

I'd gone back to work early, partly because I felt guilty for being off at such a busy time of year and also because I needed the routine, the company and normality of working. I'd spent the morning preparing the marble floor in the Painted Hall, one of the biggest jobs during the deep clean. We'd stripped off the old scratched and scuffed layer of varnish using a scrubbing machine, nicknamed Bertha. Then we'd rinsed the floor to get rid of any chemicals and taken off the residue with Victor, the buffer, leaving a clean matt finish, upon which the first thick layer of varnish was applied with a mop. We applied five or six coats, creating a beautiful, shiny marble floor. It took us five days but the result was worth it.

The very first thing I always did when I got to the forge,

was put on a CD. Soundgarden's 'Louder than Love.' I listened to it when I was working out at the gym and working here.

I turned the sound down when I saw Robbie, the sight of him making my heart jump.

'So let me get this right,' he began, as I shovelled coke. 'At midday, you swap your maid's outfit for a leather apron and steel-capped boots?'

'You got it. Most blacksmiths have a bread and butter job, when they're starting out,' I explained. 'They work as steel fabricators or welders or whatever.'

'Hmm. I can picture you as a welder.'

'Can you now?'

'Remember that movie?'

'What movie is that?' I knew exactly what he meant. Original as he was, he was by no means the first to bring this up.

'The girl who dances by night and welds by day. What was it called?'

'Flashdance.'

'Yeah, that's it. I remember watching it with my sister and I thought there was something so sexy about a graceful dancer who stripped off her leotard and leg-warmers, to put on a boiler suit and safety vizor and then fired up a blow torch.'

'Right,' I grinned. 'Anyway, being a housemaid suits me fine because mostly I'm free every afternoon, unless there's an event on.' I asked him: 'What are you doing here anyway?'

'Just passing,' he said, leaning a shoulder against the door.

'On the way to where?'

'I wanted to say goodbye,' he admitted, 'before I head back up to Scotland.'

Yesterday, he'd gamely joined in the Chatsworth litter pick, as if he was still part of our local community. An annual event, led with vigour, by the Duke and Duchess in their raincoats and high-vis vests. It was always a strangely jolly affair. Everyone worked in teams, armed with refuse sacks and picking tongs, combing the miles and miles of footpaths and roads around the estate, before being rewarded with bacon butties and hot chocolate.

'You'd have been excused under the circumstances,' the Duchess had told me kindly.

'It's just what I needed,' I said with half an eye on Robbie, who was retrieving a crisp packet from under a hedge, joking around with the Duke about it having been there so long it was practically archaeology. Picking up rubbish in the drizzle - who'd have thought it could so comforting and cheery?

Now my heart dived down to my steel-capped boots. He was leaving so soon? I stopped what I was doing. 'Come in,' I told him, overly bright.

He ducked his head under the low lintel and peered around. A smithy had been housed in the corner of the magnificent stone stable block for centuries, which was a big part of its appeal for me. I loved being the latest in a long line of blacksmiths. With Eli's blessing, I'd reorganised the tools so that all the hammers and tongs were hung on pegs on the back wall, arranged according to size and purpose.

Robbie smiled softly when he saw them. 'Neat freak at work.'

'There's no room to be anything but neat in here.'

There was just enough space for the coke forge, plus the anvil, which stood on a stump of oak. In the far corner was a bench fitted with vices and a swage block, a cast iron lump of iron with square, round and rectangular holes and grooves, for punching.

I dropped teabags into two chipped blue and white striped mugs, poured on boiling water, feeling his eyes watching me. I glanced up at him and he looked awkward, as if he'd been caught out.

'Nice trousers,' he commented, clearing his throat.

Sometimes I wore a boiler suit but today, I had on protective, tan-coloured moleskin trousers with double vertical zips either side of the waist. 'They're made for ships' carpenters, so they can be taken off super fast.'

'Useful.' There was a cheeky twinkle in his eyes.

'In the water,' I qualified. 'If the carpenter fell overboard.'

'I'm glad you've not changed your hair,' he said, more softly. 'Kept the plait. You still look like Pocahontas.'

I squished the teabag against the side of the mug, scooped it out and stirred in milk, before handing it to him. 'I'm more often called Rapunzel.'

'But you're not waiting to be rescued, are you? Not you. Of all people.' He'd picked up a tendril of metallic ivy from the workbench. 'It's like calligraphy.'

'It's part of a gate. It's supposed to reflect the decaying grandeur of the old stone posts that stand either side of it.' I indicated a sketch beside it. 'See.'

'What are the flowers?' They had trumpets and scroll like fronds.

I shrugged. 'They're fantasy flowers, I guess, modelled on hibiscus flowers and the camellias in the glasshouse.'

'What you're doing here is amazing.'

'It's really not. I'm just messing about really.'

'Doesn't look like that to me.' He gifted me a sweet

smile. 'We're both inspired by nature and by keeping alive something ancient,' he said, as if it made him happy to note the similarities between us.

They were similarities I'd spotted long before, when I'd first started working as a housemaid, I'd so wanted to write to him and tell him that my new job was just like his. He collected songs passed down the generations and the Devonshire collection reflected the passions and interests of generations of the Cavendish family and now, I was looking after this collection, helping to ensure its survival. But of course, I'd not been able to tell him any of this because I was the one who'd decided we weren't going to write to each other.

He asked, 'D'you sell your stuff?'

'A few things. Just to friends and friends of friends.'

'Commissions.'

I laughed. 'That sounds far too grand and professional.'

'You should advertise.'

I shook my head. 'What I really like doing, is working on my own ideas, rather than making things to order. Whenever I'm working up at the House or walking the dog in the gardens, I always see something new or see it in a new way, even after years of living here and looking at things. I'm currently a bit obsessed with the Boulle furniture. It's made by a cabinet maker to Louis X1V and the surface is decorated with veneers of pewter and brass and turtleshell.' He didn't need to know all this but I wanted him to know. We'd years of catching up to do. And years ago, Robbie had given me a Moleskine sketchbook, to thank me for making him the bow and arrow. I had dozens of Moleskines now, the creamy pages filled with ideas. 'I like taking old designs and crafts and reworking them, helping to keep them alive, you know? Same thing you do with the old songs you collect, right?'

'Totally. When I was a kid, I had a book about a man called Snowflake Bentley,' Robbie said. 'He spent his life photographing snowflakes.'

'Your mother told that story to us, at school. I've always remembered it.'

'Bentley said that when a snowflake melts, its unique design is lost forever: "So much beauty gone, without leaving any record behind".'

'I love that.'

'I love that you love it.'

The way he said love. It made my heart dance. It felt as if, in discussing our own passions and ambitions we were throwing out threads of hopes and dreams that might somehow weave us back together. Maybe. 'I went to see an exhibition in London, called the New Iron Age. There were all these amazing artist blacksmiths there and I thought how great it would be, to be one of them.'

'So what's stopping you?'

'For one, I don't fire-weld.'

'Hmm. I can see that's a big problem.'

I laughed. 'Trust me, it is. It's how blacksmiths tradition-ally joined metals using just the forge and anvil. With gas or arc welding, the fusion only happens at the surface of the joint, whereas with fire-welding the two surfaces of metal join all the way across, become one continuous piece. People say that you're only a true blacksmith if you can fire-weld.'

'So go to it. Fire-weld.'

'I wish it was that easy. '

'How hard is it?'

'You have to super heat the metal but if you don't catch it before it gets too hot, you scorch and destroy it. It's a fine line and I can never seem to get it right.'

'But you get so much right, clearly. Will you show me what you do?'

'You wanna watch me work?'

'I promise not to get in the way.'

'All right. If you like.' I reached behind my back to tie the leather apron straps. I'd had to have the apron cut down to size, since there was an assumption that all blacksmiths were great, strapping men. I pulled on my gloves and goggles and thrust an iron rod into the flames. 'Don't come too close or you'll get burnt. That's not a metaphor by the way.' I grasped the rod with a pair of tongs and moved it around, digging it deeper into the glowing coals.

'How d'you know when to start bending it?'

'You have to wait for forging heat. Bright orange-yellow.' I'd quickly grasped how to distinguish the different colours. Eli said I was a natural. I put on my ear defenders and handed a spare pair to Robbie. 'You'll need these. It's gonna get loud.'

I removed the rod and set it on the anvil, steadied myself, legs slightly apart, the metal tucked into my waist as I swung the hammer. Robbie watched as I angled the metal and brought down the hammer, so it rang out against the anvil like a bell. I let it bounce, raised it again, brought it down. That was the rhythm, two hits on the iron and one on the anvil. I felt the vibrations tingle all the way up my arm. I was left-handed, so they went all the way up past my elbow and into my heart, which was doing its own hammering right now.

'I imagine it's a good feeling, to pound out all your anger and frustrations that way,' Robbie said, when I broke off to thrust the cooling iron back into the heat once more and we could remove the ear defenders.

'There's a lot more to it than that,' I told him. 'It's a case of working with gravity, letting the weight of the tool drop and fall rather than hitting. It's nothing to do with strength,' I said, searching for the right words and thinking how it was the same way that he sang, with both power and restraint. 'The trick is to hit it exactly where you want to hit it.'

I liked to feel the power in my body, to know I had sinews and hard, corded little muscles beneath my skin, which I did like to soften with lotions, just like any girl might, soaking in a scented bath. But it felt good to be strong, able to take care of myself. Lizzie's little children liked me to flex my biceps and they prodded the small mounds of hard muscle that appeared in my skinny arms, giggling that they were like Popeye's.

Droplets of perspiration were running down the side of my face. I raised my arm, wiped my brow against it. Robbie was watching me so closely, it was unnerving but at the same time, I liked being the focus of his attention.

'You look so at home here,' he said, almost wistfully.

'I find it really peaceful. It doesn't look at all peaceful, I know. I go home with blisters and bruises but I'm a much nicer person, when I've been here a while.'

'You're always a nice person, Silly.'

'Thanks.'

'A nice person, who likes bending things to your will,' he grinned.

I picked up a cloth and lobbed it at him.

He raised his hand, caught it in mid-air. 'So what else can you make, besides gates?'

'Oh, I can turn my hand to most things. Nails, fire guards, curtain rails, you name it.'

'And horseshoes? Isn't that what blacksmiths used to make in the olden days?'

'Plus the odd sword and shield.'

'Now there's an interesting concept: a damsel in distress, who forges the weapons for her knight in shining armour.'

'I'm no damsel in distress, I'll have you know.'

'Joke,' he grinned. 'You're definitely more Boudicca than Guinevere.'

'Right answer.' I focused on the metal, which had now turned from red to orange. I thrust it into a bucket of water and steam hissed around me.

My dad had watched me just once. 'Aren't you afraid of botching it?' he'd asked.

'Metal is very forgiving,' I'd told him, 'not like wood or stone. Mistakes are easy to rectify. If a piece is botched, you can just reheat it and start over again.' Forging and forgiving. They were almost the same words, bar a couple of extra letters.

'So you get a second chance,' Dad had said. 'You do something wrong and you can always put it right? If only life were the same.'

I was kicking myself now. I should have probed him, asked him to explain exactly what he meant. What mistakes had he made in his life, and what second chances would he have liked? I didn't want to make the same mistakes my parents had made but how was I to avoid them, if I had no idea what they were in the first place?

'So, I asked Percy if he knew anything about Molly Marrison,' Robbie said, for all the world as if he'd been reading my mind.

'You did?'

'I asked if he'd ever heard Molly's version of 'The Runaway Lovers' but I'm afraid he was no help at all.'

'I remember he said he never sings that song, but thanks for trying. How is Percy anyway? How old is he now?'

'As old as the hills. Have you looked Molly up in the newspapers yet?'

'I'm going to go over to Chesterfield tomorrow.' My day off.

'Wanna hand?'

I stopped what I was doing and looked at him, remembering how he'd once criticised me, for never asking for help or accepting offers of it. 'A hand?'

'Two hands even. I don't fly back to Scotland until late. I've got lots of experience finding forgotten singers.'

That was true. Robbie had been travelling all over the world, collecting old songs and performing them to new audiences. That's what he did now. What he'd left Derbyshire to do. Before that, he'd spent hours, digging up old songs from archives.

Would it be such a bad idea if he went with me?

No, said my heart.

Yes, said my head.

I was fed-up of obeying my head. 'Thanks. That'd be great. I'll pick you up at ten tomorrow.'

'Oh. Okay.'

'Am I being bossy?'

'My mum always drilled it into us boys, that women should never be called bossy.'

'Because a man would be described as authoritative or a good leader. I remember. I love your mum.'

'She loves you too,' Robbie said. 'She's always going on about how lovely you are; how talented and hardworking and kind, blah blah.'

'That's nice,' I smiled.

'She's right. I totally agree with her. On every count.'

I stepped up to him, clamped my hand over his mouth. 'You'll make my head swell,' I scolded. I let my hand fall away. 'Now, I've got loads to do. I'm babysitting for Lizzie's little girls in a couple of hours.' I was Godmother to Carys, who was now nearly five and a handful. Carys's baby sister, Maria, was almost two and too cute.

'My sister says you're the best babysitter in Chatsworth,' Robbie said.

'Well, I'm certainly the messiest.'

'Freya says her little lad will only have you to look after him, when she and Sam go out.'

'That's because we make stuff. Started off with play-doh and plasticine but now it's more sophisticated.'

'Yeah, Dylan told me about your boats.'

'Really? Bless him.' Every time I saw little Dylan now, he handed me a piece of paper so I could turn it into a boat to float on the Derwent. Or in his bath if it was dark outside. 'I've promised Carys that we're making a fairytale castle out of papier-mâché tonight. I'm bringing glue, old newspapers and paint. She's been collecting the innards of toilet rolls.'

'Ha! No wonder you're so in demand.'

'I love seeing how enthusiastic little kids are about making things. They don't worry about the end result, they just get stuck in, enjoy the process. It's such a shame we lose that ability just to play.' I patted my anvil. 'Well, I guess some of us don't lose it.'

'You're doing much more than playing.'

'I'm really not. But you do need to get out from under my feet. OK? I'll see you later.'

'Later alligator.'

CHAPTER TWENTY-TWO

By the time I'd got back from Lizzie's, it was nearly two in the morning. I'd made an awesome castle with her little girls, though I say so myself. Then we'd started on pompom animals. I got the girls dressed in their Pjs, brushed their teeth and, when they were snuggled under their duvets, I read them *Little Rabbit Foo Foo*, about a dozen times. When we'd turned out their lights, I tidied up all the art mess and then sat with a cup of tea, watching a Disney film on my own because I couldn't be bothered to find the remote control, to switch channels. By the time Lizzie and Joe got back from their evening out, it was nearly midnight but Joe insisted on producing a bottle of gin and some cheese and biscuits from the Farm Shop and the three of us sat around, drinking and snacking and chatting. All the same, I was wide awake, when my alarm when off at seven.

I had a quick shower, pulled on jeans and a white shirt, quickly painting on some lipstick and mascara and arrived at Brook House ten minutes early. I was eager to find out more about Molly and also, I couldn't wait to see Robbie. It annoyed me, how I'd already slipped back into ridiculous teenage paranoia, when I over-analysed and agonised over every tiny thing he said or did, convincing myself, that when he said 'see you soon', what he actually meant was he didn't ever want to see me again. Do we ever really grow up? Or do we just learn to put on grown-up clothes? Swear to God, there was a teenager still lurking inside me, and a frightened ten-year-old child too.

In many ways, Robbie was the kind of person who disliked being ruled by a clock but although he was a free-wheeling spirit, he was too well-mannered to keep people waiting and he was ready early, too.

'So how did the castle-building go last night?' He asked, as we drove through Baslow.

'It's fit for Sleeping Beauty herself.'

'I can see you up a scaffold tower, building a flying buttress.'

I laughed. 'Mostly, I'm just rocking a hip vac!'

He frowned. 'Vac? Not flask?'

'They come in handy, when the doors you happen to be vacuuming are ten feet tall.'

'You love your job, don't you?'

'I do. Getting a close look at the beautiful wood-carvings is one of the best things about our Winter deep clean. The other day, I was dusting Samuel Watson's carvings in the state apartments. They'd have been silvery originally but three hundred years of daylight has given the lime wood a grey sheen which looks like dust. So some of the maids find it a bit of a thankless task.'

'You should be a guide,' Robbie said. 'With all your knowledge.'

'I like helping with the conservation.'

'You look tired,' he added softly.

I glanced at him as I changed gear. 'Late night. And you know what it's like at the House at this time of year, when we're so close to opening.'

'Not really. Tell me.'

'I suppose it's the same with any deadline, as it gets closer, you always long for just another day, another few hours even. We've been coming in at weekends and working in the evenings sometimes, just to get everything done. When you think you've just about got it all sorted, you suddenly realise, you've still got all the little finishing jobs to do and that's when you start to panic slightly, not too much, obviously, when you're handling priceless antiques.' I slowed down, indicated right. 'I feel like I'm skiving now, to be honest.'

'This is important.'

'It is. Bea has this recurring nightmare before the House opens, that she's going round with her big bunch of keys and she gets overtaken by the first visitors. She's terrified we won't be ready on time.'

'She'd never let that happen,' Robbie said. And then. 'Are you doing OK?'

'I'm good.' The reflexive, ready-made answer. I kept my eyes on the road, so he'd not see that it was a lie, but it turned out he still knew me too well, didn't need to look into my eyes in order to read my mind.

'Honestly?'

Most people don't really want us to be honest when they ask how we are, do they? If we replied by saying: I might look like I can cope, but I can't. I might be smiling but actually, I'm screaming inside, most people would want to run a mile. They'd definitely never ask again, might even avoid us in the future. But if we're lucky, we have one rare and precious friend, who genuinely cares. Robbie had always been that friend for me. He wanted to know the truth.

'I miss my dad,' I said, a catch in my throat. 'So much.' I gripped the steering wheel, digging my nails into the black leathery covering. 'Things happen during the day and I think, I must remember to tell him about it because he'd find it funny or interesting or just want to know but then, I realise I can't ever tell him anything, ever again. And I just can't get my head around it. We used to talk every day. I'd pop in to see him, cook dinner for us both. Or I'd bump into him somewhere around Chatsworth Park. We'd have a cider in The Club or he'd just give me a quick call before bedtime. Checking in, he called it. He'd tell me what he'd been up to and I'd tell him what I'd been doing. Just little things, nothing earth shattering, but it was nice to have someone just saying: how was your day? You know what I mean? I took that for granted and now there's nobody to say it, I realise how lovely and important it is, what a difference it makes.'

'I know what you mean,' Robbie said.

I found that hard to believe. He had Catrina after all. 'I'm also aware that I'm only a couple of decades younger than my dad. I need to make every day count.'

'You already do.'

'Not the way you do. You've always grabbed life with both hands and wrung all the juice out of it. That's so great.' I let go of the gear stick, tucked a stray wisp of hair, behind my ear. 'My dad didn't do that. I'm only just starting to realise that deep down, he was so unhappy for most of his life.'

'Because of Sukey?'

'I can't help wondering, if she'd not gone, would he have taken better care of himself? Would he still be alive?'

'You can't think like that.'

'I can't not think like that. But I'm not even sure he even loved her. Not really. They fought. About everything. All the time. That's all I can really remember about them. Bickering and shouting. Doors slamming. Plates smashing. And no making up. I have no memories of that at all. That's pretty telling, isn't it?'

'He couldn't live with her and he couldn't live without her?'

'And maybe that's not really living at all? It's a horrid thing to say but there was this oppressive atmosphere in the house, whenever she was in it. I liked it when I came home from school and she was out. But then, when she was gone for good, I wanted her to come back. It was all I wanted. Where's the sense in that?'

'At the end of the day, she's still your mum.'

I never called her that any longer. 'I always thought Dad wanted her back too, despite everything.'

'But now you wonder if it was someone else he wanted?'

'I keep wracking my brains. Where does Molly fit into the picture? How?'

'That's what we're on our way to try and find out.'.

We parked in the multi-storey and walked together, through the busy town centre and shopping precincts. When we hit the main road, Robbie switched sides with me so that he was walking on the edge of the pavement, to protect me from being hit by a reckless bus driver, presumably. It was a sweetly old-fashioned gesture, typical of him.

We walked past the Winding Wheel Theatre and the other black and white buildings that lined Holywell Street, towards the red-brick tower and turrets of Stephenson Memorial Hall, which stood on the corner of Corporation Street and St Mary's Gate and housed the public library.

Opposite, was the church of St Mary's and All Saints, topped by Chesterfield's iconic and rather sinister crooked spire, so called because it was twisted at more than forty-five degrees and leant as precariously as the tower of Pisa.

'Isn't a blacksmith supposed to be responsible for that?' Robbie teased.

I pushed against the revolving door, past a plaque commemorating the building's official opening, by the 7th Duke of Devonshire, in 1879. I threw a reply over my shoulder. 'He was from Bolsover and he mis-shod the devil, who leapt over the spire in pain and knocked it out of shape.'

'Great story,' Robbie chuckled.

We were suddenly surrounded by thousands of stories. The local studies section occupied the third floor of the library, row upon row of shelves. I could almost hear the ghostly whispers in the hushed atmosphere. Heroic acts and achievements, medals won and lives lost. A framed portrait of local hero, George Stephenson, the railway pioneer, gazed down from the far wall.

'The newspapers will be on microfiche,' Robbie said. 'That way.'

I headed over to the row of computer screens and keyboards, set up on the long, central, veneered table. I sat down on a green padded chair at one of the work-stations, figured out how to turn the machine on. Robbie pulled up another chair beside me, his elbow resting on the table, as he peered with me at the flickering green letters on the black screen. I noticed the frayed cuff of his jumper, his narrow, bony wrists, the blue ropes of veins that snaked to his palm, like tributaries of a river. My fingertips throbbed with an urgent need, just to reach out and touch him. My whole body felt charged. I wished he'd move away a little, so I could breathe, concentrate.

'I guess we just type her name in the search box?' I whispered.

'Go for it,' Robbie murmured.

I typed: Molly Marrison.

A few seconds later, it had thrown up three articles. The first one was from the *Daily Mail*.

It was a photo of my dad and Molly. She had a flower in her hair, was smoking what looked like a joint. The caption: 'Look at the folks you meet at Woburn Abbey these days.'

'Wow. My dad was in the national papers.'

The second piece was from the Chesterfield Star, dated 1978:

DERBYSHIRE SINGER DISAPPEARS

On the cusp of fame and fortune, ten years ago, in 1968, critically acclaimed local singer-songwriter Molly Marrison, vanished without trace. Royalties remain uncollected and her whereabouts are still a mystery. She was feted by Melody Maker, who called her 'a songwriter with great promise, with a voice that blends the sweet sorrowfulness of Sandy Denny with the birdsong of Joan Baez'. She had a northern authenticity that appealed to the proletarian pop culture, her Derbyshire accent speaking of sooty back-to-backs and tinkers. Signed to Albion Records, she recorded one album which was hailed as a mini-master-piece but within months of its release, she'd disappeared. There are rumours of a disastrous LSD experience and a reinvention as a teller of folk tales, in California. No theory has been proven, though none has been disproved.

Jeff Bond, the producer who was instrumental in landing Molly her record deal, recalls first seeing her perform at the Festival of the Flower Children, in the summer of 1967. "The way she sang 'The Runaway Lovers', it was like a slap in the face, stopped me in my tracks. She sang with such warmth and grace and she had bags of talent and an elfin quality that made her mysterious. The audience fell in love with her.'

But despite the excellent reviews, Marrison was in trouble, as Jeff Bond witnessed: An intense relationship with an unidentified man may have prompted her to flee. 'It was certainly not making her happy. She was a gentle soul with a big heart and I just hope she's happy now."

There is no evidence of Marrison's death and an APB put out on her in the US, has yielded nothing.

Robbie slouched against the chair, scratched the back of his head. 'So, when your dad asked you to find Molly, he was asking you to do what reporters, music fans and investigative journalists, have been trying to do for decades and have all singlehandedly failed.'

'Yeah, thanks, Dad!' I exhaled. 'So now what?'

We were still whispering, so as not to disturb the other library users.

'He believed you'd find a way,' Robbie said. 'He must have known you'd enjoy a challenge.'

'Wild goose chase, more like.' I bit my bottom lip. 'I wonder if he might be…'

'The unidentified man?'

Further down the long table, a silver-haired man in a tweedy jacket turned to scowl at us.

I dropped my voice lower still, leant in even closer to Robbie. 'In which case, he had an affair with her, cheated on my mum?'

'That would explain a helluva lot.'

'It would.'

Patterns. They were everywhere. I was fascinated by the Fibonacci sequence in nature, the way it dictated the arrangement of leaves on a branch, flower petals, spirals in a shell. Much traditional ironwork was based on repeat elements and I used it all the time when I was at the forge, designing gates and fire screens. Molly disappeared in 1968 and ten years later, the exact same thing happened to Sukey. Two women in my father's past, who'd both gone missing. Here was one of those patterns that caused TV detectives to reopen old cases, hunt down a killer who'd escaped justice. My dad was no killer. But…

'D'you think your dad was the type to have an affair?' Robbie asked.

I couldn't make that fit either. 'I don't. I really don't. But then what do we really know about our parents and who they were before we existed?'

'I know. Hard to imagine they even had a life before we came along.'

'Hmm. True.' I smiled at him. 'I'm really glad you're here.'

'Me too.'

We were silent for a moment. I fell to wondering if my dad had known, when he left me with this quest, that the only person I could turn to for help, was the person who was right here beside me now? He was canny like that.

'Hey look at this. Robbie was occupied by something else on the screen.

He'd clicked on the third index listing for Molly Marrison and it had pulled up another newspaper cutting. The article was dated 25th October 1967. The title: *Derbyshire Girls Arrested in Abortion Rights Rally.*

There was a brief mention of Molly in the second paragraph, simply stating that she was a Derbyshire singer, who'd built up a following the local pubs and clubs.

But it wasn't her who'd been was arrested.

· · ·

Mrs Sukey Brightmore, an active member of a local arm of the national Abortion Law Reform Association (ALRA), led by Vera Houghton, was arrested for uncivil behaviour, hurling verbal abuse at police officers. 'It's a woman's right to choose to have a baby or not,' she protested.

There she was in the photo, a grainy image of young women waving placards.

'Safe Legal Abortions for all Women', demanded the placard that my mother was fervently waving. It looked like an old sheet or pillowcase with two garden stakes in each corner but the homespun domesticity of the construction, was totally at odds with the starkness of the words. I skim-read the rest of the article. The rally had apparently been held the day before a decision was to be made in parliament, about the abortion act.

It wasn't at all hard to imagine Sukey as a militant fire-cracker and, despite everything, I felt a rush of pride. Good on her for campaigning for women's rights. She'd spoken out and stood up for a cause she believed in. But the date of the rally. A chill was rushing through my veins, as if I'd been injected with a gallon of icy meltwater.

When Sukey had been on that march, shouting for abortion rights, she'd been about three months pregnant. I was born six months after the photograph had been taken. Sometimes, it was so easy to fill in the gaps in a story, sometimes the dots were arranged in such a way, that they could only be joined to make one possible complete picture. There was only one conclusion. Sukey had felt so strongly about this issue because she'd wanted to have an abortion herself. She'd fallen pregnant in the summer of 1967 and had wanted to get rid of the baby. I'd believed my mother had rejected me when I was ten years old but it had happened long before that, before I was even born.

My mother's voice: *Never have kids. They'll ruin your life.*

'She didn't want me,' I said quietly. 'Not ever.'

Robbie immediately put his arm around me, pulled my head closer to his. 'You don't know the whole story,' he reminded me.

His embrace, the sudden nearness of him, completely overwhelmed me. He was only doing it to comfort me, nothing more and it was all too confusing. I shoved my chair back from the desk, the metal legs grating on the floor. 'I know enough.' There was nothing else I needed to know about Sukey now and as well as feeling abandoned all over again, I was swamped by guilt for ruining my mother's life. 'No wonder it wasn't Sukey my dad told me to find. She'd not want me to find her, would she? She'd escaped, started a new life.'

'There might be some other explanation.'

'Do you honestly believe that?'

I went to one of the librarians, who looked exactly like the stereotype of a librarian with frizzy grey hair and spectacles on a chain around her neck. She was wearing a herringbone patterned skirt and a name badge that said Eva. 'Do you have anything about the 1967 abortion act?' I asked.

'Certainly.' Eva went over to the 20th century history section, ran her fingers along the spines and pulled out a thick, blue-covered tome on feminism in the 1960s. She flicked to the index, then flicked to a page in the middle of the book, handed it over. 'Here. This chapter.'

I skimmed a dozen pages. How cruelly ironic the timing must have seemed to Sukey. The act had been introduced as a private members' bill in 1966, then the government had appointed Sir John Peele to chair a medical advisory committee. Sukey fell pregnant in the summer of 1967 and the abortion act had been passed on the 27th of October that same year with perfect timing for her to terminate her pregnancy. Only not. Because the act didn't come into effect for six months, not until the 27th April 1968. She'd known that legal abortions were imminent but just a few months too late to make any difference to her life. I had been born exactly a week before abortions were legalised.

CHAPTER TWENTY-THREE

'Want me to drive?' Robbie asked, when we were back at the car park.

'Thanks.' I handed over the keys.

We drove out of Chesterfield in silence, got snarled in heavy traffic. I didn't want to talk but I wouldn't have wanted to be alone either. I just needed Robbie to do exactly what he was doing, sitting quietly beside me, steering us home.

'It's strange how we went to find out about Molly and we found out something important about Sukey too,' I said eventually, when we were out into open country roads.

'Not so surprising, when you think how the three of them clearly knew each other well.'

'D'you think my dad was involved with them both? I mean, at the same time?'

'It's possible. It was the Summer of Love, after all,' Robbie said wryly. 'Young people were experimenting with casual sex.'

But had it been casual for Molly?

Had I got things the wrong way around? Had my dad loved Molly? But had he screwed around with Sukey, got her pregnant and been forced to do the decent thing? Had the pregnancy forced him to give up Molly and marry Sukey instead? Suddenly, that made everything make so much sense.

It was one thing feeling guilty for ruining my mother's life but it was a different matter entirely, to feel guilty for ruining my father's. Sukey had run off, abandoned her child, abdicated all responsibility, whereas my dad had stuck by me, loved me, cared for me. Even if I was an encumbrance. He'd been such a good dad, a great dad but at what personal cost? What did he sacrifice for my sake? A happy life? Love? 'D'you think free love is a good idea?'

'Genius,' Robbie joked. Then more seriously: 'I doubt it's all it's cracked up to be. It must create all sorts of complications.'

'We should be like our grannies and marry the first boy we ever kissed?' I wasn't really thinking about what I was saying.

'I'm the first boy you kissed, aren't I?'

The memory of that kiss slammed into me, along with the most powerful desire to repeat it.

'You know very well that you are,' I said, struggling to breathe normally. Did he want to re-stake his claim? Despite everything, the thought made me ridiculously happy. A kiss from him, might just make everything all right. Don't go there, I told myself. Life was already messy enough.

'Had many kisses since then?' he inquired, sliding a glance in my direction as he turned the wheel.

I had to laugh. 'None of your business.'

'Lots then, huh?'

'A fair share. I wasn't counting.' None of them counted anyway.

I'd had a few relationships since Robbie but nothing serious, on my part at least. One boy, Andy, who I'd met at an evening course at Sheffield Art College, took me to Paris for a weekend in Spring and started dropping hints about marriage. I'd ended it there and then. I'd never said I love you to anyone else, though both Andy and Matthew Redfearn had said it to me.

'And you?' I asked Robbie. 'How many girls?'

'Ohh, dozens.'

'Haha! That's not hard to believe.'

The views of the moors faded away and I was left staring at Robbie's elegant hands on the steering wheel. The simple rightness of it. It felt all wrong, that he was leaving for Scotland again in a few hours.

I gazed out of the windows as we entered Chatsworth. February could be wild in Derbyshire and also, extraordinarily beautiful. The white frosted fields and river beneath Paine's Bridge were tinged a pretty pink by the winter sunset. Moody skies and twinkling lights in the stables.

We were silent for a while longer, until Robbie said: 'You need to contact that journalist who wrote about Molly. What was his name?'

'Rick Evans. I will.'

'Have you looked through your dad's stuff? There might be something else connected with her.'

'I need to sort through everything and clear out the cottage but I can't bring myself to do it yet.'

'Let's go over there now?' Robbie suggested. 'We can at least make a start.'

'OK.'

Robbie drove over to the Farm Shop and came out with

two rustic ploughman's sandwiches, packaged in brown paper. He dropped one in my lap.

'Thanks.'

He unwrapped his and bit into it, waving it towards mine. 'Eat up.'

'I'll save it till later. I'm not really hungry.'

Opening the front door and stepping into my dad's cottage, required as much effort as pushing through a brick wall, was as painful as climbing over barbed-wire and for a moment, I couldn't go any further.

Robbie touched my shoulder. 'I know this must be really tough, Honey.'

I stood just inside, paralysed. 'That's an understatement. I'd rather be anywhere but here.'

These were the rooms where I grew up, where my dad lived for over thirty years. Where my mother had also lived for ten years.

With leaden legs, I headed up the stairs to Dad's bedroom, tried to ignore the unmade bed, the pillow still indented by the shape of his head, his checked pyjama-bottoms slung over the chair, his well-worn sheepskin slippers by the radiator, car keys, wallet. I dived under the bed, like a child hiding from the bogeyman and retrieved a sort of crate which he'd knocked up from random bits of wood.

I sat with Robbie on the edge of the bed and rifled through the contents: my cycling proficiency certificate, school reports and all the handmade cards I'd ever given to my dad. Cards for Father's Day, his birthday, Easter, Christmas. I'd designed some myself: a pop-up cake, 3D butterflies. Further down were the ones I'd made at primary school: the usual egg cartons cut up to make daffodil trumpets, cotton wool for bunny tails and snowmen.

'Your mum helped me to make some of them. I can't believe he saved them all.'

Delving deeper, I came to letters and postcards from before I was born, which I put aside to read later. Near the very bottom was a flimsy square of pale-pink paper. A ticket to the Festival of the Flower Children at Woburn Abbey. It was headed: By Kind Permission of His Grace the Duke of Bedford and listed the bands on the line-up: The Kinks, Small Faces, Eric Burdon. *Plus many other stars.* And the DJs: John Peel, Tommy Vance.

'It's like an artefact from a time machine,' Robbie said. 'Wonder why he saved it?'

'Because he went there with Molly and Sukey? Because something important happened there?' But it was not what I'd been looking for. 'I thought he kept the family papers up here too. Maybe downstairs.'

I headed for the teak veneered sideboard in the living room and rummaged through the three drawers. Meanwhile, Robbie fetched a black bin-bag into which we stuffed a rubble of ancient utility bills, receipts, bus tickets and old takeaway menus. Underneath all of that, I found the battered manilla folder. 'It might as well be stamped Top Secret. I always knew I wasn't allowed to look at anything in here, on pain of death or no ice cream for a month.'

'Now's your chance.'

Kneeling on the floor, the papers fanned out, I found my parents' marriage certificate. The wedding had taken place two months before I was born. So there was the proof. No doubt about it, Sukey and John had been forced to marry. This was a time when women were supposed to wed in virginal white with unblemished consciences but

Sukey's must have had been different. The dates meant that hers had been a shotgun wedding. I never knew that 'til now.

I put the certificate aside and sifted through the rest of the papers until I found my own birth certificate. My father's occupation was recorded as farm labourer. When it came to my mother, Sukey, maiden name Miller, there was no mention of an occupation. I had been born too early in the century for birth certificates to record a mother's work, but in any case, Sukey hadn't had time to carve out a career for herself. Her plans and ambitions would all have been thwarted by pregnancy and she'd been bitterly resentful ever since. What else was there to know?

I pushed the papers back inside the folder, shoved it back in the cupboard. Perhaps I stood up too fast but my head swam and I put my hand against the wall to steady myself.

Robbie's expression was full of concern. 'You OK?'

'I should have eaten that sandwich.'

'Told you so.'

I looked into his eyes, so kind and knowing and I felt again, the jolt of connection that had always been there between us. I knew he still loved me and that I still loved him and at that moment, it seemed like the one good, clear and simple truth that I could cling on to. 'Hold me?'

I stepped into the circle of his arms and he wrapped them around me. I could feel the fast beating of his heart as he cradled the back of my head. I pushed my face against the column of his neck, the soft, bare skin and I breathed in the outdoorsy scent of him, the clean, soap-powdery smell of his t-shirt. I clutched it. 'I've missed you, so much,' I murmured.

'I've missed you too.'

'I've tried so hard not to think about you. But I have

thought about you, pretty much every day, in one way or another.'

'Same,' he said.

I drew back so that I could see his face. 'Really?'

'Really.'

'I wondered where you were, what you were doing.'

'Same.'

'There were so many things I wanted to tell you, talk to you about.'

'Same,' he said once again.

I put my hands on either side of his hips, all the while holding his gaze, as if his eyes were guiding stars. He looked wary but not unwelcoming and I pressed my mouth against his. Our lips touched, neither of us moved and there was a moment filled with the possibility of what might happen next. But nothing did happen. Robbie's body was rigid and his mouth was unyielding. It was like kissing a statue.

I flinched, mortified, my hands dropping to my sides. 'What's wrong?'

'This is wrong,' he said. 'Here. Now. When you're upset.'

'You'd be taking advantage of me?' I wanted to laugh. 'Is that what you mean? I'm not a kid anymore. I'm thirty-three and in any case, I don't mind.'

'I mind.'

It would be untrue to say that I'd never felt so humiliated and rejected in all my life because I had felt those precise emotions before and this time I slammed the door in their face. 'Then what are you doing here, exactly?' I put up my hand, palm facing forward, like a police officer stopping traffic. 'Actually. Don't bother answering that.'

'Silva...'

'No need to spell it out. I get it. You were just being

helpful, a good friend, for old time's sake. Well thanks for that but I can manage on my own.'

'This isn't the right time…'

'It never is for us,' I said bitterly. 'Oh, just go away.'

'If that's what you want?'

'It is,' I said firmly. *It's not. Don't listen to me.*

'I'll call you later.'

'No need.'

I watched him walk from the room, heard his footsteps in the hall, the front door opening and then softly closing and I felt like I couldn't breathe. I couldn't get enough air into my lungs. I wanted to run after him, tell him I was sorry, or else run upstairs, fling myself on the narrow single bed I'd slept in until I was eighteen. I had an urge, which felt instinctual, to curl into a ball, like a person shielding themselves from bullets, a wild animal protecting itself from predators.

But I wasn't going to let myself do any of that. No. I'd go to the forge instead, do something constructive, beat hot steel against the anvil for a couple of hours, however long it took. It always made me feel better. Helped me convince myself that I could be strong and resilient in body and spirit. I overrode the voice of caution in my head, warning that fire and heavy tools didn't mix with grief and anger.

Before I left, I grabbed the ticket to the Festival of the Flower Children, slipped it into my pocket, wondering, just briefly, how Molly, John and Sukey ended up there.

CHAPTER TWENTY-FOUR
MOLLY - 1967

There's an old stone barn on John's dad's farm and there, Molly sits crosslegged, in her velvet paisley print bellbottoms and white lacy blouse, her guitar cradled in her lap. Apart from a few stalks of hay, poking through the velvet into the backs of her thighs, she feels perfectly comfortable and at ease. Piebald Jacob sheep are grazing in the field outside, the clotted golden sunlight is streaming into the lofty barn. Dancing dust motes spangle the air, creating a fairytale magic, scented with summer countryside smells and the patchouli oil that Molly is wearing. She only wears Shalimar, the exotic perfume John bought for her, on special occasions. Whenever she catches a waft of that fragrance in the future, she knows it's going to remind her of him, of this summer and of what it feels like, to be in love for the very first time, how it feels to be seventeen, the turmoil of excitement and impatience. Sometimes, there is so much going on inside her, she can barely breathe.

John has slung the microphone cable over the low,

wooden tie beam that runs the length the barn and the huge Sony reel-to-reel tape recorder is standing on a wooden crate. 'Ready when you are, Babe,' he says, his finger on the button of the tape-deck.

Molly strums the opening chords of *The Runaway Lovers*, starts to sing. She sings the whole song straight through, note perfect, while Johnny watches the lights and levels go up and down on the tape machine. Old songs and new tech.

Henry's wrestled to the ground, and with poor Clara's desperate cries
A knife is drawn across his throat; her love, her husband dies.
Then turning on this girl so dear, in one swift axe blow she too fell
Oh how good grace and justice slumbered in that dreadful dell.
Dark and darker grows the sky, through the dale the whirlwind howls
On its head the black cloud lows where hard the grey rock growls

As soon as that song is done, She goes straight into another ballad called, *Died for Love*.

Over yonder hill, there is an old house
Where my true loves goes and sits himself down
Takes another fresh girl on his knee
Now don't you think that's a grief to me
A grief, a grief I'll tell you for why
Because she has more gold than I
She lay down and she closed her eyes
She closed her eyes no more for to rise

The song tells of a betrayed girl, left to brood over the faithlessness and the transiency of love, to sigh for death to heal her heartbreak. It is a very old song, yet the emotions on Molly's face are raw and real.

'That's the saddest song I've ever heard,' John says, when she reaches the end. He sounds close to tears and she's amazed that her song, her voice, has the power to move him like that. The song is sung from the point of view of a girl who falls pregnant and then dies of a broken heart, when her lover runs off with another, richer girl. 'I hope you never get to know half of what that poor girl felt,' John says softly.

Molly doesn't tell him that young as she is, she sometimes feels as if she's experienced a lifetime of pain and shame, several lifetimes even, as if she's somehow inherited those heavy burdens, along with her voice. Sometimes she feels as if she has no skin. She feels pierced by daggers that nobody else knows have even been thrown. 'Can you play the songs back for me?'

'Sure, Babe.'

It's the first time Molly has ever heard herself sing and she doesn't sound at all the way she sounds in her own head. She wants to sound like Shirley Collins on *Folk Roots, New Roots*. Or like Joni Mitchell. But she doesn't sound like Shirley or Joni. 'The phrasing is wrong on the second verse,' she says with a frown.

'Is it?' John asks. 'Sounded perfect to me.'

She tries to be objective, to listen to herself as she'd listen to any other singer. She needs to work on the phrasing. Practise. Improve. She's prepared to accept that this is as good as she can do right now and it's OK, maybe more than OK. 'You think it'll work then? You really think the organisers of the festival will want to put me on the bill?'

John flops down beside her on the hay, leans back on his elbows and looks up at her, admiration shining in his eyes. 'If they don't, then they don't know great music when they hear it. You sound every bit as good as Joan Baez. Better. '

'You're too kind.'

'I mean it, Moll. You must know it yourself, that you're good?'

'I suppose deep down inside, I've always thought I'd be someone. When I was little, I was going to be a great ballerina or a painter. But maybe every little girl feels that way.'

'I'm not sure they do.'

'Now I've got my sights set on John Peel playing my record on the *Perfumed Garden*. My gran is still hoping I'll give it all up and do something normal; be a secretary or something.'

'But you won't.'

'I won't.'

'You've big dreams.'

'They're not dreams. They're goals.'

He laughs. 'Brilliant.'

'I just want to stand on stage and sing. Earn enough to buy clothes and a nice little house. And I'm prepared to work my butt off.'

'I know you are, Moll.'

She frowns and then rubs the frown away. 'My teachers all think I'm lazy, a daydreamer. But I'm not lazy. I just hate school. They teach you what to think, not how to think.'

'I never thought of it like that. I don't think anyone could squash the drive I see in you, Moll. Nobody will stand in your way. And you mustn't let them. You have an amazing gift, an amazing voice. The voice of an angel.'

She runs a stalk of hay slowly down the bridge of his nose to his mouth, then stretches herself out beside him, languid as a Persian cat. 'But I am no angel,' she murmurs.

'Glad to hear it.'

'If I do get to go to the festival, you'll have to come as my manager or producer, or something.'

'I'll happily be your something.' He reaches out to disentangle another hay stalk from her hair, then coils the lock around his finger. 'But I'd like to be your everything.' He holds her eyes, says tentatively. 'Maybe your husband. One day.'

She lays her finger across John's mouth, wiggles closer to him and she snakes her arm around his neck as he presses his hand into the small of her back. She kisses his mouth, his eyelids, his neck.

Oh, she loves being in love. She loves singing songs about love. Love is what inspires her. Compared to other girls, she's not really promiscuous and she loves weddings, still wants a white dress and a ring on her finger one day; to cook Yorkshire puddings and hang up curtains. All of that. But she's modern and independent and she wants to rewrite all the rules, break some too. A girl with one foot in the fifties and one in the sixties, that's me, Molly thinks. Ideals at war with themselves.

She thinks of her gran and her waste not want not attitude to life. She sees her standing at the cracked Belfast sink in her unpolished lace-up shoes, brushing dirt and slugs off their homegrown spuds before she peels them. Married before she was twenty-one, her life has been hard drudgery all the way, with regimented daily tasks that include scrubbing the front step. Monday is washday, leaving the rest of the week for the sheets and clothes to be dried and ironed. 'All I ever wanted to do was get married and all I wanted to be, was a wife and mother,' she's told Molly countless times. 'Now I just dream of fitted kitchens and fitted carpets and maybe an Electrolux refrigerator, so I'll not have to shop for food every day.'

Personally, Molly would settle for a flushing indoor toilet: the height of luxury. She likes looking through the Universal catalogue her gran keeps by the settee. It's like a book of dreams and she used to cut out pictures of pretty crockery and shiny electric goods, stick them in a scrapbook. She wants her own life to be very different to her grandmother's.

So she'd better not get married, at least not until she's made something of her life.

CHAPTER TWENTY-FIVE

SILVA - 2002

'How's she doing, Mr Brightmore?'

I opened one eye, saw that the young woman who'd spoken was wearing a blue nurse's uniform. Behind her was a plastic curtain that looked like the curtains around a hospital bed.

I felt a hand holding mine. Whose hand? Mr Brightmore, the nurse had called him. Must be my dad then. Only my dad was dead. I must be dreaming or maybe I'd died too. But the hand felt so warm and real. If I was dreaming, then it was such a lovely dream, despite the throbbing pain in my head, and I didn't want to wake up.

'Silva, can you hear me?' That was definitely not my dad's voice.

With a supreme effort, I opened both eyes.

Robbie. He was sitting on a moulded, grey plastic chair by the bed, a beeping monitor behind him. My body was covered by a pale-blue waffle blanket and on top of the blanket, Robbie's hand was holding my hand, which had a cannula stuck in it. But. He was not Mr Brightmore. He was not supposed to be here.

'You're supposed to be on an aeroplane,' I tried to say but my tongue was furred and my jaw hurt too much, a bruising ache that wrapped itself around the inside of my skull.

'Ah, you're back with us,' said the young, blonde nurse. She was friendly and capable and athletically built, with big dimples and strong shoulders, like an Olympic swimmer or champion rower. She checked the watch pinned to her uniform. 'When did she come round, Mr Brightmore?'

Why did she keep calling Robbie by my father's name? What was going on?

'She woke up about ten minutes ago,' Robbie said, as if it was the most miraculous event.

'Wish I had a husband as devoted as yours,' called the skinny, crinkly-faced old lady in the next bed. 'Sitting there for hours on end, watching over you while you sleep. How long have you two been married?'

'Not long,' Robbie said, ignoring my look of utter confusion.

Had I lost my memory? Had I married Robbie and forgotten all about it. How tragic was that? To forget my own wedding day. But if we were married, I'd be Mrs Nightingale. He was very forward-thinking and egalitarian and all that but surely, he'd not have taken my name instead of the other way round. Would he?

The nurse quickly wrote something on a chart, hanging at the bottom of my bed and said she'd be back later.

'I heard you say you're from Chatsworth,' the old lady said. 'Lucky you. My husband proposed to me at Chatsworth. It's our happy place. Is that where you popped the question too, lad?'

'It is,' Robbie said.

'Ohh, whereabouts?'

He stroked his thumb across the back of my hand. 'I took her to the top of the cascade,' he said softly. 'The sunlight on the water was like a river of gold and we slipped behind the veil of water, into the little stone temple, and I asked her to be my wife.'

'My, my,' sighed the old lady. 'How romantic.'

It is, I thought. Oh, it is. How could I have forgotten?

'I was about to check in at the airport, when Freya called to say you were in A&E,' Robbie said to me, when we were in his car. 'I had to think on my feet. Unless I said I was your husband, I knew they'd not let me see you.'

It all came hurtling back to me. After making a fool of myself, trying to kiss him and then telling him to go away, I'd gone to the smithy. I'd turned the music up loud, really loud. I'd worked like a demon, by the light of the burning coals, for a solid three hours, until my arms were aching and weak, my muscles trembling with fatigue. All I'd had to eat all day, was a couple of bananas and digestive biscuits and I felt lightheaded but I kept going, pushing through the pain, both physical and emotional.

I couldn't think about Robbie getting on a plane to go back to Scotland. How had I let him leave on such bad terms? Again? What was the matter with me? What an idiot I was. I'd banged the hammer, in time to the accusing voice in my head. Idiot. Idiot. Idiot.

Chunks of the past swirled around inside me, a caldera of confusion and that's where the tears came from, not from my eyes ,but from a pit of pain in my soul.

Robbie, I love you. Don't go. Help me. My heart hurts.

I imagined Catrina, waiting at the airport arrivals to greet him. I imagined him dumping his rucksack on the ground to hug her, kissing her the way he used to kiss me, smiling at her the way he used to smile at me. Telling her all about his trip, the way he used to talk to me.

I brought down the hammer, heard my own voice. *Oh just go away.*

The hammer nearly hit my thumb. I wasn't concentrating. I was weak and tired. I swore loudly, sucked at my thumb. I knew I needed to stop right now, have something to eat, go home to bed.

I fastened the steel tube in the vice, wrenched the handle tight. It jammed and the metal tube was suddenly transformed into a lever which whacked back, hit me smack on the jaw. My neck jerked and I felt my brains rattle in my skull. I heard someone scream, knew it was myself. Black blotches floating in front of my eyes. Blinding pain. I touched my cheek, took my hand away, to see it was covered in blood.

Once I was discharged into Robbie's care, we drove into Chatsworth, where the fading embers of the sun combined with a bright moon, to give the House an indigo glow that was unbelievably romantic.

'That story about how you proposed to me? Where d'you get that from?'

'It's how I've always imagined I'd do it.'

A beat of silence.

I turned my head to look at him. 'Do what?'

'It's how I always imagined I'd propose to you.'

I rested against the headrest, let him drive to Edensor, stop the car outside my cottage and turn off the engine.

Only then did I say: 'I would have said yes, by the way. Just so you know.'

CHAPTER TWENTY-SIX

R obbie stayed with me for a week, sleeping at night on the sofa, sitting on my bed for most of the day with Tijou curled up on the duvet between us.

We chatted for hours and hours. He told me stories about the singers, the gypsies and travellers, the sailors and shepherds, who'd shared their rich repertoires of traditional songs with him over the years. The famous Stewarts of Blairgowrie and the Copper family of Rottingdean in Sussex, who celebrated nature in their romantic plough songs and old land worker's ballads. He told me about an old lady in her nineties, called Penny Black, who grew up under tarpaulin in a bell-tent with ten sisters, had a staggering memory for lyrics and verses. 'She knew more old songs than anyone else alive today and served them up with homemade scones, jam and butter, accompanying herself by tapping cardboard boxes.' Then there was Luke Connors, a former trawler captain from Hull, who sang saucy sea-shanties. An old, old man known as The Memory, who Robbie had watched reciting his family genealogy, to a young boy sitting by his bedside, repeating back to him the names of their ancestors, word for word, without taking any notes.

'That's how the songs are handed down,' Robbie said. 'Neither could read or write. They're the last of a kind.'

I could tell how dearly he loved time spent with these colourful characters and I got a sense of what a privilege it was to hear their ancient songs, sung as they'd been sung centuries ago, an unbroken connection to the past.

I told him how I got the job at Chatsworth.

'Bea said to me at the interview: "If you know the history of something, then you'll love it more and treat it with more care." She handed me a pottery bowl, asked me, "What do you make of it?" She told me later, that it was incredible how much you can tell about a person, just by the way they handle the bowl. Some treat it like it's cheap crockery you could sling in a dishwasher, whereas other people are more respectful and notice small details about it, are interested in its craft and its history. Bea stressed to me right at the beginning, how the housekeeping team are not just responsible for cleaning but for the conservation of one of the most important, private art collections in Europe.'

'So what did you do with the bowl?' Robbie asked.

'I said it looked Georgian, which it was. And I said porcelain is a bit like people. Some people at least. If you don't care for it properly, it becomes crazed.'

Robbie laughed. 'What Bea said about how knowing the history of something, makes you treat it with more care, I think that's also true of people.'

'Maybe.'

Robbie made Tijou get up and go for a walk and when he came back, Lizzie came round and he made a pot of tea for us all. He made me endless pots of tea, ran me hot baths and brought me bowls of tomato soup and toast. Gave me a running commentary on the colour of my bruise.

'A lovely shade of yellow and green it is now,' he informed me on the fourth day. 'Bit like lichen.'

'I'll give you a bruise to match, if you're not careful.'

He did some more research and found a review of Molly's album in *NME*.

'It's like a love letter,' he said, before he read it out loud. '"Molly Marrison possesses a rare and remarkable talent and this is destined to be a landmark album, a masterwork. In her hands, these songs, by turns plaintive, sensual and grave, are filled with haunting grandeur. It's as if the doors of her heart have been flung wide and she is inviting the whole world in. Close your eyes, and you're transported to a sunlit field. Molly is standing on stage. There is dirt and wildflowers beneath her feet, stardust above her head. You might be alone, but it feels as if you're surrounded by thousands of people. Yet the songs challenge you, take you inside the darkest corners of your heart. Molly is a child of the sixties and also timeless."' He put down the photocopied sheet of paper. 'She recorded a session for John Peel too, apparently. He was a big fan.'

'You've been busy,' I said. 'While I've been lazing about for a week.'

'Are you sure you're ready to go back to work tomorrow?' he asked, seriously.

'We're opening in five days, so it's all hands on deck.' I made myself ask: 'What about you?'

'I need to get back to my own work.'

'Oh.' I felt as if I'd been hit again.

'I thought I might talk to Freya's Sam, about organising the sound recordings I've collected,' he said cautiously. 'See if we can get some funding; create a proper archive.'

He was as full of dreams and schemes as ever but this seemed different. 'Great idea,' I said, trying not to get my hopes up. Sam lived at Chatsworth, so did that mean Robbie would be sticking around for a while?

Now I was feeling better and my jaw was working properly, so I could speak without sounding like I was drunk, he gave me the phone so I could ring the offices of the *Chesterfield Star*, the newspaper that had carried the story about Molly Marrison's disappearance. I spoke to Stella Price, the editor's secretary, who offered to contact Rick Evans, the staff reporter who'd written the piece about Molly, all those years ago.

'He's retired but I can certainly pass on your address, ask him to get in touch and tell you what he knows.'

Next morning as I walked to work, I passed through a hive of activity. The hundred and five acres of world-famous gardens were still being spruced up, an annual challenge for the Duke's twenty gardeners. Robbie's dad, in a bottle green fleece, emblazoned with the gold Chatsworth logo, was shovelling compost while talking to the Duchess, who'd come to inspect.

'On a morning like this, one can't believe how lucky one is, to be alive and in Derbyshire,' I heard her say.

Ben, in matching green and gold fleece, was busy with a rake, spreading fresh gravel on the path by the Orangery. Meanwhile Bill was busy burning foliage in a metal bin. He was in his eighties, technically retired years ago, but he liked to keep his hand in as a volunteer.

'Morning,' he said, giving me a merry wave. 'How are you?'

'On the mend, thanks, Bill.'

Two of the housemen were up ladders doing something with the guttering.

Inside the House there were similar levels of activity. Two of the curators were hefting an unwieldy gilt-framed oil painting up the great stairs, Bea was dusting tiny pieces of china with a tiny brush. Matthew Redfearn was in the dining room with Hector, laying the thirty-foot-long table, in a way that recalled a historic moment in Chatsworth's history, when Queen Victoria experienced her first formal dinner here, as a thirteen-year-old child. The white linen tablecloth was decorated with sparkling silver and pink Bohemian glass. There was a charged air of expectation. The table all set for a ghostly dinner party, for guests who would never arrive. Wearing blue latex gloves, Hector was measuring the distance between the silver candelabra and place settings with a ruler.

'Hey, Hector, that glass looks half a millimetre out,' I called.

He'd admitted to me that he felt really uncomfortable if he didn't get the distances absolutely accurate and he looked really quite worried, until he realised I was having him on. 'Very funny.'

I headed to the sculpture gallery, where I'd be working with Annie Ollerernshaw for most of the day.

We worked from the top to bottom, using scaffolding to reach up to the skylights and cornices and then dusting the sculptures with brushes. I loved the sculpture gallery. It was like being in Italy, such a peaceful and serene space, yet full of echoes. I loved working with Annie too. She had a wicked sense of humour and the dirtiest laugh. Her hair was a pretty mixture of gold and silver and she turned up every morning, proudly wearing the gold watch, which marked twenty-five years of service. After ten years, women were given a Blue John necklace, backed with an engraving of the Cavendish snake, symbol of Chatsworth. I treasured my necklace, almost as much as the tiny Blue John pendant that Robbie had once given to me, but which I never now wore.

'There're beautiful, aren't they,' Annie commented, as she moved on to the statue of Mars. 'Such gorgeous bodies. I shouldn't think you'd find many like these in real life.'

I was fascinated by the statues when I was a young girl, experiencing a sweet flush of heat, as I wondered if real men looked like that when they were naked. If Robbie Nightingale looked like that.

Annie disappeared behind Mars, with a girlish giggle. 'I do love polishing his bottom.'

I laughed. 'No wonder it's shining.'

When Mars had been cleaned, we covered him with a dust sheet, making him look like a ghost. When the gallery was filled with shrouded statues, the effect was haunting.

I worked a couple of extra hours, had no interest in going back to the smithy. Since my argument with Robbie and then the accident, I'd been totally lacking in motivation and inspiration. Anyway, any spare time I had over the next weeks, was needed to sort through the contents of my dad's cottage.

Standing in my dad's living room, I realised just what a long and painful process it was going to be. He didn't actually have that much stuff but I needed to go through everything, room by room, cupboard by cupboard. I wished, as I'd never wished before, that I had a brother or sister to help me. That I was not an only child.

I emptied out the sideboard first, then the bookcase, then took down the pictures from the walls. I felt like the curator of a curious archeological dig, piecing together fragments, in order to understand a past life. There were the books my dad had read or intended to read but now never would. Pictures he'd chosen to hang up, just because he'd liked the look of them or because they were linked to some special event in his life, which I could never ask him about now. How could I throw any of this stuff out? How could I keep it all?

I tackled the kitchen next, then his bedroom. Everything looked so forlorn, a whole life, boiled down to a few chipped pots and pans, frayed blankets and towels, cupboards with creaky doors and shirts worn soft with age. They were not even good enough for the charity shop, fit only for the skip, yet even the poorest object was rich in memories. By nature, I wasn't a hoarder but I did attach great sentimental value to certain objects. There were hundreds of decisions to make about what to keep and what to throw out and it was exhausting. Every ornament had its own history, like a key to a memory I feared would be lost, if the object were discarded. I picked things up, put them down again. Cleaning up and clearing out usually made me feel lighter, refreshed, more in control of everything but now I felt hopelessly indecisive. I put something in a big, black, bin bag and then I immediately wanted it back.

The worst part was clearing out the shed. If my dad's spirit lingered anywhere, it would be there but there was nothing of him in that place, where he'd spent such long, relatively contented hours. He was gone and all he'd left behind, were abandoned tools and a heap of unanswered questions.

I packed up half a dozen boxes to take back to my

cottage, where I spread an odd assortment of objects on my bed. They really were like museum pieces in a family history. It was like attempting to assemble a jigsaw puzzle of a thousand pieces, delivered without a picture to indicate where any of the pieces should go.

Some of the items I'd brought back because I knew my dad would definitely want me to have them. A pearl-handled knife that had belonged to my grandmother, Ivy. Other things I'd salvaged for myself. His electric screwdriver was sure to come in handy. He'd always loaned me his tools. It looked incongruous against my lacy white duvet and cushions.

For about the fifth time, I picked up an old cream-coloured gravy boat, its glaze crackled from being over-heated too often. It reminded me of toad in the hole, one of my dad's favourites. I'd made it for him practically every week, like shepherd's pie. It hit me afresh: I'd never do that again. I'd never cook him a meal. I was never going to see him again.

I clutched the gravy boat to my heart as my body was wracked with sobs and tears poured from my eyes. My nose ran and I couldn't breathe. I'd not cried that way since I was a child.

I used to try to imagine what it would be like when I lost my dad but I'd always assumed that by the time it actually happened, I'd be resigned, better prepared. He'd be old and ailing and I'd be older too, wiser and more self-reliant. But this was all wrong, the timing was off. My dad was too young to die and I was too young to lose him. I didn't feel ready or mature enough to deal with any of it. Not on my own. I had no choice though, did I? Just had to get on with it. I reached for the box of tissues on my bedside table, wiped my eyes, blew my nose, pulled myself together. At least that decided it. The gravy boat was staying.

I went downstairs to make tea and was confronted by the Blue John candle-vase. It didn't look as if it belonged in the same room or even the same life as the crackled gravy boat but of course, it had belonged to Sukey, not to Dad.

The telephone was ringing and I dashed to the hallway, snatched up the receiver.

'Hi,' Robbie said.

'Hi.' The one voice I needed to hear. It was like sliding into hot, scented bathwater. All the tension left my body and everything was suddenly all right. I wasn't on my own at all. The sound of his voice instantly made me feel at home.

'Everything OK?' I asked him.

'I just wanted to ask; how was your day?'

So sweet of him to remember what I'd said, about having nobody to ask me how my day had been. I told him: 'It's been busy and pretty shitty, to be honest.'

'Come for a drink with me then.'

'So how long will all that take?' I asked, when we were ensconced in an alcove in the Devonshire Arms, half-way down a bottle of red wine. He'd filled me in on his discussions with Sam, about the archive project and making a radio documentary series, a montage of stories and songs.

'Not sure.'

He talked, too, about making a new album of old songs.

'When will you go back to Scotland?'

'Not sure,' he said again. 'Not for a while.'

'How will Catrina feel about that?'

'To tell you the truth, I don't think she'll mind too

much.' He picked up the beer mat, turned it over and put it down again. 'When I cancelled my flight to come to the hospital, she told me not to bother coming back.'

'Robbie, no! That's awful. It's all my fault.'

'It is,' he agreed.

'I'm so, so sorry.'

He looked at me quizzically. 'Are you? Honestly?'

'I'm sorry, if you're sorry.'

'I'm relieved, I think.'

I wanted to cheer, dance round the room, throw my arms round him and just kiss him.

He reached for the wine bottle, topped up my glass, then his own. 'So.' He touched his foot against mine under the table. 'This means you're stuck with me for a while longer.'

'That's a nuisance.'

CHAPTER TWENTY-SEVEN

The Saturday in mid-March, when Chatsworth opened for the first day of the season, happened to be the first day of spring sunshine, clear and warm, sparkling with the promise of summer.

Opening day was always a happy day. A relief, when at long last the deep clean was done, the mad rush was over and everything was ready and looking lovely, the House and gardens at their magnificent best with hosts of golden daffodils, swathing the grassy lawns around the canal pond. The restaurant ovens were heated and the gift shops were full of wonderful new items, including signed copies of Duchess Deborah's autobiography, which were on display in pride of place.

Lizzie's mum, Megan, was all spruced up herself in her head guide's uniform, of blue pinstriped skirt and blazer. She was busy in the Painted Hall, giving her morning briefing to the sixty room guides. Many were retired, old enough to be her parents but they respected her nonetheless.

'We've five coaches coming in today,' Megan told me. 'All arriving when the gates open at eleven.'

The Duke and Duchess stood at the top of the great stairs, to welcome the first visitors through the door and shake their hands. Then they gave an interview to the local TV station, talking into a camera positioned on the catwalk, looking down over the Painted Hall. 'I want people to come here and see that it's the most amazing place,' the Duchess said. 'We're so proud of it and just want to share it.'

Which brought its problems. Megan had to do battle with one of the young Japanese tourists, who was wandering around with a massive rucksack on his back, despite being asked several times to remove it, so he'd not accidentally knock anything.

'Drives me mad,' Megan complained. 'It's not a museum but someone's house. Show respect. You know?'

An American lady in retro spectacles stopped me to ask about the Veiled Vestal Virgin and I explained how she was inspired by a discovery in Pompeii.

On my way out, I overheard one of the visitors cheerily say to his wife: 'Always something new to see, isn't there?'

It made me go home happy too, feeling so proud to be a part of such an amazing team. But I'd not be needed now until tomorrow morning.

I said hello to Tijou, kicked off my shoes, picked up the envelope that was waiting on the doormat, the address typed on an old-fashioned typewriter. I'd almost given up hoping for a response from the journalist who'd written about Molly but now, at long last, here it was.

Short and sweet. Just a single paragraph. Rick Evans had written to say that sadly, he didn't know anything more about Molly, than what I'd read. However, he advised me to make contact with Karl Texas, who'd written several stories about Molly, in the *Melody Maker* and *Folk Roots*. He wrote that he was her first and most loyal champion in the press, throughout her brief career and had researched the original piece about her disappearance, on which Rick had based his own news item.

'Karl's a top bloke,' Rick Evans said, when I called the telephone number he'd given to me, urging me to get in touch if I had any further questions. 'He played a key role in the folk revival. Besides being a music journalist, he's a singer and a songwriter himself, a poet and a peace campaigner. A colourful character and there's nobody who knows more about Molly Marrison, than Karl. Think he still writes for *Folk Roots*, so he should be easy enough to track down.'

I put down the phone, immediately picked it up again, dialled Robbie's number. I could have waited until he called me because he phoned or called round most days now, but I didn't want to wait.

CHAPTER TWENTY-EIGHT

Next Monday, a meeting had been called for midday in Bea's office, to discuss the calendar for the coming months. I had grown up appreciating, from Dad, how big, old buildings like Chatsworth soaked up money. So throughout the year, a variety of events were put on to raise funds, to pay for the upkeep of the House and garden, all the essential restorations and repairs. Chatsworth was a glittering show that never ended, bigger than any theatre production and everyone had their role to play. The textiles team, housekeeping staff and collections department, had all been summoned.

There was a shortage of chairs and people had squashed onto the window seat and perched on the coffee table. I'd nabbed an upturned wooden crate. Coffee, pastries and French fancies were arranged on patterned china plates and everyone tucked in and chatted amongst themselves, before Bea opened up the discussion.

First, there was the flower festival in May, closely and stressfully followed by the horse trials. There was also the

Duke and Duchess's 60th wedding celebrations to think about this year. There was to be a lavish party on the Salisbury lawn, themed on the 1940s, when the Duke and Duchess had married. The events team were scouring the country to invite other couples who'd married the same year as them. Everyone was to be in wartime costume, including half the Chatsworth staff.

'Put your thinking caps on,' Bea ordered us. 'We also need a theme for this Christmas. Something a bit different. Any ideas?'

It was early spring and the fields across the estate were filling with skippy lambs, keeping farm manager, Abe and a couple of veterinary students, very busy but Christmas, when Chatsworth's halls were well and truly decked, took months to plan. It was only our second year of opening for Christmas. Until last year, the House and garden always closed after the horse trials in October and didn't reopen until the following Easter. It was the outbreak of foot and mouth disease, last February, that changed everything. The epidemic meant that the countryside was effectively closed to visitors until the summer, which had a huge impact from the loss of visitor revenue for Chatsworth and for local businesses. After much debate with staff, the Duke decided to extend our season, stay open until Christmas and introduce Christmas displays in the hope that it would encourage visitors and help the local economy.

There had been a meeting with the Duchess and colleagues from the garden, textiles and housekeeping teams, to decide what we could do in such a short time. It was a huge team effort. The gardeners made and dressed the garlands, the housekeeping team wired and sorted thousands of baubles, joiners prepared frameworks to be fitted around the fireplaces, the engineers sorted out the attachments for garlands and other decorations, the electricians took charge of safe wiring for all the tree lights and the textile team dressed snowy scenes.

The idea of only opening for one year had to be re-thought, since we had nearly a hundred thousand visitors through the door, all eager to know what we were going to do the following year. The extra income for the charity had made such a difference to what we were able to achieve with regard to restoration and conservation and all agreed we had to open again this year.

'How about the Christmas story?' suggested Lara, sounding unsure.

'Or Christmas stories, plural?' I said. 'A different room for a different tale. A Christmas Carol, The Nutcracker, Narnia, The Elves and the Shoemaker?'

'Great idea,' Bea exclaimed.

'I can be the Snow Queen,' Lizzie offered gleefully.

'Or the shoemaker even,' I teased.

Bea laughed. 'And since you're so creative and practical, Silva, we could put you in charge of set design?'

'All right,' I said. I dropped my head into my hand. 'What have I let myself in for?'

Lizzie patted my back. 'We have faith in you.'

It was just what I needed. I wasn't looking forward to a Christmas without my dad's endless supply of awful cracker jokes. *What does Santa do with fat elves? He sends them to an Elf Farm. What's a dog's favourite carol? Bark, the herald angels sing.* I'd either have found Molly by autumn or abandoned the search, so I'd need something else to keep me occupied.

'We could get hold of some fake snow and decorate the trees with paper snowflakes,' I suggested, remembering that Christmas when I was ten years old. 'We could ask all the children on the estate to make some.'

'Not just the children,' Lara protested. 'I love making snowflakes.'

~

When the meeting finished, I called *Folk Roots* and left a message for Karl Texas, who, frustratingly, was away for a couple of weeks.

I went to the gym and then headed up to the forge for the first time in a long time. I put the kettle on, along with some music. I'd given the record player back to Jasmine but I'd bought one of my own, to keep here. I'd been playing Molly's album over and over, every day, so that even when the record wasn't spinning on the turntable, the haunting songs were still spinning around in my head. The ebb and flow and sway of the drums and dulcimer. Lyrics that told of what happens, when fairytale romances come to an end. I heard her songs when I went to sleep and when I woke up. I walked around humming them. Ear-worms, Robbie called them. I propped the album cover against the wall, so that Molly's face stared back at me while I worked. She sang as if her heart was in pieces, but it was still a mighty and resilient heart. I'm doing my best to find you, I silently told her. I needed to find her, not just for my dad but also for myself. The songs were old but so intimate, songs of grief and woe, but with a message of survival. They seemed to say that to love is to suffer. It's a battle. It's carnage. I needed to know this woman. I needed to know what happened to her.

Walking home across the park, after the coaches had all left and the fountains had been turned off, I wondered how often Molly had been here. Bea had seen her on the stairs by the theatre and she'd carved her name in the trees. She seemed tantalisingly just out of reach, flitting ahead like a phantom, the corner of her floaty, lacy peasant dress disappearing round a corner, as I tried to follow her. What if I didn't ever catch up with her? I'd feel as if I'd failed my dad and I'd never know how her story ended. I couldn't bear that.

The telephone was ringing as I turned the key in the front door.

'Hello, it's me,' Robbie said.

'Hello me,' I answered, out of breath.

'Sorry, did I make you run?'

'Yeah.'

'So what have you been up to?'

I clutched the phone closer, cradling the handset. 'So here's my current challenge. It's almost summer but I have to find snow.'

'There's plenty in the Highlands. I'll pop back up there and send you a crateful, shall I? I could market it. Snowflakes from Scotland. It could take off.'

'Hmm. I think there's a flaw in that plan somewhere.'

'You think? Shame.'

I took the phone over to the sofa, settled against the cushions with my feet tucked up at the side. We chatted for ages, traded more random stories. Robbie told me about the recordings he'd started editing. Blind Bill Collins, who'd learnt the songs from his uncle round the campfire. 'I sat with him near Loch Lomond, beside a beautiful caravan his father had built himself, but he'd not sung for years, until I asked him,' Robbie said. Then there was Nelly Quinn, who told tales of the old ways, willow pegs, wagons and hawking.

Robbie always liked hearing about the people I worked with too. He said the gardeners and carpenters were like the folk from folk songs. So I brought him up to date with news from Phil, one of the joiners, who was an Elvis lookalike in his spare time. Since the Duchess was a massive Elvis fan, everyone said that's what had landed him the job, never mind his carpentry skills. Then there was Fred, my favourite character of all. One of the elderly room guides, he delighted in greeting each of the foreign visitors in their own language. 'He's fluent in French and German and Russian and Mandarin and now he's teaching himself Arabic, during his tea-breaks.'

'Maybe you could teach yourself to fire-weld. Or maybe Tijou could show you the way?'

'Doubt it very much. He's a spaniel.'

I couldn't see Robbie's face but I knew he was smiling his smile. 'I meant his namesake, Chatsworth's Master Blacksmith.'

'He's been dead two hundred years.'

'Have you had another go?'

'Not for a while.'

'If at first you don't succeed…'

I laughed. 'Thanks for that.'

We ended up discussing a recurring theme in folk songs through the ages, laments of lost love and fickle sweethearts. 'One of the early collectors called them heartoutbursts,' Robbie said.

'I like that word.'

'Me too. It's a great word.'

Over an hour later, when we eventually hung up, the word stayed with me: Heartoutbursts. I loved talking to Robbie every night, going to the pub with him, walking Tijou together. I looked forward all day, to our conversations. But these conversations, which had initially felt like a blessing, were no longer enough for me. We never talked about anything too personal and I was always left feeling dissatisfied. I hung up or hugged him goodbye and it felt like my heart was about to burst with all the things I wanted and needed to say but never did.

My sketchbook was on the kitchen table. I pulled up a chair and drew it towards me, opened it at a fresh page and reached for a pen. I enjoyed reading, cosy crime like Agatha Christie, classic novels and historical romances mostly, but trying to express my feelings on paper made me feel almost as anxious as talking out loud about my feelings. So I didn't stop to think what I was writing, I just let my heart open and release all the things I had, for years, kept locked inside. I let them flow down through my fingers, as if I was designing something, as if I was drawing with words, rather than writing.

Dearest Robbie,

You once called me a Trojan horse and I think it's a pretty good description, to be frank. Even talking to you, sometimes I feel as if there's this wild person trapped inside me. I've always been afraid that if I let that person out, people would be shocked. I'd be unacceptable somehow, too much. Do you know what I mean? So I crush myself down to size, to take up a smaller space, so I fit in.

If you ask me what's wrong, I'll smile and tell you everything's fine. However, that doesn't mean it always is fine. Sometimes, I'm sarcastic simply because I like being sassy but sometimes, it's to mask something that's really upsetting me. If I snipe about trivial things it's usually because of something much deeper that's troubling me, that I'm afraid to admit, in case it makes me seem vulnerable or because I haven't worked it out myself yet.

When I don't touch you, it doesn't mean I don't want to touch you. If I seem cold and uncaring, it's not because I don't care, it's because I care too much. I don't often cry but that doesn't mean that I don't hurt like hell. I send you away, when what I really want to do is hold you tight and never let you go. I want to touch you and taste you but I'd feel so weird saying things like that, unless I've drunk about a gallon of wine!

When you leave, you take a part of me with you. This beautiful place in which we both grew up is so much less beautiful when you are not here. The only person I want beside me in life, is you. It's only ever been you.

All my love always, Silly xxx

CHAPTER TWENTY-NINE

When I eventually spoke to Karl Texas and told him that my late father had asked me to find Molly Marrison, that John had known Molly, might even have been involved with her romantically, Karl jumped at the chance to meet me.

'Whereabouts are you?' He had a deep, gravelly voice that spoke of whisky and cigarettes, rock and roll and late nights.

'I live in the back of beyond,' I smiled. 'Up North. But I'm more than happy to come up to London.'

'By car or train?'

'Train is probably easiest.'

'You'll come into St Pancras Station then. D'you like tea?'

'I love tea.'

'Excellent. In that case, let's meet in the Hansom Lounge of the St Pancras Hotel or the St. Pancras Renaissance Hotel, to give it its la-di-da name. I'm free tomorrow if you are.'

There's something so romantic about train journeys. Even just travelling from Chesterfield to London, I half-imagined myself on the Orient Express. I'd brought a magazine to read but spent most of the time just gazing out of the window, sipping strong coffee from the buffet car. I may be a country girl but I still found the cosmopolitan energy of London exciting and endlessly inspiring and when I stepped off the train, I gazed like a tourist at the intricate iron and glass roof of the station, wishing I had time to sit somewhere and sketch.

The Hansom Lounge was part of the soaring masterpiece of rich red brick and creamy stone. Located in the cobbled driveway of the original Victorian train station, it was a huge, vaulted space with towering traditional archways and modern blue painted girders, conjuring up the glory days of steam. It was welcoming and noisy with plush sofas in taupe and pale-green velvet and low, highly-polished wooden coffee tables, decorated with exotic, long-stemmed purple lupins in tall glass vases.

Karl Texas wrote biographies about rock stars now and with his craggy face, shaggy white hair, and white beard, he looked like an ageing rockstar himself. He was sporting a black wool fedora, black cowboy boots, bootlace tie with Indian eagle motif and various badges, which all marked him out as a rebel and radical.

'My mother took me on my first demonstration when I was seven, against Neville Chamberlain's appeasement of Hitler,' Karl told me with a wry grin. 'As if that doesn't make me sound like a relic.'

I liked him instantly. We made fascinating small talk, after ordering a pot of Earl Grey tea. I had asked him a question about his career and off he went. So much to tell. 'I did publicity for Billy Smart's Circus, then I wrote for a local paper for a while, became a staff reporter at *Melody Maker*. I walked with giants there, interviewed all the greats, Pink Floyd and Frank Zappa, Jim Morrison and Janis Joplin.'

I felt grateful to Molly, for giving me a reason to meet Karl. 'You need to write your own life story,' I told him.

'Argh, most of it could never appear in print,' he chuckled. 'Molly Marrison could have been right up there with the greats,' he added. 'Jeff Bond agreed with me about that.'

'The producer of Molly's album?'

'Oh, he's more than that. It was Jeff who discovered her.'

'Are the two of you in touch? Would he have any idea where she might have gone?'

Karl sucked in his breath, like a builder asked for a quote. 'Molly developed a cult-following after that album. It's stood the test of time and as a result, many people have tried to find her. I actually went up to Castleton myself and asked around, talked to people who'd known her. By all accounts she was a happy child, full of life, free spirited and impetuous. I spoke to one of Molly's primary school teachers. She remembers Molly singing *Away in a Manger*, very sweetly in a school nativity play, going from door-to-door with her dad, singing the old Derbyshire carols. She said Molly was smart but not academic and knew her own mind from an early age. A kindly way of saying she didn't like being told what to do. One of Molly's classmates, a girl called Julie, elaborated: She said Molly hated school, every minute of it. She wanted to kick against authority in general. She was always in hot water, never did her homework on time, didn't pay attention in lessons.' He chuckled.

'There was one story I liked, about how she poured out a jug of custard on a jam roly-poly, then took it to the serving hatch and asked, what's this? The dinner lady told her it was custard and she said, it can't be because there are no lumps in it. She got caught nicking a lipstick from the local shop apparently. She was a bit of a tearaway, wild and wonderful, by all accounts, a force of nature but with a sparkling personality. Julie said Molly was raised by her grandmother, Lavinia, who was very strict but if her gran said 'not under my roof', Molly threatened to find a different roof.'

'She sounds fabulous.'

'Doesn't she just. There was one guy, called Pete, who'd been to what seems to have been her first gig, a sort of gathering of local musicians and music fans in Peak Cavern. Apparently, you could have heard a pin drop while Molly did her floor spot. He said she had an extraordinary voice and she knew how to use it, even then. When she walked into a room, she grabbed everyone's attention. He said she was a go-getter and definitely wanted fame and fortune, so it was inevitable she'd get picked up by a record label. But I guess he would say that, in hindsight. Everyone likes to think they can spot talent. Pete claimed to have had a bit of a fling with her, described how sensual and free she was with her body, like a goddess of love. She liked to smoke and flirt and have a good time. Like a lot of brilliant people, she didn't stick to conventions. They didn't mean much to her, in spite of the fact or because, her upbringing had been fairly conventional.'

'Thanks to her grandmother. Lavinia?'

'She was still alive then but she flatly refused to talk to me.'

'You found Molly's grandmother?'

'Finding her wasn't the hard part. There were plenty of

people to point me in the right direction but getting her to talk to me was a different matter. I explained to her that I was a music journalist, not a ruthless hack but to her mind, we're all the same and not to be trusted. She must have been ancient and she was very frail but I imagine she was a fearsome character, in her day. She spoke very proper, as if she'd learnt how to do it. You know what I mean? The definite impression I got, from everyone, was that Molly had a restrictive childhood, until she saw there was a good time to be had out there and she was determined to have it, to live life to the full.'

'What about Molly's father?'

'I had a very brief conversation with him too, at his door. Charming old fellow. I'd have loved to sit down with a few beers and talk to him all evening. Listening to him speak about his lost daughter was as heartrending as hearing her saddest songs. You could tell he adored her and missed her but bore her no ill will for the great anguish she'd caused. He was no help at all though. But you have your own links to Molly.' Karl leant forward a little, as if he didn't want to miss one word. 'You think she was involved with your dad? Romantically?'

'Maybe.'

'John Brightmore. I have to say, nobody mentioned him.'

'Did they mention anything about Molly having a friend called Sukey?'

He shook his head.

'The three of them went to the Festival of the Flower Children together, I believe and Molly came to see my dad in Chatsworth. I don't know how often. He recently passed away, as I explained and my mother and I are...we are estranged.'

'Just like Molly and her folks maybe?'

'I'd not thought of that, but yes. I can't ask either of my parents anything and I'm stumped.'

'The first rule to follow, when you're trying to track an elusive rock star, is generally to follow the money,' Karl said. 'But Molly's label, Albion Records, were very vague about where royalties from her album were being paid. I guess they would be. It became a treasured rarity among record collectors and bootlegs appeared over the years. Then the master tapes were located and an imprint was reissued, which sold in good numbers but if the record label can't find anyone to pass the money too, they get to keep it. I was given a telephone number for an accountant and I called it and left a message but the next day, the number had been disconnected. I made a kind of spider diagram of all the people involved in Molly's career and I attempted to speak to them all, each and every one but there were so many dead ends and closed doors, in the end I was forced to give up.' He set down his tea-cup. 'Sorry. I'm not being much help.'

'You've been incredibly helpful,' I assured him. 'She's so elusive but I feel that I know her a little better now, thanks to you.'

'I felt like that after I interviewed Jeff Bond,' Karl recalled. 'He told me all about the festival and seeing Molly for the first time on stage. And then of course, Jeff gave me a blow-by-blow account about making the album with her. He said she loved being in the studio just as much as she loved being on stage. It was a wonderful space, mind. I was fortunate enough to hang out there on a couple of occasions. It opened in the sixties, in a renovated milking parlour in Chelsea. Set up by Jeff and his friend Ralph. Jeff liked to tell the story of how they had no money to buy equipment, so they built it all themselves, complete with four-track and mono mixing machines, housed in cast-off consoles from the BBC. What with his electronic wizardry and Ralph's perfect ear, they were credited with creating some of the finest music in Britain. Jeff has always claimed that *Died for Love,* was one of his greatest achievements.'

'D'you know how I could get in touch with him?'

'Argh, you'll be lucky. He moved to New York many moons ago.'

'Can you remember any of what he told you about working with Molly, about the festival and...everything. Anything at all?'

Karl grinned from ear to ear. 'Oh, I can do far better than that.'

'You can?'

'I'm a journalist,' he said proudly. 'A diehard, dyed-in-the-wool, journo. I recorded the whole damn thing. The whole interview. I have it on tape.' He reached down to the floor, retrieved the canvas bag that had been slung over his shoulder when he came in. 'I also always come well-prepared.' He dumped the bag on his lap, rummaged around and produced three cassettes. 'Here you go. Have a listen.'

CHAPTER THIRTY

K arl Texas had given me three cassettes and I took the first one from its case and slotted it into the cranky old machine I'd borrowed from the Ashwells. Maggie told me that it was from their era and that George still liked to listen to his Shirley Bassey cassettes on it.

'Seeing Molly Marrison sing at that festival, is one of the highlights of my career,' Jeff said. 'She was one of the most exciting acts I'd heard for years. You knew even then she was special, a one-off. I couldn't take my eyes off her and that's no understatement. She delivered the songs with an almost unbearable sensitivity and empathy. It was transcendental, as if she was occupying another plane. An innocent, experienced, girl-woman. She was spellbinding with a voice that could reach inside you and wring out every ounce of feeling, reduce even the toughest man to tears. She spoke of tortured souls everywhere, gave language to mute misery. 'He broke off. 'Sorry, I could talk about her forever.'

'Please carry on,' Karl encouraged.

'She could make you totally believe in what she was

singing, even those ancient ballads. She made them seem so relevant, even more relevant than modern songs. In her hands, they were like anthems of doomed love or hymns perhaps, is a better word. To my mind, there's been no-one to hold a candle to her since. She had it all, great timing, great musicality. She could tell a story, paint a picture in a minor key. She had total star quality. But of course, there's always a downside to that. Living with that kind of brilliant gift can be tough.'

'What was she like to work with?'

'Oh, she was a complete pro. The real deal. That's not to say there weren't challenges. She always got nervous before doing a vocal in the studio, just as she got nervous before going on stage. She had a huge dynamic range as a singer, an ethereal, expressive soprano, like a fairy princess. She could slide from a whisper to a wail in one phrase, which meant it was hard to mic her up. Back then, my production method was just to switch on the tapes and record live. I expected an album to be completed in a single three-hour session with no retakes, unless there was a technical problem. With Molly, we quickly laid down tracks straight to master–tape. It's almost like she channels, she's gone for hours. She was physically right there but not there. A one-take wonder.'

'So it didn't take long?'

He laughed. 'I was a tad disappointed, to be frank. Reluctant to let her go, you know? I remember her, wafting around the studio in hip-hugger bell-bottoms with her killer body. She seemed totally unaware of how drop-dead gorgeous she was. But she had something that made women love her too. They felt like she was singing their secrets out loud. There was a vulnerability there too. She smoked like a chimney, four packets a day, from the moment she woke up to the moment she fell asleep. And she didn't sleep well. I used to nag her to lay off the fags, for the sake of her voice. She said she'd tried to cut down but became so bad-tempered, people begged her to smoke again. I found that hard to believe. She had a genuine warmth and sincerity, a wicked sense of humour. I don't know anyone who didn't love her.'

'You sound like you were a little in love with her yourself,' Karl commented.

The tape clicked off.

I'd been sitting at the kitchen table with the machine for over two hours. My shoulders ached and my eyes were scratchy. It was past midnight and tomorrow was the Duke and Duchess's diamond wedding celebration. It would be full-on. But I couldn't stop now. I made another cup of tea, rolled my shoulders to ease the tightness, took out one cassette and slotted in the next, hit the play button and Jeff Bond's laconic voice filled my little kitchen once more, as he continued his story.

'Sadly, she wasn't interested in me, or anyone at that time. She was off limits. Her excuse was that she'd decided she just wanted to focus on her music, didn't want any distractions but there was more to it, I'm certain. My guess is that something happened to her at that festival. She wouldn't talk about it but I think she'd had her heart broken, badly and was struggling to put it back together. There was a darkness. It wasn't visible usually because she seemed a happy soul, like I say with a big, generous laugh. If you are going to fully inhabit those dark songs, as she did, there has to be a release button. But the anguish and pain was always there, underneath and it fed into her songs. She poured all her heartache into her music, which is why it communicates so well. Those songs set off synchronised weeping sometimes.'

Karl says: 'If you hear someone singing about heartache, it eases your own.'

'Molly has been compared to Sandy Denny and Joni Mitchell and, what all three of them have in common, is that they were all caught between ambition and creativity and a longing for love, a strong desire to settle down, have a baby. Whoever it was who broke her heart, Molly was trying to go on talking to him in song. She once said to me that you should record songs when you believe in them the most and her genuine pain is what makes that album one of the classic break-up albums, but with a difference because the songs are so old. They carry hundreds, thousands of years of learning and wisdom and have been shaped by generations of suffering. Modern songs just can't ever match up to that. I remember sitting with her, in the studio, deciding which tracks should go on the album. She was very strong-minded and when I suggested she choose a few of her own compositions, she was adamant, that they must all be old songs. She was right, of course. Dead right. Joan Baez had a remarkable impact with her repertoire of traditional songs, collected by Francis Child. But Molly had her very own repertoire, time-honoured songs she said her father had taught her.'

'Her father?'

'Apparently he sang to her all the time.'

'So what did she do, after she'd recorded the album?'

'She played a few open-mic nights in basement clubs,' Jeff said. 'Soho had a folk club on every corner in the sixties, seedy joints, down among the strip clubs. At Kingston, every other pub along the Thames had a regular folk club or folk night. Molly liked Kingston Folk Barge but her favourite place was Les Cousins. She loved it there. It was open all night, everyone wore black. We all sat in the dark most of the time. Just the glow of cigarettes. It was very hip and she felt at home, I think. She'd found her tribe. She hung out with art school dropouts. With Martin Carthy, Anne Briggs, Peggy Seeger, Donovan. The clubs didn't pay much but if you got three or four bookings a week, that wasn't so bad. Having a record out was a big deal, a real feather in Molly's cap and she got her first billing and review in the *Melody Maker*, thanks to you.'

'It was a round-up of established folk singers, alongside some of the new crops,' Karl recollected. 'I remember writing it. I called it a sublimely original collection of songs that rewarded repeated listening. I said she was destined to be one of *the* great voices. I stand by that.'

'She was so psyched to read it. Then there was a glowing review in *Gramophone* too. I can still quote it: "Exquisitely powerful stories and melodies and a voice that's tender and trance-like, an ornate traditional folk voice. Molly Marrison has an incredible soul and we are going to hear much more of this captivating young singer."'

'But nothing more was heard of her, was it?' Karl points out.

'Indeed.'

'Have you any idea why? Do you have a theory, even? What do you think happened to her?'

'I don't like to speculate but it's true to say that she recorded a great album and great albums are often made in a point of crisis. She bared her soul and it was a soul in torment. But all I know for a fact is this. In 1968, Peter Kennedy from the BBC, wrote to me because he wanted Molly to arrange a date with him, to record some songs for his *Folk Song Cellar*, the series of very prestigious programmes he made for the BBC's World Service back then. They were recorded live, in the basement of Cecil Sharp House and set out to reflect what was happening in folk clubs, juxtaposing established singers like Martin Cathy with younger performers like Shirley Collins and the like. The Molly I knew would have jumped at the chance. She'd have been so honoured to be on that show, would have done anything to take part. But she'd not replied, so Kennedy wanted me to forward the letter on to her. I'd have been glad to do so, obviously, only I had nowhere to send it. No forwarding address. I had no idea where she was. And thirty years later, I'm afraid to say that I'm none the wiser. All we have left of her is that album. And I'm just glad I recorded her. It was a privilege.'

'You said she'd had her heart broken?' Karl probed. 'But was she stable, mentally, would you say?'

'Depends how you define stable. I've noticed in life that insecurity and massive belief in one's abilities often go hand in hand. She had both in spades. She knew she was good but she was also incredibly insecure. She had terrible stage fright, was sometimes paralysed with fear, yet she was compelled to perform. She had great drive and determination and she was a much better musician than she ever gave herself credit for. She was very self-effacing. However, the only thing that struck me as really odd about her, were her weird tastebuds.'

'Her tastebuds?'

'She had a liking for marmite and strawberry jam. Together. She kept eating these revolting sandwiches, slabs of white bread, oozing red and black goo. Yuk. I happened to mention it to the girl I was seeing at the time and she asked me if Molly might be pregnant.'

'Pregnant?'

'Means expecting a baby,' he chuckles.

'Might she have been?'

'You're asking the wrong person, my friend. As in, you're asking a man.' He laughs deeply. 'How the hell would I know a thing like that? What I do know though, is that the Festival of the Flower Children was a pivotal moment for her, not just in terms of her career. She never spoke about it. But something happened. Just wish we knew what.'

CHAPTER THIRTY-ONE

MOLLY - 1967

They're travelling in John's unreliable old Austin and they've ended up giving a lift, not only to Sukey but also to Johnny's two bandmates, Pete and Mike, who are squished into the backseat with Sukey. Pete is sporting a Jimi-Hendrix Salvation-Army jacket with gold braiding and brass buttons, from Portobello Road Market. Molly's been admiring it.

'You're more than welcome to wear it on stage,' Pete tells her. 'In fact, it'd make my day.'

'He's got the hots for you,' Sukey whispers.

'Nonsense,' Molly tells her.

But Pete's never made any secret of the fact that he wants to sleep with Molly. 'You're going to be on the same stage as The Faces and The Kinks,' he sighs.

She'll perform on Saturday afternoon, just for twenty minutes, but it's like a dream.Needing a costume she'd headed, with Johnny, to Lift up Your Skirts and Fly, had trailed her fingers along the fantastic gear hanging from the red clothes-rails, suspended by chains from the mirror-tiled ceiling. A trouser suit by Ossie Clark, in black crepe with scarlet silk edging, cost £10 10s. For £5 5s you could buy a dolly dress in flame satin. She didn't have £5, nothing like, but she got chatting to the tiny red-haired shopgirl called Sandra and immediately she heard about the festival, Sandra fetched the manager. On the spot, she offered to let Molly have something for free.

At the end of the rail was a flowing pin-tucked white gown with bell-sleeves, an elevated waist and a ruffled flamenco-style skirt, embroidered round the hem and neckline with tiny, wildflowers.

'It's a Mexican peasant wedding-dress,' said Sandra, as Molly held it up against her body. 'It's perfect for you. Go try it on.'

In the communal changing room, divided at one end by a heavy wine, velvet curtain, Molly stripped down to her underwear, stepped inside the dress, pulled it up over her shoulders. The fabric was cool and light against her skin and though it was romantic and feminine, the dress made her feel strong and brave.

It's going to take them four hours to drive from Chatsworth to Woburn Abbey, straight down the new M1 motorway, so the plan had been to leave early on Friday morning. John had picked up the other boys first and then collected both girls from Molly's house.

In the passenger seat of the Austin, Molly is supposed to be navigating but the OS map has rips and tears and coffee stains all over it. She wrestles with it, turns it this way, then that way, folds it and refolds it, swears under her breath. Through no fault of her own, she gets them lost, twice, somewhere near Birmingham. 'I'd be better driving.'

Pete is aghast. 'You can't drive. You're a girl.'

'Women should be able to drive a bus if they want and play football,' she scolds him.

'Let's swap places,' Sukey simpers. 'I'd be a hopeless driver but I can read a map.'

'Let her try,' John agreed.

Molly narrows her eyes at him. She can't decide if he's just being diplomatic or if he really wants Sukey riding up front with him, instead of her. 'Fine,' she huffs.

'Come and sit on my lap,' Pete tells Molly.

'Leave it out, Pete,' John retorts, good-humouredly.

Molly clambers over into the cramped back seat, as Sukey squeezes herself out of the way, practically climbing into Mike's lap as he shoves himself up against the door to make room. Her skirt up around her hips, Sukey provocatively hooks her tanned bare leg over the back of the passenger seat to scramble over to the front.

Molly is now squeezed in between Pete and Mike and Pete's leg is pressed up against hers. His right hand slips across onto her thigh. She picks it up, between her thumb and forefinger, like something infected and unceremoniously, deposits it back on his own leg.

'Spoilsport,' he mutters, then starts talking about the heartless patriarchy.

'Meaning women are superior?' Molly asks. 'Totally agree.'

'Pah,' Pete grunts. He enthuses about a magical substance called lysergic acid or LSD 25. 'You take it on a sugar cube and it's like you go to heaven. Nirvana. I can't wait to try some.'

'Sounds far out,' Molly says.

'I just need a burger,' John says. 'I'm starving.'

They stop for sausage, egg and chips at the Blue Boar

transport cafe and Molly plays around with the contents of her plate.

'You've hardly touched it,' Sukey notices.

'I'm not hungry.' Molly pushes her plate away. She's only had three bites but if she has one more, she'll throw it right back up.

'How can you not be hungry?' Pete asks, reaching across to nick one of her chips.

'Nerves, I expect.' She lights a Camel cigarette instead.

'You sure that's all it is?' Sukey says, challengingly.

'Yes.' No. Now another possibility hits Molly full on and she feels sicker than ever.

The boys pay the bill and they head out to the car, eager to get back on the road. They've made the mistake of parking in blazing sun and the leatherette seats are red-hot, practically melting, searing the backs of Molly's legs. They wind all the windows down but inside the car it remains like an oven and as the miles slide by, Molly feels sicker and sicker. Glancing in the mirror, Johnny looks concerned. 'You're as white as a sheet, Moll. Want me to pull over?'

She shakes her head. 'Just keep going. I'm fine.'

She's not fine. Anything but. Can she really be pregnant, expecting Johnny's baby? Hellfire, it might be true. She missed her period last month but then that's nothing new. She's regularly irregular. She's paralysed with fear, horror, shock. It's the worst thing that could happen to her.

They turn off the motorway and run straight into a traffic jam and crawl along in the queue for upwards of an hour. With no wind blowing through the car now, it gets hotter and hotter. The map gets passed around as a makeshift fan and Pete complains that he's gagging for a beer now.

Finally, they arrive at Woburn early in the afternoon. There are Checkpoint Charlies, bizarrely dressed in karate outfits, guarding the gates to the festival site but once inside, it's all very relaxed. Woburn has been transformed into a magic kingdom of flower children and butterfly bohemians. There are thousands of them, wandering around or sitting under the shady trees, laughing, drinking, smoking and getting high. The air is heavy with the aromatic smell of hashish. Everywhere you look, there really are beautiful people. Everyone looks like a romantic poet or Shakespearean hero-ine, festooned in Eastern jewellery, beads, floppy hats, feathers and flowers. There are boys who look like girls, in ruffled pirate's blouses and long curly hair, guys wearing bandanas and girls with ostrich and peacock plumes on their heads, flowers painted on their faces, sticks of incense between their teeth. Molly finds herself staring at an attractive young man, in purple satin trousers covered in frills with a sleeveless Afghan jacket, his hair freaked out into a huge frizzy halo.

The grounds of Woburn are as bewitching as the gardens at Chatsworth, with a Chinese pagoda, hornbeam maze, pavilion and an aviary. There are stalls selling paper flowers, hot dogs and Pepsi. Jefferson Airplane's trippy chart hit, *White Rabbit*, blares out from speakers on either side of the stage. Johnny buys a string of bells to wear around his neck and when he leans in close to Molly, he smells of Old Spice and soap and cigarette smoke. It's all so incredibly stardusty and glamorous and it feels as if nothing bad can happen here.

If she's pregnant, then there's absolutely nothing she can do about it today. She'll just chill out, put everything out of her mind and enjoy all this.

A giant hot air balloon sails overhead, bright-red and green against the blue sky and then, thousands of red carnations are falling from the basket, drifting down into the outstretched hands below. Johnny catches one of the flowers, plucks it out of the air like a magician and tucks it behind Molly's ear. He lights a cigarette and hands it to her, just as a photographer, who says he is from the Daily Mail, snaps a photo. Molly, with the red flower in her dark hair, smoking a Number 6, except it will look like a spliff.

'I can see the caption already,' the photographer drawls, drawing two parallel lines in the air with his thumb and forefinger 'Look at the folks you meet at Woburn Abbey these days.'

'It's a far cry from Chatsworth, that's for sure,' Johnny laughs.

The weather is scorching and all the musicians seem to know each other so there's a great, social atmosphere. The performers are mingling with the audience, as if they all belong together. Alan Price and Jeff Beck are sitting on the grass together, just chatting.

'So d'you wanna try my jacket on?' Pete asks Molly.

'Oh, let me, let me,' Sukey jumps in.

'Sure.' He takes it off and like a matador's cape, he drapes it with a flourish, over Sukey's shoulders.

'You look great,' Johnny tells her.

'Moll's turn now,' Pete says, taking the coat from Sukey and helping Molly shrug her thin arms into the sleeves.

She flips her long hair out from under the collar, so it falls like a dark river down her back. 'Can I really wear it on stage?'

'Course you can. What time are you on?'

'In half an hour. I should probably go and get ready.'

'I'll go and get us all some more Pepsi,' Sukey offers sweetly. 'I'll come and find you.'

The backstage area, such as it is, is cordoned off with

metal fencing and is chaos. A chap with a beer gut sits at a big mixing desk, smoking a joint and flicking ash all over the knobs. Lights on gantries trail cables. There are amps and guitars and keyboards, musicians sitting around on flight cases, smoking and drinking from bottles of brown ale and Jack Daniels. Empty cans of Double Diamond beer litter the grass. Two guys are unloading huge speakers from the back of a van. The group who are on stage are Beatles soundalikes but not lookalikes, which is disconcerting.

Molly feels out of place, out of her depth. She loves being on stage. It feels like home but here, suddenly, she is so unsure. Then Johnny drops a kiss on her brow. 'You're going to knock 'em dead.'

Sukey reappears, hands Molly a warm bottle of Pepsi with a straw.

'Take this as well,' Pete says, and drops a tab of acid into the cola. 'It'll make you sing better.'

'Thanks.'

Molly's mouth is so dry, she ditches the straw and empties the bottle of warm liquid down her throat in one go, craving the refreshment as well as the sweetness.

Soon after, a sweaty young man in Indian pants with a long beard and a clipboard says: 'Your turn now, babe.'

Johnny gives her a kiss.

Molly kicks off her shoes, loops the guitar strap around her neck and wearing her lacy white dress and Pete's military jacket, she walks out barefoot onto the stage, looks down into a sea of expectant young faces.

There are three thousand people, maybe more, sitting on the grass, dancing, standing, waiting at the front of the stage. It's overwhelming. But she can do this. She shuts her eyes, places her fingers on the frets and starts to sing the opening verse of *The Runaway Lovers*.

Over moors and valleys deep, through the Dark Peak and the White
There two tragic lovers sleep in gritstone, blood, and lime.

The microphone and the speakers amplify her voice in an alarming way, make her sound so much louder than she expects. In her head, her own voice distorts.

But these five most murderess men, all fell foul to fates revenge
One tumbled down that self same dell, and one was crushed to death
One with guilt his own life took and one died mad before his time
And the last, on his death bed confessed this terrible crime.

She opens her eyes and sees that people are listening to her, really listening and at the end of that first song, the applause is deafening, like nothing she's ever heard before. They are applauding her and it's impossible not to smile.

Images flash through her head. She feels as if she has a sixth sense. There are luminous fibres connecting everything. She can see right through to people's hearts.

The sky looks weird and wonderful and she searches and searches for Johnny's face in the crowd as she sings another song. One girl near the front of the stage has her arms in the air, her long, straight blonde hair falling like a curtain over her face as she sways balletically, as if she is lost in the music or it has taken her to another world.

Molly sees him then. He is standing with Sukey, over by one of the drink stalls. She has her arm draped around his waist and her head is resting on his shoulder. But that's not all that's wrong with what Molly is looking at. Their faces. Everyone's faces, in fact. Their features are twisted out of shape, noses and eyes in the wrong place. The beautiful people have turned into an audience of grotesques.

Molly closes her eyes again and there are lights

shooting across the backs of her lids. She sings *Died for Love* and she remembers Johnny saying how he hoped she never felt like the girl in the song. Betrayed and abandoned. She feels like that right now, like a premonition. She feels as if her heart is cracking. She forgets that people are listening to her and she sings the song, just as she sang it before, in the barn. She sings to Johnny, for Johnny, as if only he can hear her.

There are lights all over the sky now, like an early sunset but much brighter and with more colours. The grandeur of it is awesome, mind-bending and she thinks how beautiful the world is and how infinitely sad but even the sadness is beautiful. She feels like a shaman, a witchdoctor.

When Molly comes off stage, there is a man waiting to talk to her. He is young and slim, with straight blond hair, a long floppy, fringe and sad brown eyes that turn down slightly at the corners. He's wearing a paisley shirt and an oversized black donkey-jacket with silver buttons. She thinks how he must surely be too hot.

'Jeff Bond,' he says sticking out his hand. 'Music producer and manager.'

He is cocksure, laddish and swaggery. There seemed to be stars, dozens of stars, revolving around his head. And the sky is the brightest sapphire-blue, the grass emerald-green.

Molly takes hold of Jeff's extended hand, to steady herself as much as anything. His handshake is strong and his skin dry and cool. 'Hi,' she says.

'You were extraordinary, just now.'

'Thanks.'

'I want to make a record with you,' he tells her simply. 'Put out an album of those songs you just sang.' He thrusts a business card at her with an address in Denmark Street. 'We're on Tin Pan Alley.'

Molly looks at the business card, then at him. 'Are you serious?'

'Deadly serious. Call me.'

'I will.' She feels her lips stretch into a smile. She is sure she is grinning insanely, like the Cheshire cat. She is mesmerised by the beautiful patterns on his shirt and enraptured by the slurred, slow-motion resonances of a guitar solo being played behind her. She feels just joyous now. 'Excuse me,' she says.

She has to find Johnny. She has to tell him what just happened, what's going to happen. He recorded the demo tape that has got her this far. She couldn't have done any of it without him.

She walks away from the stage, is swallowed up in the crowd. Lights are flashing everywhere now, not just in the sky but in the trees and the grass and in the air itself. Everyone is dancing but Molly can't hear any music any longer. It's so weird. Peaceful, but strange. Like heaven might be. She stands for a moment and shuts her eyes and it's as if images from a dozen different movies are being projected onto the backs of her eyelids.

She wanders round for what feels like hours and she looks everywhere and there are just all these strange faces. Very strange faces with little buttons for noses and eyes like kittens.

Dantalion's Chariot take the stage, wearing gleaming white robes with a brilliant white backcloth. The music sounds amazing and there is an equally amazing light show. Zoot Money lets rip on the keyboards as they belt out *Madman Running Through the Fields*. Molly feels like a madwoman herself. Strobes make everything flash in and out of view. The silent, pounding rhythm has turned everyone around Molly into marionettes, their limbs jerking, as they are engulfed first by darkness and then by bright white light. The night is like a montage.

'Free sparklers for all,' the lead singer shouts from the stage and he starts to throw lighted sparklers into the crowd. Of course, the crowd toss them back and some of them land on the canopy, which instantly catches fire. Tongues of lurid orange flame leap in the dark sky and to Molly, they look like pouncing lions or crashing red ocean waves, rivers of fire. She hears a voice she recognises from the Radio. John Peel, speaking loudly and urgently over the tannoy, appealing for everyone to move away from the stage. But people just laugh, while the attendants try to rip down the burning canvas.

When the panic dies down she feels so tired and she just sits down on the grass. Eric Burdon from the Animals walks out on stage and gives a sermon, about how they should all love each other. Everyone cheers.

Suddenly there is Pete. Does he want his jacket back? He takes Molly's hands in his and pulls her back onto her feet, pulls her close to him. He whispers in her ear: 'Eric said we should all love each other. So how about it, how about you give me some love?'

'You know I'm with Johnny,' Molly says.

'You're with me for now,' Pete slurs, as the Animals start to sing *The House of the Rising Sun*.

'Leave me alone.' She pulls away from him, runs, goes to sit by herself under a sycamore tree.

The bass thump of the music is softly punching her in the chest. She stares at the roots of the tree going down, down into the earth, like the veins on an old man's hand. She stares at the whorls in the bark and the tufts of grass. Time has taken on a strange elastic quality, so she can't tell if she's been sitting here for twenty minutes or two hours but she feels herself sinking, as if she is following those roots, is being taken down into a tunnel in the earth. She doesn't mind, she just wants to sleep. She lies down under the tree and closes her eyes.

She half wakes several times to hear The Doors, *Light my Fire*. Jim Morrison isn't actually here, it's just the record, playing on repeat. When she opens her eyes properly, Pete is there again. He is sitting on the ground beside her, staring down into her face. Above them, all the leaves are dancing like demented fairies.

'You're hot stuff,' Pete says, stroking her hair.

She feels a fantastic sense of benevolence, an open-mindedness towards all humankind. She feels light-headed and light-hearted. She loves everyone right now.

Pete leans towards her and he starts kissing her. He's a very good kisser, very gentle and Molly reminds herself that free love is supposed to be a wonderful thing and totally cool. They are supposed to be throwing off the confines of previous generations. They are supposed to be making a new world, one where people are liberated. She doesn't want to be like her teachers, like her grandmother, like everyone over the age of thirty. Heaven forbid. They're so square. And straight. How can square and straight mean the same thing? Like an old person.

'I'm never getting old,' she proclaims.

'Me neither,' Pete says. 'I'll shoot myself when I get to fifty.'

Molly thinks: I've barely drunk anything and I've not been smoking pot, so why do I feel so out of it? She thinks it must be the sun and the music and the elation of being on stage and being in this amazing place. It has all gone to her head. Then she remembers the tab Pete dropped in her cola, before she went on stage. That guy who wanted to make a record with her. Did she dream that? No, she still has his card, clutched and crumpled in her hand.

All around, couples are snogging and making out on the grass, lying down together with their tongues down each other's throats, deep kissing and rolling about, shirts unbuttoned low and skirts hitched high. Before she knows it, she is lying on her back too, her dress half off, her shoulders bare, one of her breasts exposed. Pete is lying on top of her, playing with her nipples, still kissing her, fondling her, his leg hooked over her leg. He smells sweet, like summer grass.

Something, some sixth sense, makes her twist her head away from him and that's when she sees Johnny's feet, a yard or so away from her. Her eyes travel up his long legs, up his body, to his handsome face. He is just standing there, watching her and he looks cut to the quick. He's forgotten that they're not supposed to be jealous or possessive. That nobody belongs to anybody anymore.

What has she done?

CHAPTER THIRTY-TWO

SILVA - 2002

Everyone had made a huge effort with their costumes. Arthur and Hugh were both dressed as army officers, bedazzled with medals. Bea and Robbie's mum were looking lovely in vintage floral tea-dresses, their hair styled in victory rolls. Freya had hired a WRAF uniform, scratchy blue wool with a tight straight skirt and a jaunty little hat. Robbie matched his sister and made a very raffish airman, a squadron leader no less. He looked unbelievably handsome. In honour of my dad's agricultural background, I'd gone as a land girl, in khaki dungarees and a spotty red and white headscarf.

Lizzie was in her element, playing the part of a Red Cross nurse, complete with a starched white uniform with a red cross branded on the apron. 'I'm worried I might be called on to actually do lots of nursing,' she said, casting her eyes around at the elderly guests dotted across the sunny Salisbury Lawn. Half of them were tottering on walking sticks or being pushed in wheelchairs. Like our Duke and Duchess, they'd all married during the war, which meant that the youngest amongst them, were knocking eighty. 'What are the odds of someone falling over and breaking their hip or having a heart attack?'

'Probably quite high, I'd say.'

A week's wartime rations was laid out on one of the trestle tables, two ounces of bacon for seven days, a stark contrast to the banquet that was being served. There were pork pies and canapés, champagne and cheesecakes. The Squadronnaire's orchestra, inspired by the original RAF dance-band, played songs made famous by Vera Lynn: *We'll meet Again* and *You'll Never Know*. Flora played piano for them for two of the numbers. The ancient guests joined in the singing with great gusto, holding hands and dewy-eyed. They seemed to be from an entirely different world, not just a different era.

I watched the dancing couples, tried not to dwell on why Robbie hadn't even mentioned the letter I'd sent to him, several days ago now. I'd poured out my heart and he'd just ignored it. I wished to God I'd never sent it. What was I even thinking?

'I can't imagine what it must be like, to be married to the same person for sixty years,' I said to Flora. 'Thirty, even.'

'I imagine it must be extremely hard work,' Flora replied. 'But I do also think it would be wonderful, to share your whole adult life with someone you love and who loves you back, to grow up and grow old together, raise a family. When you think about it, romantic films about finding your soulmate, have it all wrong. That's not the interesting part, is it? It's not will they or won't they *get* together that's the most fascinating story. It's will they or won't they *stay* together.'

'These lot have all managed it.' I noted. 'What's their secret? How did they do it?'

'How did they do what?' Robbie asked, overhearing my question as he strolled over.

'We're wondering how you stay married to the same person for sixty years,' Flora explained.

Robbie took off his airman's cap, ruffled his hazel curls as he tucked the cap under his arm. He said to me: 'Shall we try and find out?'

I stared at him, my heart racing, head spinning. What was he proposing? Was he actually proposing? Right here? I blinked. 'Excuse me?'

He gave me a dazzling smile. 'Let's ask someone who knows how it's done, shall we? What better chance will we ever have?' He scanned the elderly crowd, all made up of couples who'd been married more than half a century. 'That pair over there, they look like a good bet.' He nodded towards a tall, shapely lady in a mid-blue tea dress and an elderly man in RAF uniform, under the horse chestnut tree. He was probably an inch shorter than his wife with a round face and a bald patch on the back of his head. They were sipping champagne and the gentleman gave Robbie a mock salute as we approached.

'Good afternoon,' Robbie smiled.

'Afternoon to you.'

'Are you having a good time?'

'We're having the time our lives, lad.'

'I'm Robbie,' Robbie said, reaching out to shake hands. 'This is Silva.'

'Captain Max,' the man replied, introducing himself. 'And this is my wife, Barbara.'

'So, my friend here was wondering,' Robbie began with a disarming smile. 'What's your secret? To staying married for so long, I mean? If you don't mind me asking?'

Max glanced at his wife fondly, as she tucked her arm

into the crook of his elbow. He rested his hand over hers, patted it. 'Well now,' he said. 'I've actually pondered this quite a lot.'

'Oh dear,' his wife sighed with affection. 'Spare them the lecture, Maxie.'

'No, no, we honestly want to hear,' Robbie assured her.

'The older you get, the more you realise that real love is not about the fluffy, fuzzy first days when you fall for each other,' Max said. 'It's not about your wedding day.' He looked lovingly at his wife. 'It's about what happens afterwards, isn't that right, Babs? It's about two people, meeting as youngsters, thinking they know everything but knowing nothing at all. A couple who marry with a homemade dress and a pub supper and are still going strong when their teeth fall out.' He chuckled. 'It's about sticking together through thick and thin, through sickness and health, for richer and poorer, through misery and joy. It's about getting bored and frustrated and hating each other for a time, taking each other for granted when life gets busy. It's about fighting and making up and fighting again. It's about two people, who go through all of that and at the end of their days, they still love and care for each other enough to hold hands on the seafront. If you ask me, there's your real romance.'

'That's lovely,' I said.

'It's about kindness,' Barbara told us. 'Just being careful of one another's feelings. It's as simple and as complicated as that.'

'Thank you,' Robbie said to both of them. 'That's wonderful advice.'

'You're welcome, lad.' Max glanced at me. 'Good luck to the pair of you.'

'Oh, we're not…'

Robbie hooked his arm through mine and steered me

away, before I could finish my sentence. 'Come for a walk with me.'

'May's my favourite month,' he told me, as we headed over towards The Crobbs.

'I know. You've told me that nearly every May.'

It was inevitable really. He had a spirit like springtime, bursting with possibility, full of optimism, defined by warmth and tenderness, as well as a kind of sexy, fertile restlessness.

At Chatsworth, plump beech buds were unfolding into vivid green crimped leaves and the trees that lined the broad walk were a myriad of glorious fresh greens, arching above like a cathedral. The hawthorn was a froth of white, like snow, sycamore and horse chestnuts were dusted with green and the cherry blossom was at its very best, while plum blossom littered the ground, nature's own confetti.

Robbie led the way to the bottom of the cascade. 'Have you ever listened to it?' he asked me. 'I mean properly?'

'I'm not sure.' The cascade comprised twenty-four wide steps and if you studied the design closely enough, as I'd done, you could see that each was a slightly different height or shape. I'd watched the way the water flowed over them in ripples of sparkling gold, but had I listened?

'Close your eyes,' Robbie said. 'It helps you to hear better.'

'Is that right?'

'Don't argue.'

Unusually, I just did as I was told.

He gave me his arm to hold, encouraged me to take a step. 'Don't worry. I won't let you trip.'

I gripped him tight as he led me slowly up the grassy bank. 'Can you hear? Music?'

I could. I really could. The different sized steps each created a different sound as the water flowed over them. It was like stopping to listen, properly, to the dawn chorus and being able to identify the song of each bird. 'That's so cool.'

When I opened my eyes again, we were outside the little temple at the very top of the Cascade. A perfect miniature building, it was crowned with a carved river god and watched over by statues of nymphs and griffins sporting gilded plumes. Keeping hold of my hand, he led me behind the veil of water, into the small stone building. Above our heads, the cupola was adorned with scrolls and shells that had been carved over two hundred years ago.

My heart was hammering so hard Robbie must surely hear it. How could I not be acutely aware that this was where he'd told the old lady in the hospital that he'd asked me to be his wife? 'Robbie, what are we doing here, exactly?'

'Thank you for your letter,' he said, turning to face me, looking into my eyes. 'It was a beautiful letter.'

'I was beginning to wonder if you'd even read it.'

'I've read it dozens of times.'

'Really?'

'I loved you when you were sixteen years old,' he said. 'And I love you still.'

I could see love in his eyes. There was love in his voice and the vibrations of that beautiful voice of his resonated softly around the stone walls, echoed inside my body. It was such a soothing voice and yet it didn't always soothe me. On the contrary, sometimes it stirred me up, set off all kinds of confusing longings and yearnings. His words seemed to fill the air, bounce around me and envelop me. *I love you.*

'I love you too.'

'I think we were too young, before,' he said carefully. 'I think we both needed time, to work out what we want, who we are, where we're going. I love you now, more than ever but I love you as a man, not a boy. I love the girl you were and the woman you've become. I know that wherever I'm going in my life, I want you with me too.'

I focused on his mouth, the little creases at either side of it, like parenthesis, framing such beautiful words. I wanted him to stop talking though and kiss me. I should say something but I didn't know what to say and anyway I couldn't speak. I was afraid I might cry. I'd never imagined Robbie or anyone, saying such lovely words to me and meaning them wholeheartedly, as I knew he meant them.

He put his hand in the pocket of his jacket and took out a small, dark-blue box, held it out to me.

My heart was racing full pelt now, as if from fear.

'Open it,' he told me.

I knew what was inside. An engagement ring.

It was not an engagement ring. No diamonds or sapphires. But something far lovelier. Nestling on a bed of black velvet, was a ring made of Blue John, set within a delicate frame of old gold.

'D'you recognise it?'

I did. Of course I did. It was almost identical to the ring I'd admired in the dimly-lit shop window in Castleton, a lifetime ago. I took it out of the box, was about to put it on my right hand but Robbie stopped me.

'Wrong hand, wrong finger.'

I looked at him. 'I don't understand?'

'Yeah, you do. It's not complicated. I'm asking you to marry me.' He paused. 'Will you?'

It was an engagement ring then, just not a regular kind. It was the most perfect engagement ring I could imagine.

'We don't have to do it right away,' he added quickly. 'Whenever feels right. And it can be a small occasion or a grand event, whichever you'd prefer.'

'Why do you even want to marry me?'

He pressed his lips together, as if to hold back laughter and yet he looked so earnest. 'Because I love you and I want to spend the rest of my life with you. What other reason is there nowadays?'

The 'nowadays' was typical of him. Everyone else would have ended the sentence before that word. But he was no doubt thinking of girls from times past, girls immortalised in folk songs, who'd been forced into a marriage arrangement, not for love but for financial, dynastic reasons. There was a farm or a stately home or castle to upkeep. That's why young lovers like Clara and Henry had been forced to run away.

'This is insane.' I laughed, but there was nothing amusing about where my thoughts were veering. I tried to yank them back on track but didn't manage it. 'I have no faith in marriage. Neither do you.'

We'd both said as much at times. We'd both come from homes where a marriage had catastrophically failed and neither of us really understood why our parents weren't able to make a success of it. We had no understanding of where it all went wrong, for John and Sukey and for Flora and Jim. Being married, being a wife or a husband, it sounded so normal and staid and safe, yet for me, getting married felt dangerous. Maybe not so much for Robbie, because his mother and stepfather were happy. But all the same, we'd both seen how the failure of a marriage could be devastatingly destructive. We knew how a journey that began with such love and hope, could, with a few wrong turns, lead to agonising pain and great suffering on both sides.

'I always wanted my life to be full of adventures,' Robbie said, 'and I think that being married to you, would be the most wonderful adventure of all.'

'Robbie, you say the sweetest things.'

'But? There is a but?'

I looked down at the ring, imagined him slipping it onto my finger, where it would glow like a tiny fragment of rainbow, with all the colours of the Derbyshire moors in late summer: purple heather and blue sky, golden sunshine and soft white clouds. Blue John. The distinctive zigzag pattern was particularly clearly defined in this piece. It ran right across the middle of the oval, like a child's drawing on an Easter card, of a cracked egg with a fluffy yellow chick popping out. Something broken but giving life to something new. I'd always hated the term broken-home but the truth was that my home, my family, had felt broken. Robbie's too.

I wanted the ring on my finger but it terrified me.

'There are good marriages,' Robbie said. 'We can make a good marriage.'

I looked into his face, more dear to me than any other face. 'You really think so?'

'Here's what I think: Marriage is like art.' He was talking slowly, giving weight to every word. 'It takes a lot of hard work, to create something beautiful and lasting. All those sculptures and paintings you clean every day.' He cast his eyes upwards to the miraculous carvings above our heads. 'The amazing metalwork you make yourself, you of all people can understand all the effort that goes into creating something that's worthwhile creating. It's worth all the hard work, isn't it?'

'I'm not afraid of hard work. I like it in fact.'

'I know you do. Me too.'

Stepping behind the veil of water above the cascade had been like stepping from one world to another and I thought how marriage would be the same. I wanted to do it. Suddenly, I wanted all of it. Deep down, I realised I'd always wanted it. Who had I been kidding? I wanted to wander with Robbie, through the daffodils and bluebells in springtime, walk home with him through the park at dusk, when the sheep and deer were silhouetted against the sunset. I wanted cosy evenings in front of the log fire with a film and a bottle of wine, trips to the cinema, dog walks under an umbrella in the rain and lazy Sunday mornings in bed. I wanted to cook breakfast with him and light candles in the evening. I wanted several children and a soppy golden retriever. I wanted all the things I once swore were not for me. I wanted children, to bring my own son and daughter to the Duchess's magical annual sheep service in Edensor church, when a flock of lambs was carried in by Chatsworth children, blessed by the vicar as the lambs of God. I wanted family life like a television advert: beach holidays and rock pools, strapping Christmas trees to a car roof, Sunday roasts, making costumes for school nativity plays. I wanted picnics in the park by the river and buckets and spades on the seashore, collecting pebbles and shells and sea glass. Christmas morning and sledging, conker fights, lullabies, bikes with stabilisers, train sets, fairy wings.

These were such ordinary things, such ordinary dreams. I was not asking for fame and fortune with a mansion and supercars. But I might as well have been. Normal family life had always felt so unobtainable to me. Ordinary yet extraordinary.

When my friends had started having babies, I'd embraced it. I'd visited Lizzie and Freya in the maternity ward with teddies, two pink and one blue. I'd cooed over prams and marvelled at first steps and first words. I'd enjoyed building bricks and reading nursery rhymes, making a mess with glue and paint. But I'd never felt broody, never let myself yearn to experience these things first-hand. But now, I forgot all about the only family life I'd ever really known, how stressful and miserable it had been, the shouting and the sad silences. My father's unresolved grief. My own. I wanted to be Robbie's wife. I'd not be the kind of wife my mother had been, not with Robbie beside me. I always felt like a nicer person when he was around, as if he raised me up, to be the very best person I could ever be.

How would it work though? Train sets and Sunday mornings. Robbie had not changed. He still wanted to wander. He'd just said that he wanted his life to be full of adventure. I was not adventurous.

And yet…

The saddest thing in the whole world, is if you meet the right person at the wrong time and then you let them slip away. If you don't know what you've got until it's gone.

I felt churned up inside.

Robbie's face was overlaid with my dad's face, on the night Sukey walked out. What if he'd loved Molly, had wanted to spend the rest of his life with Molly but had messed up and lost her? He'd not wanted me to make the same mistake. I knew I'd have his blessing to marry Robbie. It would have made him so happy, to know he was not leaving me alone. He couldn't be there on my wedding day to give me away but I could feel him, urging me on.

I rehearsed the words in my head: Yes. I will marry you.

I couldn't say it.

Robbie and Molly both sang songs that told how love took you straight from heaven to hell.

Robbie was such a restless soul.

No. I can't marry you.

I couldn't say that either. No way could I say those words to this man.

If he was ready and willing to make a lifetime commitment, then why couldn't I? I wanted this future, stretching on forever, with Robbie. But it wasn't fair to mess him around. If I said yes to him, then it would be as good as a vow. I had to be certain.

'Don't give me an answer now,' Robbie said, seeing my jumbled thoughts as if I was projecting them onto the wall of the temple. He laid the ring in the palm of my hand, wrapped his own hand around my fingers, closing them over it, as Percy had done with his ring, making Robbie the keeper of songs. If I didn't keep this ring, if he had to take it back, what would he do with it? Stow it in his sock drawer, return in to the shop?

'I'll keep asking until you say yes,' he said.

'All right.' I wanted to laugh with relief. 'That's fine by me.'

'And you will say yes, eventually, I know you will.'

Amazingly, I knew it too. So why couldn't I just say it right away? What was stopping me? *What's your problem, Silva?* I wanted Robbie to ask me that, to probe and press me for an explanation. But he was prepared to be patient with me, so I should be patient with myself, right? At the same time, I willed him: Please don't be too patient. Please don't just let me go. This time, please fight for me.

Had my dad fought for Molly?

The penny dropped as we were walking back towards Chatsworth House and made me stop dead in my tracks. 'Robbie, what if Molly really was pregnant? What if my dad was the father? What if I have a half brother or sister somewhere?'

'Might your mother know?' Robbie ventured. 'If you got in touch with her and...'

'No. Never.' I set off walking again. 'Dad told me to find Molly. Maybe this is why. But it was definitely her he told me to find.'

CHAPTER THIRTY-THREE

Ted was busy emptying the bins by the orangery, tipping rubbish into plastic bags to be loaded into a white pickup truck, emblazoned with Chatsworth livery.

'You have such a glamorous life,' I joked as I strode past. I felt like joking around with everyone. I'd woken up so happy, because the sun was streaming through the little mullion windows in my bedroom, Tijou was curled up in a ball right beside me and Robbie had asked me to marry him.

'It makes it much more fun, when there are a few pesky wasps about,' Ted grinned. 'I get to dance like Madonna. But I won't ask the lads to do jobs I'm not prepared to do myself.'

'How about helping with the flower arranging?'

'Nah. I'll leave that to the WI ladies.'

This year, the floral designs were inspired by the bulb fields of Holland and there were wheelbarrows full of brightly coloured cut tulips all over the garden, yellows, purples and oranges. A volunteer army from the local Women's Institute was coming later in the week to help with arrangements that would bring all the rooms at Chatsworth alive with thousands of blooms.

In preparation, Lizzie and I spent the next few days moving things around, dusting all the blue and white Delft tulip pyramids with their myriad of little spouts and holes. To ensure the safety of fragile ceramics, we fastened them down with museum wax at the base.

Somehow, I managed not to say anything to Lizzie while we were at work but when we went out for our drinks at the Devonshire Arms with Freya, nearly a week later, I was fit to burst with the news that Robbie had proposed. Yet I hesitated. Freya was Robbie's sister after all and I knew both my friends would start squealing with excitement. They'd want to crack open the champagne, assuming I'd said yes.

Robbie had left two messages on my answering machine, said he needed to talk to me but I'd been putting him off, stalling for time. Why? Did that mean I still had doubts? Or was I just being a coward?

'You look different,' Freya said to me.

I was watching the young waitress taking orders and I saw the ghost of myself as a teenager, working here with Robbie. 'Different how?'

'I can't work it out,' Freya said. 'Have you changed your hair?'

'It's not plaited, if that's what you mean?'

I'd stopped dressing up to go out because Lizzie and Freya complained that by the time they'd fed and bathed their babes and put them to bed, they barely had time to put lipstick on and I made them feel dowdy, not that either of them could ever be dowdy.

'I dunno?' Freya frowned. 'You seem sort of…sparkly.'

Lizzie peered at me. 'Freya's right,' she decided. 'I've noticed that too. And, I caught you humming songs to yourself while you were dusting the staircase the other day. If I didn't know you better, I'd say you had a secret lover. Do you?'

I glanced at Freya. Had she given up hope of me and her brother ever getting our act together? 'As if.'

'Pity,' Lizzie said. 'We could do with some excitement. All me and Freya have to talk about is nappies, nursery places and nits.'

'Don't put her off,' Freya chided, opening another bag of crisps. 'Take it from me. Being a mum is the best job in the world. Messy and exhausting, but lovely.'

I ate the crisps.

Later that evening, I was standing quietly in my kitchen, stirring pasta sauce, thinking about Robbie and about Molly, about the Chatsworth Flower Festival and the Festival of the Flower Children, when there was a knock at the door.

I wiped my hands on a tea-towel, turned the heat on the hot plate down to let the water simmer, went to see who it was. I was expecting a neighbour. Bea maybe. Or Robbie.

A strange man was standing on the doorstep in the dusk. He looked to be in his mid-sixties and he was wearing the standard uniform of men of that age, who lived and worked in the countryside; checked shirt, v-neck woollen tank-top, brown corduroy trousers and muddy green wellington boots. He was of average height and build with a long, thin face.

'I'm Simon Miller,' he said.

It took a moment for it to click into place. 'My mother's

brother.' My uncle, in other words. 'That's right.' He stood up straighter, as if to give himself courage. 'Sorry to drop by unannounced but after your young man paid me a visit the other day, I've not been able to rest.'

'My young man?' I frowned. 'What visit?'

'Ah.' He shuffled his feet. 'I've gone and put my great big size twelves right in it, haven't I? He's not told you, has he?'

'You'd better come in?' I stood back to let him through the door.

'After you,' he said and followed me to the kitchen, where he stood looking around him, in much the same the way that visitors to Chatsworth did, finding themselves in the splendour of the Painted Hall. 'Nice place you've got.'

It was, though hardly the Painted Hall. 'Would you like a drink?'

'I'll pass on that.' He seemed jumpy, as if he was the suspect in a crime, who'd been taken into an interview room at a police station and knew he was about to be presented with evidence that proved him guilty. 'I'll not keep you long. I'll just say what I've come to say and be on my way.' But then he said nothing more.

I reminded myself that he might be a blood relation but I didn't know him from Adam and there was something fishy about him. He was hiding something. 'What is it that you wanted to say to me, Mr Miller?'

I half expected him to tell me to call him Uncle Simon or just Simon. He didn't. 'You'd best sit down.'

I pulled out one of the kitchen chairs and he did the same. 'What's going on?'

'Your mam,' he began, then hit the buffers again. 'I'm afraid to say it.'

'Afraid to say what?'

He took a deep breath and I saw beads of sweat glistening at his receding hairline. 'There's no easy way to tell you this, lass.'

'Tell me what?'

'Thing is. Sadly. Our Sue. She's…well…she's no longer with us.'

I could feel the pressure of blood rushing to my head, as if the world had spun out of control, flipped off its axis and turned me upside down. 'What do you mean?'

'Sue's dead. She died. Almost two years back now.'

'No.' I shook my head. 'That can't be right.'

'I'm afraid it is.'

'We'd have heard. They'd have let my dad know. She was his wife.'

Now it was Mr Miller's turn to shake his head. 'Was his wife, yes but not when she died, she wasn't. Maybe he never told you, in order to avoid upsetting you unnecessarily, since it would make no difference to you whether they were still married or not. But Sue filed for divorce, nearly six years back. You can hardly blame her. Your dad and her, they'd been apart for well over a decade and it's not as if there was any likelihood of a reconciliation.'

I shot to my feet, felt propelled by some explosion deep within me. I strode over to the cabinet above the sink and took down a glass, pulled the cork out of a half-drunk bottle of red wine and sloshed in a large measure. 'You sure you don't want a drink?'

'I don't drink.'

I'd always consoled myself that things hardly ever turned out as bad as you feared they might. But this. In all honesty, I'd never once considered that the last time I ever saw my mother, would be the last time I would ever see her.

'I'm sorry to be the bearer of bad tidings.' Simon Miller

rubbed at his stubbled chin, a bristly sound. 'Dearie me, I'm really not very good at this kind of thing.'

'I appreciate you taking the trouble to come and see me,' I said, sitting down again, trying to order my thoughts. They were jumping about, a riot in my head and I needed them to sit back down too.

'Well, you're family after all, even though we weren't acquainted until just now. Pity. I've two girls about your age. Cousins of yours.'

'I never met anybody from my mother's side of the family,' I said absently. 'Not even your parents. My grandmother and grandfather.'

'You wouldn't have done. Sue and our ma, they had big falling out a while back.'

'About what?'

'Oh, women's business. Sue was tricky, chippy, it has to be said. She fell out with lots of folk for no good reason.'

'Are either of your parents still alive?'

'Sadly not.'

I was about to take a slug of wine but I put the glass down again before it reached my lips. I needed to keep a clear head. 'How did my mother die?'

'She'd not been well for years. She had a lot of problems, did Sue.'

'What kind of problems?'

'She always thought the grass was greener, always wanted what she didn't have, hankered after the high life. And it did for her, in the end.'

'What do you mean?'

He looked pointedly at my wine glass. 'She had a drink problem. She was boozer, a lush, a drunkard, call it what you like. I'm afraid to say, it was alcoholism that killed her.'

It didn't come as a huge surprise. 'Did nobody get her any help?'

'Alcoholics are notoriously hard to help.'

'What happened?'

'Argh, I'm sure you don't want all the gory details?'

'I do. I need to know. Everything.'

Simon Miller shifted in his seat. 'When Susan left your dad, she hooked up with a solicitor, called Gary something or other. He had a big flashy house over in Whirlow and a flashy sports car to match and she had a wild time of it. Pink champagne and furs, days at the races, gala dinners, jetting off to St Tropez. She was always dressed to the nines, designer labels, dripping jewels. But none of it made her happy. She'd been drinking heavily, since long before she and your dad parted company, I reckon. And then Gary chucked her and it got much worse. She shacked up with a builder chap but that didn't help because he was a drinker too, by all accounts. A rough diamond. Alcoholics lie to themselves and they lie to everyone else. Sue hid it so well. Neighbours noticed that she got withdrawn but she still seemed her usual herself, most of the time. When she lost tons of weight, we made her go to see a doctor.' He paused, as if to check that I wanted him to continue.

'Go on.'

'They told her that her liver was packing up but that the damage was reversible and she would recover, as long as she stopped drinking. She did stop for a while but then she started again. About a year later, she was admitted to hospital and they warned her that if she touched one more drop, it would kill her. That scared her good and proper and we really thought she'd take note and pull through. Then we got a call to say she'd been rushed to A&E and had started haemorrhaging inside her and that was the beginning of the end. I'm so sorry,' he said. 'It's a tough thing to have to hear.'

I stared into the wine glass, suddenly drenched with sadness. 'Why did she drink so much?'

'We've all wondered that but maybe it's pointless to wonder. How many of us go home after a hard day and pour ourselves a drink, eh?' His eyes drifted back to my own wine glass again. 'But why some become addicted and others don't, is a question it seems that no one can answer.'

It was as if I'd been punched in the chest. I'd lost my mother over twenty years ago and I'd grieved for that loss as well as a ten-year-old child could grieve but losing her again now, so soon after losing my dad, it was not so much like reopening an old wound as stabbing the knife in deeper. The cumulative effect was too much. It felt as if my innards had been scooped out and stamped on.

I gripped the table. 'Where is she buried?' I managed to ask, thinking that at least now I'd have a place to take flowers.

'She wanted her ashes to be scattered in the South of France,' Simon said with a wry tut. 'Chance would be a fine thing. I mean. How do you get human remains through customs, I ask you? That was just like her, making unreasonable demands. Getting grand ideas. She's had to make do with the top of the great ridge, I'm afraid. It's close to where she was born after all and it's not such a bad place to end your days, looking out into Hope.'

'I can't believe I didn't know.'

'How could you know?' Simon reached out and patted my hand. 'Don't be so hard on yourself, ducky.'

When my dad died, it had a direct impact on my

everyday life, left a gaping hole but my mother's passing should make no difference to me, on a day-to-day basis. Except that it already did. Because a startling truth gate-crashed my thoughts. For all these years, since I was ten years old, I realised that I'd been fantasising about meeting my mother again, reaching some kind of understanding. One day. But now that one day could never come. I could never rekindle any kind of relationship with her. All those wasted years. And at the centre of it was the guilt which had now turned so much darker. If I'd never been born, my mother's whole existence would have been very different. She sounded so very unhappy and if things had gone differently for her, she might have been alive now. In a different place altogether. All the anger that I'd harboured for so long, dissipated. What did it matter? All that mattered was that Sukey had now gone to a place where I could never follow, from which there was no hope of return. I could never talk to her. Never call her Mum, never call anyone Mum.

Robbie had told me, years ago, that I should try to find my mother and if only I'd listened to him, I might have found her before it was too late.

'You said that my young man paid you a visit?'

'Nice, polite lad. He's clearly smitten with you. He said he'd asked you to marry him but he didn't think you'd be able to say yes. Unless your mum could come to the wedding.'

I shut my eyes, pressed my fingers against the closed lids, as if I could block out thoughts and images. What had Robbie gone and done? He shouldn't have interfered. He had no right.

It was like being trapped in a cosmic game of grandmother's footsteps. I'd always made a concerted effort to leave the past behind and I believed I'd succeeded, mostly, but all this time it had been creeping up on me, while I'd had my back turned and now it had pounced. Frustratingly, Robbie was right. I had always pictured Sukey at my wedding. I realised that it had been a sort of unacknowledged goal. When I got engaged, *if* I got engaged, that's when I'd finally find my mother. I'd find her and I'd invite her to my wedding and in my fantasy, she'd have been delighted to come. The two of us would be reconciled, reunited. We would do what mothers and daughters were supposed to do at such times. My mum would help me choose my dress, help me with the invitations and the planning. When the day came, she'd help style my hair, arrange my veil, just be there, sitting in the front pew and on the head table, looking chic in a posh frock and hat.

Robbie should have asked me, before he meddled in my family.

How could I marry him now, under this cloud?

Simon Miller let himself out and after he'd gone, I didn't have the strength to even move. I felt paralysed, crushed by a melancholy so dark and heavy it frightened me. A double grief. I was grieving for the mother I'd lost but underlying it, was a far worse grief, for the mother I'd never had, the kind of mother, friend, carer, confidante, who I'd needed and wanted as a child and needed and wanted still, but had never known and could never now know. I felt as if I'd not really grown up at all. My body had grown but inside, there was a child still. I still wanted my mum, someone to love me unconditionally.

'I'm sorry,' I said out loud to Sukey. 'I'm sorry if I ruined your life.'

Eventually, standing and moving very slowly, like a person who'd recently come from an operating theatre, I walked through to the living room. Without turning on the light, I took the flowers out of the Blue John candle-vase. Delphiniums and sweet peas. They were past their best but would have been good for another three or four days. I shoved them in the bin and inverted the finial. I put a slender, white candle in the holder, struck a match and held it to the wick to light it. That's what you did, wasn't it? You lit candles for the dead. My dad was dead and so was my mum. I sat on the arm of a chair and watched the little flame valiantly flicker and gutter, the droplets of wax dripping as the candle slowly burned down.

The phone rang and I let the answering machine click on.

Robbie's voice filled the darkness around me, both acutely familiar and wholly strange.

'Hi you,' he said. 'Hope you had a good day. Please call me, darling, when you can.'

I stared at the phone and suddenly all my grief and rage and disappointment was funnelled towards him. I snatched up the receiver. 'When were you going to tell me? Did you intend to keep my mother's death a secret forever?'

'Whoa. Hang on a minute. I said I needed to talk to you.'

That took the wind out of my sails. 'You should have said it was urgent,' I argued but with less bite and fight.

'I'm sorry,' he said, disarmingly. 'I'm so sorry, Sweetheart. Do you want me to come over?'

'No,' I said quietly. 'I need to be on my own.'

'OK. I understand.'

'No, you don't.' How could he? 'I'll talk to you soon.'

'OK,' he said gently. 'Bye for now.'

'Bye.'

In no time, it seemed, the candle had shrunk to a stub. I snuffed it out, then I picked up the candle-vase. When I touched it, I could feel her, my Mum. Very tenderly, I wrapped it in a fleecy blanket and tucked it into a rucksack, ready for morning.

CHAPTER THIRTY-FOUR

Bea was taking a tour of the flower arrangements with the Duchess, stopping to worry about a stain on the tablecloth in the dining room. The explosion of bright blooms inside the House presented huge challenges for the housekeeping team, who had to clear up dropped leaves and pollen dust, along with the regular dust. Just keeping the flowers watered was a full-time job, at the same time ensuring the water didn't overflow onto the any of the antique furniture.

In a house filled with flowers, all I could think about now was weddings and funerals.

'You OK?' Lizzie asked me, handing me a watering can. 'You've gone and lost all your sparkle.'

'Robbie asked me to marry him.'

'Oh, hurrah,' Lizzie was beaming from ear to ear. 'About flipping time.'

'Wrong time.'

She frowned. 'Silva, whatever's the matter?'

'My mother died. I just found out.'

'What?' Lizzie put down her can, instantly wrapped me in a tight hug. 'That's too much.' She moved back, studied my face. 'What happened to her? When did she die?'

'Two years ago. She was an alcoholic.'

'I'm so, so sorry.' Then: 'So were you going to say yes to Robbie?'

'I think so. Probably. I don't know. I don't know anything anymore.'

'Listen, this is huge. Massive. Give yourself time. You just need to do whatever you need to do, to help you come to terms with this.'

'I will do.'

When I had half a chance.

It turned into another mad day. Coach loads of pensioners arrived en masse, to ride around in garden buggies, eating ice creams. Two buggies were off the road, awaiting repairs and there was a bit of a skirmish when two American ladies tried to jump the queue and people got irate. My dad would once have been called to the rescue, to fix the broken-down vehicles. I didn't possess his technical knowhow but I did have his practical attitude, a knack for thinking on my feet, coupled with his determination, that nobody should leave Chatsworth with any negative experiences. If people complained about anything, he always took it to heart. It wouldn't do, to have people queuing for something that wouldn't arrive. I radioed through for the Duke's personal buggy and the American ladies were thrilled, thinking they'd been given real VIP treatment.

Bea thanked me: 'You saved the day.'

'How many times did people say that about my Dad?'

'Many, many times, love. Silva, are you all right?'

I forced a smile. 'I will be.'

At lunch time I made my way along the service passage

that served as the main artery of the House, connecting the north wing. It was here that I'd always felt the presence of the ghosts of the previous estate workers most strongly, the girls, aged twelve to fourteen, including my grandmother Ivy, who'd once lined up across the corridor, on hands and knees and scrubbed from one end to the other.

Carrying my weighted rucksack hooked over my shoulder, I climbed to the third floor, which had been converted to a suite of offices. Feeling more positive and purposeful, I took the steps two at a time, knocked on the oak door of the office that belonged to Matthew Redfearn, Keeper of Collections.

It was a hugely important role at Chatsworth, since the keeper oversaw the curators, textiles team, archivists and a host of other people, who cared for the thousands of historic objects in the Devonshire Collection. Matt was still young, in his late thirties and he was very unpretentious, despite his grand title. He drank cider with me in The Club, played pool with me, usually lost. We had a short history of our own, the two of us. When I turned twenty-one, Matt had taken me for a celebratory bottle of fizz at the Devonshire Arms, which had led to a dinner in the Cavendish Restaurant. I'd enjoyed talking to him, hearing how from a young age, he liked nothing better than to wander off for hours around stately homes. We'd ended up in bed together after a Christmas staff party, which had felt like a mistake, only not for Matt. He made no secret of the fact that he would jump at the chance to have a chance with me. I really wasn't capitalising on the fact that I knew he'd do anything for me. I was only going to ask him to do this one small thing.

He called out for whoever was knocking to come in.

I peaked round the door. The hushed old room exuded

warmth and comfort, with a colour-scheme taken from the natural beauty beyond the window. There were oil paintings of the countryside on the cream painted walls and a large photograph of Matt's beloved black Labrador, Bono, on the wide, oak desk. Which needed polishing, I noted. I'd pop back later with my duster.

'D'you have a moment?'

'For you I do.' His smile was as mellow as his surroundings.

Despite being of medium height and build, Matthew had an imposing presence. He dressed in well-cut English gent suits and shirts. Only recently, he'd grown a short pointy beard that made him appear more European than English, as if his ancestors had sailed in with the Spanish Armada.

He stood and offered me the seat at the other side of his desk. 'What can I do for you, lovely lady?'

'My mother left something for me. An heirloom, I guess. I'd like to know more about it and I wondered if you could help.'

'Those sound like the kind of questions I most like to be asked.' Matt frowned. 'But it's your dad who recently passed away.' Matt had come to the funeral.

'I just found out my mother died too. It was two years ago actually but I didn't know, until a few days ago.' It felt careless somehow. Tragic.

'That's really tough. I'm so sorry.'

'Thanks. Anyway. Like I say, she left me this one thing. It's all I have of hers. It's made of Blue John.'

'Blue John?' That piqued his interest, as I'd known it would. Matt made no secret of the fact that the important collection of Blue John at Chatsworth was one of the main reasons he'd come to work here in the first place. He'd written about Blue John for several specialist journals. I had never told him about my own prized possession because I didn't want to dredge up the whole sorry tale of Sukey. I felt differently about all that now.

'D'you have it with you?' Matt asked.

'I do.' I opened my rucksack, took it out, rested it in my lap, as I carefully unwound the blanket, which I then used to give the desk a quick dust before I stood the candle-vase on it.

Matt looked at me and at it, dumbfounded. 'May I?' he asked, before touching it.

'Feel free.'

I watched as he picked it up with great reverence and examined it. 'How long has this been in your family?'

'I've no idea. I was hoping you might be able to tell me when it was made.'

'And by who? Since you're a craftswoman yourself, you must be interested in that?' Matt often stopped to chat to me at the forge. People had noticed and there had long been gossip about the two of us in the staff-room. 'The discovery of Blue John and its potential for turning into ornaments is shrouded in mystery,' he said. 'But we do know that it was Henry Watson, son of our own master carpenter, Samuel, who first invented a lathe for turning Derbyshire Spar, as it was called back then. Besides him, the most important craftsman was Matthew Boulton of course, not forgetting James Shore, who made the Chatsworth Tazza. But sadly, few pieces can be attributed to any craftsman and fewer still can be dated.'

'Might this have been made by Watson? Or Boulton or James Shore?' Could one of these illustrious men be my ancestor?

'Matthew Boulton was the first to exploit the new

passion for the antique taste, as it was called, which created a craze for vases,' Matt said.

'But you don't think this is his work?'

He gave a definite shake of his head. 'Influenced by him, certainly.' He stopped talking, in order to concentrate better as he carefully lifted the top off the vase, turned it upside down. 'It's most probably from the same period.'

'The eighteenth century?'

'Mid to late eighteenth. But there are differences to Boulton's work. Pleasing ones, to my eye at least. The omission of gilding is the obvious one. Boulton was all for showy extravagance and opulent flourishes and there's a simplicity to the lines of your piece that I must say I like.'

'Me too.'

He peered at the bottom of the vase more closely as a slow smile spread across his face.

'Care to share?'

'I was going to say that since Matthew Boulton worked with ormolu and also specialised in Sheffield plate and silver, his pieces are generally easy to identify, since the metalwork is stamped with a maker's mark. But your piece, though it has no metalwork, also has a mark of a kind. See?'

He showed me a kind of engraving. Three lines, two vertical and one horizontal, like a loose capital A with the two upright lines not quite meeting at the top. Or else it was a capital H with the two lines a little slanted towards each other, like the walls in a house of cards. It was small but clearly visible, once you knew what you were looking at.

'It's more like a stonemason's signature,' Matt said. 'The kind you see on church walls.'

It felt as if a gap was being bridged, a circle closing. 'So you know who made it?'

'Indeed I do. Because we happen to have an almost

identical piece in the collection here, bearing the same signature.'

'Do we? I've never seen it? Never cleaned it.'

'You won't have done. It's in storage, up in the attic with lots of other items we have no room for. But I went to great lengths to trace its provenance a while ago. We have masses of documents relating to the Blue John industry in the archives here, of course, since Castleton and the Blue John mines were all part of the Duke of Devonshire's estate, back in the eighteenth century. There's lots of paperwork here, originating from that period.' He glanced at his watch. 'Look, Lara's coming to see me in ten minutes to talk about cleaning the tapestries but come and find me after you finish work tomorrow and I'll show you something. You're gonna love it.'

I felt I was letting my dad down, getting distracted with Sukey, when I should be out looking for Molly, doing as he'd asked me to do. But right now, I needed to do this for myself.

CHAPTER THIRTY-FIVE

Next day was a typical rainy spring day in Derbyshire, visitors under umbrellas, waiters in the cafes upending the outdoor chairs to tip off the puddles. The archives housed the Chatsworth weather books, which had been kept daily by the gardeners since the nineteenth century, with rainfall, hours of sunshine, temperature and barometric pressure recordings, collected at the so-called weather station on the big lawn. Robbie's dad saw keeping these books up to date as an obligation stretching back decades, so I'd heard plenty about the archives from him but I'd never actually seen them.

They were stored on the ground floor of the North Wing but it felt like entering an underground vault. The vast space was partitioned into long, narrow alleyways, by shelves stacked from floor to ceiling with numbered box files, battered lever arch files and great leather-bound tomes.

'There are six thousand boxes here,' Matt commented. 'Two miles of estate papers and correspondence, diaries, inventories, account books, scrapbooks and all sorts of other papers relating to Devonshire family life and estate management. So much of it is hasn't been looked at for centuries.'

'Really?' I was astounded. 'I assumed everything had been sorted and catalogued ages ago.'

Matt shook his head. 'Our volunteers are painstakingly going through each box and listing the contents. We're unearthing wonderful gems all the time.'

Hundreds of colourful characters from Chatsworth's long and illustrious history were no doubt gathered here, details of the great dramas that had played out within the gracious old walls of the House. So many stories, just waiting to see the light of day. It made me think of Robbie. Everything made me think of Robbie, annoyingly. The stories here, even if they were hidden, were at least already safely preserved. It was just a case of finding the time to dig them up and dust them off. Many of these documents might have lain here for decades, had waited a hundred years or more to be unearthed and read but they would wait another hundred if need be. Whereas for Robbie, time was running out. He was always saying how the songs and stories he'd made it his mission to collect, were held only in the heads and hearts of the elders, as he called them. The tradition bearers and keepers of the flame, people who were not long for this world. And when they were gone, their songs would be gone with them, their wisdom and tales of the old ways, would be lost for all time. The death of both my parents had suddenly brought the urgency of his work home to me so forcibly. I understood it now, what he was doing. And I wished with all of my heart that I'd done it too. That I'd sat them both down, my father and mother, not together obviously but individually and asked them to tell me about their lives, while there was still time. Maybe the Blue John candle-vase could at least tell me something.

'The documents are all being sorted chronologically,' Matt explained. 'They're assigned reference numbers, then the details are entered onto a spreadsheet with identifying dates, provenance and a brief description of contents. That's what Heather here is doing. She's a postgrad student from Sheffield University and she's making a study of the household accounts, for her PhD on female servants through the ages.'

A young girl with dyed pink hair was sitting at a small square desk, piled high with bundles and piles of letters, which had practically buried her.

'I bet it's fascinating,' I said.

'And time consuming. We have to read each document,' Heather explained, adjusting the heavy black-framed glasses on her nose. 'But that's the best part. The way the personalities leap at you from the page sometimes. They feel so close, so alive.'

What stories might be waiting for me, about the person who'd made the candle-vase, who might be a blood relation, a real connection to Sukey?

'We'll let you get on,' Matt said to Heather. She buried her diamond studded-nose once more in the papers and Matt led me to another tiny wooden desk, sheltered on three sides by more tall shelves.

'Sit yourself down,' he said, dragging out a box file.

He put it on the desk and leafed through it for a minute or so, evidently hunting for something. Eventually, he handed me a single sheet of paper. 'Here. It's a receipt from 1777. Duchess Georgiana was a great collector of Blue John, as you know.'

The writing was elegant but indecipherable. 'How come everyone in olden times wrote like they'd learnt calligraphy?' I was sure that writing styles played a large part in creating the impression that past ages were more genteel. The ink had faded to sepia-brown, so I struggled to make out a single word, anything much beyond the date.

Matt helpfully read it aloud. 'Ten shillings, for two Blue John bodies for Cleopatra vases. Paid to Widow Hall of Castleton.'

'Widow Hall?' I could make out the name now, it leapt out of the page and almost gave me a friendly wave.

'You were right about the maker's mark representing an H,' Matt said. 'Matthew Boulton was a manufacturer, an industrialist. The Blue John bodies he used for his candle-vases weren't made by his own fair hand. Sometimes he bought lumps of raw Blue John and had it transported to his manufactory near Birmingham, where the bodies were shaped by his craftsmen. But often as not, he bought the shaped bodies direct from the Blue John workers in Castleton. Georgiana, being the local landowner, would have known the workers and would have her pick of their pieces.'

This was all very interesting. But. 'How do you know my candle-vase was made by Widow Hall?'

'Several reasons. Boulton was a prolific writer of notebooks and journals. In one of the many notebooks he left behind for us, he carefully listed all his suppliers. The journals are kept at the museum at Soho House and I've studied them. She's in there, plain as day: Widow Hall from Goosehill, Castleton. Blue John bodies were usually made with two or more pieces of stone, held together with projecting pegs and holes and a threaded rod, which screwed into a base plate inside the stone body. Many of the signatures on Boulton's candle-vases aren't visible, unless you dismantle them and know what you're looking for but the experts at Soho have done that on numerous occasions. Excitingly, they've confirmed that they've seen a fair few bodies with the self-same mark as on your candle-vase.' He paused. 'So, it's pretty conclusive.'

'Amazing.'

'Thought you'd like it. But there's more.' Matt opened a manilla folder and drew out a tiny, tattered piece of paper.

It was another receipt, this one from Henry Watson and I could read this without Matt's help. I could read the name Hall and the name which proceeded it, a name with a pattern, a palindrome. The receipt was made out not to the Widow Hall but to Anna Hall.

'Anna?'

'Anna.'

'Are they..?'

'One and the same? They must be. The maker's mark.'

Of course. It was neither an A nor an H but was meant to signify both those letters in one. Her initials. Anna Hall. There was an artful playfulness to it that I admired and it brought Anna suddenly to life. 'How clever of her to think of that.'

'Ingenious.'

Anna. It felt wonderful to be on first name terms.

'So we know that Widow Hall, Anna, was selling Blue John to both Watson and Boulton,' Matt said. 'She was supplying the two pre-eminent Blue John manufacturers of her time. Which means, that she must have been highly-skilled and a good businesswoman.'

Irrespective of whether or not we were blood relations, I was linked to Anna. She'd lived over two hundred years ago but I had in my possession, something she'd crafted and created, had doubtless been rightly proud of. When I started at the forge, I used to dream about how some of my work might live on, after I had gone. I imagined the people who might pass through gates I'd made and sit on my benches in the sunshine and I felt bonded to those people from a future I would not live to see but who would, I hoped, see what I had crafted and take pleasure from it. Even if Anna turned out not to be kin, we were kindred spirits

'Was she very unusual? Were there many craftswomen in those days?'

'Until the Industrial Revolution, cottage industries ruled,' Matt said. 'Husbands, wives and children, all working together, making things in the home. But we know that Anna was a widow, so she would have additional pressing need to bring in an income. I did do some research on her and I found out that she had three children. Her husband was a lead miner, so chances are he died in an accident down the mine. They were such lethal places to work that death was commonplace. And having been left a widow, Anna would have been forced to find a means to support herself and her brood. A single, working-mother, centuries before the label was bandied about in tabloid newspapers. All that was new in our century, you know, was the concept that mothers should *not* work outside the home, that they should find complete fulfilment at the kitchen sink.'

I laughed, remembered where we were and quickly shut up. 'Dear Matt, God love you, you sound like a feminist.'

'I take that as a compliment.'

I looked down at the two receipts. It was humbling. To think how over two hundred years ago, a lead miner's widow, who was likely to have been uneducated, had found a way to support herself and her family through her craft and from a life of extreme hardship, she'd crafted the most exquisite pieces of work, which were treasured centuries later. How wonderful to be related through blood and genes, to someone so gutsy and skilled. Far better than being related to Matthew Boulton even. The fieldwork Robbie did, delving into a rich heritage of song and story, amongst tinkers and travellers and the descendants of farmworkers and fishermen and the story of Anna Hall, all confirmed people's ability to create a rich culture in the poorest circumstances.

'Do you have a maker's mark?' Matt asked.

'Kind of. I've a stamp. A little oak tree. As in Silva. From the forest.' Robbie's idea.

'That's quaint,' Mark said.

'Quaint?'

He grinned. 'I hope your Blue John piece is well insured.'

I felt like I'd inadvertently stumbled into an episode of 'Antiques Roadshow.' One of Sukey's favourite television programmes. She'd watched it avidly, every week.

'Why? How much d'you think it's worth?'

'At a rough estimate, I'd say it would fetch anything up to £30,000 at auction.'

I wished I was sitting down. That was a life changing amount of money. I should have felt elated to learn that I owned something so valuable but instead, I felt like a burst balloon.

That's how you see me. A thief. Who stole what was not mine.

'Could I do some sort of family tree, to prove how Anna Hall is related to me? I'd so love to know for certain. Prove that the vase could have been handed down as an heirloom.' It wasn't only that I needed to know that Sukey hadn't stolen the Blue John. I'd lost Sukey but I wanted to make absolutely sure that Anna was mine. Lose a mother but gain a several times great-grandmother.

'Reverse genealogy,' Matt smiled.

'Beg your pardon?'

'You want to go from the past to the present, rather than from the present to the past, as generally happens?'

'Is that possible?'

'There's a whole government department dedicated to that sort of genealogy.'

He must be having me on. 'A government department?'

'The Bona Vacantia Division, it's called. Heir Hunters, in other words.'

'Cool job title.'

'Isn't it just?'

'So would it be possible, to trace forward from Anna, find out if my mother really was descended from her?'

'How wide d'you want to spread the net?'

'How do you mean?'

'Well, say Anna had four children and each of them had just two kids, that's eight families and say each of them had another two children, that's sixteen, and so on. There's six or seven generations between the late 1700s and present day, so you're talking about a family tree involving hundreds of people. However, you could simply follow the main blood-line, like the heir hunters do: find out who would most likely inherit, in each generation. Follow the most likely journey of an heirloom, in effect.'

'Yes,' I exclaimed. 'Exactly.'

'Leave it with me.'

'Oh, I can't ask you to do that.'

'You didn't ask. I offered. I actually insist. You'd be doing me a favour. This is what I like doing.' He gave me a smile, identical to the smile he'd smiled at me, that one time we'd ended up in the same bed. 'Call me a geek if you like.'

'Geek.'

'Come for a drink with me?'

'I'm sorry, Matt. I've stuff to do.'

'Another time.' He looked disappointed and I knew that there wouldn't be another time, that he wouldn't ask again. 'There's a good chance your Anna came here, you know,' he added brightly. 'Chatsworth House has been open to the public since it was built and in Anna's day, the housekeeper had instructions to show people round.' We were at the door to the Orangery now. 'Anyway, you have a fun evening.'

'You too and thank you so much for letting me pick your brains.'

'You're very welcome.'

CHAPTER THIRTY-SIX

I'd vacuumed all the carpets in my cottage, which didn't need vacuuming. The bath didn't need cleaning either but I'd cleaned that too. I'd stripped the bed and pushed the sheets into the washing machine, even though I'd only put clean ones on two days ago. None of it had been therapeutic or even satisfying, the way cleaning was generally satisfying for me. It used to make me feel calm and in control, but this time it wasn't working.

Matt had wished me a fun evening and now here I was, sitting alone on the sofa, nursing a cup of tea. Even Tijou had taken himself off, to sit up on my newly made bed.

Outside it was pouring with rain, the drops splattering against the windows, giving the room a subaqueous glow. The weekend stretched ahead and I felt an onslaught of loneliness. Maybe it came from the dawning realisation that both my parents were gone. I was thirty-three, single, with no children and no family. I'd plenty of great friends though, belonged to a tight-knit community, who were all as good as family. From the outside, people often thought it must be odd, so many people living and working together in close proximity, but really, it was wonderful. Still, I had nobody who was directly connected to me by blood or law, nobody who was first and foremost mine. If I had to fill out a form stating next of kin, who would it be?

Robbie wanted to be my husband. I could be his wife. Why was I so reluctant?

I turned my thoughts to Anna Hall instead. My relationship to her seemed less complicated. I reached for the comfort of my sketchbook and pencil, started doodling the letters A and H and then underneath them, I drew the amalgam of the letters as they appeared in Anna's inventive maker's mark. So clever, how she'd turned her initials into an emblem, an early example of a logo.

Drawing always made the cogs in my brain turn in a totally different way and this time, they released a memory. The signature on the photograph of Molly Marrison that hung on the wall in the Rambler Inn. The signature that was also more like a symbol. It looked like four petals of a flower or a four-leafed clover. I doodled that too. The petals or leaves all tilted upwards, so they appeared like two hearts, side by side, their tips almost adjoined but not quite. Now, this was pleasing. And I was reassuring myself and my dad, if he was looking down on me, that I'd not forgotten about Molly.

Then it hit me. They were not petals or hearts. They were initials too. MM. Like Anna's emblem. AH for Anna Hall. MM for Molly Marrison. The two Ms side-by-side but tilted, one to the left and one to the right, with the downward strokes of the letters brought almost together to form tips. An autograph and a little drawing all in one. It made me smile, made me like Molly more than ever.

It was hardly a major discovery but all the same, my

first instinct was to share it with Robbie. Should I ring him? I was still cross with him for going behind my back. But I'd wanted him to fight for me, hadn't I and that's what he'd done, wasn't it? His motives had been entirely good, as ever. He'd only been trying to help me. That's all he'd wanted to do. He'd known what the problem was for me, even if I'd not known it myself. My dad couldn't come to my wedding, so he'd wanted to make it so that my mother could be there instead. He'd tried to put things right and inadvertently made it so much worse, but that wasn't his fault. And aside from all that, I missed him. Nothing felt right without him.

I picked up the phone, dialled his number.

'I was just about to ring you,' he said.

'You were?'

'All right if I pop round?'

'What? Now?'

'It that's OK with you.'

'It's OK with me.'

Less than half an hour later he was standing my kitchen, opening the neat draw of utensils and helping himself to a corkscrew, opening a bottle of red. It was still raining outside but the evening had just got a whole lot brighter. He was wearing black jeans and a white t-shirt under an open khaki utility-shirt and his hair was freshly washed, a tumble of chestnut curls. He looked unbearably cute.

If I said I'd marry him, I'd be able to touch him, kiss him, take him to bed, whenever I wanted to, like right now.

'I've been thinking,' Robbie said.

'Dangerous,' I smiled, taking down two glasses.

'We need to look at the lyrics of Molly's song about the Runaway Lovers.'

I held out a glass for him to fill. 'OK?' I'd assumed we'd talk about Sukey and my uncle, weddings. I'd never expected him to bring up Molly, even though of course that was what had prompted me to call him. It was as if he knew that it was easier and better for me to talk about this right now.

'The key, the clue, it's in that song,' he said. 'The more I think about it, the more I'm certain of it. It's in that odd last verse, the one that only Molly appears to know.'

Enthusiastically, he took a piece of paper from his pocket and unfolded it on the kitchen table, flattened it out with a sweep of his hand, then leant over with his palms on the tabletop, studying it like a General might study a strategic battle map. I'd seen his bold, arty handwriting on countless greeting cards and little notes over the years and it always made me inordinately happy.

He'd not written out the whole song, just the lyrics of that mysterious last verse.

Shamed and damned, blood on their hands,
An eye for an eye, a life for a life,
A widow, where once was a wife,
Then from the darkness of Waterhull,
Something so rare and beautiful
With this ring, I give you a song to sing

'The rest of the song is about Henry and Clara,' he said. 'But not this verse. This part is different.'

'Hmm, it's like a riddle,' I said, sliding into a chair, toying with the end of my plait.

Robbie pulled out a chair opposite me, spun the piece of

paper towards me, so it was the right way up for me to read again. He jabbed it with his finger. 'The tone, the point of view, everything. This verse is not about Henry and Clara, it's about the men who murdered them.'

'Blood on their hands. I get that. But what's Waterhull?'

'Don't know.'

'Matt might know.'

'Matt?'

I filled Robbie in on what I'd just learnt about Anna Hall.

No response.

'Isn't that fascinating?'

Still no reply.

'Robbie? What is it?' He was looking at me so oddly.

'I reckon I know how Anna Hall became Widow Hall.'

'A mining accident?'

Robbie shook his head, drank some wine, looking at me over the rim of his glass. He was enjoying this now, prolonging the suspense. 'Hall,' he said. 'Did that name not ring any bells?'

'Erm, no. Should it?'

'What were the names of the five men who murdered Henry and Clara?'

'I thought we weren't supposed to name names?'

'But they're listed on the plaque by the saddle in the museum.'

'Like I'm supposed to remember?'

'One of the miners was called Tom Hall.'

'Which is not an uncommon name, especially round here.'

'True. Hall is a Castleton family name. And Tom was also a very popular given name for a man in the eighteenth century.'

'But?'

'But,' Robbie said. 'Remember that I've been obsessed with this song for years, same as my mum. I know the story of it, inside out. First of all, it's important to point out, that even though they're commonly referred to as a gang of miners, the five men were not actually all miners. There were two blacksmiths.'

'Really?'

'Yeah. And one of the blacksmiths who murdered Henry and Clara, was called George Bradshaw.'

'You've lost me.'

His eyes locked with mine for a moment as if to say: Please tell me I haven't lost you. 'George Bradshaw has always been described as Tom Hall's brother-in-law. A historian, researching the story fifty years ago for a pamphlet for the local history society, asked to see the register of baptisms and marriages at St Edward's Church in Castleton, to find out more about the murderers and their families. And guess what? George Bradshaw had a sister named Anna, who married a man called Tom Hall. Now, there may have been more than one Tom Hall living in Castleton at the time of the murder but there surely can't have been more than one Anna Bradshaw, with a brother called George, who married a man called Tom Hall?'

'That does seen...unlikely.'

'So you know what this means?'

I screwed up my eyes, rubbed at my brow. 'Anna Hall, who made my candle-vase and may be one of my ancestors, was left a widow because her husband, who would of course be another of my ancestors, was a cold-blooded murderer. What happened to Tom?'

'He took his own life after killing The Runaway Lovers.'

'It's a Shakespearian tragedy.'

'Hmm.'

'And these are possibly my ancestors?'

'Isn't it crazy?' Robbie said.

'It's all completely crazy. Especially if you believe there's no such thing as coincidence.'

He looked at me for the longest time, as if he might never see me again and needed to fix my face in his memory. 'Do you believe that?'

'I don't know what I believe anymore.'

'But you don't believe in us?'

I stretched my hands across the table and took tight hold of his hands. 'I just...I can't think about us right now.'

'You're still angry with me?'

Was I? I shook my head. 'No, not angry.'

'You just don't want to be with me?'

'I can't be with you but only because I can't be with anyone. I don't even want to be with myself, most of the time.'

'Don't say that.'

'It's true.'

'Take it from me. You're the best company.'

If I had three wishes which could all come true, what would they be? I didn't have a clue. 'I don't know what I want, or even who I am anymore.'

'You're the most amazing person. That's who.'

'You're a sweetie.'

'So are you.'

I emptied my lungs, raked my fingers in my hair as I slumped down the back of the chair. 'Sometimes I feel like I'm at war with myself. I feel so...'

'So?'

'Screwed up, I guess.'

He looked troubled and then he looked as if he'd just

been struck by a funny thought.

'What?'

'I was about to say that I'd like to unscrew you. But that sounds all wrong.'

I giggled. He always knew how to make me laugh. 'If anyone could unscrew me, it would certainly be you.'

'Well, that's good to know. Thanks for that.'

I saw then how we could so easily be just friends again. Forget proposals of marriage. Everything back the way it had always been. Maybe our time had passed. We'd just missed each other, romantically. But it would all be alright. I'd still have him in my life. Lovers came and went, husbands and wives too for that matter. But the best friends were the best. Could be friends forever.

'Promise me we'll always be friends,' I said.

'Promise.'

I wanted him to tell me that he wanted me to be so much more than that. This was the moment, his cue and he'd just let it slide by.

'Here's another thing,' Robbie pointed out gently, steering us back to more solid ground. 'Anna's brother George was a blacksmith, like I say and since that craft generally ran in families, it's highly likely that their father was a blacksmith too. Naturally, it follows that if Anna is your direct ancestor, then so is her father. So that would mean it's not just artistic flair that runs in your family but actual blacksmithing.'

'Oh my goodness, yes.'

Robbie had always been a person who took more pleasure in giving gifts than in receiving them and he grinned at me. 'Knew you'd get a kick out of that.'

I picked up the piece of paper, the lyrics that lay between us. 'I wonder what else this song can tell us?'

CHAPTER THIRTY-SEVEN

Dusting the seventeen thousand books that lined the shelves in Chatsworth's impressive library, provided ongoing work for me and the other housemaids. Not that I thought of it as work.

I loved being in the library. The sixth Duke, having inherited his mother Georgiana's passion for books, had converted the long gallery, commissioning his architect to remodel it with bookcases around all four sides, beneath gilded plasterwork ceiling. The enormous Persian carpet and shaded lamps made the grand room also surprisingly intimate and cosy.

I had spent countless hours, taking the books down one by one and carefully brushing the dust from their jackets and the tops of the pages and I'd often imagined what it must be like, to actually just sit and read within those hallowed walls. The turquoise and gold silk brocade settee looked far too lovely to actually sit on but it would be such an atmospheric setting in which to learn about history or practically any other subject. The thousands of volumes covered every topic under the sun: art and music, science and natural history. Just being there, cleaning, made me feel more learned, as if I was absorbing the wisdom and knowledge contained within the millions of pages through my hands, breathing it in.

Today, I was up the scaffold tower again, dusting the very top shelf and my eyes were drawn to one book in particular, a slim volume entitled, *The Ballads and Songs of Derbyshire* by Llewellyn Jewitt.

You could tell, just from the spine, nut brown leather embossed with faded gold lettering, that it was an old book, very old. I slipped the slim volume from the shelf and with utmost reverence and care, I opened the cover. The spine crackled alarmingly and the pages were foxed and mottled, the edges rough cut. I held it open like a prayer book in my hands, breathed in the evocative smell of ancient paper, as I leafed through the pages of lyrics, past a wonderful woodcut illustration of a wandering minstrel named Singing Sam, from whom a great many of the songs had been collected.

Towards the end, there it was. *The Runaway Lovers*. The version that Robbie had always sung. The one that everyone else sang too. Everyone but Molly.

Later that morning, I was sitting on a red carpeted step of the grand staircase, dusting Tijou's intricate ironwork with a hogs-hair brush, a painstaking task that had to be done every day before the House opened. Tijou and all the craftsmen who made all the intricate decoration at Chatsworth, never thought about how hard it would be to keep everything clean. Or maybe they did think, but didn't let that put them off. Thank goodness. The craftsmen and women of old had a different take on time. They devoted so much care and attention to their craft, to creating objects of beauty. I thought how, in the modern world, we'd lost that patience and ability, that pride. Nobody had the time to perfect a craft and nobody was willing to pay them for their time.

Everyone was still very busy here. The flower festival was over but there was hardly any breathing space before it was on with the Horse Trials. Two years ago, the Duke and Duchess's daughter-in-law, Amanda, took over the running of the event and it was now the highlight of the social calendar, attracting the world's leading riders. The course designer was an Olympic gold medallist and seventy-five fences had been erected, with marquees and tents going up all over the park. In the kitchens the chefs, sous chefs, cooks and bakers, plus fifty catering staff were busy preparing canapés for a champagne reception in the Painted Hall, a thank you to the hundred vets and officials.

In the midst of all the hubbub, Matt had made time to do what he had promised to do and he came looking for me, sat himself down on the stair beside me. He said: 'So, good news. I've found Anna Hall's living descendant for you.'

I put down the brush, sure I'd misheard. 'Say again?'

'I've found…'

'Is it…me?' But I knew already that it wasn't me.

'Chap called Percy. He lives up near Peak Cavern.'

Now I stared at him, literally agape. 'What? What did you just say?'

'I said that Anna Hall's descendant is a fellow called Percy who lives…'

'That's insane. No way! Percy is descended from Anna Hall?'

'You know him?'

'Yes,' I said. 'At least. I think I do. Of course I do. He's always known as Percy of the Peak. Percy Peak for short. I'm not related to him. As far as I know. I mean. I can't be. That would be way too weird.'

'He married a girl called Esme .'

Karl Texas said that Molly's mother was called Esme. Not exactly a common name.

It was just as well that I had been sitting down on the stairs because it felt as if all the energy had left my limbs and been diverted to my brain, which had gone into overdrive.

Molly had been friends with Sukey and John, so say she was roughly the same age as them, born twenty or so years before me, in the mid 1940s. That meant that Molly's own parents would have been born around the 1920s. Which would put them now in their eighties. Could it be true then? Was Percy Molly Marrison's father?

In which case, the Blue John candle-vase had belonged to Molly's family, not Sukey's. The Blue John was Molly's heirloom, not mine.

That's how you see me now. A thief. Who stole what was not mine.

Suddenly, all the pieces fell into place and it all made sense, a sickening kind of sense. Sukey had stolen the valuable vase from Molly and my dad wanted her to have it back. That's why I needed to find her. I needed to give back to Molly what was rightfully hers, something worth tens of thousands of pounds. I felt as if I'd been steamrollered. Was that all it had ever been about? I didn't have a lost sister or brother? I simply had to give up an object that had always been very precious to me but for all the wrong reasons?

Percy and Molly though. Molly and Percy. My dad had loved Percy's daughter? My dad had loved the daughter of Robbie's teacher. It felt like a bad precedent somehow. What went wrong for Molly and Johnny?

'He's here again, Moll,' says Molly's dad, addressing her closed bedroom door. 'I've a mind to call the police station. Get them to tell him to stop being such a nuisance.'

'No, Dad,' Molly orders from behind her door.

It's December. Four months, a hundred and five days to be precise, since Molly hitched back to Derbyshire from Woburn Abbey. This is the fourth time that Johnny has come to their house and politely but persistently, knocked on the door and waited, then turned around and gone home again.

She gets up off the bed, goes to the window, hides to the side but shifts the curtain a little with her finger, so she can peek out. See but not be seen. She looks down into the lane and there he is, waiting by their front door. Her heart twists. She used to see him nearly every day and she misses him so much. She feels bruised inside. He looks dejected, head bowed, shoulders hunched into his greatcoat, as if it's cold and raining, only it's a bright, breezy day. Maybe she should just let him say what he wants to say. Get it all over and done with.

'Ask him to wait while I put my shoes on.'

She walks down to the hallway. 'Wouldn't it be best to invite him in?' Her grandmother says. 'You don't want folk to gossip.'

'Folk will always gossip, Gran.'

She slips out to join Johnny and with barely an acknowledgement to one another, they walk away from the house in silence, more a march than a walk. The breeze is making the clouds race high above them and Molly doesn't think where they're going. She just keeps her head down as she makes for the edge of town. Johnny follows her, the tails of great coat flapping like a cloak, as they walk out towards Winnats Pass, past the old Odin Mine and round to the Blue John Cavern.

Eventually, Molly is forced to stop short. They've reached the A road that lies below Mam Tor. It was built back in the 1800s, linking Castleton to Chapel-en-le-Frith, by crossing the side of the Shivering Mountain. But bumps and cracks kept appearing in the road, due to the force of millions of tons of shale that had been moving down the hillside, for thousands of years. The civil engineers finally admitted they were fighting a losing battle and the road was permanently closed to traffic, abandoned to nature. The broken road has been left where it lies, snapped and buckled, contorted into the most unimaginable shapes and structures within the perilous cliffs.

The clouds continue to scud overhead, wheeling around the two figures, the young man and woman, standing together on the ruined hillside. Molly knows that the words each of them say to each other next, will seal their fate.

'You might as well just spit it out.' The wind snatches at

Molly's words. 'Call me a slut or a trollop or whatever you want to call me. Get it off your chest.'

'That's not why I'm here.'

The original white road markings point in haphazard directions now, separated by deep fissures in the tarmac. A good line for a song: We've run out of road.

The disused road quickly acquired another purpose, has become an adventure track for scooters and cyclists, who use the cracks to perform stunts and jumps. Right now, a father in a peaked cap has parked his Cortina estate in a lay-by and is unloading two bikes for two little boys who are jumping up and down with excitement. Molly wonders if the baby growing inside her is a boy or a girl. Johnny should be there to teach their child to ride a bike. They could come here for a fun day out. Could they go back to how they were before the festival? It was a crazy time. Time out of time. Could they just wipe it, pick up where they left off? Will Johnny forgive her? Would he ever trust her again?

Molly watches as the two boys set off, pedalling fast and furiously, racing down to one of the cracked sections of tarmac. Their dad leans against the bonnet of their car, drinking from a steaming thermos. He's watching the boys intently but they look as if they come here often and know what they're doing, how to gauge the jumps, though the cracks are permanently changing, shifting and slipping. Molly holds her breath, as the eldest boy reaches a part of the road that's been thrown up at a particularly steep angle. She wants to call out for him to stop but he doesn't brake or even slow down, so his bike keeps going, takes off into thin air. She really does hold her breath as the bike becomes airborne, then she shuts her eyes tight for a second too. The boy's father cheers as the lad pulls off a perfect landing and lets go of one of the handlebars, to raise his arm in a victory salute.

This is a turning point in her life. Two roads lie ahead. Both broken. Which to take?

She thinks how she's responsible for the life of another human being now. She doesn't feel responsible. She's going to have a baby and it will change her life forever. She needs to start thinking ahead, read up on what to eat, what to expect. She needs to start knitting a shawl. Isn't that what you do? Her grandmother should do that. Fat chance.

If she tells John she's pregnant now, will he believe the baby is his? Will he suspect it's Pete's child? How would she convince him? What about all his dreams and plans? To travel and study to be an architect. He can still do that. She'd not stop him. She looks at the road that leads nowhere, with its haphazard white lines and she thinks of the road that she and Johnny might set out on together. It's cracked and broken too but it's still there, leading onward. No road is ever straight. If they could jump across the crack that's opened up in front of them and torn them apart, they might continue on their way. They just have to be brave, be prepared to race headlong and take a leap into the unknown. But there are so many obstacles in their way. One of them was a girl who had once called herself a friend.

'I heard you're with Sukey now.' Just saying it makes her feel peculiar, erased and replaced. She hates Sukey with a passion, she really does.

'D'you have a problem with that?'

Right answer: Of course not. She wants to think she's above jealousy but she's not. Oh, she's not. She's consumed with resentment and a dark sort of emptiness and fear. A fear of being pregnant and alone. This is no love story. She turns her face Heavenward for a moment, as if seeking forgiveness from God. All she has to do, is just say it: *'I'm pregnant. We made a baby.'*

'Sukey wants to get married.'

'Of course she does.' *But I'm pregnant.* If she speaks those life-changing words out loud, he'll overlook what happened at the festival. He'll ditch Sukey. If she tells him she's pregnant and he believes the child is his, he will ask her to marry him, he will insist they marry. He'd want to do the right thing by her. He's a good person. Responsible, honourable, kind. If she married him, there'd be no shame. Could they be happy? A regular little family. Could she be a regular mum? If Sukey is sleeping with him now, she'll be pregnant in no time, if not already. It's the age-old way for a woman to entrap a man, a good man and Sukey will use every tactic at her disposal. 'Why aren't you angry with me? For what happened?'

'That's by the bye.'

She looks at him. 'I don't understand.'

'I love you,' he says simply, stating an irrefutable fact. 'I'll always love you, Moll. Forever and a day. But I always knew I'd never get to keep you for very long.'

The wind whips at her hair. 'What on earth are you talking about?'

'I knew you were destined for greater things.'

There's a sort of wonderment in his voice and it chokes her. His chocolate brown eyes look so warm and sweet, she wants to weep. He'd make the loveliest dad. She has no words.

'Right from the start, I knew one day I'd have to say goodbye to you,' he goes on. 'When I saw you on that stage at Woburn, I knew our chapter had closed. We had our time but now this is a new time. I am in awe of you Moll. I have always been in awe of you. But I am a talentless nobody, no more in your league than a sheep is the size of an elephant. I wish you all the success and happiness and luck in the world. You deserve it. I promise I'll buy all your records, every single one.'

Emotion is suffocating her and all she manages to say is, 'Thank you.'

Johnny leans towards her, kisses her mouth, then he pulls away. He turns and leaves her there, on the windy hillside, on the broken road that now seems to lead to nowhere.

A fortnight later, Molly has found a new road.

She has to keep pinching herself, reminding herself that she is actually here. In a recording studio. In London. Not just any recording studio. Martin Carthy and the Incredible String Band recorded albums in this very place. It's a converted cowshed in Chelsea, very funky. The rhythm section is positioned in the middle, and the strings are under an old lath–and–plaster ceiling which does amazing things for their sound. It's all wonderfully makeshift and the atmosphere is laid–back and sociable. The young studio engineers, Malcolm and Roger, know how to put everyone at ease and the session musicians are slick and friendly. Danny on drums, Tim on keys, Ray on guitar. When they take a break, everyone troops over the road to The Black Lion pub for pints of cider or bottles of Mateus rose, and there's a constant supply of snacks from the cake shop next door.

Jeff Bond has secured digs for Molly with three other girls, in a shared flat in World's End. The house, with a crumbling stuccoed porch, is conveniently located just around the corner from an American style Wimpy bar and

an Italian coffee bar with a juke box, where actors, beat-
niks, art students and musicians smoke Gauloises. One of
her new flatmates, Karen, is studying cello. She's a Jean
Shrimpton lookalike with unkempt tresses of hair and
massive cornflower blue eyes, while Lisa, a dancer, is a
coltish Cleopatra with black-lined cat's eyes and black hair,
styled by Vidal Sassoon in a short, cropped helmet. The
flat is furnished from Habitat, with pasta storage jars and
tubular frame furniture. Clothes and magazines are strewn
everywhere, a teetering stack of vinyl LPs on the coffee
table, Sergeant Pepper, Hendrix, The Kinks. There's a
tambourine, lamps draped with scarves, a Moroccan rug.
It smells of joss sticks and patchouli oil. They make spag
bol with tinned mince and brandy and stay up all night
eating peanuts and listening to music. Tonight, Molly is
going to see Fairport Convention at Middle Earth in
Covent Garden and tomorrow, Paul Simon is at the
Troubadour.

It's all like a dream, but a dream that's shadowed with
the recurring nightmare of her grandmother's stricken face
when she told her about the pregnancy. She'd been in the
sitting room, listening to the radio when Molly said: 'I'm
going to have a baby.'

Molly's dad was half-way through drinking a cuppa and
the cup started rattling in the saucer as his hand trembled.
Molly couldn't look at him.

'What have I done to deserve this?' Her grandmother's
voice had been frost and ice.

Molly feared she wasn't too old to get a whack on the
bottom with the flat-backed hairbrush.

'Will you help me?' Molly didn't plead but asked politely,
with pride.

'You can't stay here and disgrace us all,' her grandmother decided, her sense of propriety ringing out in every word. 'Nobody must ever know.'

Molly turned, at last, to her dad.

'The shame,' he whispered, setting the cup and saucer down with care, then hiding his face in his shaking hands. 'Oh Molly, the shame.'

She knows that pregnancy out of wedlock is a terrible thing. She may as well have murdered someone. But she didn't expect this. She'd never felt so alone.

But in the studio, when she sings the old songs, songs like *Died for Love*, it reminds her that she's by no means the first girl to find herself in this predicament. There's an undertow of melancholy and despair in the old songs that consoles her. She knows how it feels to want to give up, just curl up and die.

But she will not die. She has too much to live for. She's petite, and with the help of a stretchy hold-in corset she should just about manage to hide the pregnancy until she's seven months gone. Then, she'll go to the home for unmarried mothers in Highgate, where she'll give birth to her baby before it's put up for adoption.

'We'll just tell everyone here that you've gone to London to be a musician,' Molly's grandmother had said, before Molly left with her suitcase. The subtext: Nobody need ever know her granddaughter is a fallen woman.

In the night sometimes, Molly feels a rawness inside her, an inconsolable sorrow. But she can use the darkness and demons when she's singing. They are the sand that makes pearls.

Molly rests her hand on her stomach and she feels the baby wriggle as she sings into the microphone and she wonders if the baby is dancing. Are unborn babies comforted by the sound of their mothers singing to them, just as newborns are soothed by lullabies? She wants to sing lullabies to her baby, to teach her child the old ballads her father taught her. Songs that have entered her bloodstream. She is surprised by the fervency of this wish, because she also wants to go on living this great life she is living right now. She wants to lounge around on floor cushions, smoking pot and listening to records. She wants to hang out at The Speakeasy, go with her new friends to the Roundhouse to see the light shows. She wants to be taken seriously as a singer, to honour the ancient songs she is singing. They are her core. They belong to her and she belongs to them. She revels in them, tastes the words that take her back in time, into other people's lives. She wants to follow her star and be true to herself. She wants to keep her baby.

Basically then, she's hoping for some kind of miracle.

CHAPTER THIRTY-NINE

SILVA, 2002

Silver foil trays covered in cling film, crates of champagne and boxes of napkins had been arriving all morning. On my way out of the House I bumped into Haydn, a young apprentice chef, just seventeen years old, from Bakewell. Fresh-faced in his white apron, he was the same age that I had been when I started working here. When Haydn first met the Duke and Duchess at a staff party it was me who'd assured him that he didn't have to bow to them.

'How's it going, Haydn?'

'I'm buzzing,' he beamed at me, spinning the tray into the air and catching it on his fingertips. 'I've made bases for six hundred lemon cray fish canapés. The Duchess tasted one and she said it was delicious.'

'Well done you. It'll be a great night,' I smiled, picturing Haydn adding last minute garnishes, the catering staff all smart in their white shirts, black waistcoats and name badges, lined up with their trays in the Painted Hall, where the duke's son, Stoker, and his wife, Amanda, would shake hands with all the guests. But for once, I couldn't wait to get away. Since Matt had told me about Percy and Molly that morning, I'd been desperate to talk to Robbie.

He was in the barn at Brook House, rehearsing for a concert with Kirk and Sofie. They were playing a song I didn't recognise, with a daring jazzy arrangement, like nothing I'd heard before. They stopped playing when I strode in and my entrance instantly changed the atmosphere, making me wonder if Robbie had confided in his friends, if they knew that he'd asked me to marry him and that though I'd not exactly turned him down, I'd not accepted either. What would they think of me? That I was a tease, an idiot, a coldhearted witch? All of the above?

'Hi, Silva,' Kirk said, friendly enough. He'd grown a beard and moustache, looked as rugged as a lumberjack.

'Hiya.' I turned to Robbie. 'I'm sorry to interrupt but I need you to come with me.'

'What's wrong?'

'Nothing. I'll explain on the way. Can you come right now? Please? It's really important.'

'Sure.' He grabbed his khaki jacket which was hanging over a chair. 'Back soon,' he said to his friends.

'We need to talk to Percy,' I said, when we were in my Jeep. 'You'll never guess why, not in a million years.'

'Gimme a clue.'

'We've been looking for someone, and a member of her family has been there, in your life, right in front of us, all this time.'

'I don't follow.'

'Your teacher. Friend.' I took my eyes off the winding country road for a moment, to glance across at Robbie in the seat beside me. 'Percy is Molly Marrison's father. Molly is Percy's daughter.'

'What?' He had turned to face me, incredulous, half laughing. 'No way.'

'Yes way.'

'But I asked him about her,' Robbie sounded confused and a little cross now. 'I asked Percy if he knew anything about Molly. I played him her record, for heaven's sake.'

'And he denied all knowledge. I know. Let's see what he has to say now.'

We parked in the car park and Robbie led the way, up the high street towards Peak Cavern. It was drizzling with rain. We followed the path that ran beside Peak's Hole Water, the brook flowing right past the front doors of a row of quaint stone cottages, which lay in the shadow of the great rock face, upon which the ruins of Peveril Castle stood sentinel. We crossed over a little arched, packhorse bridge and Robbie stopped outside a tiny house, around which the river babbled. An etched wooden sign read Bridge Cottage and Robbie knocked on the wooden door.

It opened, and there stood Percy. He hadn't changed one bit and he didn't seem surprised to see me on his doorstep. He took my hand in both of his and I felt the warm, gnarly roughness of the old man's skin.

'You've come a long way,' he said to me.

I didn't correct him, didn't say that I lived but ten miles from Castleton, had travelled for less than half an hour to be there. He wasn't talking about geographical distances but something else entirely. Robbie swore Percy was practically psychic, so he probably knew exactly why we were there.

'You've still a long way to go though,' he added.

'Have I?'

'Both of you.'

I was struck afresh by the ancient sort of magic that still clung to him like a cloak, an almost supernatural power. He must have had his reasons for not talking about Molly before.

He stood back to let us in, showed us through to a cosy front room with floral wallpaper, a gas fire, shelves crammed with china ornaments and dozens of photographs in silver frames. There was a well-worn chintzy armchair and two wooden chairs, by a small teak table in the corner. 'Take a pew,' he said. 'Back in a tick.'

He disappeared through a door, through which came the sound of a whistling kettle. I scanned the photos. Working horses and stocky cobs, an elderly couple, the man in a cloth cap and the woman with a deeply wrinkled leathery face, wonderfully expressive, a shawl wrapped around her shoulders. Percy smoking a pipe, leaning on a rake. There was a soulful looking little girl in a pinafore dress and socks falling down around her skinny ankles, her long hair in dark pigtails. Molly as a child? It could be? She had a look of Percy.

He reappeared with a tray bearing cups, saucers, a strainer, creamy whole milk in a gold topped bottle, white sugar in a stainless steel dish, a plate of McVitie's digestive biscuits. 'So what can I do for you today?'

'Will you tell me about your family?'

He didn't seem at all put out by my question. 'I married my Esme when we were sixteen,' he began. 'She was the daughter of the last of the rope-makers, the hardworking folk who'd continued to live and work in the Devil's Arse, long after the gypsies and tinker families had moved on. My family were linked to that place too but we were metal workers, had a house and a garden. Esme thought she was moving up in the world. She ignored my wild ways, believed she could tame me, as women always do believe they can tame their men.' Percy smiled wryly, with love. 'She was pretty and good in the kitchen. I thought I was the luckiest man alive. She died on the same day our daughter was born.'

'I'm so sorry.'

'In the midst of life, we are in death. She blessed me with the most beautiful, bonny little lassie.'

'Molly. You called your daughter Molly?'

'Lovely Molly. Everyone loved her. I always said she could have married the Duke of Devonshire. But she captured the heart of the Duke's young ploughboy.'

This sounded like a story straight from the ballads but I knew it was all true. The ploughboy. 'John? Johnny. My father?'

Percy nodded. 'Aye.'

I leant forward a little. 'Where is she now? Where is Molly? Can you tell us?'

'The world was a very different place back then,' he said, cagey now. 'I did what I thought was right at the time. Which is the best that any of us can do, isn't it?'

'What did you do?'

He put his hand over his eyes, dragged it down his face, as if he wanted to wipe away dark thoughts, unwanted memories. 'My mother, Molly's grandmother, Lavinia, she agreed to raise Molly. She did a good job. Strict but fair. She brought Molly up to abide by the ten commandments, taught her that a person's good name is their most valuable possession. So it was bad enough that the lass, a young, slip of a girl, was singing alone in dodgy bars. Terrible, wicked places, dens of iniquity, according to her Granny Lavinia.' His smile was full of a sorrowful kind of pride. 'It was the sixties and in my mother's mind, the whole world was going to hell in a handcart. She couldn't stand to see her grand-daughter shamed.'

'I don't understand.' I did though, or I was beginning to. So it was true. 'Molly was pregnant?'

'In those days, single mothers were seen as scroungers and sinners and I didn't want that for my girl or for her poor wee baby either.'

'My father…John Brightmore. Johnny. He was…was he…the father of Molly's baby?'

'That's what she claimed.'

So I'm not an only child.

'I believe my dad loved her. Very much,' I said.

'Pah. If he had, he'd not have hooked up so fast with that dolly bird.'

'My mother? Sukey? You mean Sukey?'

'Her parents christened her Susan. Jezebel would have been more appropriate. I mean that as no insult to you, lass.'

I leant forward on the stool, my heart hammering against my ribcage. So this *was* what it was all about then. Not the Blue John after all. This was why I had to find Molly. 'So you're saying, Sir, that somewhere out there, I have a half-sister, or brother, roughly the same age as me? Where is he, or she? Percy, do you know? Where is Molly's child?'

The old man shook his head. 'That I can't tell you.'

'Can't or won't?' Robbie asked, but kindly.

'Can't,' Percy said, regretfully. 'I know you asked me about her before, son, and I dodged the question and I'm sorry about that but it's something I don't ever speak of, if I can help it. Her grandmother sent her away in shame and I now am ashamed to talk about how and why she was sent away. I should have stuck up for her, but I didn't. That's the truth of it. That's my cross to bear. Besides, I can't help you. I don't know where our Molly is, let alone the baby. I let her Gran take care of it all. And Molly never forgave either of us. She broke off all contact, told us that as far as she was concerned, we were no longer family.'

I sat back, exhaled. 'Did you teach Molly the song about *The Runaway Lovers?*' I asked after a moment, to lighten the mood and because I knew Robbie would be interested to know that. 'Did that last verse come from your family?'

Percy nodded. 'Molly was such a good little singer,' he recollected, his piercing blue eyes growing dewy and distanced, as if he could look back through time and see his daughter plain as day, hear her song. 'She learnt the old songs so diligently but she had a broad taste and for a while, she preferred pop music. I remember her buying a Billy Fury record, *Halfway to Paradise* and playing it over and over, when she wasn't listening to the pirate radio stations. She loved Jim Morrison and The Doors and the storytelling in Bob Dylan's songs, but she once said the pop world was phoney and she could never imagine singing a song that didn't mean anything to her. She made jokes about the dark, old songs I taught her but when you're singing a song that's hundreds of years old, you know it's bigger than you. There's power in it.' Percy looked at Robbie. 'She wasn't like you, lad. She didn't have the hunger for the old songs. But she cared about them, loved them and they came to be a great comfort to her, I like to think. Especially a mournful song about a girl, who was jilted by a man who got her with child.' He recited a line: 'I wish, I wish that my baby was born, sat smiling on her daddy's knee and the green grass growing over me. She put that song on her album,' he added proudly.

I recognised the heartbreaking lyrics of the title track, *Died for Love.*

'There's such power in those old songs,' Percy said. 'When Molly sang them, she'd have seen that she wasn't alone. They were her solace. She saw that people have always been abandoned and wounded in love and have lost all hope, have wanted to die for love. How Sweet William on his deathbed lay, for the love of Barbara Allen.'

'Lovers in the songs die because love is worth dying for,' Robbie said.

I glanced at him. He glanced away.

'Those songs will have saved my Molly,' Percy said. 'I need to believe that.'

I could see how much the old man had suffered and was suffering still, how sorely he regretted what he'd done, when he sent his only daughter away or let her be sent away. He stood up, went over to the windowsill, picked up the photograph of the little girl with her hair in pigtails and handed it to me. 'There she is, my lassie. My Lovely Molly.'

The girl who'd been born Molly Hall, a name tainted with a terrible legacy.

'Where does Marrison come from?'

'Her mother's maiden name.'

Molly Marrison. It had more of a ring to it than Molly Hall but there was surely another reason that Molly changed her name. The name, Hall, was tainted.

The ballad of *The Runaway Lovers* had been handed down through generations of Percy's family and they sang a different version to everyone else, because of their personal connection to that story, the stigma of being descended from one of the murderers. Percy probably hadn't joined the dots. He came from a generation that was less inclined to navel gazing and introspection, was unfamiliar with Freudian psychoanalysis. He'd not see that the effects of that horrific murder were far-reaching, had cast dark ripples and echoes that had lingered for centuries.

But these five most murderess men, all fell foul to fates revenge
One tumbled down that self same dell, and one was crushed to death
One with guilt his own life took and one died mad before his time,
And the last, on his death bed confessed this terrible crime.

Shame and the fear of shame, the wish to avoid more of it, had surely made Molly's grandmother act the way he did when Molly fell pregnant. Easy to see how having a murderous black sheep in your family would make generations of their descendants hypersensitive to shame. You'd feel the need to compensate for the ignominy that had been handed down from father to son, mother to daughter.

To this day, the Hall family in Castleton believe their name to be tainted. And it would have been worse, far worse, the further back in time you went, when Lavinia married Percy's father and took his name. That disgraced name. She had tried to raise her son and granddaughter to live blameless, moralistic lives, to compensate for the crime and shame that blighted their family's reputation.

That song really did hold the key, to everything.

'She was my little princess.' Tears glittered in Percy's eyes and I could see that now he'd started talking about his daughter, he didn't want to stop. It was as if he'd gone back in time. He stared down at his hands, the knobbly knuckles, liver spots and blue veins, meandering under the paper-thin skin, as if he didn't recognise them as his own hands. 'She used to come and sit on my lap when I was singing and she'd beg me to keep on. She had such a memory for songs and if I changed a line, she knew it. When she started singing our songs back to me, it was the greatest day. When that gentleman from the BBC wrote to her, Mr Kennedy, the record company forwarded the letter here. I was so proud that he wanted to record her, to have her on his programme. I never missed an episode. Molly had grown up listening too and now she had a chance to be on it, on the wireless. My songs, her songs, our songs, were to be played on the BBC. Just imagine. So of course, I sent the letter on to her.'

'Where did you send it?'

'Pelagia House.'

'Where's that?'

'London.' He looked shamefaced. 'It's a home for destitute girls. It's the last address we had for her. But she wasn't there and she left no forwarding address. They sent the letter right back, along with a letter from her doctor.'

'What letter? What doctor?'

'Doctor Martha Epstein,' he said quite grandly. 'Funny the stuff you remember but I remember her name. She wanted to speak to Molly, for some paper she was writing.'

'What kind of paper?' I asked. What was wrong with Molly? Or her baby?

'Search me,' Percy shrugged.

CHAPTER FORTY

The Chatsworth Horse Trials lasted for three days and with over five hundred competitors and ten thousand spectators, the Duke and Duchess's army of three hundred and sixty staff had their work cut out. We started work at seven and by nine, Ted was manning the gate, crackling walkie-talkie in one hand, as he simultaneously checked tickets and cooked bacon butties in a frying pan in the back of his van.

'Smells delicious, Ted,' I said.

'Best meal of the day,' he grinned, taking a ticket off a young couple in wellington boots and gilets. 'Have a good one,' he told them.

Visitors poured in to watch the best riders in the world and I stayed on after work, to watch the cross country with Freya, with its thrilling, high-risk, water jumps. 'The horses don't know if the water is six feet deep or six inches,' she told me gleefully.

'I hardly dare watch,' I admitted, clutching Freya's arm. 'I just hope everyone gets home in one piece.'

We went with Flora to the big marquee, to watch the Duchess present the winner with a red rosette, telling her she was a fine horsewoman. Freya looked wistful, almost envious.

'You're a fine horsewoman too,' I assured her. Watching her fearlessly ride Starlight, her glossy black mare, I often wondered if she'd inherited her horsemanship from Jack Willis, the Chatsworth groom.

'We're both awesome,' Freya grinned. 'So let's celebrate our awesomeness with a glass of bubbly, shall we?'

I grimaced. 'I'd love that, but I can't right now. I'm so sorry but I have to be somewhere.'

'Where?' Freya inquired suspiciously. 'What's going on with you?'

'You can tell us,' Flora said with a worried glance at her daughter.

Robbie's family. They still felt like my family too, always had. I didn't want to keep secrets from them. 'I promise I'll explain soon.' *When I've worked it all out.*

Robbie knew what I was up to. He knew that I was going to do some research on Martha Epstein, but I knew he'd not say anything until I was ready. He was the keeper of secrets as well as songs.

As I walked past Tudor Square and up the narrow street that led to Sheffield City Library, I couldn't help but admire the decorative mouldings, in pale Portland stone, that adorned the impressive Art Deco building.

Inside, the Library housed an art gallery, a basement theatre and countrywide trade databases. With the help of a smart-suited young librarian, who looked more like a banker, I looked up Martha Epstein in a directory of the British Medical Association, found out that she'd been the president of an organisation called the Voice Research Society, which had consulting rooms at Abbey Road in London. Current presidents and patrons included a mixed bunch of opera sopranos, vocal coaches and musical directors, as well as ear, nose and throat consultants, surgeons, and psychologists.

Dr Epstein was a speech and language therapist, who specialised in disorders of the voice. She'd passed away five years ago but through another database, of the Wellcome Medical Library, I managed to trace a paper she'd written, in 1975, entitled: 'When it isn't just physical: The effects of stress and emotion on the voice.'

The photocopy arrived promptly in next morning's post and I skim read the first part, while eating a slice of buttered toast and drinking a cup of coffee.

The paper focussed on a condition called Muscle Tension Dysphonia.

Muscle Tension Dysphonia (MTD) occurs as a result of inappropriate use of the muscles around the larynx, during speech or singing. MTD may occur on its own, called primary MTD, or as a result of another underlying disorder, called secondary MTD. In secondary MTD, there's an underlying problem, such as nodules or polpys. However, the cause of primary MTD is often unclear. It may be triggered by illness, allergies and in some instances, the cause may be related to underlying stress and anxiety or a significant emotional event. The present study examines the emotional characteristics of ten female primary dysphonic subjects, suffering from depression, anxiety and the affect of trauma.

. . .

Dr Epstein cited two well-known female singers who'd been affected: Shirley Collins and Linda Thomson. A young singer simply referred to as Molly, was one of her case studies.

I put down my toast, left my coffee to grow cold.

Molly came to me very distressed. The severity of the symptoms of Muscle Tension Dysphonia (MTD) can vary enormously. Some people find they can barely whisper, while others can sound relatively normal but suffer tightness, pain in the neck or throat and fatigue, whenever they have to use their voices. Molly complained of altered voice quality and effortful voice production, only when singing. Her speaking voice was quiet and soft but when she tried to sing, she experienced soreness and her voice became rough and raspy.

She'd been examined by an Ear Nose and Throat (ENT) Surgeon, who established no presence of disease or abnormality on the vocal folds which would explain the symptoms. Molly was shocked to be told that nothing was physically wrong with her, when her symptoms sounded and felt so severe. Like many in her position, she struggled to understand and believe the diagnosis, when the specialist suggested that her voice problem might be caused by a psychological trauma or other emotional issue. Treatment of secondary MTD involves addressing both the MTD and the underlying condition but I could not assure Molly as to when and if, she would ever be able to sing again.

I told Robbie what I'd discovered.

'There's your reason why Molly had never recorded a follow-up album or sang on the radio show either.'

But it was only half a reason. Because frustratingly, there were no details of the 'significant emotional event' that she had suffered.

CHAPTER FORTY-ONE
MOLLY - 1968

'This is your stop,' says the smartly-dressed, middle-aged woman sitting beside Molly on the bus, pointing sanctimoniously through the grimy window, to a huge, forbidding red brick building. Molly feels her cheeks burn hot from shame. She's not asked for directions but she is seven months pregnant now and from one look at her belly, the woman knows exactly where she's going and why.

In essence, mother and baby homes have replaced the workhouse as refuges for so called fallen women and Pelagia House looks like something from a Dickensian novel, a depressing orphanage. But at least inside its walls Molly can stop having to lie and hide her condition, give birth away from prying eyes. But as she steps up to the tall painted door, she feels only fear and a sick, cold dread. She almost runs away but where can she run to? Not to Johnny. Not to her family.

For weeks, she's concealed her growing bump beneath lacy smocks and flowing skirts. She's performed at folk clubs in Soho and Richmond and for a while, she's allowed herself to imagine that her career as a singer will take off and she'll have work, money, will be able to keep her baby. But deep down she knows very well that mothers who work, who are performers, are especially frowned on. She's trapped. She also fears she's not up to the task. She can barely take care of herself. How can she care for a helpless baby? But she wants to try. Oh, she wants to try. There's another little person inside her, who she passionately and fiercely loves already, more than she has ever loved anything or anyone. It's just the two of them, against the world.

Molly spends the next two months on her hands and knees, cleaning floors with a scrubbing brush, as if that will clean her filthy soul. She learns to listen for the gong that signals lunch, as if watery, scrambled eggs is anything to look forward to. The spartan dining room has a long refectory table that makes it feel even more like a Victorian orphanage. Each evening, Molly washes herself in a bathroom shared by a dozen girls with a chipped cast iron bath and freezing cold water, and then she lies in the dark, on a thin mattress with springs poking through and she feels her baby kick and wriggle inside her. She rests her hand on her taut belly, feeling little feet kick. Sometimes the baby gets hiccups. Sometimes she sees a great hump moving under her skin, a little heel or elbow jutting out at the side of her stomach. A little alien.

'We'll get through this together,' she whispers.

How could they ever be separated? The thought of it is unbearable.

There's a common room with a lumpy sofa and some evenings, the girls watch the flickery, old black and white

379

television set in the corner. Cathy McGowan in her cuban heels on *Ready Steady Go*. When The Faces come on, a girl called Linda squeals with excitement and jumps up, pulling Molly to her feet. Linda starts dancing along to the song about handbags and gladrags and Molly tries to forget that not a year ago, she sang on the same stage as The Faces.

More girls follow Linda's lead. A girl called Niamh rebelliously turns the volume up as high as it will go and soon, all the girls are dancing and singing along at the tops of their voices, just like regular teenagers. Until Sister Agnes appears in the doorway.

'Stop that this minute,' she scolds. 'You wicked girls. Have you not learnt your lesson?'

Clearly Molly has not because a life without music, is no life at all and the next night, she huddles under the blanket with a transistor radio tuned to Radio 1, the BBC's new pop music station. Linda creeps in beside her and they huddle together at midnight to listen to *Night Ride*, on Radio London, presented by John Peel, a voice from the Festival of the Flower Children, from that other, brighter world. Molly is instantly transported back to Woburn Abbey. She feels as if she's been evicted from her life, sent into exile. What's happened to the age of Aquarius, the Summer of Love? Peel plays Captain Beefheart, Pink Floyd and the Bonzo Dog Doo-Dah Band. Then he introduces a record by a young singer who he says he's had the privilege of seeing live. 'She's going to give Sandy Denny a run for her money,' he says.

Molly hears her own voice drifting out on the airwaves.

Over moors and valleys deep, through the Dark Peak and the White
There two tragic lovers sleep in gritstone, blood, and lime.

'Molly Marrison,' John Peel says at the end of the song.

In their blanket cave, Linda turns to Molly, her mouth forming the shape of an astonished O. 'You made a record?'

'Don't be daft,' Molly whispers back. 'That's not me. It's just another girl who happens to have the same name as me.'

Molly's waters break while she's on all fours with the scrubbing brush. The first contraction grasps her stomach, the pain reaching round to her back. She keeps scrubbing. Eventually she staggers to her feet, clutching her belly, leaning against the wall for support, as contraction after contraction grips her and rips her apart. Doubled up, she screams for help and one of the other girls runs to fetch one of the nuns.

Molly is taken to the labour ward on the ground floor, where she's left to get on with it. She's already been told not to bother asking for pain relief because part of the girls' punishment is to suffer as much as possible. The contractions grow stronger and stronger, tightening like a vice around her, cracking her in two. She cries out for the woman who was like a mother to her. Where is her granny now? Does she even care? No.

They've rigged Molly to a monitor and she can hear the galloping of her baby's tiny heart coming from inside her. Every time a new contraction brings a clench of pain, the heartbeat gallops faster, so that Molly worries her baby must be suffering too, distressed at being pummelled by her muscles.

'It'll be alright, little one,' she murmurs. 'We need to

help each other and then we're going to meet each other at last.'

There are no spaces between the pains now, the contractions are relentless. Molly reaches up and grips the iron bars in the bedhead, yells in agony. Still nobody comes, nobody cares. Perspiration pours from her skin, sticks her hair to her face. She must stay strong for her baby's sake. Whether or not the poor little thing wants to be born into such misery, it's going to be born and Molly is all it has. Her body takes over, becomes a great pump, designed to push the baby out of her. She screams at the top of her lungs as a rush of tearing pain engulfs her. And then she hears a little wail.

'A girl,' a midwife says flatly. 'Born at three thirty-three.'

It's April 22nd. Molly knows that this is a new anniversary, that she will mark every year, a date that will haunt her for the rest of her life.

She's shivering, soaked in sweat and the baby is unceremoniously dumped in her arms. She has a thick mop of black hair, sticky with blood and tiny wrinkly fingers. All Molly can think is that this tiny girl, this little person, is part of her. Her little fingers wrap around Molly's thumb and she melts. She is a child with a child, but all she feels is love, a love so huge that her body no longer seems big enough to contain her heart. How can the birth of a baby, any baby, not be something to celebrate?

'Jeannie,' she whispers, stroking the baby's silky cheek. Jean is the female version of John and at the last minute, she wants her baby to take her father's name. 'Shhh, Jeannie,' Molly soothes. 'I'm here, my little sweetheart. Everything's alright.'

Only it's not alright. It's far from alright. The pain of childbirth will be nothing compared to the pain that must follow. Molly hugs the baby and rocks her and she cries and cries.

Her little daughter is sleeping soundly in the crib beside her bed but Molly cannot, will not sleep. She is beyond exhausted but she just wants to gaze and gaze, at the precious little bundle. She's fascinated by everything about her. Her minute, shell-like fingernails, the perfect whorls of her little ears, her expressions, the snuffling sounds she makes, like a kitten. She's impossibly tiny and pink and delicate, so helpless and innocent and trusting.

Linda shows Molly how to put on a terry nappy. They have so many corners and are all rough and scratchy but Linda shows Molly how to lay the material under her baby's little pink bottom, how to lift her up by her ankles while she dabs on a little zinc and castor oil cream, folds the nappy neatly and avoids stabbing Jeannie with the big, nasty pins.

Molly's breasts fill with milk, grow agonisingly hot and rock hard and Molly aches, just to feed her baby. But breast-feeding is forbidden at Pelagia House. Her breasts are bound tight against her body, forcing the milk back.

Molly gave birth knowing she might not be able to keep her baby but she had imagined being able to nurse her at least, cuddle her, play with her, love her, just for a few weeks. Instead, when she is just three days old, Jeannie is hastily baptised in the chapel by the visiting priest, who preaches from the pulpit about the moral corruption of unwed mothers, how the decline of Rome began with sexual depravity. Then she is transferred to the nursery, a long dingy room with twenty cots lined up along the walls.

The babies look so tiny against the metal bars and Molly

thinks how she really has fallen back in time, to a more brutal age. Even in springtime the room is freezing. Dozens of babies, all howling at once, ear-splitting, distressed wails. All Molly wants to do is go to her little girl and pick her up. It's a form of torture, to be forbidden to comfort your own baby.

'They're being punished too,' she weeps to Linda in the dormitory, 'when none of this is their fault.'

There's no night feed, so the babies are starving with so many hours in between their bottles. By half past five in the morning, when Molly is finally allowed to go to back to the nursery, Jeannie is almost blue with cold.

A new routine. She gets up to feed Jeannie at six, feeds her again at 10am and 2pm, working until 4pm. She eats supper and then does the 6pm feed and another at 10pm. These are the happiest moments in her day, the happiest moments in her whole life, holding Jeannie safe and secure in her arms, as her little mouth tugs at the bottle and she gazes up into Molly's face with such trust. But the nuns are so zealous about the mothers doing anything for their babies, beyond the bare minimum necessary for their survival. Once, Molly tickled Jeannie's belly when she was changing her and was instantly rebuked.

'What do you think you're doing?' Sister Agnes hissed. 'Hurry up and get that baby dressed and back in the cot. If you'd wanted to have a baby of your own, you should have got married first.'

Molly wants to scream: I do have a baby of my own. She's mine.

But Jeannie seems to know that Molly is her mother and she doesn't care how sinful she's been. She stops crying when she hears Molly's voice, grows calm the instant she picks her up. Molly cannot imagine letting someone else care for her.

The following day, she notices that all the babies have changed cots and that both her baby and Linda's baby son, have moved further down the line.

'The cot at the far end is for the newest baby,' Linda explains. 'The one nearest the door is for the oldest. They move up the queue, until they're in the last cot and then they're gone.'

St Mary's no longer feels like a prison but a refuge that Molly never wants to leave. She no longer cares if she's shunned, ostracised, treated as no better than a prostitute. She doesn't care for her own sake but she does care for Jeannie's sake. Linda is a realist. She tells Molly how there's a severe housing crisis in England and as an unmarried mother, she'll be at the bottom of the pile when it comes to deprivation, unlikely to be housed by the local authority, prey to unscrupulous landlords, left to live in a slum. She'll not be able to find work. 'You'll condemn yourself to a life of destitution and you baby to life as a destitute bastard.'

She cannot begin to think of a future that will not include Jeannie but she has to face facts: Jeannie will be better off without her.

When Jeannie is moved into the last but one cot in the row, behind Linda's baby, Molly goes down to the local shops, withdraws all the money from her post office savings account and buys Jeannie a fluffy pink bunny rabbit. On the way back, she passes a little girl in a fairy dress and wings, trotting along holding her mother's hand and she feels a piercing misery, knowing she'll never see Jeannie at that age, will never walk beside her, holding her little hand in hers.

When it's Linda's turn to hand over her baby, Molly

listens to her agonised sobs, as she gives him the last bottle of milk she'll ever give him. 'I can't bear it,' Linda weeps. She tears at the hair on her own head as if she would pull it out. 'I can't bear it.' She's cried so much, she's hollow-eyed and exhausted. 'I know this is for the best, but I just want to run away with him. I just want to pick him up and run and run.'

Then Linda's baby is gone and Linda herself is gone and all too quickly, it is Molly's turn.She's taken to the Mother Superior's office and made to sign a document.

I, Molly Hall, hereby agree that the administrator shall have the powers of legally appointed guardian. I hereby declare, that there is no history of tuberculosis, mental illness or other disease in my family. I am offering my child for adoption because I am unable to provide a comfortable and stable home. I was not married to the father of the child. The father of the child does not object to adoption.

Is that true? That last sentence? No. On the contrary. If she knows anything at all, she knows this. Johnny would object very strongly to what she is about to do. But he will not have the opportunity to object because he has no idea that this child, his child, even exists.

When Molly leaves that place, leaves her baby there, her heart does not break, it shatters into a million pieces.

CHAPTER FORTY-TWO

SILVA - 2002

I'd arranged to meet Linda Wilson in the Children's Farmyard at Chatsworth and the weather was on my side. The blue sky was like a nursery rhyme, decorated with fluffy, cottonwool clouds, a timeless sky, except for the criss-cross of vapour trails left by aeroplanes. The Farmyard was busy as ever; pigs and shetland ponies, goats and chickens, and hundreds of children.

It had been Linda's idea to meet here. She lived near Liverpool but said she'd seen Chatsworth on television and had wanted to visit for ages, so this was the perfect excuse. She'd brought along her grandson, George, a two-year-old toddler, dressed in little shorts and a baseball cap over his mop of white-blonde curls.

'I look after him every Tuesday and Friday while his mum's at work,' Linda explained, as we watched George squatting by the rabbit hutches and petting one of the little brown rabbits. 'My son's a microbiologist,' she added with huge pride. 'He works in a lab with test-tubes and micro-scopes. I missed out on watching him grow up but he came looking for me four years ago, when his girlfriend was pregnant herself, so I'm making up for lost time.'

'How did he find you?'

'Same way as most people go about it, through the adoption contact register. From 1976, it made it so much easier for adopted children to be reunited with their birth parent.'

Could Molly's child have found her the same way?

It had been surprisingly easy to find Linda. I'd got in touch with the Catholic Children's Society, who'd helpfully given me the contact details for a girl called Niamh, who'd been at the mother and baby home in the spring of 1968. Niamh now ran a support group for other former inmates, as she called them and she remembered that Molly had been friends with Linda, with whom Niamh had been in brief contact.

Slender and well-dressed in a fawn trench-coat with tortoiseshell buttons, Linda had flyaway brown hair, streaked with grey. She was in her fifties but looked a decade younger. It would have been easy enough to believe that she was little George's mother, rather than his grandmother. She looked so content, wheeling a buggy, with a packet of disposable nappies and a plastic dinosaur peeking out of her roomy leather handbag.

How I envied little George's dad. I'd never be able to call on my own mother if I needed a babysitter. If I married Robbie, of course, if he was the father of my children, then we'd have Granny Flora to babysit. Robbie's proposal was there in my subconscious all the time but I could only think of it abstractly now, not as something that could ever really become real. It was so much easier just being friends. I'd told him I was meeting Linda and he'd told me to call him immediately I'd spoken to her, was as eager for news as me.

He also had a personal interest in Molly now, because she was Percy's daughter and because she was a singer who had lost the ability to sing.

'I'd like to make up for lost time too,' I said to Linda, as we watched George helping one of Freya's colleagues to collect eggs from the Duchess's prize chickens, placing them in a little wicker basket. 'I'm certain now, that's why my father wanted me to find Molly. He wanted me to find her baby. She's my sister, half-sister. He knew how much I hated being an only child. He didn't want to leave me on my own, with no family.'

George came toddling over, grabbed hold of his grandma's hand, started dragging her over to the barn. 'See baby cow,' he pleaded. 'See baby cow.'

'Calf,' Linda corrected gently. 'A baby cow is called a calf, Love.'

'This one's called Buttercup,' Freya told George, stroking the shorthorn's nose. She'd been born a few days earlier and Freya was giving its mother a bucket of feed.

Freya looked over at me questioningly and I felt guilty again, for not having told her what I was up to, that I was so many steps closer to finding Molly Marrison.

'Molly called her baby, Jeannie,' Linda said.

'Jeannie.' Jean. The French for John.

Linda smiled. 'I used to hear her singing to her baby when the nuns weren't listening. Lullabies and strange ballads that were rather dark and sad but so pretty. I knew she wasn't telling me the truth, when we heard a singer on the radio who had the same name as her. She said it wasn't her but I knew it was. So when I met up with her a few months after we'd both left Pelagia, I asked her if she was going to go back to being a singer and she said that she couldn't sing any longer. Once she'd mentioned it, I could hear the rasp in her throat even when she was just talking. I'd assumed she had a cold or tonsillitis or something.'

'It's called dysphonia,' I said. 'It can be caused by severe emotional trauma.'

'Such as having her baby taken off her? That's about as severe and traumatic as it gets. Poor Molly,' Linda sighed. 'She spent ten years hoping and praying that she'd be reunited with Jeannie.'

I felt sick. 'Why only ten years? What happened to make her give up hope?'

But maddeningly, she would say no more. She looked as if she regretted that she'd already said far more than she should have done. 'Look, this isn't my story to tell. Molly needs to tell you this part herself.'

'You know where she is?'

'We lost touch for ages but then she got in contact with me again. I was so happy to hear from her, I can't begin to tell you. She's a very special person and I'm blessed to call her a friend.' She broke off, as if to work out what to do. 'If it's alright with you, I'll give her your phone number and address, let her handle this whichever way she feels most comfortable.'

'What if she doesn't want anything to do with me?'

'Oh, my dear, there's no fear of that. No fear of that at all.'

'I so hope you're right.'

'Trust me. I'm right.'

'So all I can do now is wait?'

'That's what I did for thirty years,' Linda said.

'Did Molly ever talk about my father?' I asked. 'John? Johnny?'

'Oh yes, she talked about him all the time. She said he was her first love and she'd wanted him to be her last. She could be quite scathing of other people, but John Bright-more was a sacred subject. In any other era, theirs was like a fairytale romance. A beautiful singer and a handsome shepherd who adored her and wanted to live happily ever after with her, in a cottage with roses round the door. But everything in the world was changing in 1967. She had not one bad word to say about him though. She said she treasured the memory of his love, as something that occurred only once in a lifetime.'

I bit my lip, feel tears prick my eyes. 'That's just so sad.'

'She never would explain what went wrong but then she had little Jeannie and she said she'd never felt love like that before. When she lost her, it left her completely broken. People often talk about their heart or their spirit being broken, something intangible, but with Molly, there was real physical evidence of the break. A noticeable part of her that actually stopped working. The most important part of her, some might say, the part that defined her.'

'Her voice.'

CHAPTER FORTY-THREE
MOLLY -1968

M olly opens her mouth to sing and the most awful sound comes out, as if she's being strangled.She's sure it's just nerves, tightening her throat. She just needs to forget where she is, forget that she's in a broadcast studio, a real broadcast studio, recording an episode of a legendary radio programme. She's standing in front of a large, silver and black microphone with the letters BBC on it. A dream come true. She clutches her guitar and everyone waits, the producer and the sound engineer and Peter Kennedy himself. The microphone looks intimidating, demanding.

'When you're ready,' the producer says over the monitor, a hint of impatience in his voice. He's middle-aged, greying and distinguished, with longish hair and a weary look about him, as if he's sick to the back teeth of dealing with unpredictable divas.

She strums a chord, tries again to sing. Still nothing. She's like a television with the volume turned right down.

She shuts her eyes, takes a deep breath. Her diaphragm lifts, her lungs fill. She can hear the opening lines of *The*

Runaway Lovers so clearly inside her head, word for word, note for note. In her head, she can hear her own voice, singing the song she's sung hundreds of times. She tries to push it up through her throat and out of her mouth. This time she manages a hoarse, raspy croak. It's as if someone has gagged her. Tears blur her eyes and she fights down panic. She's trapped in a nightmare in which she's screaming for help at the top of her lungs, while people just walk by, unconcerned, not even able to hear the scream.

The producer's voice cuts through over the intercom again. 'Everything all right?'

'Please could I get a glass of water?' She is shocked to hear herself speak. Her vocal cords haven't been severed then. She can still talk nearly normally, just not sing. She'd far rather it was the other way around. What use is speaking if she can't sing?

Someone brings her a plastic cup and she sips the tepid water, half-expecting not to be able to swallow, but it slips down fine.

It's not fine when she tries again to sing. Mute, standing there in the studio, Molly experiences the frustration of a toddler in distress or discomfort, trying to make themselves heard and understood but lacking the means to communicate. The only thing they can do is cry and stamp their feet.

It hits her like a juggernaut. She's lost Johnny and she's lost her child. And now she has lost the one thing she had left. She looks at Peter Kennedy and it feels as if she is becoming transparent, all bare bones, with her heart and guts all on the outside of her body. She feels as if she has no secrets. There is no point pretending to be strong or happy because everyone can see right through the pretence.

'Take your time,' Mr Kennedy says.

But after another agonising ten minutes, three more

aborted attempts to sing, she has to admit defeat. She can't do it.

'I'm sorry,' Molly manages, stepping back from the microphone. 'I'm sorry.'

In the privacy of her little bedsit in Camden, Molly tries again and again to sing. She keeps picking up her guitar and the ease with which the strings and the wood make their sweet sound seems to taunt her. Sometimes she can sing along in fractured cadences, but sometimes she just opens her mouth and nothing comes out but that dreadful croak. Sometimes her voice cracks half-way through a song. She has absolutely no command over it anymore and it causes her the most extraordinary anguish.

She goes to one of the folk clubs in Richmond, down by the river and she makes herself stand up and take a floor spot. It doesn't feel like being on stage here. Members of the audience are close enough to touch. Centuries ago, someone probably sang from this corner, to a room full of friends. But it makes no difference. The same thing happens there. She has made a fool of herself and steps down. The worst of it is that she still wants to sing. In fact, now that she can't do it, she wants it more than ever. She realises she's always taken her talent for granted. Only now that it has been taken from her, does she realise how much she loved singing, how much pleasure and sense of fulfilment it gave to her. It's who and what she is.

The more she tries and fails, the worse it becomes. There's a pressure building up inside her and no way to relieve it. What if she can never perform, never record another song? She is a singer. But what if she has lost the ability to sing? She's like a marathon runner who's had his legs cut off. A bird with no wings. Singing for her, had been like soaring and now she's permanently grounded.

The songs haven't left her though. On the contrary. They're in her head all the time, the lyrics and the melodies and the messages growing louder, more urgent and insistent. Around and around they go, like angry wasps trapped inside a room, battering themselves against glass windows, desperate for escape. Eventually they'll drive her mad.

Music is everything to her. Singing was her way of communicating and now she is cut off, unable to express herself. Singing was her solace, her safety valve, the source of so much beauty and joy in her life and now she has no solace. Singing was her way of making sense of the world and now nothing makes any sense at all. Singing made her feel in control, made her feel brave and safe and now she feels none of those things. She is lost, reduced, invisible. It is as if she is living but half a life. As if she has died inside. It's like a curse from a dark, twisted fairytale or parable. A girl is given a precious and rare gift, the gift of song but then she commits a sin and is forever silenced. The princess who had her tongue cut out.

She needs to sing now more than ever because singing was the only way she had to process her grief, so now she's certain it will destroy her. She's lost her means of earning a living. But it's more than that. Much more. She's lost her identity. If she is no longer a singer, then who is she? What will become of her?

She wanders the streets aimlessly, crossing roads without looking. People are going about their everyday lives and she wants to scream at them: You have absolutely no idea what I have been through, what I have been forced to do, what I have lost. It's as if she's lost her mind. She knows she will never feel whole again.

But nobody cares, not even Molly's family. She should go home but she has no home. She never wants to see her grandmother again. Or even her beloved dad. He should have helped her.

She sits on a bench in a bus stop.

Where is her little girl now? What is she doing? How bewildered she must be, not knowing where her mummy has gone. Molly's arms ache, her whole body aches just to touch Jeannie again. Selfishly, the very worst thing is knowing that Jeannie will forget all about her.

I am a mother without a baby.

A tide of despair threatens to drown her. She wants to die. She thinks if she can only die, there will be no more pain. But then it hits her. No. What on earth is she thinking? She must not die. If she dies, she will definitely never see Jeannie again.

She will take the lowly heroines of folk songs and make them her role models. The poor, the downtrodden, the heartbroken, girls who long for a better life, but who meet hardship with resilience and are ultimately, unbreakable.

She will take this experience and rather than let it destroy her, it will put iron in her soul.

I am her mother. If ever she needs me, then it's my job to be here.

'I so want to talk to Percy about Linda, but I feel I need to wait until I've heard back from Molly. If ever I do.'

'I agree,' Robbie said. 'No point getting his hopes up.'

My hopes were already up. But Spring turned to summer and I heard nothing from Molly.

Robbie told me that he was planning to go touring Scotland and Ireland with Kirk and Sofie. He was leaving in three weeks and would be gone for months.

'I understand,' I said.

Once a wanderer, always a wanderer. In a romantic movie, he'd be cast as a gentle poet with a beautiful soul, an accidental breaker of hearts, adorable, maddening, fascinating and forever unattainable. He could never really marry me and settle down, could he? He was the sort of boy I thought I wanted to marry, once, but no longer. Things had turned out for the best.

June was flaming and I took little Carys, Maria and Dylan, to splash about in the cascade. Scientists said that running water made people happy and so it seemed. There was plenty of squealing and laughter.

At the south end of the canal, the magnificent bronze statue of the war horse looked out over the park. The present Duke was reviving the Cavendish tradition for collecting contemporary art and the horse was the first new sculpture to be placed in the garden for a hundred and fifty years. Appropriately, he'd arrived in a horse box, then journeyed to the canal in the bucket of a JCB. The sun warmed his bronze back and children pretended to ride him while their parents snapped photos for family albums. Carys wanted a turn, then Dylan. I lifted one off and one on.

I let Dylan hold Tijou's lead and we made our way down the hundred steps to the monkey puzzle tree, past the Spanish chestnut, struck by lightning years ago. I thought how there was such generosity in planting trees, never seeing the results in your own lifetime but planting them anyway, for future generations to enjoy.

We always seemed to end up at a different kind of tree - the willow tree fountain. Dylan and Carys laughed and darted in and out of the spray with the other children and I saw a ghostly boy and girl from a sunny summer's day years ago, the boy with brown curls and the girl with a long dark plait. I saw Robbie, grabbing my hand and dragging me, giggling and squealing in mock protest, through the deliciously icy sprinkles, so that in minutes we were both soaked to the skin. I remembered feeling self-conscious of the way my ribbed vest top clung to the outline of my small breasts, acutely aware of my own body and how it had been undergoing changes, some subtle and some not so subtle, so that sometimes I felt as if I didn't belong in my own skin. I remembered wiping sticky tendrils of wet hair from my face, crossing my arms in front of me and noticing the way

Robbie slid his eyes away. I remembered how I'd struggled not to stare at the way his t-shirt clung to his ribcage, riding up slightly to show an inch of his bare flesh above the belt of his jeans. So much for cold showers. I'd felt consumed by desire, but had no idea what to do with it.

I thought about Robbie and trees. The ease and speed with which he climbed the boughs of the crooked apple tree at Brook House and the Douglas fir tree near the grotto pond. The importance he'd always placed on the past, on old songs and stories, handed down through hundreds of years and countless generations. I thought a lot about family trees.

As I unlocked the front door, the phone was ringing.

'Thank you so much for your letter,' said the woman at the other end of the line.

CHAPTER FORTY-FIVE

She had the softest trace of a northern accent but I recognised the sweetly haunting voice that I'd been listening to obsessively for months.

'I tried to write to you,' said Molly Marrison. 'But I didn't know how to even begin. I started literally dozens of letters to you and I threw them all in the bin. I was a singer, once upon a time and I suppose I still find it easier to reach out and connect with my voice, or what's left of it.'

'I've listened to your record hundreds of times,' I told her.

'Have you?' She sounded amazed and deeply touched.

I wondered about taking the phone over to the sofa but I felt afraid to move, as if Molly was a rare butterfly that had alighted on a nearby flower and any movement might scare her off.

'Where to begin?' Molly said.

She sounded so nervous. Did she think I'd judge her? 'I know who you are,' I said, wanting to spare her the awkwardness of having to explain it all from scratch. 'I know you're my sister's mother. My half-sister's mother.'

'No,' Molly said carefully. 'No darling, I'm not.'

'But Jeannie…'

'It was Sukey who took Jeannie from me.'

My heart slipped out of its proper place and plummeted through my rib cage, into the pit of my stomach. 'What? I don't understand?'

'Oh, this is so hard. Maybe we should be doing it face-to-face after all.'

'This way is fine,' I assured her hurriedly. 'Tell me. Please. Where did Sukey take Jeannie? Why did she take her?'

Silence at the other end of the line, so that I worried Molly had hung up.

'There was only me,' I said, my head swimming. 'Growing up. Just me. What happened to your little girl? Where is Jeannie?'

'I'm talking to her. Right now.'

'Oh, no. No. I'm so sorry. There's been some terrible mistake. I'm Sukey's daughter.'

'I understand. Of course you're her daughter. But I'm your birth mother,' Molly said.

'How is that possible?' I thought perhaps she was crazy, deluded.

'In an ideal world, children grow up with both their parents,' she said, sounding wholly rational. 'But the world is far from ideal and at least you got to grow up with your dad, instead of being adopted by total strangers.'

'Adopted?' The word stabbed at me. I still couldn't make sense of what she was saying.

'They wanted me to sign papers to say that the father of my child agreed to her being put up for adoption,' Molly

401

said. 'I stood there, pen poised, about to sign but I knew I'd be lying. I knew that the father of my child would never agree to an adoption. No way. Johnny was engaged to Sukey by then but I knew that if I wrote to him, told him the truth, he'd agree to come and collect you from Pelagia House immediately. In fact, he'd insist on it. I knew, beyond the shadow of a doubt, that he'd love you, care for you. You'd get to grow up at Chatsworth, the most beautiful place in the world.'

It felt like vertigo or claustrophobia or a concoction of the two, a horrible suffocating panic, that made me feel as if I was trapped inside my own body and falling from a great height, all at once. I felt winded, dizzy, sick. 'But. My birth certificate,' I stammered, grasping at facts like life rafts. 'Sukey is named on my birth certificate. I have it upstairs. It says very clearly that Sukey is my mother. Not you.'

'It's a forgery,' Molly said with infinite gentleness, as if she knew that with every word she spoke, she was destroying my whole identity, my sense of myself, dismantling the foundations of my life, piece by piece. 'The certificate's a forgery, Silva. It was easy enough to do, back in those days. Scandalously easy. There have been all those stories in the newspapers, about mother and baby homes selling babies to America, taking so called donations, falsifying birth certificates. It was common practice.'

'But why? Why would she do that?' She had never even wanted me.

'I told Johnny that I was happy for Sukey to adopt you officially but that was not enough for her. All she had to do was turn up to see the registrar with a new baby and claim it was hers. I didn't know she'd done it. Had no idea. Your dad didn't know anything about it either, not at first. So she began her married life with this huge, dangerous, dark secret. She was building her future, your father's future and yours, on a crime. The punishment for putting false information on a birth certificate, is a decade in prison. But I think that having to hide that deception from her husband was a far greater punishment. One that ate away at her.'

The world was spinning around me and crumbling. It was like being in an earthquake, the ground behind and in front of me was cracking, opening up with gigantic fissures. No way back and no way forward. The past was gone and the future too.

Who was I?

I needed a life belt, something to hold onto. Someone. But at the same time I felt suddenly so far removed from myself, so cast adrift, that when I ended this call, I wouldn't even be able to call Robbie and tell him what had happened. Was it even true?

I remembered standing in my dad's shed, showing him the photo of Sukey and Molly at the Festival. 'It's mum, isn't it?' I'd said. He'd told me it was.

Not Sukey but the other girl in the photo. Molly.

The Blue John candle-vase. *Your mother wanted you to have it. It was made by one of her ancestors.* Anna Hall was Molly's ancestor. Therefore my ancestor too, if Molly really was my mother.

'But you knew where I was all along. If you knew, why didn't you contact me?'

By way of a reply, Molly asked me a question: 'Do you know the story from the Bible, about The Judgement of Solomon?'

Molly was a born storyteller, I knew that much, but I didn't want to hear a story now. I didn't want another riddle or parable or allegory. Just the truth. But Molly was not to be rushed. 'Something to do with two women fighting over one baby?' I said. 'Isn't that what it's about?'

'Two mothers who both had infant sons,' said Molly. 'They came to Solomon because one of the babies died and each claimed the remaining boy as her own. Solomon called for a sword and declared that the baby would be cut in two, so each woman would have half. One mother didn't contest the ruling but the other begged Solomon, "Give the baby to her, just don't hurt him!" The king declared the second woman the true mother because she'd willingly give up her baby to save it from harm.'

Molly took a steadying breath and her voice, when she spoke again, sounded hoarse, constricted, making me remember all I'd read about dysphonia and how Molly's had been caused by the emotional trauma of losing her baby. Losing me. 'Your dad sent me photos every year. He let me know how you were getting on. Then when the government opened up the adoption contact register, I made sure I was on it. It was not that I didn't trust your dad to tell you the truth one day but I don't think I quite trusted Sukey, even then. It prompted me to look up your birth records and that's how I found out that I was not registered as your birth mother. According to the register, your father had one daughter and her mother was not me but Sukey. But the birthdate was the same. I worked out what Sukey had done and I couldn't bear it, for it to be denied that I had even given birth to you. I lost you all over again and this time, I lost you utterly. I felt so powerless. Unless you father told you about me, you'd never come looking for me because you'd never even know you were not being brought up by both your birth parents. In order for Johnny to tell you about me, you'd have had to find out about Sukey's crime and I thought he'd avoid facing that, for as long as possible. I wasn't wrong, was I?'

'He asked me to find you just before he…'

'Before he died?'

'Yes.'

I heard Molly swallow grief. 'So we have his blessing. I wonder then…would you like to come and visit me? Or I could come to you? Whichever you'd prefer.'

O n the leather-topped mahogany desk in Bea's office, the dominant item was a bulging file marked in large red lettering: Christmas. Bea talked about how everyone would have to work extra hours on baubling duties, starting in September, since over two thousand baubles would all be supplied without anything to suspend them. 'We'll obviously need a scaffolder to hang them on the tops of the trees,' she said, looking at me.

'I know my place,' I said. It was often ten foot high up a ladder. There were to be thirty trees, including a pair of huge Norwegian spruce that would stand in the Painted Hall. I'd be climbing up and down the portable scaffold tower for the best part of a week, hanging the baubles on the uppermost branches and placing golden stars on top. 'We mustn't forget the tinsel either,' I said.

Last year, Duchess Deborah had walked round the House with Bea, on the day before Christmas opening and said, 'Aren't we having any tinsel?'

We'd decided against it but had to re-think because she

was adamant, that although some people might consider it 'rather vulgar', it was also a lot of fun. So all the marble busts in the House, were duly crowned with tinsel wreaths.

'We need to get Santa back in The Stables,' Lizzie said. 'Remember that little lad who arrived clutching a scrap of paper with the Argos catalogue number of the gift he wanted, written down?'

As usual, the meeting ended with tea, buns and gossip. Bea chatted about recipes for the sloe-gin she was making for the forthcoming horticultural and produce show.

'Do you mind if I take tomorrow off?' I asked her.

'I can't see that being a problem.' She looked concerned. 'Are you alright?' I hardly ever asked for time off at short notice.

'I found her. I did what my dad asked me to do. I found Molly.'

'Goodness. Where is she?'

'In Gloucestershire. I'm going to see her.' That was all I could share for now. The rest just sounded too far-fetched and until I actually saw Molly, met her face-to-face, I couldn't wholly believe any of it. I'd not even told Robbie about this.

'Incredible,' Bea said.

'It certainly is.'

I set the alarm for 6.30am, had a shower and then changed my outfit half a dozen times. What would Molly expect her daughter to look like? What would she want her to look like? In the end, I decided to wear the clothes I felt comfortable in. Black jeans, converse trainers, a baggy black and white striped jumper. I made coffee but then had second thoughts about drinking it and put the cup down before it reached my lips. My stomach felt jittery enough as it was and I was already wide awake and wired. I'd barely slept, was ridiculously nervous and excited. My mother was not dead. My mother was not Sukey. I was finally going to be reunited with the woman who'd given birth to me, it was just not the woman I'd always hoped to meet again one day.

The journey took nearly three hours, skirting Birmingham and on into the rolling limestone hills and honeyed stone cottages of the Cotswolds. Village after village, all with a similar chocolate box charm as Edensor. Was that why Molly had chosen to settle here? Because it was far enough away from Derbyshire and yet still felt like home?

Molly had suggested we meet at 10.30am in a little coffee house called New England, in Stow-on-the-Wold, an ancient market town centred round a market square, with a stone cross marking the last battle of the English Civil War, which had been fought close by. The coffee house was just off the square on a narrow lane. It was the quaintest little place. The higgledy-piggledy rooms were on four floors, all decorated with vintage furnishings, old typewriters, box cameras and gramophones, the rooms lit with lamps with fringed silk shades. There was music playing in the background - Van Morrison.

I arrived half an hour early and ordered a cappuccino at the counter, went up the narrow, twisty stairs to find a table, liking the fact that I had a few minutes to prepare myself. But there was Molly. She'd arrived early too. She was in a little room on the second floor, sitting in a winged armchair by the window. She was wearing a mossy-green corduroy coat, her long dark hair tied loosely back from her face. She was gazing out on the rooftops of the little market town, as if she'd never seen it before.

She stood when she saw me and instinctively I went to give her a hug. Molly hugged me right back, a tight, warm hug, full of love. We both sat down but Molly reached out her hand, a hand with fingers encircled by more silver rings than I could count. She kept hold of my hands and for a while we just looked at each other. We looked and looked.

Tears shone in Molly's dark eyes. 'I've always dreamt of visiting New England.'

'Me too.' I thought of the paper snowflakes I'd made at school, Robbie's story of Snowflake Bentley, which I'd heard the day before my mother had gone away. No. Not my mother. I'd lost her long before that. But now, here she was. It was all too hard to grasp. For years, Robbie had urged me to find my mum, had tried to do it for me, while I'd been busy trying to find Molly. But in trying to find Molly, I had, in fact, been looking for my real mother all along. It blew my mind.

'I'm shaking,' I said.

'Me too,' Molly told me.

An attractive blonde teenage boy, with short cropped hair, a silver crucifix around his neck and pristine white trainers, brought us two frothy cappuccinos. We'd ordered the same. The boy had a lovely, sunny smile which made me want to smile back.

I couldn't stop smiling. Molly couldn't stop smiling either, seemingly. We had the same smile. Our eyes and mouths were the same shape. It was extraordinary, how similar we were. It was like a dream. This woman, my mother, seemed like a mirage, intensely romantic.

I took a sip of my coffee and Molly did the same, our actions mirroring each other. The coffee was hot, milky and strong. It was the most delicious coffee I'd ever tasted.

'I never wanted to give you up,' Molly said in a rush. 'I

had no choice.' She reined herself in, dashed tears away, almost impatiently. 'Sorry. I promised myself I wouldn't get all emotional and blurt it all out the minute I saw you. But I'm just so very glad to see you.'

'I'm glad to see you too.'

'I've waited so long for this day. I pretended I wasn't waiting because I was so frightened I'd die waiting, that you'd never come looking for me.'

'I've been waiting too,' I said. 'I just didn't know who I was waiting for.'

'Dear little Silva.'

'You called me Jeannie. French for John?'

'And there's a theory that Blue John was originally known as Bleu jaune. Blue yellow. But Silva suits you better. Your daddy's choice.'

'It means from the woods. Dad always told me that's where I came from.'

'We used to meet in a little house in the woods, up at Chatsworth. It was our special place. The grotto.'

'I saw your names carved in the trees.'

'Heavens, yes, I remember doing that.' Her eyes searched mine. 'I just wanted what was best for you,' she said. 'In the sixties, mothers who worked, who were performers, were frowned upon by the courts. It wasn't just me, Judy Collins lost custody of her son. Joni Mitchell had to give her baby up for adoption. I was in good company. I had no way to make a living. Someone once said to me, the best I could hope for, was getting £25 at clubs and headlining the occasional festival. I had no idea where it was all going, how I'd pay the rent from one week to the next. I wasn't very practical either. If the sink got blocked or there were mice in the house, I didn't know what to do. Not a clue. I was sort of uneasy with everyday life. It felt selfish to keep you. But I kept on loving you. I thought about you every single day. I longed just to see you and know that you were happy. D'you believe me?'

'I do.'

'When I found out that Sukey had forged your birth certificate, I wrote to your dad and I told him I was coming to see him. When I got to the cottage, he said you were at a party with Father Christmas.'

'I saw you,' I said. 'I'm sure of it. On my way to the party, I saw you leaving our house.'

'Did you?'

'Sukey left us,' I said quietly. 'That night. Right after you came to our house. She and Dad had a massive row and she left.'

'I'm so sorry. But even if I'd known that, I couldn't have marched in and announced who I was. It would have been too unsettling, too cruel.' Molly stroked my hand. 'On the windowsill in your kitchen, there was a little pottery eggcup you'd made. I imagined you coming home from school with it in your satchel, rushing to show your dad. He told me how good you were at making things and I knew then, that you had something from my side of the family, a talent, even if you never realised it. That's why I wanted you to have the Blue John candle-vase because it was made by another wonderful craftsman, who we're both descended from, you and I. I wanted you to know about him, even if you didn't know anything about me.'

'It's a her,' I said.

'Excuse me?'

'Not a craftsman but a craftswoman. Her name was Anna Hall.'

'Oh my goodness, how wonderful.'

'I talked to the journalist who wrote about you in the music papers. He told me you were good at art at school.'

'I'm not sure how good I am, but I'm a potter now, of sorts.'

'I'd love to see your work.'

'Would you? Well, I'd love to show it to you.'

Overhearing this conversation, the elderly couple who'd sat down with toasted teacakes at the small table behind us, would take us for strangers. We were strangers. Only not. I really did feel as if I'd known Molly all my life and in a way of course, I had. I couldn't remember meeting her but we had met, briefly, a long time ago. I felt like I'd been given a fresh start, a second chance. My whole body felt lighter and at the same time I felt fuller somehow, where once I'd felt empty. Already, Molly felt like family. I thought: I love her.

Molly had finished her coffee. 'Would you like to come home with me?'

We walked down a narrow lane to a row of old terraced cottages, not unlike the cottage in Pilsley where I had grown up and where Molly must have hoped to live one day with John.

The cottage was tiny, with a low beamed ceiling, a fireplace stacked neatly with logs. It was so cosy. The walls were painted in old white but there was colour and pattern everywhere, prints hanging on the walls, fairy lights around the mirror, ethnic wool cushions and patterned throws, fringed shawls on an old leather sofa with a tabby cat curled up on it, beaded lamps, a battered pine trunk used as a coffee table with fresh picked wildflowers in a green glass vase, an overflowing ashtray. On the shelves, native Indian figurines competed for space with books; Joseph Conrad, Mary Renault. No sign of a guitar.

For all its comforts and pretty, arty touches, Molly's living room was a bit of a mess though, littered with cardboard boxes filled with bits of broken pottery. More broken pieces were stacked on the coffee table, on the little desk and on the bookshelves. I feared that something was terribly wrong with Molly, that she'd created pots only to smash them.

'I'm not a regular potter,' Molly quickly explained, half-laughing at my obvious dismay, so that I got a flash of her famous joie de vivre. 'Follow me.'

With some trepidation, I let her lead the way to a back room, that served as a studio with a long, scarred wooden work bench, brushes in all shapes and sizes and little pots with some sort of paint in them. There was no potter's wheel or kiln in sight.

'People bring me their broken things to mend,' Molly said. 'It's called Kintsugi, a traditional Japanese art. Kintsugi translates as golden repair. When a bowl is broken in Japan, it's put back together with the cracks filled with gold, to emphasise the beauty in what was once broken.'

'That's the most beautiful idea I've ever heard.'

'Isn't it?'

On the workbench was a blue glazed jug that was shot with thin golden seams, like gilded lightening. It reminded me of the saffron veins that run through Blue John.

'When I lost your Dad it broke my heart,' Molly said simply. 'It was broken again when I had to give you up. I felt like I'd been shattered into a thousand pieces, smashed violently on the ground. I had no idea how to rebuild myself, how to go on. I felt like I'd never be the same again. And that's true. I'm not the same. Kintsugi is not about repairing things so they look the same as they were before they broke. It's about not only making a repair visible but highlighting it. The object's past transforms it into a precious and unique thing. There are so many broken hearts and broken homes and broken dreams. We are all damaged in some way, but with patience, we can make our scars beautiful, if we see them as proof that we've suffered but are strong.'

'That's amazing.' There was a framed art poster on the wall behind Molly's head, a quote from a song, about how cracks were what let the light get in. 'I love Leonard Cohen,' I said.

'He's a genius. It was your dad who first introduced me to him.'

'He never listened to music when I was growing up.' It was Robbie who'd introduced me to Leonard Cohen.

'He told me music made him too sad,' Molly said. 'Stirred up too many feelings he couldn't handle.'

'He never stopped loving you.'

'I never stopped loving him.'

'But he cheated on you. With Sukey.'

'No. No. It was me who messed up.' There was so much regret in Molly's eyes. 'It's a long story. Not a very edifying one. Would you like some mint tea?'

'Yes please.'

She made a pot with real mint leaves she plucked from a little plant that was growing in a silvery pot on the windowsill in her prettily rustic kitchen. She stirred in a small measure of brown sugar, then sat down with me on the worn brown leather sofa, the cushions softened with age.

'There was a music festival,' Molly began. 'It's been largely forgotten now but it was the height of the Summer of Love and I think it was one of the first ever open-air festivals, before the Isle of Wight and Glastonbury, all the famous ones. It was called the Festival of the Flower Children. I'm not making excuses for myself. But the Summer of Love and the counterculture, practically made it a duty rather than an option, to say yes to casual sex. Nowadays people think the sixties was all about utopian dreams, peace and love, a psychedelic light show. But it was so confused and confusing, such double standards. There was freedom in the air and I thought I was being a rebel. I wanted to do whatever I wanted to do, help change the world, change the way people thought about things. But I was domesticated too. I wanted love and I wanted to be free. I wanted to roam but I also wanted a home. Can you understand?'

'Yes. Totally.' But Robbie would understand her better.

'1960s ideals were so screwy. I was restless, had to keep moving but I longed for what I'd left behind. Relationships were so complicated too. It seemed churlish not to sleep with someone, if they gave you a light for your cigarette. I wanted to practise free love. No such thing. You pay later, always. And Sukey paid the highest price.'

'Sukey? Really? How?'

'She wanted you to be hers, to all intents and purposes, because she knew she'd never be able to carry a child.'

'She was so young. How could she possibly know that?'

'Because she'd been pregnant when she was just fifteen. She told me all about it, one night when she was stoned. It's only thirty or so years ago, Silva but it really was a different world. You couldn't win. It was OK to sleep around but at the same time, it was not OK for single women to get pregnant, which happened all the time because the miraculous contraceptive pill was only available if you were married. People talk about a woman's right to choose but what a choice? Between a rock and hard place, the devil and the deep blue sea. Illegitimate pregnancies were a catastrophe. Such a stigma. Until the abortion act, a woman caught terminating a pregnancy faced life imprisonment. It's hard to believe now. But no doctor who valued his career would perform an abortion. So women tried all kinds of ways to end unwanted pregnancies. A pint of Epsom salts, gin and ginger, turpentine. Jumping down stairs was often recommended, or violent skipping, crazy as that sounds.

'When Sukey found herself pregnant, she was desperate. She went to a woman who charged her a fiver, a week's wages back then, and gave her a carbolic douche but it didn't work, so she resorted to a knitting needle. The law encouraged backstreet abortionists to flourish, Knitting Needle Noras, they were called. The horrors are beyond imagining. No anaesthetic or sterilisation. The operations were done on kitchen tables, by medically untrained people with no real knowledge of anatomy. How a woman can push any instrument up inside herself is more than I can imagine. Sukey said there was so much blood, she bled and bled. She was screaming and bleeding wads of blood for six hours, sure she'd die. She was rushed to hospital but they brought the police to question her. They told her she was lucky, that a large number of women did die. She would live and they wouldn't prosecute but her womb was perforated. She'd never carry another child. I've thought about that so much. It must be like the very worst kind of hangover, when you know it's all self-inflicted.'

I saw the woman I'd grown up calling mum, who could never be a mother and I saw the grief in her eyes, a grief that had turned to bitterness and blighted her whole life. 'It explains a lot.'

'She guessed I was pregnant,' Molly said, lighting a cigarette. 'Having experienced the early signs herself, she recognised them right away. I broke Johnny's heart when he saw me making out with Pete. But then he broke mine right back and I used to think mine was much more broken than his because he shacked up pretty fast with Sukey. I don't blame him. I don't blame her. Not really. Sisterhood as a concept hadn't been invented then; most women were essentially rivals and enemies. It's the age-old story, recounted in hundreds of ballads. Two women fighting over one man. The 'someday my prince will come' dream. In truth, we all just wanted love, the security of being married, Sukey more than most.'

That's how you see me now. A thief. Who stole what was not mine.

I knew then what it was that Sukey had stolen. Not a vase made of Blue John. Nothing with any monetary value. She had stolen something truly priceless. Sukey had stolen the most precious thing a person ever can have. She had stolen Molly's child, the man she loved. She had stolen Molly's family.

'It was my fault,' Molly said. 'If the folk songs tell us anything, it's that if you make the wrong choices, white dresses can turn into funeral shrouds. The urge to destroy and the urge to create are closely connected. I had a massive self-destruct button, I think. I used to do things that would cause a relationship to end and then I felt sore and unjustly abandoned when it did.'

Same.

I saw how Molly had struggled with the notion that if only she had not been so reckless with my dad's heart, she might have got to live with him at Chatsworth and raise a family together.

'When I messed up and lost Johnny, singing was my one consolation and being heartbroken about him actually made me a better singer. When I made the record, I was in pieces.'

'That's why it touched people the way it did.'

'Perhaps. But then when I lost you too, it was too much.'

'You couldn't sing anymore.'

'And I didn't know how to do anything else, how to be anything else. I'd never wanted to do anything but sing. It was everything to me. There's a story about a man who caught a nightingale for his dinner, but when he plucked it, there was barely anything to eat. He said: you are just a voice and nothing more. That's how I felt about myself.'

How funny, that she'd told me a story about a nightingale. That she'd related herself to that little songbird that shared a name with my dearest friend. 'What did you do? How did you live?'

'Oh, I drifted about, worked in bars and shops, did a secretarial course, like my grandmother had always urged me to do. I got temp jobs in smokey offices and spent my days taking dictation and typing on sheets of carbon paper. All I wanted was for you to know, one day, that I was your mum. But after I found out that Sukey had written me out of your history, I had to leave England.'

I had a sense then of the extreme pain she'd been through, all the lost, childless years, devoid of love and hope. It all seemed immeasurably cruel.

'Where did you go?'

'Here, there, everywhere. Our ancestors were wandering minstrels, travelling tinkers and tinsmiths who sheltered in Peak Cavern and the life of a gypsy seemed so appealing to me then, the bohemian romance and freedom of it, campfires and birdsong. Making a home under canvas, on a beach, in a camper van or a painted wagon. I went to India and learnt to meditate and play sitar. I had a few relationships but they never lasted. I don't think I could let myself be happy and I could never imagine having another child. It would have felt disloyal to you. Then I ended up in Japan and for five years I studied Kintsugi with the masters in Tokyo and it felt like a calling, what I was meant to do, if I couldn't sing.'

'It seems that lots of people still listen to your album.' I couldn't tell her yet, that my dad was listening to her album when he died. I would tell her. But not now.

'It was only when I came back to live here, that I discovered the intrigue I'd left behind.' Molly smiled. 'To be honest, I found it bewildering that people had spent time and effort, concocting all these elaborate theories about what had become of me. But enough about all that. Tell me about you. What are you passionate about?'

What a lovely question. So much better than asking a person what they did for a living.

'I love Chatsworth,' I said. 'I love helping to look after the beautiful collections there. The art and history. I love making things too.'

'And is there someone important to you, a person that you love?'

'Yes,' I said, without hesitation. 'He's a singer too.' It was surely no coincidence. I'd been draw to Robbie when I first heard him sing and maybe I was drawn to singers because my mother was one. 'That's how we found you. Robbie knows Percy, your father.'

'Your grandfather.'

I laughed, delighted and astonished. 'I never even thought about that.' I'd gained not only a mother but a grandfather. Not just any grandfather. The person who'd inspired Robbie, who'd had such a profound influence on his life. 'He will be so happy to see you.'

'I won't ever see him again,' Molly said with a flash of acerbity that seemed almost out of character.

'You can't forgive him?'

She shook her head. 'I wish…but no, I'm afraid I can't. He never spoke up for me and he should have done.' Molly was looking at me, as a mother will look at her daughter when she understands what's causing her sorrow, without having to ask one single question. 'Tell me about your Robbie.'

I picked up a once broken terracotta vase, now mended by Molly and shot with seams of gold. 'You'd love him. He'd love you. And I know I love him. But knowing and feeling, they're two different things sometimes, aren't they?'

'They can be. Does he love you?'

'I can't seem to let him, if that makes sense.' I laid the palm of my hand over my heart. 'Sometimes I can't feel anything. It's as if I've died inside, like a tree struck by lightening.'

'We all accept the love we think we deserve.'

'Sukey made me feel like I was just tolerated, an irritant who didn't deserve her love.'

Molly touched her fingers to another piece of pottery that she'd mended, a beautiful green vase with bolts of gold running all over it. 'The masters of Kintsugi believe that when something has been damaged, it becomes more beautiful. You're not broken beyond repair and you must wear your scars proudly, a badge of honour, as if to say, look what I've been through, it's made me who I am. Nobody has a perfect life,' Molly said. 'The moment we accept that and find what's useful in the pain we've been through, that's our way of painting the cracks in our broken pieces with gold, turning something that could be ugly into something beautiful, worthwhile and inspiring. Every next level of your life will demand a new you and sometimes, it takes being broken, in order to become that new version of yourself.'

I saw then a flash of the beautiful spirit and charisma that had won Molly so many admirers, people who'd gone on admiring her to this day. I saw why my Dad had never recovered from the loss of her.

'Tell him,' Molly said. 'You have to tell him how you feel.'

I shook my head. 'I can't picture us together anymore.'

She took my shoulders in both her hands, made me look right at her. 'You're an artist, Silva. You can picture anything, if you put your mind to it.'

'It's too late,' I said. 'Too much water under the bridge and all the bridges burnt.'

She let go of me. 'That's a beautiful line. I might put it in a song. For someone else to sing, obviously. But why is it too late?'

'He's going away. And… I don't want to ask him to stay.'

'That's wise.'

'It's who he is,' I said. 'What he does. I see that now. Freedom is so important to him. He's a wandering minstrel, a troubadour, just like you.'

'Then take it from one who knows. Distance is nothing. If you love him, part of your heart goes with him and if he loves you, part of his heart stays behind and he will always come home. Just tell him.'

CHAPTER FORTY-SEVEN

Biting my lip in concentration, I waited for the metal to turn bright yellow-white, start to emit sparks. Hardly daring even to blink or breathe now, I gripped the tongs tighter and cautiously withdrew the sparkling metal from the fire. The surface was boiling, liquid. It swam and wavered, started to scintillate. It was astonishingly beautiful to see, like mercury, a tiny shimmering lake of molten flame.

I raised my hammer and struck.

When I'd come back from the Cotswolds, I'd walked and walked and ended up at the willow tree fountain. I stood beside it for ages, the spray and the sun making fractured rainbows around the children who played there. It was as if something inside me was being unknotted and uncoiled, unlocked and unblocked. An idea was taking root in the back of my mind and then it grew, budding and blossoming, as fast as a flower in a time lapse film, until I ran to the smithy and grabbed my sketchbook.

The idea was fully formed in my head, even before I started transferring it to paper.

I was going to make a contemporary version of the Chatsworth's willow tree, made not of copper but stainless steel, our local alternative. It was the city of Sheffield's specialty, known as poor man's silver. To look at a living tree, is to look at living history, just as every person alive today is the living history of their ancestors, with inherited talents, songs, inherited shame and trauma too. The past mattered, as Robbie had always insisted it did and so my tree would be made with the craftsmanship that had surely been handed down to me from Anna, my blacksmith relations, the tinkers and metalworkers who'd once lived in the Devil's Arse. It would be a mirrored tree, so that Molly and I could stand before it and see our faces reflected back at us in the shiny branches, along with all the dead people who lived on inside us, who looked out through our eyes.

This tree would be my memorial to family, my family. It would be a memorial to my father, and his love for my mother, Molly. Because a child is the most exquisite result of passionate love. No matter what had happened to Molly and Johnny as a couple, they were bound together forever in me. Their little family may have broken but because they had a child, because of me, it could never totally shatter. I would set in motion the legal procedure to get my birth certificate changed, so that Molly Marrison, Molly Hall, would be recorded as my birth mother. So that people from my future, researching our family history, would find Molly and Johnny together forever.

'The two parents of a child are linked for all eternity,' I told Robbie, when he stopped by to see what I was doing, why I was not returning his calls. 'No matter if they separate or divorce, they're always a family.'

'They are,' he said. 'Silva, are you alright?'

'If two people have children, one child, then they're part of the same family tree, for all time.'

'And you're creating a piece of art that celebrates the everlasting beauty of that fact?'

'A family tree.'

'That's such a simple, beautiful idea, Silly.'

He looked at me, trying to figure out what was going on with me. I wished I could tell him what I'd found out. I wished I could share it with him, as I'd shared everything else. I wished I knew how to put it into words. But I had no words. This was the only way I knew how to process it. I looked at him and I thought: This time next week, you'll be on an aeroplane.

'Now I just have to figure out how to make my metal family tree more than just an idea,' I told him.

I'd made a good start. I'd been determined to join the branches to the trunk using fire-welding because what better way to symbolise the way families are connected, at the very deepest level?

And now, at last, I'd worked out how to do it.

It took me five days of near manic activity. I didn't stop to accept Robbie's invitation to come for coffee, or a drink at the pub, or just a walk even, before he left on his travels. I barely stopped to eat or sleep.

On the fifth day, when the tree was nearing completion, I walked up to the forge and there was Duchess Deborah, standing outside it in her wax jacket and Wellington boots, with two of her sheepdogs sitting obediently at her feet. All three of them appeared to be admiring the shining metal tree that stood just inside the doorway. It was seven feet tall, towering above her.

'Silva's Silver tree,' the Duchess said. 'Remarkable.'

One of the dogs lifted her head, pink tongue lolling and licked my hand as I came to stand with them. 'Thank you, Your Grace.' I reached down and fondled the dog's black velvet ears.

'Tell me. Do you have any plans for it?'

'Not really, not yet.'

'Then I wonder if you'd agree to it being displayed in the gardens here.'

I was dreaming. I must be dreaming. The Duchess couldn't really have said what I thought she'd just said. Could she?

'My husband and I have been saying for a long time that we should make more of the gardens, use them as an outdoor gallery, for contemporary artwork on a grand scale,' the Duchess said. 'My son, Stoker, believes that tradition is important, but changing things is important too.'

'My friend, Robbie, would agree.'

'Good,' she smiled. 'We need to make this a place where people know that they'll see our wonderful old collection but are also likely to find something thrilling and new. This is a perfect example. So. Please may we make a permanent feature of it?'

'I'd be honoured.' For my work to be on show, for generations to come, for it to become a part of the Devonshire Collection that had inspired me and that I helped to look after…it was beyond my wildest dreams.

But something wasn't right. When the Duchess had gone, I should have wanted to jump for joy, punch the air but instead I felt oddly deflated. I stood and looked at the tree and I wondered: What about the next branch?

I laid my hand on one of the fire welded joints. You could no longer see where one piece ended and another began. They were fused into one. It wasn't just blood that joined you to a person at the deepest level, it was love too.

I'd longed for a mother to advise me and Molly had advised me and so far, I'd ignored her advice. Was it too late? Robbie would be leaving for the airport soon, if he'd not left already.

I ran all the way to Beeley, pounded along the leafy lanes, past the brook, that also ran through the otherwise peaceful little village. I burst, breathless, into the kitchen. Nobody there. I thundered through the empty rooms, flung myself back into the garden. I was already imagining acting out an archetypal scene from a romantic movie, the mad dash through traffic to the airport to stop the love of your life getting on a plane, the race to the departure gates as the last call to board was announced, the impassioned argument with airport security and then…the tear-jerking reunion. It was usually the man who did the running, but hey.

I found Robbie sitting up in the tree at bottom of the garden.

'Shouldn't you be packing, preparing, doing something at least?'

I'd expected him to swing down to talk to me but instead he leant forward and reached his hand down through the branches, smiling at me like a dryad. 'Come on up.' He shifted position to make room. 'OK, put your right foot there and your left one there,' he pointed.

Dangling our legs over the bough and facing each other, we were like children on a see-saw. He was wearing a crum-

426

pled coffee-coloured linen shirt, the top two buttons undone and in the dappled green-gold light filtering through the leaves, I was struck, as if for the first time, by how beautiful he was, inside and out and how very dearly I loved him. How much I desired him too. Just looking at him, it did things to me that no other man ever had.

'Penny for them?' Robbie prompted.

'There's something I wanted to say to you.'

'I'm listening.'

His eyes drew me in, pulled me close and held me. Why did people talk about falling in love? It was the opposite of falling. More like being raised up. I felt like a hot air balloon and one by one the tethers were being released and I'd floated up here without effort and could float far higher, right up to the sky and beyond, to heaven.

'I don't know where to start.'

'The beginning,' he said helpfully. 'That's usually the best place.'

Were we soul mates? Did they even exist in real life? I wanted to believe so. We were more like magnets, maybe. There'd always been a powerful attraction pulling at me and Robbie, pulling us together but at the same time, there had always been an undercurrent, an equally powerful opposing force pushing us apart, like a deep-rooted conflict.

I couldn't blame Percy for what he'd made Molly do. It didn't start with him. His family, Molly's family, my family, we had been burdened by shame and the fear of shame, and the ripples of that shame and fear had become a tsunami for Molly and so inevitably, had repercussions for me too. But once a secret was out in the open, was it stripped of its destructive power?

'Before a piece of iron enters a magnetic field, the polarization of its atoms is random,' I said.

He chuckled, sat back. 'Right.'

'But when they're exposed to the magnetic field, the atoms align their electrons with the flow of the field. That's what makes the wonderful patterns in iron filings.'

'I'm following you,' Robbie said.

'That's how I feel. Without you, all the atoms inside me are random but when I'm near you, everything is aligned. You make me feel…' I looked up into the branches of the tree to help me out. 'I feel like I have the power of a compass that can be used to navigate the earth; the power to change electrical energy into sound and music, just like magnets can.'

'I align your atoms?' He was smiling at me but not as if he was making fun of me in the slightest. 'That's definitely the sexiest thing any girl has ever said to me. Or probably ever will, I imagine. Impossible to beat.'

With every atom and fibre of my being, I wanted to kiss him. I let myself be drawn towards him, didn't resist the pull of it at all. I leant forward and he put his arms around me and it felt as if no time at all had passed between our first kiss and this one. But this time, we weren't inexperienced teenagers. Our tongues touched, entwined, then our limbs did the same, our bodies pressed closer with a heat that was like fusion. We might have been two pieces of metal in the forge, melting and reshaping and joining into a different form.

'Don't you need to leave for the airport?' I murmured.

He cupped my face, stroked my cheek with his thumb. 'I already postponed my flight.'

'You did?'

'There's somewhere we need to go, you and me.'

CHAPTER FORTY-EIGHT

'We should really be on horseback,' Robbie said, as he drove us though the towering peaks and pinnacles of Winnats Pass.

'I can see that.' Only there was no way I'd be riding this route, side by side with Robbie, on horses. It would feel as if we were carrying out some kind of reenactment and, pragmatic as I generally liked to consider myself, I was still too superstitious to do anything like that. Aside from the small fact that I'd never learnt to ride anything beyond a bicycle. All the same, I felt Clara and Henry riding along side us in the moonlight.

He turned left at the top, at Sparrowpit and on past the wonderfully named Wanted Inn.

The Royal Forest of the Peak, as this area was once known, was a misleading name, since there was scarcely a tree or bush, just tracts of wild moorland and heath. It lay so high in the hills of the White Peak, it was often lost in the clouds and shrouded by mist. An otherworldly place. When we stepped inside the remote and picturesque little chapel, I felt as if we were stepping through the pages of a storybook.

Robbie picked up a printed leaflet from an oak bench, dropped a pound coin into the honesty box, as I read over his shoulder, all about how the chapel had the unusual name of The Parish Church of King Charles the Martyr, dedicated to the king who'd had his head cut off, a hundred years before Clara and Henry set out to come here.

Robbie read the rest out loud: 'Christian, Countess of Devonshire, was very loyal to the crown and much troubled by the killing of the king. Seeking some way to show her devotion, she decided to build a little church in the Royal Forest, for the use of the next king's foresters. Built during a time when there was a ban on church building, her little chapel fell outside church law, so the minister could wed people here without the usual formalities. Peak Forest became Derbyshire's own Gretna Green and the minister became accustomed to being roused from his bed in the middle of the night, to perform a hasty candlelit ceremony. There were so many runaways that a second register was begun for these so called 'foreign marriages'.

I walked down the aisle to the altar, my footsteps echoing on the old stone and I stood before the huge silver cross, looking up at the stained glass window. 'If this was a movie, we'd do what Clara and Henry were prevented from doing and this is where we'd get married.'

Robbie came to stand close beside me, as if we really were about to say our vows, dressed in t-shirts and jeans. 'We could do that, if you like.'

I thought about how Henry and Clara were by no means the only runaway lovers to set out on a journey here. There had been many eloping couples, who'd made it safely and actually got married.

'Silva?'

When someone loves you, the way they say your name is totally different. I turned to him and I thought how little his face had changed since I first spied him, up in the attic with his headphones on, singing that haunting song of two people who died for love. There were faint lines around his eyes now, laughter lines but the eyes themselves were still the same: a poet's eyes, windows to an old soul. In many ways, he was even more attractive than his younger self. How would I feel, I wondered, if I were to see this face of his for the first time now? If we'd both found ourselves in this haunted little country chapel and struck up a conversation? I would have struck up a conversation with him, I felt sure of that. I'd not want to let him walk away without talking to him. How would I feel if I received an invitation to his wedding one day and sat in the pews to watch him stand before another altar, vowing to love and cherish a woman who was not me?

'When will you be back? From your travels, I mean?'

'In no time.'

'When?'

'Christmas.'

I waited a while, then said: 'You're not going to ask me to come with you?'

'Travel is not what you see in glossy magazines, you know. It's traffic jams, airport delays and launderettes, late nights and early mornings.'

'Your point being?'

'It's darker. It's about escape, restlessness, dissatisfaction, running away, yearning. For me at any rate. It can be exhausting. There's no refuge on a motorway.'

'But you'll always be a gentleman of the road.'

'You once asked me about nightingales, so here's

another thing. They always come back to exactly the same spot they left. Their homing memory is incredible. They use magnetic fields to navigate.'

'Aligned atoms?'

'Yes.'

'You've not answered my question. You don't want me to come with you?'

He shook his head.

I should feel hurt, indignant but I didn't. 'Why not?'

'Because I don't think it would make you happy.'

'Because I'm not like you? Because I'm not adventurous like you?'

He just smiled at me, enigmatically, infuriatingly.

'What?'

'Silly, you're the most adventurous person I know.'

I laughed. 'You do talk nonsense sometimes, Nightingale.'

'I'm being serious.'

'I'm adventurous? Me?'

He stroked the side of my head, left his hand against my hair. Nobody touched me like he did. I tilted into his touch, put my own hand over his.

'In here, in this head of yours, this is where you do all your exploring and adventuring. Your imagination takes you to the wildest places. Nothing is safe about you but you need to feel safe.'

'Since when did you become my psychoanalyst?'

'Hear me out, will you?'

'Go on then. If you must.'

'I've said before, that you keep so much hidden. But I can see what you hide. I see an inventive, fearless artist and she lives within this beautiful, quiet, grounded woman, who is wary of change, who needs the solid

432

certainty of a home, in order create beautiful, unre-strained art. '

Fleetingly, I saw myself differently. I saw myself as he saw me.

'I will always come home to you,' he said, 'because I've never met anyone like you and I never will.' His smile was playful, happy. 'You and me. We are meant to be. Nightin-gales live in woodland thickets, and you are Silva. From the Forest. We are meant to be together.'

Christmas. It was months away. Months and months. But I felt no panic or distress, just a sweet sort of ache at the thought of being apart from him for so long, coupled with the heady excitement of looking forward to him coming home. Unlike the lovers who'd come here in past centuries, we would not lose touch with each other if we were in different countries. I could still talk to him on the phone every night. Still hear his lovely voice. I could catch a train or a plane to see him within hours if I needed to. I could trust him. I could wait. It all felt so easy. Like fire-welding. Everything was easy all of a sudden, everything that had once felt impossible. I couldn't even understand what my problem had been before. Since I met Molly, it was like someone had hit a reset button in my head. We could make this work. He would travel and I'd stay here but we would still be together, in all the ways that mattered. Just not geographically. And what was a bit of geography?

'So would you like to get married at Christmas?' He asked.

'Not here?'

'No. God no. Edensor. It has to be Edensor.'

'Yes.'

'Yes you will marry me?'

'Yes. I will marry you.'

CHAPTER FORTY-NINE

Most girls dreamt of a fairytale wedding but our wedding truly was a fairytale.

It began in the bridal-wear boutique in Chesterfield, a tiny timber-framed shop with white painted beams and walls, little rooms filled with beautiful white gowns, veils, silver tiaras and silk slippers. There were two other future brides trying on gowns. They both had their mothers with them and it was like a dream for me, to have my own mother there with me too. To have a mother like Molly.

On the morning of my wedding, Freya came to my cottage with curlers and pins and she restyled my hair into a cascade of inky ringlets, woven through with sprigs of cloudy baby's breath flowers. Molly fastened the dozens of tiny silk buttons that ran down the back of my dress and just before she left for the church, she arranged the veil over my face, handed me a bouquet of scarlet camellias, freshly cut from Chatsworth's Victorian glasshouses.

'My beautiful daughter,' Molly said, with tears shining in her eyes.

'You look like a princess and a goddess all in one,' Freya smiled.

Molly and Freya both looked stunning too. Freya, chief bridesmaid, was spectacular in scarlet taffeta. She'd complained that redheads should never wear red but I'd been determined to prove the old maxim wrong. The red of Freya's dress was deep and dark, with a dash of purple in it and it suited her magnificently. In jade green shot-silk, her black and silver hair held back from her face with two thin, plaited ropes, Molly looked like the girl from the album cover. A girl who might ride in on a unicorn.

'All set then?' Molly asked.

I felt a tremor of nerves. It was not unusual for young brides to feel nervous about their wedding night but it wasn't the prospect of going to bed with Robbie that made me anxious, obviously, it was something else that was to happen beforehand. It had taken a huge amount of planning and persuasion to make it happen and now I wondered what on earth had possessed me. Whatever had I been thinking? I tried to put it out of my mind for now. Too late to back out.

Molly escorted me down the aisle and we walked past so many of my friends. Friends from primary school, secondary school, art school, people I'd worked with at Chatsworth. The gardeners, oddmen and shop assistants, were almost unrecognisable in their fancy hats and smart suits.

Percy had scrubbed up too. He'd had a haircut and a shave and he was sitting proudly on the front pew, on the bride's side. He glanced at Molly as she walked down the aisle, the first time he'd set eyes on his daughter in over thirty years and his expression was a kaleidoscope of emotion, love and pride, regret and sorrow, apology and hope, all competing and colliding. I'd tried to engineer a meeting between the two of them, my mother and my grandfather, before today but Molly had remained firm. She didn't ever want to speak to her father again. I trusted them both not to make things awkward for me and Robbie on our wedding day but still, the rift between them was a great sorrow, in the midst of all the joy. They were my family. My dad wasn't there and his absence made me realise how short life is, how important it is to forgive and make up while there's still time. Family was all that mattered. It made me so sad that two people who, unlike John, were able to be there, two people who I loved and who I knew loved me, two people who had been lost to me and to each other, who should be enjoying the day together, were at best just going to ignore one another.

Until later of course, when my harebrained plan was going to leave them no choice but to do otherwise.

The church was decorated for Christmas, with holly, ivy and dozens of candles and there was Robbie, waiting at the altar, looking as dashing as a courtier, in his crisp white shirt and charcoal grey waistcoat and jacket. His curly brown hair was shining with chestnut highlights and there was a dark red camellia in his buttonhole, to match my bouquet.

The ceremony began. I listened to Robbie promising to love me until death parted us and I promised to do the same. I meant every word. I was going to love and cherish this man with all of my heart. Impossible not to love and cherish him. He had the kindest, most generous spirit. He was not just in cahoots with me about the plans for later, he had been fundamental to those plans. None of it was remotely possible without him. I was suddenly so certain that it couldn't go wrong, that nothing could possibly go wrong today. When he kissed me, there before the altar, in front of everyone, I felt blessed. I felt cherished and loved. I'd never thought it was possible, to feel so full of happiness and hope for the future.

The photographer took us to pose together for photographs on the Paine's Bridge.

'I'm sorry if it's cold,' he said. 'But that has to be the most picturesque little bridge ever.'

What could be more romantic than a young bride and her handsome groom, standing there in the sparkling sunlit frost, with the gilded majesty of Chatsworth House as a backdrop.

More photographs were taken of us in the Painted Hall. Even though I'd helped to design the scenery and set everything up, hang baubles, make paper snowflakes and scatter fake snow, it was amazing to see the results of our months of planning and hard work; Bea's Christmas file made real. The House had been transformed into a winter wonderland.

There were garlands up the staircases, a beautiful kissing bough suspended from the chandelier above the Oak Stairs, a sumptuous display of silver gilt on the Great Chamber table. The State Drawing Room housed two beds from the 1940s, complete with hot-water bottles and bulging Christmas stockings, which were actually Duchess Deborah's shooting stockings, hanging alongside the wartime painting of the Penrhos College girls, using the room as a dormitory. The Norwegian spruce stood twenty feet high in the Painted Hall. The final touch, and my favourite, was the addition of hundreds of real candles throughout the House. It was a mammoth task to light and extinguish them all every day but it was worth it because the atmosphere they created was truly magical.

Molly said that the picture of me, lifting the hem of my

skirts to descend the wide staircase to the black and white marble floor, was like an image that might so easily have been captioned: and they lived happily ever after.

A wedding is where all the best fairytales end. But to me, it was just the beginning.

Every year lots of people want to marry at Chatsworth because they know everything will be perfect, that the bride and all her guests will always be wowed. I knew that the cutlery would have been polished so there was not one fingerprint. There were bottles of Chatsworth spring water on the tables and Haydn and the rest of the catering staff were so smart in their white shirts and black waistcoats. The Dining Hall had been decorated with more camellias.

So far, so traditional. But instead of a traditional string quartet playing in the corner, which would have been too conventional for Robbie, Sofie and Kirk were a playing a dulcimer and Irish harp.

Guests mingled, chatted. There was only one thing still marring the occasion.

'I didn't expect them to chat to each other but they've not even looked at each other once,' I said. The delicious wedding breakfast suddenly weighed heavy in my stomach and I felt sick with trepidation. 'Have I done the right thing? This evening? Oh Robbie, what if they both hate it?'

He reached out and took hold of my hand. 'They won't, Sweetheart. It'll be fine.'

Molly and Percy were not the only two people who were doing their best to avoid each other though. Robbie's real father, Jim Munro, had arrived late, slipping into the church unnoticed and standing alone at the back. I hadn't needed

Robbie to tell me who he was. He was unshaven with a stubbly beard and he was wearing a crumpled dark-blue linen jacket over a black t-shirt. His hair was shortish but I could imagine it longer and tousled like Robbie's and I thought how it would suit him better. As the guests all filed out, I noticed how Jim Munro's eyes followed Flora, who had the grace to come across and say hello to him, touching his arm as she spoke. I watched Robbie's stepdad who was watching them but not with any jealousy, as if he was genuinely glad, for Robbie's sake, that Jim had shown up.

When we were sipping champagne in the Painted Hall, Robbie had taken me over to Jim to introduce us and I couldn't help but notice how out of place he seemed. Robbie might have been Jim's younger brother. Their expressive grey eyes and their mannerisms, the way they walked, it was just the same. Only Jim was a shadow of his son, a negative, the dark to Robbie's light. He seemed unsure of himself.

'I hope you'll be very happy,' Jim said, looking at his son and then at me. They were not empty words but full of... what? Regret? As if the chance for happiness had passed Jim by or he realised that he'd squandered it. He seemed almost in awe of Robbie, as if he knew himself to be the lesser man perhaps. He looked as if he believed, or at least sincerely hoped, that Robbie might achieve things in love and in life, that he himself had not managed to achieve. It was as if he was passing on a baton and his son's happiness could go some way to cancelling out his own unhappiness. Rectifying his own mistakes. I liked him far more than I expected to and I also felt terribly sad for him. He'd slipped away before the first course of the wedding breakfast was served.

'Your dad is not at all how I imagined him,' I said to

Robbie, as we took our seats together at the head of the table.

'How did you imagine him?'

'I'm not sure. More swagger, I guess.'

'I think he was like that once.'

After we'd eaten, cutlery was tapped against glasses and the speeches followed - genuinely amusing speeches from Hugh and from Kirk, who was Robbie's Best Man.

Robbie stood by my side to make his speech, which ended with him unbuttoning the cuff of his shirt, to reveal the cryptic date from the future that he had tattooed on his wrist. He never had explained its significance but now at last, he did.

'I had it done on my eighteenth birthday,' he said. 'It's a random date, when I'll be in my fifties. I wanted to be able to look at that date each day and make sure that I'm living my life to the full, so that when I reach it, I'll be where I want to be, with no regrets.' He spoke softly, like a prophet. 'I've always tried to make sure that each day is better than the last,' he said. 'That can be hard because shit happens.' He looked down at me. 'But I know that with Silva, each day will be amazing and when the 21st November 2025 finally comes around, I want to be spending it with her.'

There was not a dry eye in the room. Men, women, young and old, if Robbie had not won all their hearts before, he'd won them now.

But I'd get to take him home at night.

Before I could do that though, instead of the usual dancing and disco, something different…

∾

The little theatre beneath the Belvedere Tower, dormant for so many decades, was one again filled with excited chatter, the air alive with the heady scent of perfume and wine and the expectation of the entertainment to come. The wedding guests in all their finery had taken their seats in the plush red rows and in the boxes. The candlelight was warm and golden. It was as if we'd stepped back in time to the Edwardian age.

The tiny stage, framed by the heavy crimson velvet curtains and richly decorated proscenium arch, was empty for now, except for two microphone stands placed in the centre of it. A splendid backdrop depicted Chatsworth House in Elizabethan times.

Two seats in the front row, beside Flora and Freya, had been reserved for me and Molly. We made ourselves comfortable and I clasped my hands, my second finger, displaying the new band of white gold beside the Blue John ring, resting prettily in the tulle skirts of my grown. I couldn't have felt more nervous if I had been about to walk on stage at Wembley Stadium.

But Robbie had nerves of steel and as ever, he stepped out from the wings to stand in front of the audience, as if it was what he was born to do. He started with a couple of traditional Derbyshire carols, his rich, soulful, straight-to-the heart voice, resonating somewhere deep within my body. I relaxed, let myself be transported, as I had been that first time I'd heard him sing, when I was ten years old. It was such a timeless voice. You could close your eyes and imagine you were in a different century. Yet the way he reinterpreted the old song he was singing, made it sound as if it was written yesterday.

I slid my eyes sideways to glance at Molly, saw that her black eyes were filled with unshed tears and I wondered if it was because of the beauty of the occasion and the song, Robbie's voice, or was she mourning the loss of her own voice? I was certain, somehow, that Molly was wishing she could be up there with Robbie, maybe even standing in his place.

It was Percy who stood up and joined Robbie on stage and for one horrific moment, I wondered if I'd made a massive blunder. This was Molly's father, the man who'd stood by while her grandmother banished her to a home for fallen women, as a result of which, she'd lost her child and lost her voice. Yet Percy could still sing. He could do what Molly could not now do. Would that make her despise him? Instead of ending the rift between them, would it widen it?

But Percy told stories that made Molly smile and at one point, she actually laughed out loud. Percy saw her laughing and he smiled down at her, as if that was his greatest achievement. Molly reached out and took hold of my hand, as Percy entertained the whole theatre for about half an hour, just playing spoons, tapping them against his legs. It was surprisingly tuneful.

He sang a song called *Tinkers' Corner*, which he said was about the vagabonds who once lived and earned their living, in the Devil's Arse. I thought how wonderful old voices were because what came through, was the character of the person. There was a directness to Percy's singing. He was not trying to impress anyone or put on a show. It was the song that was important to him. He was just the conveyor.

'That's a song about where my family come from,' Percy said, looking directly at me and at Molly. 'There was a little concert there, over thirty years ago,' he said very gently. 'I went along, not to sing, just to listen and I remember this girl who got up to sing. Oh, I wish you could have heard her. She brought the house down. She had the most beautiful voice and I was right proud of her then and I'm still right proud of her now.'

I didn't know that Percy had been there in the crowd, the night when Molly sang in Peak Cavern. By the look on her face, Molly had had no idea that her father had been present either.

'The song that she sang then, is one that we're gonna sing tonight,' Robbie said, picking up the story seamlessly. 'It's not a carol or at all Christmassy and though it is about a wedding, it's not the most appropriate song to sing on someone's wedding day. Except. This song, though it's about a tragedy, has magic in it. It brings people together, in a way that I like to think is redemptive. It brought me and Silva together and it led me to Percy, her grandfather, who as well as being my dearest friend, is also my inspiration. It's the song that helped us find Molly.'

Over moors and valleys deep, through the Dark Peak and the White
There two tragic lovers sleep in gritstone, blood, and lime.

I listened to my grandfather's voice and my husband's voice, lifted in unison and I had a sense of light being shone into the darkest corners. They reached the end of the tragic song or rather the end of the version of the song that Robbie had always sung. The music stopped and both men looked down into the audience at Molly. Percy glanced at Robbie, nervous, afraid. He looked suddenly very old, a tired old man, who'd made mistakes he wasn't sure he could even begin to rectify. He looked like someone who wondered if maybe this was all far too little and too late.

I held my breath but Robbie held out his hand to Molly. He'd always believed in the power of music, to unite and heal and bring people together.

My heart in my mouth, my mouth parched, I waited to see what my mother would do.

Molly didn't hesitate. She put her hands on the arms of the chair and she pushed herself to her feet. In her swishing jade silk dress, she walked, unhurried and serene, to the end of the row of seats and around to the side of the stage and, lifting her long skirts, she climbed the few steps that led up to where Robbie and Percy were standing in the spotlight. She went to stand between the two of them. Robbie had told me the legend of Philomela, who had her tongue cut out by Tereus. Unable to speak, she wove her story into a tapestry, but was eventually turned into a nightingale. Please let Molly sing.

I could barely breathe, but Molly breathed deep, filling her lungs.

Then from the darkness of Waterhull
Something so rare and beautiful

She sang with not one crack or rasp in her lovely voice. She sounded like she did on the album. She sounded young and strong, with the future before her and the world at her feet. It was a voice that didn't even seem to go through her mouth or her throat at all but came direct from her heart. It was the sound of someone's heart singing.

With this ring, I give you a song to sing

Everyone applauded. I jumped to my feet to clap, followed by Freya and then, everyone was standing and applauding.

Robbie smiled at me, a conspiratorial smile, as if to say: we did good; we make a good team, you and me.

Molly hugged Percy and he hugged her back, then he stroked her hair, as if she was the little girl he'd sat on his lap to teach her the old songs, the young woman he'd watched singing those old songs in Peak Cavern, before she went on to preserve them on vinyl. It was as if the intervening years, the sorrow and loss, had not been telescoped or wiped away but the cracks and been filled with gold, to emphasise the beauty in what was once broken: Kintsugi.

'Nothing can stop you singing those songs' Percy said. 'They're in our bones.'

I made a silent toast: Here's to you, Henry and Clara, whoever you were. I still wished I knew.

EPILOGUE

SILVA - 21ST NOVEMBER 2025

The strangest of anniversaries. We were marking the date that Robbie had randomly chosen and tattooed on his wrist, over thirty years before.

Raffi had caught the train up from London, where he was acting in a film being shot at Ealing Studios and Kizzy had driven up from Brighton with her twin boys. Me, Robbie and our grown-up son and daughter and two little grandsons, had gone for a walk to Chatsworth House. It was the first day of the Christmas markets and I remembered all the Christmases past. Our wedding day, the annual outings with the children as they were growing up.

I was in my fifties now and life felt, if not slower, then steadier. Sometimes I missed the intensity of youth: the extreme highs and lows and endless possibilities, listening to a song on repeat and totally identifying with the agony of the lyrics. That sense that one song, could literally change your life. Late night telephone calls with Robbie that had gone on for hours, crossing off the days and hours until he came home from his travels, then staying up until dawn, talking and making love. I had no energy for that any longer. But I was content and it was a good feeling. I was perfectly happy, just to wander with my family around the stalls, drink mulled wine, eat stollen and mince pies, watch my grandsons' little faces when they entered the winter wonderland in the Painted Hall. Chatsworth was full of Christmas stories again.

'Once Upon A Time,' Kizzy said.

Back at home, sitting beside a flickering log fire, Kizzy gave us our Christmas present, wrapped very quaintly, in old-fashioned brown paper tied with gold ribbon and red starry bows. Everything Kizzy did was beautiful. When our little family had grown to four, we'd moved to one of the gracious Italianate houses in Edensor and over the years, Kizzy had helped with the interior design, picking out antiques, soft furnishings and paint colours. She also had an extraordinary knack for choosing the most special and appropriate gifts.

'It's for you both to share,' she said, 'and you have to open it today.'

Robbie let me do the unwrapping and inside was a book, a notebook, beautifully bound in Chatsworth Blue leather. Written by hand, on luxuriously creamy paper, in elegantly scrolled blue-black ink, the lettering looked more like calligraphy than regular handwriting. Art and words, shapes and patterns, combined in a timeless document.

'There's no point looking back,' my mum used to say. 'You're not going that way.'

Which is ironic because she grew up and then went on to work, at Chatsworth House, the most beautiful and famous stately home in

England; a place that's steeped in centuries of the richest history. It's a place that inspires respect and love for the past.

I understand now though, that my mother had good reasons for wanting to leave her own past behind her. But she came to realise that people live freer and happier lives, if only they understand the sort of history that's never taught in schools. The private history of our own parents and grandparents and great-grandparents. The history of the ordinary, extraordinary people who made us who we are. Percy, my great-grandfather, used to talk about learning to see through the eyes of a skull. About the importance of finding an access point with a view back in time.

There are so many things that can be passed down through the generations. So many legacies that you can hand on to your children and your children's children, so many gifts which might be bequeathed to you, sometimes inadvertently. The colour of your eyes and hair and the shape of your mouth. A wild imagination maybe or skilful hands or a voice to sing with. A kind nature or a fear of the dark. There are heir-looms too, jewellery and antiques, rare and valuable objects and other treasures that are valuable purely for sentimental reasons. There are also the old stories and songs, the lore and legends, that my dad has spent the best part of his life collecting and recording for posterity.

But there's something else. Another legacy, dark and hidden. Bad things that have happened, events that were too distressing and over-whelming to be resolved in one person's lifetime. It's fascinating to learn that scientists have proved that trauma can be passed on through genera-tions, sometimes buried deep and seemingly forgotten but still with the destructive power to cause much pain and suffering. We all walk around with ancient memories and mysteries, locked deep inside of us, along with our DNA. We're troubled with terrors and torments, that we can't even begin to understand because they didn't begin with us.

And some of us are burdened by age-old debts that, sooner or later, must be repaid.

You see it all the time. The patterns that keep repeating.

My mother's past is also my past and by unravelling it, she was able to pass on good things to me and my brother. She delved deep and dug up secrets, both ugly and beautiful, so in that way, she was just like the eighteenth century lead miners in the Peak District, who stumbled upon the rare Blue John gemstone, while they were out looking for lead to make water pipes and cannon balls.

My mum works with her hands and by her own admission, she is no writer. Even drafting a letter to my schoolteachers, used to bring her out in a cold sweat. So it's fallen to me, to relate what she discovered, to write it all down. Now that I'm old enough to fully understand, she's told me her story and I recorded our conversations and then transcribed them all, in just the same way my dad records and preserves ancient songs.

We had the loveliest time, Mum and I. We sat for hours at a little table in the teashop in Edensor or in the cafe up at the Farm Shop, nattering and drinking pots of tea and eating scones and cake. Mum can still eat whatever she likes and never put on a pound, since she burns it all off, literally, working at Chatsworth and at the forge. My dad likes to tell the story of how, when he first heard his mother mention a little girl called Silva, he expected to meet a woodland sprite and instead, there was a little amazon, a girl with a warrior soul.

And the rest is his story and her story. The love story of Silva and Robbie, my mum and dad. Which is also the story of Flora and Jim and Molly and Johnny. Henry and Clara.

Granny Molly's story I have pieced together, from what Mum told me and what Granny herself told me. I have written her story in the present tense. Because the past is always present.

But this story goes far beyond all of us, with roots deep in history, stretching back over two hundred and fifty years, beginning in tragedy and blood and murder. And ending...well...we shall have to wait and see.

I've written it all down, just as Molly and Mum told it to me, so that it can be passed on. And because writing can be an act of exor-

cism. I want my children and their children to know who they are and where they've come from. For there to be no more secrets. So this is for them and for my parents, of course and for anyone who's interested in family history and in old songs.

My mother learnt to see through the eyes of a skull and this is what she saw.

Kizzy Munro, 2025

'I want to earn my right to wear that ring one day, Dad,' Kizzy said.

'You've already earned the right, Petal. More than earned it.'

It was Kizzy, as an inquiring teenager, who'd asked her great-grandfather, Percy, about the origins of the crested pewter ring her father always wore, which Percy had given to Robbie long before she was born. It was Kizzy, who wondered if it was connected to their last line of *The Runaway Lovers*.

With this ring, I give you my song to sing.

'All I know is that it was handed down through the singers in my family,' Percy had told his great-granddaughter. 'From father to son, from mothers to daughters. The ring was handed down along with the songs.'

So Kizzy had researched the origins of the crest. She'd visited museums and archives and consulted experts in heraldry and eventually, she cracked the code. She discovered that it was the family crest of the McVurichs. They were seanachies, the Gaelic word for storytellers. In Scotland, a seanachie was a chronicler of family history and tradition and they were attached to the household of a clan chieftain. The McVurichs were attached to the Clan Gordon and sure enough, there were reports that of one of the Gordon's daughters, Clara, had gone missing from their Highland castle in the 1700s and there had been a McVurich boy, named Henry, who was a similar age to Clara, whose baptism was recorded in the register at the local church.

With this ring, I give you my song to sing.

Tom Hall must have stolen the ring from Henry McVurich when he killed him.

Historians had pondered the identities of Henry and Clara for centuries and it was there all the time, not written down anywhere but passed on in a song. The song really was the key, all along, just as Robbie had said it was.

Not long after we were married, Heather, the pink-haired PhD student from Sheffield University, who'd been working in the Chatsworth archive, had come to tell me that she understood the lines about the beauty that came from the darkness of Waterhull.

'Nobody knows exactly where Clara and Henry's bodies were found,' she said.

'No,' I'd agreed.

'Nor do we know exactly how or when Blue John was first found, just that it was supposedly discovered by someone called Joseph Hall. I believe he is Anna and Tom's son. We found a file of old papers in the archives, which we've called the Oakes Deeds. They're the family papers of the Bagshawe Family, who lived at Oaks Hall at Norton, near Sheffield. They show how in the quest for new veins of lead, miners began exploring the cave systems of Treak Cliff Hill and in 1709, they broke through into a series of passages and caverns, which they named the Waterhull Mine. They stumbled upon rich veins of then worthless Blue John, but no lead was found there, so the mine was abandoned, decades before Henry and Clara were murdered. Tom Hall was a lead miner, so it would have been known to him and to the other murderers.'

A shiver ran down my spine when I heard that. 'It would have seemed like a safe place to deposit two dead bodies, with no risk of detection.'

'Until of course, the growing popularity of Blue John, caused miners to revisit Waterhull.'

'And along with the huge supplies of Blue John, they'd have found the remains of the Runaway Lovers. The dates tally.'

'The dates tally perfectly,' Heather said. 'Waterhull was renamed Blue John Cavern.' Anna Hall had chosen to make something beautiful, from the Blue John that came out of such darkness. Her family had commemorated that in song.

Then from the darkness of Waterhull.
Something so rare and beautiful

Kizzy had drawn a diagram of our family tree in the front of her storybook, as if it were a family bible. There was me and Robbie; Molly and Johnny; Percy and Esme; Lavinia and her husband, Jack, Percy's father; Anna and Tom. Henry McVurich and Clara were there too, since they were inextricably linked to the Halls.

Kizzy said: 'Did you know, that symptoms of lead poisoning include anti-social behaviour and aggression? Maybe Tom and the other men, the lead miners, were terribly sick.'

'Perhaps they were,' I said.

'Even if that's not the case, sometimes just having a story, some kind of explanation, lets you turn the page and start a new chapter, doesn't it?'

'How did you get to be so wise?'

'It's not what happens to us that counts,' Kizzy added vehemently, 'but how we remember our life, in order to recount it. It's the stories we choose to tell ourselves.'

'And if we understand our history, we can be better wives, husbands, better lovers and parents,' I agreed. 'Instead of spending so much money on therapy, people should be doing genealogy as well.'

The title of Kizzy's book: How to Mend a Broken Home. Only she'd crossed out 'Home' and written 'Heart' instead.

'I was thinking how you and dad both came from broken homes but this is a much bigger story, isn't it? It spans centuries. It's epic.'

When she was about eleven, epic had been Kizzy's most favourite word.

'I think heart is the right word,' I told her, 'because if you can mend a broken heart, then everything else follows.'

~The End~

AUTHOR'S NOTE

To say that *The Keeper of Songs* is inspired by the music and work of singer and song collector, Sam Lee, is an under-statement.

While thinking about this story, researching and writing it, I have been on a rollercoaster, rocket ride through divorce, three forced house moves in four years with four young children in tow, plus various other family, romantic and career-related dramas, that resulted from the fallout of marriage breakup and the breaking up of the little family that has always been the mainstay of my life. I had to focus on my children, so writing took a backseat but I realise now, that I also suffered from a kind of temporary writerly dysphonia, very similar to Molly's affliction. It was not writer's block because I was still putting words and sentences on pages, but they would not sing.

Then, when wandering around on YouTube, wondering how best to shape a contemporary romance around the Derbyshire folk tale of the Runaway Lovers, I discovered Sam Lee's songs, starting with *Lovely Molly*, which Sam performed at the Royal Albert Hall, accompanied only by the voices of the Roundhouse Choir. It's no exaggeration, to say that it felt like a life-changing moment. Firstly because in those old, old songs that Sam has so lovingly collected, preserved and reimagined, there are so many tales of heartbreak and betrayal and they struck a powerful chord with me. They made something exquisitely beautiful out of grief and sorrow and they were, are, so comforting and uplifting and they pulled me out of a hole.

Lovely Molly led me to explore Sam Lee's work. I read an enchanting interview with him by Ed Vulliamy in The Guardian (28th October 2012) entitled, 'There is a difference in the songs the gypsies sing.' I also discovered the story of folk singer Shirley Collins, who lost her voice as the result of a broken heart or 'an emotional fracture', as she perfectly described it. I went to see Sam sing ancient songs and ballads backed by an orchestra in a lovely old London church, in a forest in Kent at night accompanied only by nightingales and in a tiny seaside shack in Cornwall in midwinter, completely unaccompanied, except for the sound of the waves. I spent a fascinating five-hour train journey with him all the way to St Ives, listening to his magical stories and I knew then, the story I wanted to tell. I'd decided on Robbie's surname and drafted my novel before Sam brought out his wonderful book, *The Nightingale, Notes on a Songbird,* but it provided some additional sources of conversation between Silva and Robbie.

Singer and songwriter Bella Hardy, from Derbyshire, also offered me some wonderful observations about folk singing, Castleton and the murder of the Runaway Lovers. It is her haunting version of *Henry and Clara* that I've used throughout, taken from her beautiful album *The Dark Peak & The White.*

The legacy of craftsmanship in Silva's family, embraces gemstones, blacksmithing and kintsugi and I have to thank the craftsmen and women who gave me an invaluable insight into their work. John Turner at Treak Cliff Cavern gave me a tour of his Blue John workshop; Bex Simon and Beth Forrester are two inspiring female artist blacksmiths and David Joy taught me how to forge a poker at the Cotswold Discovery Centre. From Kristina Mar I learnt about the painstaking art of kintsugi, at Robin Walden's pottery. Molly's explanation about mending breaks with gold, is borrowed from Sean Buranahiran's video 'Be Proud of your Scars.' It's a philosophy that I know my strong, kind and wise friend, Mel Brunyee, embraces and Silva is modelled (in part!) on her.

For the history of Blue John, I referred to *Derbyshire Blue John* by Trevor D Ford with a Foreword by the Duchess of Devonshire (Landmark Publishing Ltd 2005). It was my sister Kirsty, who pointed out that I couldn't possibly write a story about Derbyshire and Blue John, without mentioning Chatsworth which, growing up, was our family's favourite destination for days out. It was my mum's very favourite place and she was a huge admirer of Duchess Deborah. The 'mention' of Chatsworth grew to a takeover, as Chatsworth became the obvious backgdrop to the whole story and I came to see the House (always with a capital H!) and estate as one of the main characters. I'm hugely indebted to former Head Housekeeper, Christine Robinson, who has lived and worked at Chatsworth for over forty years. I've spent lovely afternoons chatting to her, at her enchanting home in Edensor and her guided tour around Chatsworth House as preparations for Christmas were underway, was an experience I will never forget. Christine's entertaining and informative books, *The Housekeeper's Tale*

(Bannister Publications, 2014) and *Chatsworth: The Housekeeper's Tips, Tales and Tipples* (Bannister Publications, 2017) give a real feel for the work that goes into making Chatsworth the wondrous place that it is. I also have to thank Christine for ace fact-checking and proofreading. Any remaining errors are mine! Deborah, Duchess of Devonshire's two books *The House: Portrait of Chatsworth* (Macmillan, 1982) and *The Garden at Chatsworth* (Frances Lincoln, 1999) also capture it perfectly and I have drawn heavily on these and on the DVD of the BBC documentary *Chatsworth House*, for colour, characters and conversations concerned with the modern-day workings of this great estate. Bea Waterfield is a real person, who bid her name for this book at an Auction of Promises.

The folklore of the *Murders in the Winnats Pass*, is the subject and title of a book by Mark Henderson (Amberley Publishing, 2010). Since the murder took place in Castleton, at the height of the Blue John craze, the 'mysterious' discovery of the fluorspar had to be part of this story. So it was a gift, to discover the receipt for Blue John bodies, made out from Matthew Boulton to a Widow Hall, who shares her surname with one of the murderers. It's the kind of nugget of fact that sends tingles down my spine when I'm constructing a plot. Other tingles came from finding the engraving of 'Singing Sam' in an old book of Derbyshire ballads, learning about the abandonment of the Waterhull Mine and the Oaks Deeds and seeing how Clara's saddle was bequeathed to the Speedwell Cavern Museum by a Chatsworth groom.

Thanks also to early reader, Jemma McDonagh, for suggesting an important scene to insert.

The music biz scenes, set in 1967, were great fun for me to research and write. The story of an enigmatic, missing folk singer is inspired by Charles Donovan's article in *The Independent* in 2005, about Shelagh McDonald, who released two albums before her mysterious disappearance in 1971. (She has since reappeared!) The Festival of the Flower Children really did happen and featured John Peel and Tommy Vance, two radio presenters who I had the great honour of working with at Radio 1, along with Mark Radcliffe, who has become the figurehead of UK folk music and whose Radio 2 'Folk Show', has been a soundtrack to this book. I got rather carried away with researching the 1960s folk music revival, thanks to a bunch of great books, all published by Faber: *Folk Song in England* by Steve Round, (Faber and Faber 2015); *Electric Eden - Unearthing Britain's Visionary Music*, by Rob Young (Faber & Faber 2002); *I've Always Kept a Unicorn - The Biography of Sandy Denny*, by Mick Houghton, (Faber & Faber 2015); *First Time Ever*, by Peggy Seeger (Faber & Faber 2017); *The Lark Ascending: The Music of the British Landscape* by Richard King (Faber & Faber, 2019) and *Singing from the Floor, A History of British Folk Clubs*, by JP Bean (Faber & Faber 2014). The latter begins with a foreword by Richard Hawley, who has given atmospheric concerts in the Devil's Arse cavern (available to watch on YouTube). *White Bicycles: Making Music in the 1960s* by Joe Boyd (Serpents Tail, 2006) has a wealth of information on recording processes. Virginia Nicholson's *How Was it For You?* (Penguin Random House, 2019) is packed with the most wonderful and necessary period detail and gave me an invaluable insight into how things were in the sixties, as did Jenny Diski's *The Sixties* (Profile, 20009). I was also inspired by *Kate Bush, Under the Ivy* by Graeme Thomson (Omnibus Press, 2015). The details about mother and baby homes comes from *The Baby Laundry for Unmarried Mothers* by Angela Patrick (Simon & Schuster, 2012).

I need to flag up one significant liberty that I've taken with dates. The Duke and Duchess of Devonshire were married in 1941 and their diamond wedding anniversary was therefore celebrated in 2001. However, that's also the year that the foot and mouth epidemic broke out in the UK, which had a significant impact on Chatsworth that spring and which lead to the genius idea of decorating and opening the House for Christmas. If I'd set these scenes in 2001, I'd have had to include foot and mouth and it would have been a very different story and not one I particularly wanted to tell right now, in this year of another pandemic.

I have to close by thanking my sister Kirsty, for being our rock, financial advisor, bank and research assistant, including sitting in the rain to listen to nightingales with Sam. Also, my amazing agent, trusted friend and ace editor, Broo Doherty, who has been unfailingly supportive and encouraging, offering invaluable advice, constructive criticism and gently but firmly, chivvying me along! Broo's confidence in me and in this book and her boundless good humour, kept me going and I could not have done it without her. It has been a great pleasure once more to work with Rosie DeCourcy, who lent her editing prowess to this manuscript. Thanks to Steph Freeland for proofreading and to Heike Schüssler and Laura Barrett for the beautiful jacket. Thanks also to Jules Russell for the SnowGlobe logo and tattoo tale!

Huge thanks to everyone who has bought and read this book. Your support means so much to me.

Three of my children have become adults while I've been working on this story, while working as a mum. All four of them, Dan, James, Gabe and Kezia, have made me prouder than I can ever say and this, like everything I ever do, is for you guys.